PRIVATE
MATTERS

PRIVATE MATTERS

A Novel

M. H. MUNDY

Kuyomi Books Tucson

2022

Published by Kuyomi Books
kuyomibooks.com

Library of Congress Cataloging-in-Publication Data
Names: Mundy, M. H., Author.
Title: Private Matters – A Novel / M. H. Mundy.
Description: First Edition. | Arizona: Kuyomi Books, 2022
Identifiers: LCCN 2021921603 (print) | ISBN 9781956997026 (hardcover)
| ISBN 9781956997019 (paperback) | ISBN 9781956997002 (ebook)

LC record available at https://lccn.loc.gov/ 2021921603

Cover design: Kuyomi Books

This is a work of fiction. Names, characters, places and
incidents either are the product of the author's imagination
or fictitious. Any resemblance to actual persons, living
or dead, events, or locales is coincidental.

To Matapatira,

my sister, my friends

and

my mother

PART ONE

Schisms

Some people do what they want. Others do what they must. My mother did both and in between, she broke down. She was an enigma. Although she complicated things, we were a team. Our firm, Foster & Co. has been a part of the Brackwood community in New Hampshire for almost a century. We are a family of accountants. My father had been an accountant, his father's father and his great grandfather were too. My mother and I are also accountants.

Every Wednesday evening, we conducted business at my house, where my obsession with unlinking us began after one of our dinner meetings. My mother blurted out, "I don't want them looking at my hoo-ha."

Mourning the end of a pleasurable meal, I scraped my fork over the plate to capture the last bits of flavor. Loaded with creamy sauce, flecks of spinach and sprinkles of pepper, I shoved the last fork of scrumptious pasta into my mouth. When I looked across the table my mother scowled at me. Clad in a silvery-blue blazer and a cream blouse buttoned up to her neck, she looked formidable. Why wouldn't she relax?

Delaying as long as I dared, I plunged into the conversation. "What's a hoo-ha?"

"It's my possible."

"What's a possible?"

"You know what I mean, Portia. That place, making it possible, for women to have babies."

Mom fidgeted with her blouse. Although she is powerful, enterprising and considerate with a unique specificity, her frigidity bled me of my compassion. I had never heard her say vagina or penis or any sexual term.

"Are you talking about your vagina?" I asked.

"Yes, that place down there."

Leaving the table, I pushed stray foodstuff from our plates into the sink. My mother put our glasses into the dishwasher. The water spiraled down as it flushed the food particles away. I turned on the disposal to pulverize the food bits, giving myself time to think. I thought about remaining silent, but I couldn't.

"Why not say vagina?"

"Because... I don't think it's the easiest word to say."

My mother is brilliant. Nothing seemed too technical, detailed, or broad for her to grasp. Why was she so prudish? The day had been long but pleasant; an argument would spoil it. While loading the dishwasher, I surrendered to the upbeat music playing in the background. One of our favorite songs started playing. I sang along wishing to avoid a confrontation.

"Sing Mom." I held out a spoon for a microphone.

Mom gaped at me and then went back to the table; the moment lost to us. With our glasses in her hand and tears rolling down her cheeks, Mom came back to the sink. Turning to her, I adopted my father's gentleness.

"What's wrong?" I asked.

"Don't worry yourself—you go on—sing your little song."
Classic Mom. She kept on cleaning. First, she wiped down
the table. Next, she took the spoon I carried, brushed by me
and then tucked it into the dishwasher. After turning on the
dishwasher, she scrubbed the counter.

Life taught me to refrain from showing affection to her.
Pushing down my reservations, I mustered my goodwill.
Standing with my arms open, I implied she needed a hug. My
mother backed away. She stood rigid with a look of disgust on
her face.

Feeling rejected, I spat out, "I'm tired. Can you let me relax?"

"Sorry, but you know—"

"Just forget it Mom."

My mother swung around. Her veins popped out on her neck
like little snakes. "Don't go expecting me to change at fifty-six."

"You seemed upset. I was just trying to help."

"I'm fine. Don't let me stop you from relaxing."

Fleeing the dramatics, I left her standing at the sink. Sunset
filled the living room windows as I stared into the woodsy
outdoors. The clack of Mom's block heeled shoes reverberated
as she walked across the wood floor. My body tensed as she
approached me. When my mother reached me, she glanced my
way, crossed her arms and then gazed out the window. We stood
side-by-side like strangers in Times Square on New Year's Eve.

Taking slow deliberate strides, so as not to appear angry, I
went to the other side of the room. I sat in Dad's armchair. My
father had been Mom's only friend. After he died, Mom refused
to cultivate new friendships. Our codependency suffocated me,
yet I was afraid to let it be any other way. With my eyes closed,
I stroked the velvety suede covering the chair. Rubbing the soft
arms quelled my thirst for Mom's affection like a drink of cool
water after a long run on a hot day.

Clack, clack, clack, those shoes echoed as Mom came forward.
The clatter ended when she stopped right in front of me. I felt
trapped. Mom removed her blazer, draped it over the chair,

unpinned her hair and then letting out a heavy sigh, she sat in the chair next to me.

Dodging the catch-twenty-twos of Mom wasn't going to be possible that day. Overwhelmed by her intrusion, I appreciated the barrier formed by the table separating our chairs because it prevented me from feeling boxed in by her.

Mom looked over the vase sitting on the table. "I know the devil will get me there," she said.

"I thought you didn't believe in the devil."

"It's a saying, Portia."

"Can we talk tomorrow?"

"I'm trying to talk to you now."

I slipped out of my shoes and then lifted my legs into the chair. "It's been a long day and—"

"You don't care at all… do you?"

I exhaled, letting my shoulders drop. "Go ahead. I'll listen."

"Well, I know it's going to happen."

"What will happen?"

"Having a problem down there."

"Down where?"

"There, in my private place."

"What makes you say that Mom?"

"It's probably cancer."

"Now you're scaring me. What's going on?"

Mom twisted her mouth and then looked at her hands. "Tomorrow, I have a female exam."

"Do you mean a pelvic exam?"

"That's what I said."

"Women have pelvic exams all the time."

"I've survived for years without one."

"Why are you worried?"

"My doctor says it's important."

A chill washed over me. "Are you having a problem?"

"None of your business what's happening to me in that way."

I scrutinized Mom. She had never discussed her medical problems with me. I stood in front of her. Softening my voice, I said, "Please, tell me what's going on. Who knows, maybe I could help?"

"What could you possibly do?" Mom crossed her arms.

I squatted to feel closer to her. "I don't know. Maybe, I could drive you there tomorrow."

"Fine, be ready by nine."

I stood up. Mom stood up too. We were face to face. I looked into her eyes hoping she'd discuss her concerns. "Is it serious?"

Mom tugged her sleeves to cover her wrist. She almost whispered, "I just don't want them roto rootering around in me."

"You were married. Certainly, you've had a pelvic exam."

"Don't be crass. Your father is dead. I did what I had to do."

I sighed. "No problem, I'll take you."

"You mind if I sleep over?"

I shook my head.

My mother left the room, only to stand in the entryway minutes later with her travel bag slung across her body.

"Goodnight," she said and then headed down the hall.

I had been gullible. My mother's words often cut into me. More than that, I was accustomed to her uncharitable attitude. I'd learned not to reciprocate her unkindness, but she had duped me into driving her to the appointment. She probably rehearsed the scenario in her head. She could have asked me. Had she just asked, I would have agreed to take her without the drama. Instead, she power played me, bewitching me to offer my support.

Thinking about Mom's antics caused me to fear she had a major illness. I figured she might have some kind of cancer. If she did, caring for her wasn't going to be easy and we were going to have a tough road ahead of us. My father had a long, slow and painful death. Watching him waste away devastated me. How could anyone prepare for a trudge down that road? I wasn't fit for the job.

One of the obscure truths about me, is how my parents contributed to the duality of my person. I was warm and friendly or icy and detached. My mother underwrote the latter. Sometimes, it took days to balance myself after an encounter with her.

My father, he was different. He had been my champion and best friend. He died two weeks before my seventeenth birthday. Ten years later, I missed him as if he had just died. Yearning to express my woes to him, I rested against Dad's chair and inhaled deeply, searching for a remnant of his scent. None lingered.

I tuned into the sounds of day's end while I stared out the window. The branches, with their budding leaves, moved in a synchronized dance. The swaying trees mesmerized me and I let the room darken around me as I meditated in Dad's chair. Twilight passed and the moon rose while I thought back to the beginning of my father's illness.

On the day he went for the first of many hospitalizations, I was eight years old, and my father was fifty-nine, energetic, strong with well-defined muscles. He didn't look sick to me. Together, we waited for Mom in the living room. Dad rested in his chair while I sketched at the coffee table staying close to him.

At some point, Mom called out, "Time to go."

Then my father said, "Portia, help an old man."

"You don't need help Daddy," I teased back.

I loved calling him Daddy, but my mother insisted only Southerners called their fathers daddy, so I stopped calling him Daddy years before he died.

"I'm going to miss you. Come over here." Dad held out his hand. I went to him. When we clasped hands, he embraced me. After letting go, Dad slipped his feet into his shoes. I knelt to tie them before he could give permission.

When Mom came over to us, she put her purse on the sofa and then draped Dad's coat over it. Although I had limited understanding, I sensed Mom's sadness. My father remained as chipper as always, but I'm certain he hid his fear from us.

"Are you ready?" Mom asked.

"In a minute, my dear." Dad winked at me.

"When are you coming back, Daddy?"

"He'll be home in two weeks," Mom answered.

"Why so long?"

"They're going to remove a lump from my lung."

"We'll visit every day," Mom reassured me.

"I don't want you to go."

"You want me to be as good as new, don't you?"

I hugged him. "I do. May I come with you?"

When I released him, Dad leaned close to my face with his finger pressed to his lips. I silenced myself. "Let her come." Dad touched Mom's cheek. "Please?"

"Ramona is already here."

Dad turned to me. He cupped my face. "Go get your coat. I'll clear things with Mom." They argued while I fetched my coat.

"Howard, hospitals are dangerous places…" I heard Mom say. I didn't know it at the time, but my dad had lung cancer. His battle lasted nine years. The day he died, my mother mournfully said, "Your father saved my life." She never discussed him again.

Having recalled my father's illness, I regretted my contemptuous attitude. If she died, there would be no one left. Right then, I embraced my duty to support Mom. I knew, even if supporting my mother drained my soul, I would be there for her anyway.

I forced myself out of bed at six, still feeling groggy, I went downstairs to do a set of energizing exercises in the den. My mother had already settled in there. The chirp, chirp, chirp of birdsong welcomed the day as rays of sun illuminated the room. Mom had her back to the windows. The sunbeams enhanced the red highlights in her hair. She'd pinned it into a tight bun that rested at the back of her head, and she sat there waiting in one of her dark gray business suits.

At daybreak, Mom looked immaculate. How did she do it? I felt substandard compared to her. My jumbled hair was all over my head and my pajamas were rumpled. I walked over to her.

"You're dressed. Did you sleep?"

"Of course not; but I'm sure you did a fine job."

Her vitriol soured the morning, I froze to calm the thumping in my chest. For that day, I had one goal. Get through it, without upset or drowning in Mom's drama.

"Please, I can't do this so early in the morning," I said.

"We have a forty-minute drive. I hope you'll be ready?"

"It's only six o'clock." I walked away.

Mom called out, "If I must do this, I want to get on with it."

I smelled coffee. Ignoring my frustration, I did an about-face yielding to the aroma. In the kitchen, brewing coffee sizzled as it dripped on to the hot pad while I filled my cup. I drained the pot and then replaced it without wiping up the spilled coffee.

By the time we reached the doctor's office at nine forty, the caffeine had perked me up. Everything in the little anteroom where we waited for the doctor was beige or white. The walls were white, the tiles on the floor were white, the cabinets were white and everything else, like the couch we sat on, was beige. The magazines on the table added pops of color. Those magazines and the soft music streaming into the sterile room assured me we were still on the planet called earth. Even so, things were topsy turvy and weird.

"Breathe Mom," I said, noticing her shallow breathing.

"Hold my hand."

Mom turned up her palm, her hand laid between us on the sofa. I slipped my hand into hers. Fourteen years earlier, when I turned thirteen, Mom forbade me to touch her, and she seldom touched me. Holding hands might have been normal for other folk, but not for us. Things couldn't have gotten weirder.

"What's wrong, Mom?"

"Why do they need to probe around in there?" Mom said, *in there*, as if she referred to a scientific exploration into an Egyptian tomb.

"What's to be afraid of? You pushed me out—didn't you?" I teased to lighten the mood.

Mom jerked away. "I never liked it. I swear, I never liked it. I'm glad for you—that's all."

I snatched a journal from the magazine table. I felt nauseated. Mom's surly outlook infected me like a virulent pathogen. As I flipped through the pages, I doubted my ability to support her and struggled to regain my composure. Soon after, the doctor entered the room with the nurse.

Mom introduced Dr. Mitchell after they greeted one another. The doctor's energy spilled into the room. When we shook hands, I focused on her. Her dark chocolate skin radiated, her eyes were friendly, her braided hair wrapped around her head forming a crown and with her lab coat on, she looked like a goddess.

"I'm needing permission to discuss your medical matters in front of your daughter." Dr. Mitchell said after she sat in the chair across from us.

Mom nodded her approval.

"Today you're having a pelvic exam and a Pap test to check for cervical cancer. Are we in agreement?"

Mom nodded again.

"Next, there will be the bi-manual exam to check for abnormalities in your ovaries and uterus." Dr. Mitchell leaned forward, bringing herself the tiniest bit closer to us. "Do you have any questions?" she asked us.

"Do you suspect my mother has cancer?"

Dr. Mitchell shook her head. "No, this is routine, but we do want to rule out cancer with the testing."

"Are you ready Mrs. Foster?" The nurse asked.

Mom stood up, pressed her lips together and then straightened her blouse. As she entered the exam room, I declared my support. "Everything will be fine. I'll wait here for you."

Mom stopped. "I'd prefer you came in with me."

"Me?" My eyes blinked like running horses.

"Yes. Hope you don't mind."

"Sure, I'll come in," I said feeling as though I had no choice.

The doctor, the nurse and I waited in silence while Mom changed. A few minutes later, the ready light glowed. The nurse tapped on the door, poked her head into the room and then went inside with Mom. Later, she came back for me.

Mom sat there covered by a cool-mint colored sheet that concealed her hips and thighs. With her right hand, she clutched the medical gown to her neck. Mom pointed to the chair next to the exam table with her left hand.

"Move that chair over there," she demanded still pointing and then swung her arm to the opposite side of the room.

The chair scuffed the spotless white tiles when I dragged it across the floor. Feeling somewhat mortified, I carried it to the other side and then went to stand next to my mother.

"Please, sit over there when the doctor comes in," Mom said.

I smiled, hoping to ease her distress and then I noticed how puny Mom looked. Although she is six-feet tall, in her exam gown, Mom resembled a frightened child. My very fit, strong-willed mother appeared weak—even helpless. It seemed all the blood had drained from her face. Her legs dangled over the exam table, every few seconds, she swung them back and forth, flexing her feet each time.

My face flushed when I focused on her. Until that day, I had never seen above her calves or elbows. Even her pajamas hid her neck, legs and arms. A tap on the door startled her.

"Everything is fine. I promise." I touched her shoulder.

Mom swatted my hand. "What do you know?"

"Sorry Mom," I lowered my eyes.

She scooted away from me, exposing the black exam table beneath her as the thin paper crinkled and ripped with her abrupt movement. During that whole ordeal she held on to the gown. She still clutched it to her neck when the doctor came over to her.

Mom asked the nurse for a blanket. While the nurse fetched a hospital blanket, Mom ordered me to sit down. Refusing to behave like an obedient dog, I remained where I stood and turned my back to her. I gazed out the window. Keeping myself tuned in, I listened to Dr. Mitchell's soft lyrical voice as she performed the breast exam.

"Everything seems fine Ma'am," she said finishing the exam and then she rolled her stool to the end of the table.

The nurse instructed Mom to lie back and then she draped the blanket over Mom's body.

"I'm starting with the pelvic exam now."

After hearing Dr. Mitchell's words, I moved to the other side of the room, took a deep breath, relaxed my body and then sat down.

Using the blanket to create privacy, the nurse instructed my mother to move to the edge of the exam table, place her feet into the stirrups and to keep her back on the table. As Mom positioned herself, I became selfishly thankful for the blanket.

"I'm checking the thighs for lumps and lesions."

"Portia, please hold my hand."

I sprung out of the chair, went to Mom's side and then took her hand. The doctor retrieved a speculum from the metal tray. I turned away after the nurse squirted goop on it. As I stared out the window, the late morning sun warmed my face. To protect my sanity, I escaped, heart and soul, into the pale blue of the little bluets clustered along the pathway in the park below us.

"There's going to be some pressure," the doctor warned.

I turned when Mom squeezed my hand. She placed the blanket over her face. Her breathing got louder. Seeing the blanket go up and down over her mouth as she hyperventilated caused me to keep my eyes on her.

"You're going to feel a pinch now. Almost done here."

The nurse flattened her hand over my mother's belly and peeled the blanket away from Mom's mouth. "Push your lower back onto the table," she instructed. "Now, take a deep breath." The nurse looped through a set of directives, she said, "In through your nose... out through your mouth." Her soothing cadence calmed me too. I took several deep breaths.

At the other end of the table, the doctor placed a small vial on the tray. "With two fingers, I'll check the ovaries—" she began.

Mom jerked her feet out of the footrest. Her eyes blinked without delay. Her breathing quickened. Mom gripped the blanket and then sat up. "That will be enough," she said.

The doctor's sudden movement caused fear to sweep over Mom's face. In a panic, she shrunk away like a caged animal. After she collapsed onto the table, she brought her knees to her chest. I stepped back. As the nurse ushered me out, I glimpsed Mom lying there in the fetal position with her eyes wide open. My stomach knotted. Nothing made sense but I didn't ask any questions. I waited in the anteroom.

After a while, Dr. Mitchell came out. I motioned to go inside, but she shook her head. I sat down, letting her explain how Mom had had a panic attack in there. To calm her, they gave her a Librium injection.

Mom refused to stay with me after leaving the doctor's office. I felt awful, but there was no way to have foreseen her melt down. I'm not a psychic. For some unknown reason, she became overwhelmed. Before going into her house Mom said, "I thought I could finally manage it." Those were the only words she spoke and then she shut me out of her life for more than five weeks.

Although, it shouldn't have been true, at twenty-seven, I had made only microscopic insights into Mom's character. Consoling her moved beyond the range of my abilities. Unlike me, my father had understood her. He had also attended to her problems as if they were his own. After Dad died, I pleaded with Mom to feel better, to eat or go outside for fresh air. Those actions marked my limited ability to support her.

Nothing would prevent me from fulfilling my role as her dutiful daughter; yet I questioned my fitness to nurture my mother through any kind of illness. She needed a friend. Someone who could support her through whatever turmoil she might face. Although I doubted she had cancer, I wondered about her mental health, and I braced myself for a nightmare.

Throughout my childhood, Mom demanded periods of isolation from time to time, but I had never seen her cruise from lucidity into an inexplicable stupor. When Mom quarantined herself, those sequesters sometimes lasted a week, never more. After her episode at the doctor's office, things were different. For the first time, my mother shutdown for weeks and I began to fret. In the years after my father died, I grew to respect my mother's coping style, but I decided her time was up.

Six weeks after the appointment, I stormed into Mom's home office. I unlocked the door, entered and then walked right over to her. She grimaced when she saw me, perhaps because my unannounced visit annoyed her or perhaps because I hadn't knocked—it might have been both.

High stress always caused my mother to lose weight. That day, she wore a tawny, high-necked blouse, one of her favorites. It slipped down her shoulder. She seemed to have lost about fifteen pounds. Assessing her overall well-being or lack of it wasn't difficult because my mother never wore makeup. Her natural look made it easy to see that she wasn't doing well, and I knew she'd resist whatever support I offered.

"Glad to see you're alive." I opted to say.

"I am. Thank you."

"Well Frances, I'm worried about you."

"You know I don't want you calling me by my first name."

"This is business Mom."

My mother swiveled to sit behind her desk putting her back to me. I exited the channel between her worktable and desk. I studied her face. She looked past me. "Mom," I blocked her view, "we need you to work your accounts."

"We... who says I'm not?"

Without cause, I had accused her of slacking off, so I paused to examine her office. She had open documents on her screens, her untidy desk had folders everywhere and the cabinet on the back wall where she kept her reference books was ajar. I turned back to her.

"I see you're working. What about your deadlines?"

"Have I missed any deadlines—ever?"

"I don't think so."

"Well, I haven't. I was an accountant before you were even born. Don't try to track my responsibilities."

She flung a file folder onto her desk.

"I'm not here to track you."

"Then, what do you want?"

"I want you to stop ignoring me."

Mom sighed.

"I'm serious Mom."

"Well, you can't always get what you want," Mom said.

She offered a truce. During my childhood days, she played that Mick Jagger song countless times. On occasion, we held hands and danced around while it played. The song had been special to us. After her line, she expected me to say the next one. Saying those two lines became our private little game but over the years, it morphed into our way of patching things up after an extended disagreement.

Mom always presented the first key. My stubborn, rebellious, often angry, teenager self would impede her efforts for weeks if possible. That day, I didn't have the luxury of defiance. Releasing the tightness in my throat, I substantiated our respite by saying, "No, but if you try... who knows."

With the gorge of silence officially ended, I continued. "I'm worried about you."

Mom stared up at me. "I'm fine."

"You keep canceling our meetings."

"What's the problem? Anything burn down?"

"No, of course not. Do you have Reconciliations for the HS&M account?" I tried to legitimize my visit.

"I have two days—please, let me do my work."

"Mom, we're up to the deadline now. I'm managing the office for you because—"

"Are you about to accuse me of being incompetent?"

"You work from home now. If you wanted, you could still—"

"What do you mean—still?"

"I don't mean anything. If you were sick—about to die—or dead, then things would fall on my shoulders regardless. Right now, that's not the case."

"You think I'm dying?"

"I hope not. My point is… you're the CEO, not me."

"You want to fire me—don't you?"

"I can't fire you. You're the CEO."

"But you would fire me, if you could."

"No, Mom, I wouldn't."

"Then why are you here?"

I planted my hands on her desk, bent my elbows to make eye contact with her and then said, "I haven't heard from you. You refuse to answer your phone."

"I'm dealing with my life issues."

Her foray into powerlessness flummoxed me. "You could take sick leave," I suggested, hoping she'd consider the option.

"Like I said, I'm doing my best. Don't try to run me."

"You're accountable to people."

"Of course, I am. I know that."

Mom faced her screens. I moved into the aisle between the desks to prevent her from shutting me out. "Fine, I'll trust you to handle the business side. The other thing is the problem."

Mom turned her chair my way. "What other thing?"

"You know. The issue you had in your doctor's office."

"Talking about that, with you, will never happen."

Her flat, leave-me-alone tone deflated me. She needed to confide in someone, whatever her trouble. I readied myself to listen. "If you want to talk… I'll listen. I'm here for you."

Mom sneered, "What do you think I need?"

"I don't know… someone to confide in?"

"You're my child. We can't have a heart-to-heart talk about my private matters."

"You should talk to someone."

"I take care of myself. Sorry you don't like it."

"You had an awful experience. It disturbed me. Why can't we talk about that?"

"I see. We're talking about you now."

"No, I'm talking about us."

"What horrible thing happened to you?"

"Seeing you collapse like that… I felt awful."

"I'm sorry you felt bad. But I'm not going to chitchat with you about those things."

At the time, I trusted my mother in business; yet her personal life remained cryptic. For unknown reasons, she wouldn't share the tiniest detail of her personal life with me. During my college years, Mom had become more elusive. I found myself in a curiously odd predicament because her clandestine manner kept me guessing. Somehow, Mom's atypical lifestyle made us inseparable, and all the emotional wrenching sucked me into her madness.

After a long pause I said, "You must have confided in Dad. Now you're closing yourself off."

"How would you know? I protected you from my problems."

"Protected? We lived in the same house. I figured things out."

"Well, you're not figuring anything out right now. I'm not asking for help or support. Please respect my choice."

"What would you have me do Mom?"

"I will get past this… I always do."

"But… I feel like we need to talk."

"I can't tell you how to feel. I'm living my own life. You should do the same."

"That's crazy. We can't go our separate ways."

"Crazy?" Mom pecked at her keyboard. "Things will get back to normal soon enough."

"Normal? What I saw wasn't normal."

Mom twisted her face as if she were in pain. She seemed to freeze in place but then she rubbed her wrist. A second later, her face reddened, giving away her embarrassment. Both my worry and confusion took hold of me. I stepped away from her. If my inquiries made her feel worse, then I wasn't helping at all.

"I'm leaving now. Please eat," I said opening the door.

Our encounter disturbed me for days. I had earned my MPA as my mother advised. Even so, I didn't qualify for her job. Taking on CEO duties put a lot of pressure on me, and I had stepped up. Mom's dismissal hurt deep down. She seemed to find me lacking as both a daughter and a colleague. Whenever she commanded me, I wanted to say, I'm not your puppet. Instead, I always clammed up.

My father inspired me to become an accountant. He groomed me to love everything about it. So, I loved it. I unreservedly loved it, but nothing could change my temperament. Management just didn't suit me. I'm the kind of person who finds underlying causes. If things don't add up or make sense, I can't let go until they do.

Had I followed my true passion, I would have defied Mom to study forensic accounting. I'd made my career choice as dictated by my mother, but I had also grown weary of being her stopgap. Acting CEO had been a useless role anyway, because my mother wielded the power of the position, and every single employee knew it.

There's no way to quit a family, but I did consider quitting the Firm. It wasn't possible. Although my dad had died years before, my perception of his disappointment pressed upon me the importance of staying at our firm. Imagining his disapproving scowl, I realized a workable solution eluded me.

I'd never stop being an accountant and starting a competing firm would have put a permanent wedge between my mother and me. Our dispute would have lasted for a lifetime. Absent of a winnable solution, and without any leverage nothing could change. Like always, I just did what Mom wanted.

Not until the following Wednesday, when Mom showed up unpredictably for our canceled meeting, did I rethink my options. Mom walked into my house carrying dinner. I stood in front of her.

"What's this?" I asked.

"It's from Maydan Taverna." She pushed past me.

"Wait a minute; I want to know why you're here?"

"It's Wednesday, four o'clock. Don't we have a meeting?"

"You've canceled for weeks now."

"According to the office, you still leave early on Wednesdays."

"Mom you can't—"

"A mother can't visit her daughter; keep a scheduled appointment?"

"You haven't spoken to me in days."

"Time is time. You hungry?"

"I'm already preparing my dinner."

"Have that later."

Mom unpacked the food, and I itched all over. Becoming quarrelsome would have heightened my nervousness. I yielded the kitchen to her and then retreated to my father's chair. While I watched the sun twinkle through the trees, I imagined myself to be a squirrel living in the woods.

Out there, living as a small creature, would have meant never having to battle with my mom again. I lived my fantasy until Mom rang out, "Let's eat."

Every part of me wanted to ignore her. Unable to resist, seduced by the smell of lamb, I headed for the kitchen. While Mom transferred rice from a foil container into a serving dish, I set two dinner plates on the kitchen table.

"We're in the dining room, my dear." Mom smiled.

I cringed at the news. Eating in there would make me miss my father, his parents and all the big gatherings we had when they were alive. Mom scooped out the last bits of rice before heading to the dining room. I followed.

"Why did you choose the dining table today?"

"I know you prefer to eat in here."

"These days, eating in the kitchen is better."

"You don't want to eat with me. Do you?"

Although I couldn't tell her, she had it right and I also wanted her to go home. "I'm missing Dad right now. That's all."

Mom studied my face. "Fine, let's move."

I carried my plate away. I sat at the kitchen table in front of my empty plate letting Mom ping-pong between the dining room and kitchen until she brought everything to the table.

"You couldn't help?" Mom asked when she finished.

"This is your show."

I served myself. Mom filled her plate with lamb, rice and vegetables. Seeing her eat lightened my heart. I dipped a piece of pita bread into the hummus, closing my eyes as the tang of the nutty spread filled my mouth. I enjoyed my meal for a few minutes.

"This is delicious Mom."

"I sent an intern to get your favorites."

"You were in the office today?"

"We had a board meeting."

"How is the ACC Foods account coming along?"

Mom spread hummus on a piece of pita bread, chewed slowly and finished her little bite before responding.

"They're apprehensive about the audit."

"If you work this out for them, they might sign as a new client."

"Right now, I'm preparing responses to the IRS questions and gathering the supporting documentation."

"This account fits you. You are definitely the most persnickety." Mom laughed. "On this I agree."

Her eyes were lively. I loved hearing her laugh. In her own way, she could be good-natured. Ending our laughter, I lowered my eyes and risked asking a personal question.

"Have you resumed your regular schedule?"

"Not one hundred percent."

Mom touched the collar of her blouse. Her uneasiness made me nervous. I reverted to Foster & Co. business. "Any board decisions I should know about?"

"Just one," she said. "Would you like to lead the 2008–9 budget planning sessions?"

"It would be an honor. I'd love to."

"Then, the job is yours."

Mom smiled and then we cleared the table. Years before, we had a cook, a housekeeper and a driver. They all lived on the property. Whereas I preferred driving myself around, having someone else take care of our meals and the kitchen duties pleased me.

"I miss the days when we had a cook," I told Mom.

"Not me. I let everyone go a few months after your father died."

"You wanted privacy, but I liked having a busy house."

"Well, then… shall I sleep over?"

I cleared my throat. "I think you should sleep at your house."

Mom held her hand to her chest. Her eyes blinked like a turn signal. "I thought you said I'm always welcomed."

"You are, but… What about our conversation? We—"

"Haven't we settled this?"

I wondered if my mother actually thought things had gone back to normal. I took a deep breath. "We haven't talked. How could we have settled anything?"

Mom looked past me. "I don't believe there's anything I can say to fix this obsession you're having."

"Maybe not, but until we talk, let's stick to business matters."

"Are you saying, I can't be your mother, if I'm not willing to discuss my private matters with you?"

"Nothing could stop you being my mother. We both know you had a breakdown during your pelvic exam."

"Why is it important to you?"

"You went berserk. Don't you think I should know what happened?"

"I didn't go berserk."

Wiping down the table and avoiding her eyes, I asked, "Where are your friends? Who do you talk to?"

"I'm at my best when I'm alone."

"If you want to be alone... why stay here?"

"Fine, Portia. I'll go home."

"Go ahead... go. Shut me out. It's what you do."

Mom began to cry. I felt drained. We hadn't patched things up. Pretending otherwise didn't work for me. I walked away, thinking she was old enough to care for herself. Even so, the hullabaloo surrounding her threatened to consume me.

Mom walked straight to her room, clicking the door shut behind her, ignoring my wishes. She had a right to stay, the room had been my parents' until my father died. Before my final year in college ended, my mother renovated the house. She kept all the things I treasured, Dad's chair, the kitchen and dining room tables and she left my father's office untouched. Those things reminded me of life with my father in it.

I loved my house because it connected me to him. When I graduated, she bestowed it to me. Had Mom wished, she could have sold everything. As a loving gesture, I gave Mom the room saying, it was a *forever deal*.

Unable to ask her to leave, I went into my father's study. It had been his haven. Everything remained as Dad had left it, minus the smell of his cologne. A mahogany desk sat in the middle of the room atop a hand knotted Oriental rug. I passed my fingers across the desktop before sitting in his chair to feel closer to him.

The leather chair had a tufted seat, tufted back and sat on a five-prong base, with fixed leather armrests. I touched each brass stud, moving my fingers down the arms, counting each one as I had done since childhood, as I did the day my father died. Sixty studs per arm. I knew without counting but counted anyway.

I fixated on the bookcases lining the back wall. Rows of accounting journals filled the shelves. They had been in my family since the 1800s and I had looked through them since childhood. Somehow, they grounded me. In the past, those journals had reaffirmed my link to the Foster family, always reminding me of how I belonged to something bigger. But all the Fosters I knew, had died. There wasn't a single Foster for me to connect with and I needed to know that someone—anyone cared about me.

After a troubled sleep, I headed to the office around five o'clock to avoid another confrontation with my mother. Our tussle grieved me, and my irritation caused me to question how she'd managed to alienate her parents—people I learned about from my father, after my thirteenth birthday.

Dad delivered me to them months later, on the first Sunday after summer break began. Without any fanfare, he drove me to the Miller Farm, walked me to the door, hugged me and then said goodbye before my grandmother took me inside. There were a series of firsts that day. My grandparents welcomed me into their home, I saw their faces, heard their voices, learned about the farm and felt betrayed by my father.

At the office, I phoned Grammy Miller. Hearing her voice caused tears to stream down my face. My mother's mother loved me, and she also connected me to the world outside of myself and Mom. During our short conversation, Grammy invited me for a visit the following weekend, but after hanging up, my loneliness spread.

The planned visit sparked my need to belong to someone or something outside of myself. I remembered how the Miller farm had been my refuge. I loved it there. Picking up the phone, I called back to ask Grammy if I could extend my visit. She delighted in the idea, inviting me to stay for a restful break. Without hesitating, I accepted. No matter my intentions, I had to stand up to my mother before taking off.

Out of fear, I scripted what I wanted to say. No matter what, Mom was going to try to stop me from going forward with my plan. I had to be ready. I vowed not to consent to any deviations or compromises.

Wednesday afternoon, my anxiety prevented me from concentrating at work. I went home to prep everything. I laid out copies of my weekly report, tabulated our quarterly projections, cooked, set the table and as much as I hated to do it, cleaned the kitchen too.

Later, my mother burst through the door full of positive energy. "Did you have a good week?" she asked.

I turned away from her.

Mom sighed but didn't challenge me.

We sat across from one another, using the middle chairs as we always did during our meetings. I pushed my weekly report over to her. Feeling my palms get sweaty, I said, "I'm going to take some time off from work." I spewed out my words like a child regurgitating an undigested secret.

"What do you mean by time off?"

"I've worked almost non-stop since graduating four years ago."

"Maybe we do need a vacation."

Her response bewildered me. I couldn't have her making vacation plans for us. I concentrated on her face when I replied.

"I'm going alone," I told her.

Mom jumped up. She paced back and forth on her side of the table. After a sigh, she relaxed her face and then took a deep breath before sitting down again. Emotionless, with a blank expression, she said, "Are you trying to punish me?"

"Not at all, I need a break."

"What kind of break do you want?"

"I need an unspecified amount of time away from everything."

"Unspecified? You can't take off on a whim."

"It's not a whim."

"What would you have me do? Let anyone take unplanned time off?"

"I'm not anyone. I'm your daughter."

"Certainly, this is some kind of punishment."

"That's not true. Besides, Jarod or you can do everything I do."

"You may be right."

"Thank you, that's a start. Perhaps—"

"Remember, in a few years, the Firm will pass to you."

I paced the kitchen. "I know but right now—"

"Where are you going?"

"I'd rather not say." I turned away.

"Let's talk about this next week."

After sitting down again, we ate in silence. Thinking back, I saw how Mom had become my whole life. Absent of any desire to harm or disappoint her, I became an obedient child and unwittingly turned into a servile adult. We were tangled up in a fourteen-year-old nightmare. One I hadn't created. I wanted it to end. Unfortunately, nothing changed the barriers she placed between us. None of my efforts punched a hole through or even made a pin prick in her defenses. "Mom, I leave Saturday morning," I said when we finished eating.

"You can't leave so soon. We need to plan this hiatus of yours."

"Promote Jarod McKinley to CEO."

"I will never do that."

"He's a worthy person. He's worked for us over fifteen years. He deserves a chance."

"I need time to reflect on how to make your time off work."
Her remark caused me to abandon my script. I spoke firmly
to put things back on track. "I'm not changing my plans."
"You're being ridiculous."
"Just promote Jarod. Think about all the freedom you'll have.
You could travel the world."
"I've already seen the world. I don't like it."
"Mom, I trust you'll figure things out."
"And I'm telling you to wait because—"
"Telling me? I'm not asking your permission." I interrupted
her, ensuring she couldn't pressure me to stay.
"You're putting me in a very difficult position."
"Seriously, think about Jarod. He has his MBA. I trust him."
She studied my face. "I'd like you to give me a month before
you go."
"I can't—I leave Saturday."

My mother appeared in my office Friday morning. She wore
a black business suit with a white round collar shirt. She looked
stunning. I had forgotten how commanding she appeared in the
office. Her stature combined with her hairstyle and her strong
resonating voice warranted respect. "I cleared your calendar. My
office in ten minutes," Mom commanded.
"Sure thing," I spoke in my professional voice.
Mom tapped my desk and then walked out. My hands were
shaky. Suspecting she wanted to stop me from leaving, I enumer-
ated my reasons for taking a break. To avoid panicking, I told
myself, I'd quit if necessary. Once I gathered the papers on my
desk, I locked my computer and then headed down the hall.
When I walked into Mom's office, she pushed a document
across her conference table. I sat in front of it. I read the title,
Strategic Plan 2008–9, flipped through the pages and studied

the new organizational chart. Mom had added two top-level positions. In addition to the CEO, the Firm would have a COO and a CFO.

"Who will fill these positions?"

"I will remain CEO until you're ready. You'll be the CFO. Jarod will move into the COO position."

I grinned. "CFO?"

"You'll get away from operations. I know you struggle with it."

Mom had it right. I more than struggled. Starting out, she made me the Assistant Director of Operations. Jarod mentored, coached and listened to my fears too, but nothing helped. I was fresh out of school, unlike my fellow employees who had years of experience. I should not have been their boss. Telling those people how to do their jobs wasn't fair to them and it was spectacularly uncomfortable to me.

"This is brilliant." I flipped the page.

"Always remember, this is our firm. We needn't make ourselves subordinate to anyone."

We discussed the duties and responsibilities of the CFO position until Jarod knocked. When he came in, my mother stood up. Jarod was almost forty, but his creamy brown skin gave no sign of aging. He looked nervous and pensive at the same time. His nervousness surprised me because it contradicted his calm nature.

"Is there a problem?" he asked.

"Should there be?" Mom joshed before extending her arm. She said, "Jarod, you're our new COO." Mom released his hand.

His eyes blinked fast; his thick eyelashes swooped like palm trees in the wind as Jarod rubbed his low-cropped hair. His handsome face became more wonderful when he smiled.

"Oh, wow. Not what I expected."

"You earned it. Shall I assume you accept?"

"Yes, I accept. I whole-heartedly accept."

"Congratulations," I said, while shaking his strong hand.

My mother took her seat. "Let's go over everything."

We dug into the strategic plan. Jarod interrupted when he saw the new organizational chart. "When will you advertise for the CFO position?"

"Portia is the new CFO."

"I see. How's that?"

"Let's be clear, you currently oversee our business operations. Portia, with a bit of help from me does the financials."

"Yes, I agree. Isn't she the acting CEO right now?"

"Not anymore, I'm returning full-time."

Jarod leaned to his left. "Congratulations."

His shoulder nearly touched mine when he spoke. Months earlier, I had confided to him how I disliked being the CEO. I had expected to get years of experience first. Had things happened according to the original plan, I might have had the needed courage to take over the Firm. Not having the proper experience unsettled me but Mom's organizational change remedied the situation.

Once we finished our meeting, Mom asked Jarod to give her a minute with me. He nodded and walked away from the conference table. I watched him go to the door, arms swinging, in his perfectly fitted blue suit.

Mom's singsong voice brought me back into the room. "You can't always get what you want," she was saying. Her smile melted away my fears and her eyes were charitable.

I replied, "But if you try, sometimes you do."

"Satisfied?" she smiled again.

I nodded. "Yes, I am. Thank you."

"Good. Go do whatever you need to do."

Mom allotted six months for me to figure myself out. I wanted to hug her.

Promoting Jarod proved she had considered my advice. She also managed to formulate a better plan. As we exited her office, Mom clapped me on the back, letting her arm linger on my shoulders for a few seconds, making her action the closest she'd come to hugging me in years. I appreciated what she had done for me, but my mother's breakdown changed something between us.

There had been no medical problems to worry about. I figured she'd probably live to be at least a hundred. Whatever caused her panic attack had nothing to do with her physical health, but questions lingered in my mind when it came to her mental health. I craved emotional space. Somehow, I needed to stop acquiescing to Mom's every whim.

For years, I had sampled alternative ways to better communicate with Mom. Nothing worked. My exodus would give me time to figure out how I wanted to live my life.

PART TWO

Family Secrets

Early Saturday morning, I headed to Connecticut. Jarod phoned after I'd gotten a few hours away from Brackwood. He sounded doleful when he asked if our hike was off. Absorbed by my own problems, I forgot about the hike. He'd waited an hour at the meet up place before giving up on me. Guilt swelled in me like a love song when I realized my selfishness. I offered a rain check and then expressed my gratitude when he accepted.

Once we passed that hurdle, we talked for over an hour. Jarod told me his promotion would allow him to stop avoiding a few things. He didn't elaborate. I chose not to pry. Our secrets were ours alone. My visit—no, my escape to the farm was mine. When Jarod questioned me about my trip, I changed the subject to keep my whereabouts private. That decision marked my endeavor to protect Jarod. I protected him from feeling uncomfortable around my mother, protected my mother from the truth and protected myself from my guilty feelings.

Minutes later, to stop feeling awkward, I ended our conversation and then turned my thoughts to the farm. My grandparents ran the Miller farm with Uncle Jack, my mother's brother. On occasion, I phoned them, but our conversations were always short because they weren't the kind of people who talked on the phone. The best way to converse with them was stopping by to see them. Getting my first car let me do just that—my first solo road trip led me straight to the farm. During my undergraduate years, I spent innumerable weekends with Grammy because attending Cornell made visiting even easier. Just a three-hour drive and boom, I was there.

Grammy Miller's name is Margaret Ann, but everyone calls her Peggy. My Gramps is Jack Henry. His son, my uncle, is Jack Henry too. My uncle also named his first son Jack Henry. I called him Jack because Gramps was Gramps. Uncle's parents call him Junior, but I call him Uncle to avoid confusion and only his parents call him Junior anyway. Finding myself somewhat judgmental, I've wondered why anyone would pass on such a name. No matter my qualms, there were three Jack Henrys on the Miller farm, and I was eager to see them.

In my mind, farm life had its advantages; work was in your backyard, life was slow, and it kept the family close. Five years had passed since I last visited. Uncle's youngest son wouldn't remember me, but I didn't care, because I remembered him. Looking forward to my visit put me at ease and I envisioned a carefree break at the farm.

Denten snuck up on me. At noon, I passed through the farm gates and drove around to the back of their new house. Grammy's wide brimmed hat fanning in the wind caught my eye. She stooped next to a strawberry bush. When Grammy stood up, she leaned back, stretched her arms into the air, letting the wind blow over her body. A gust of wind stuck her cotton dress against her legs like a wet sheet. In her shadowy farm dress, she blurred into the landscape like a whisper.

As she straightened herself, she saw me and then waved. I waved back. Putting her pick basket on the ground she spoke to the farm worker next to her. I hurried along until I turned into her row of strawberries. Reaching Grammy, I opened my arms to embrace her. Instead of crying away my misery, I squeezed Grammy tight.

After our long hug, she took her hat off. Her rosy face radiated with a healthy inner glow. The laugh lines around her eyes deepened when she smiled.

"How are you my sweet one?" she asked.

I glanced at a farm worker who plucked ripe strawberries. "I'm fine." I answered feeling guilty for being a liar.

"Sorry I wasn't inside," she said as her crow's feet disappeared.

"No problem, I'm a big girl. How are you these days?"

"I'm fine too. Need to get more work done. Looks like I got myself another set of hands."

"Sure, I'll help."

"Not now, we'll get there. Go say hello to your grandpa. Take those." She pointed to a crate jam-packed with harvested strawberries. The pickers had stacked them like jigsaw puzzle pieces, and they peeked over the edge without falling out.

At the house, I left the strawberries on the porch, went inside where the mingling smell of apple pie mixed with baked chicken made me hungry. A cornucopia of farm produce filled the kitchen. There were heaps of cherries, pounds of potatoes, onions, green leafy vegetables and asparagus. To tame my hunger pangs, I ate a handful of cherries and then grabbed some soda.

Carrying two root beers, I followed the hack, hack, hack of wood splitting. I navigated to the sound until I found Gramps behind the barn next to the woodshed. He didn't notice me. Perched on a stump about fourteen feet away from him, the sun warmed me while I drank my soda.

Gramps took wood from the pile to his left, split it and then cast it to his right. He whacked out a steady beat, *clunk-hack-thump—clunk-hack-thump*. He had a wide reach like a basketball player, but his bulging biceps looked as though he'd swung a baseball bat for a living instead of his occasional ax swinging.

His hair had gone all white like fresh snow. He kept it cut short. According to him, "like any good Christian would do." Even at seventy-five, Gramps seemed young because his vitality emanated from him. Strangely, he only lost his sour countenance when he worked or prayed. At those times, he looked childishly peaceful.

During an extended pause, I went over and handed him the root beer. Gramps put the soda on the tree stump, threw his arms around me, patted me on the back and then squeezed my shoulder. "Let's thank God for bringing you safely." We almost banged foreheads when he bowed his head. He laughed after saying his prayer. "You getting taller or am I shrinking?"

"I'm six-two. Same as last time you saw me."

"Guess I'm shrinking."

"Maybe a little."

"When you getting yourself married off?"

His tone caused me to feel guarded. "Summer's coming," I said with a smile. "You already planning for winter?"

"Stopped for lunch. But ain't no lunch."

"I'm super hungry. I drove six hours without stopping."

"Well, I'm bout as hungry as a pregnant filly myself." Gramps gulped his root beer.

"Why all the chopping?"

"I ain't one for wasting time. Got to apply my hands to something."

"Not me. I'm looking to take a long break from work."

"Yeah, you working on becoming a famous painter?"

"No. I paint for pleasure. I'm an accountant now. I work with Mom."

Gramps frowned, then picked up another piece of wood. He hadn't alleged anything, yet I deciphered he had an issue with my life choices. Gramps had been an artist, but at eighteen, he took over the farm after his father died, working to care for his mother and younger brother. From then on, he never painted again. When Grammy tells the story, she says he went sour. Strangely, they got married the same year he went sour.

Uncle walked up to us. He hadn't changed a bit. "Where's Mama?" he asked Gramps.

"Harvesting strawberries."

"I'm starving," Uncle said.

"We all starving," Gramps grunted and then went back to building his pile of firewood.

Uncle turned to me. "Hey Portia, Mama's all excited about you coming. Sorry for being rude earlier."

"Unmistakably, you're just too hungry for niceties," I chuckled.

"I am." Uncle patted his belly.

"You came around to see me?"

"Sorry, no. I eat lunch with my folks on most workdays. Today the food isn't ready. I'm going to have a word with the cook."

I laughed. "How's everyone?"

"We're doing fine. How's my one and only niece?"

"I'm well. But need a rest."

Uncle shaded his eyes while he looked me over.

"You let your hair grow."

"Took two years."

"Long hair is nice. Yours makes you more beautiful I think."

All the talk about my looks made me more self-conscious. I couldn't tolerate the attention. "How did your renovation project turn out?"

"Don't ask me. That's my wife's territory. You should come by while you're here."

Uncle shoved his hands deep into his pockets as little boys like to do. No one would mistake him for a boy though. His stature alone would stop anyone having such thoughts, if anything, people might mistake him for my father. We are both over six feet tall—we have thick black hair, high cheekbones and straight-edged noses—Uncle has hazel eyes, whereas mine are golden like dollops of honey. Unlike me, Uncle is brawny and I'm just athletically skinny.

"Everyone, come eat," Grammy called out to us.

In the house, Gramps went upstairs to clean up while Grammy showed me to the guestroom. "Much better room," she said before opening the door. "There's a bathroom and a door to the patio. It's very private."

"Thanks Grammy. Let me freshen up a bit."

"Lunch is waiting. Hurry along now."

After Grammy went out, I placed my bag on the built-in bench under the window and then paused to look at the apple blossoms in the orchard before cleaning up. Although, I had never slept in their new house, the room seemed cozy and familiar. The same blue and yellow patterned antique quilt I'd slept under since my first visit long ago, covered the queen-size bed. I always wondered if it had belonged to my mother. A large painting, I'd given Gramps years earlier, hung where a television might have been. It depicted the farm landscape with their old house in the background. It was a pleasant room and the coffee-colored walls made me want a scoop of my favorite ice cream.

"Want some help?" I asked when I walked into the kitchen.

"Everything's under control." Grammy stood behind the chair at the head of the table. "This is my chair. It's closest to the stove."

Gramps sat in the chair to her right.

"Table's too long for a king and a queen. We let Mama be the sole ruler," he laughed. So did the rest of us.

"How long is this table?" I asked.

"A little over eight feet." Uncle pulled out his chair.

"We got a perfect place for farm work." Grammy smiled, "You can help hull strawberries after we eat." She put a bowl of string beans on the table and then pointed to the chair next to Uncle.

"Sit there," she said.

Once she'd set all the food on the table, everyone held hands. We formed a chain with me reaching across the table to hold Gramps' hand. I studied the wood grain in the thick table as he prayed. He ended the blessing saying, "Bless the hands that prepared it."

Grammy and Uncle said, "Amen."

Uncle loaded mashed potatoes onto his plate. Gramps smiled when he said, "Give those to Portia when you done. She needs meat on her bones."

"Portia, I killed those chickens this morning. Just for you."

"Thanks Grammy."

"She didn't kill no chickens. I did," Gramps said.

"I told you to do it." Grammy objected.

"Your grandma would starve if she had to kill a chicken or anything else for that matter."

"No, I wouldn't. I'd have to become one of those modern types. I'd stick to fruits and vegetables."

Gramps smirked. "Peggy, you know you love meat more than anybody. Everybody knows you do."

Grammy laughed, then picked up her chicken and took a big bite. I did too. "This chicken is so fresh." I stretched out the word 'so' until Uncle bumped my shoulder.

"That's how you fix a broken record," he said.

I laughed hard. During the meal, I allowed myself to dismiss my worries. Removing the pressures of Brackwood from the equation made it easy.

After lunch, Gramps hoisted a crate onto the table. "Church tomorrow—you coming?" he asked.

"I'm not big on church."

"Well, you got to figure—"

"Let's get those strawberries going." Grammy cut him off.

"Are you going to make strawberry pies?"

"City girl." Gramps put a knife next to his cutting board.

Grammy patted my hand. "No, sweetie, these are for preserves."

"I'm glad you can cook. I'm useless in the kitchen."

Gramps laughed. "See what I mean? City girl through and through."

"That may be, won't stop her from carrying in strawberries." Grammy pointed to the back door. "Go get at it," she said.

We all had assignments. Gramps hulled. Grammy washed, sliced and cooked strawberries. Uncle took down the cooking pots, dragged over a barrel of sugar and carried in boxes of canning jars. Finding a measure of enjoyment in the work, I merrily completed my task.

"I cleared the porch."

I stood there holding a crate of strawberries.

"Your city arms tired?" Uncle kidded me.

"Nope." I felt my laugh grow from deep down, releasing my stored-up tension. Since arriving on the farm, I had laughed more in a few hours than I had in months. Recovering from my hearty laugh, I looked at the crates bursting with strawberries. The red-specked fruit engulfed us. "How can we finish this today?" I asked.

Gramps looked at me. "Got somewhere to be?"

"I'm just wondering—"

"We got the rest of the day. We'll do what we can. Same as every harvest." Gramps twisted his knife to remove a strawberry top.

Uncle prepared the canning jars. Grammy dumped a load of strawberries into the pot. "You mind bringing in three crates from the cold room?" she asked pouring a heap of sugar into her pot.

"Not at all."

"Hurry back, so you can help hull," Gramps hollered before I stepped outside.

I trekked out to get the strawberries. The cold storage is at least fifty feet from the house, and I consigned myself to wrangling as much pleasure out of the experience as possible. The fragrant scent of ripening fruit spread across the farm. I sniffed in the purity. Everything about the bucolic environment lifted my spirit. The cloudless sky bordered on deep blue enhancing the delightful mixture of farmhouses, cultivated crop and green-houses scattered throughout the farm.

For me, the rustic landscape foreshadowed a renewal of my spirit. The day had been warm but not too hot, the breezes were cool but not chilly. I had happened upon a perfect day to begin my adventure. In minutes, I reached the insulated storage room where they housed the farm's harvested produce. They kept it at thirty-nine degrees all year long. Going inside was like stepping into winter.

I cheerfully hustled each crate from storage back to the house, until with a tinge of sadness, I hauled in the last crate. I felt invigorated. Gramps called me over to him to stop me from pacing the kitchen. "You got a bug up your butt?" he asked.

I didn't answer but I sat next to him. He taught me how to hull strawberries. With a paring knife, he used a circular motion to remove the stem and fibrous core. Once he gutted the strawberry, he put his knife down. "Easy as pie." I used my knife to do the same. Gramps inspected my work. "See, even educated folks can do it."

Something about Gramps' jab irritated me. Perhaps the demeaning tone made me feel small. I didn't laugh. Uncle and Grammy did, and I wondered if I was being too sensitive. Even so, I ignored his ridicule. I hulled strawberries.

Throughout the evening, Uncle and my grandparents exhibited a familiarity with one another causing me to feel like an outsider. They laughed at jokes I didn't get, they talked about things I didn't know about, they discussed business as if I weren't in the room. I fought for space in their arena. I asked about growing strawberries, harvesting, planting or any aspect of farming where I had genuine curiosity.

Even with lots of tomfoolery, we managed to process the whole load of strawberries. I'd guess there were at least a hundred jars. Around eight o'clock, we added labels and then placed them into storage crates. Two days later, Uncle carted them off to the Miller Food Market.

Overall, I'd had a pleasant evening. Lying in bed, that night, I itemized all the reasons why the farm had been the best choice for a getaway. First of all, my grandparents were decent people and they made me feel welcomed. Being on the farm made it easy to relax, but most of all, I hadn't thought about my mother. I drifted off to sleep thinking about how much I loved my Denten family.

Monday morning, Gramps shook me awake. "Can't waste away your life in bed," he said loud enough to wake a dead cow.

I rolled over. "It's my vacation."

"Sleep's for city folk. Come on, wake it up."

At seven thirty, I should have felt rested, but I wanted to stay in bed for at least another hour. On most days, I ran at 5:00 a.m., but that day I had to drag myself to the shower. Thirty minutes later, I walked into an empty kitchen. Gramps' chair squeaked out on the porch. For a good minute, I stood at the kitchen door watching him. He rocked himself in his beloved rocking chair, a slow, meditative, life is grand back-and-forth kind of rocking. He just stared out on the farm.

When I stepped out, he used his final rock as momentum to come to his feet. I felt a little guilty for disturbing him. He glanced at me and then headed down the stairs. Following him, I stretched my arms over my head to get the blood flowing through my body. The cool air had already begun to make me feel more alert.

There was a tractor humming off in the distance and I wondered if Uncle drove it. Several steps away from the porch, Gramps said, "At supper yesterday, you told us you needed time to think. I'm gone give you plenty of work today."

"I did say that; I didn't mean hard labor."

Gramps chuckled. "Ain't nothing better for thinking than farming." I couldn't refute him. He had never asked me to do any farm work. From my childhood days until then, he had left me to do as I pleased. Aside from Grammy dragging me around town to shop, go to the market or some other thing she thought I'd enjoy, they both gave me the freedom to just be me. There were visits where I spent most of my time painting, other times, I read, or worked on my own projects.

This was especially true during my college years, on those visits, I ate, slept and studied. Mealtimes and Sundays marked my time with them. Even then, we didn't talk much. The farm was a second home to me. Yet, for the first time, Gramps and I walked together in the fields, strolling past rows of earth extending out like braided hair. Spotted patches of green highlighted the work ahead. It was time to plant the summer crop.

We passed a group of farm workers and then went into one of the barn-style greenhouses. The muffled light calmed me. Tuning out when Gramps gave details about the plants we passed, catching a few words, I heard, beans something, something— onions something, something and seeds something, something. Without my morning coffee it was impossible to pay attention.

Halfway down, we stopped at a nest of small plants on a series of grow tables. Light green leaves sprouted out of the cubes of soil. Rows of seedlings stretched out from where I stood to the back of the greenhouse.

Gramps picked up one of the seedlings. "Portia, I want you to give farming a chance."

"I'll try. Should I say thank you?"

"In time, you just might." He pinched off a tiny leaf. "Taste it."

He put the bud into his mouth. I clipped a sprout as he had done. An earthy bitter taste filled my mouth. The leaf tasted like beets without the crunch or wetness. Right after, Gramps rolled out a farm cart; it looked like a cross between a wagon and a baby stroller.

"Your job for today is to work this area. Time to get these beets in the ground. Turn the plant into your hand like this. Then place it in the cart. Make sure not to break or bend the leaves."

I watched his rugged hand lift another plant from the grow table. With the gentleness one might use to hold a newborn baby, he turned the plant into his other hand. Once he righted it, he put it into the cart. Banishing the serenity from his face, he turned to me.

"You got it?"

"I think so."

"Once you fill this cart, you'll take it on out to the planters. Let me show you where." We walked until Gramps pointed. "You see that cart?"

I looked past the neat rows of buttery brown earth.

"Yes, I see it."

"It's your job, to fill your cart, before that one empties."

We turned around, just about halfway to the greenhouse. Gramps stopped, clapped me on the back and then veered off into a row of deep green crop. As he walked away, he said, "Remember to thank God for His goodness." Gramps knew I didn't believe in a god, but I masterfully choked down my objections to his directive.

Inside the greenhouse, I turned over a plant. The soil spilled into my hand causing the sweet earthy smell to tickle my nose. An hour passed while I loaded the cart. When I schlepped out my first batch, the planters weren't working. With his hand shading his eyes, Gramps watched me coming up to him. I honestly feared he was angry or disappointed with how long it had taken me to complete the simple task. Getting close enough to see his expression, I lowered my eyes, focused on the plants vibrating in the cart, readying myself for his justifiable reprimand.

"Did I take too long?" I traded carts.

"They had a good break. You done good pumpkin."

I smiled. His reaction made me feel special because Gramps had never given me a nickname. He tagged along while I walked back to the greenhouse. I gleefully pushed the empty cart in front of me with hopes of getting to know him better.

"You plan to marry soon?" he asked.

"Not any time soon. Why?"

"You must have a man you could marry. You pretty enough."

"No, there's no one and I'm not looking for a man."

"You're not? The Lord commands you to get married and make some babies."

"I'm not religious so I don't agree with you."

Gramps stopped, forcing me to do the same. I turned to face him.

"It's still truth. Even if you don't agree."

"There are lots of truths, Gramps."

We started walking again. "Matter of fact, there's only one truth. You should be married with a baby already."

"Don't you think I should be in love first?"

"Lord says, be fruitful and multiply. Didn't say nothing about love."

We stepped into the greenhouse. At the grow table, Gramps removed a seedling from its tiny cube. When he placed it into the cart, I cleared my throat. I said, "I think the human race has already multiplied enough."

Gramps paused. "You do want a husband, don't you? A man?" He popped out another seedling.

"Perhaps, I'll marry. Maybe have kids. First, I have to fall in love."

"There you go again with the love stuff. Be fruitful and multiply. That ain't hard to obey."

"Maybe I'll find someone. Maybe I won't."

"If you come to my church… you'll get married off quick."

"No thanks, Gramps."

"Someday, you might just come along to my church," he said.

A sinking feeling made me want to hide as I often did when I first visited the farm. If only Gramps would have stopped blasting me with his questions, everything would have felt better. Flashes of my favorite spots came to mind. I was ready to hide from him. His religious notions about women perturbed me and his skewed ideas would never become my plight. I had never been to his church and as far as I was concerned, I would never go. I turned to him.

"Why are you interrogating me?"

"Well, I'm gone trust you mean what you say, about wanting a husband—a man." Gramps put the plant he held in the cart and then left the greenhouse.

By lunchtime, my appetite had soared. I filled up on the meal Grammy prepared and then rested in my room until two o'clock. Afterwards, I worked the rest of the afternoon without a break. Right after sunset, I showered, checked my email and called Jarod. After a quiet evening with my grandparents, I went to my room. By ten o'clock, I had fallen asleep.

On Tuesday, I woke at 5:00 a.m. Before breakfast I drank a cup of coffee to kick-start my brain. We were all somber while we ate. I supposed, at 5:00 a.m. everyone needed a bit of time for the body and the brain to turn up the volume. For the next four days, the pattern of up at five, shower, farming and a ten o'clock bedtime continued without deviating.

Gramps was right, farming had given me time to think. Mostly, I thought about my mother. As a child, I had been full of spite and the farm had been my reprieve from Mom's gelid detachment. Tending to my self-preservation, while in Denten, I learned not to think about Mom. On that trip, having seen Mom's psychological breakdown prevented me from emptying my mind of her. After a few days, I morphed from not thinking about her at all, to thinking of her several times each day.

After lunch on Saturday, Gramps released me for the day. I moseyed around the house looking for pictures of my mother. There weren't any. In the living room, framed pictures of Gramps' dead brother, Uncle, his kids and even me sat on top of their upright piano. A week with a different perspective opened my mind to the truth. We had collectively amputated my mother from the Miller family. We never uttered her name. Because I preferred my mother as an invisible element, I too had expelled her from the Miller farm, thinking she belonged only to my Brackwood life and to the Foster family.

It had taken me fourteen years to notice that my grandparents had callously erased every trace of my mother from their lives. The truth burned into my brain like formaldehyde sticking an image to paper. Suddenly, my tranquility eroded, leaving me ashamed, confused and repentant over how I'd gleefully ostracized my mother whenever I visited Denten.

Running always balanced my mood. I had had a seven-day break. Already feeling overwrought, I laced up my shoes, tied my hair back and ran out of the house hoping to evaporate my agitation and to gain insight. Running worked instantly. The facts were simple. Those Millers had stripped away the past, and I hadn't cared. There were no pictures, no stories and no curiosity about my mother.

At the farm, a void had formed in the spaces Mom used to fill. In Brackwood, there had always been a void where Mom's family should have been. The silence screamed out from both sides.

I ran again on Sunday. I went east until I reached the farm boundary where I crossed the road to enter the woods. The ground softened with pine straw, and I became tranquil again. Thirty minutes later, I looped back to the farm, staying in the zone until I trotted up to the house. Uncle's voice ended my meditative silence. "There you are," he greeted me.

"You're not home for lunch today?"

"I brought some folks by to see you."

I put my finger to my mouth. "Give me a minute, I need a shower." I entered my room from the patio.

The house had become loud with people. Voices drifted to my ears, giving me time to grow my excitement at seeing Uncle's family again. Once dressed, I joined everyone. Uncle passed by carrying the Sunday dishes into the dining room.

"Where's Lillian?" I asked him.

"At home."

"Why didn't she come over?"

"You kidding? She's stoked." Uncle chuckled as he started setting the table. "Maybe she's taking a bath or eating ice cream. Who knows, either way, she's happy."

His older son Jack filled out the high-backed chair facing the picture window. His messy hair fell around his freckled face as he focused on his gaming device. When I came into the living room he hadn't bothered to stop playing or look up. I rustled his copper hair.

"Hello cousin Portia," Jack greeted me.

"Good afternoon. You've grown up. How old are you now?"

"I'm twelve. My dad says you're rich."

Uncle stood in the entryway between the living room and dining room. When I looked at him, he cocked his head to one side, shrugged and then turned away.

Robert, Uncle's youngest son, sat on the sofa with Gramps. His milk chocolate hair hung down to his neck, but he'd pushed it behind his ears to keep it out of his eyes. He was a scrawny boy with square glasses. The narrow rectangular frame made his round face look smaller. I sat next to him, putting him between Gramps and me.

"I'm eight. What you getting me for my birthday?"

Robert closed his book, keeping his finger inside to mark his page. His innocent eyes landed on me like a vulture scoping out roadkill.

"Um, hello to you too."

"Oh yeah—hello cousin Portia. So how about it?"

"How about what?"

"My birthday?" He pushed his glasses onto his face.

"When is your birthday?"

"It's July sixth. I'll be nine."

"I'll give you the same thing you gave me last year."

Robert scrunched his face. "What did I give you?"

"Nothing stupid," Jack laughed.

"I'll get you something."

"She's too rich. You can't afford what she wants." Gramps patted Robert's leg.

Nuzzling into the couch, Robert turned his head, bringing his ear closer to my mouth while I whispered to him. After hearing my suggestion, he ran over to his dad. "She's getting me a birthday present," he shouted.

Robert had misunderstood. I hadn't promised him anything. What I told him was... "You could make something for me." Somehow, he turned it into a gift exchange. The deal was set. Not knowing him, I jetted into the kitchen to ask Grammy what type of things he liked, but she didn't know. Although I had less than two months, I intended to find a suitable gift for him.

About ten minutes later, Grammy's sturdy body appeared in the living room. She had removed her apron, freed her silvery hair allowing it to flow over her shoulders. On her day of rest, she stood there in her Sunday best, beckoning us to consume the meal she'd prepared. I dutifully obliged. Prompted by her summons, everyone filed into the dining room.

Gramps sat at the head of the table. Robert replaced me as Uncle's sidekick. Jack played his game. Without looking up he plonked his chunky body into the chair next to me. During the blessing, he wrapped his pudgy, clammy hand around mine. With unbeatable effort, I conquered an urge to release it.

Robert argued across the table before anyone tasted their food. He wanted to see Jack's gaming device. Their spat continued until Uncle said, "Let him have a turn."

Jack hollered, "He doesn't even want to play. He wants to break it."

"No, I don't. I want to see how it works."

Robert hadn't raised his voice, but Jack screamed when he replied, "That's how you break it."

"Cut it out. You boys know better. Shouldn't have that thing at the table anyway. Give it to me." Uncle put the device next to his plate.

Robert and Jack pouted. Grammy restored harmony by telling a story. During her chronicle of Uncle's boyhood adventure the jollity at the table infected all of us. Pulled in by their laughter, I said, "Grammy, do you have more photos stored somewhere?"

"We only got what you see around."

Unable to believe they didn't have at least one photo of my mother somewhere in the house, I pressed her. "Certainly, there must be at least one picture of my mom around here."

"There ain't none."

"Are you sure? You have pictures of Uncle."

"Sorry sweetie. Grandpa is right. Ain't none."

A flash of truth made my body feel heavy and my heartbeat thumped in my throat. They all hated my mother. I sat there feeling dazed hoping my insight was an overreaction to the rejection I felt. Jack kept his green eyes pinned on me. He seemed to detect how Grammy's words affected me.

"Cousin Portia, do you work?" he said trying to appease me.

Although he meant no harm, I wasn't a twelve-year-old girl who could be made to feel better by changing the subject. Using the respect of age, I turned his question around on him.

"What do you plan to do for a living?" I asked him.

"I'm going to be a farmer like my papa."

Robert focused on me, pointed to himself saying. "I'm not going to do farming."

"What are you going to do?"

"I want to make stuff."

His announcement made him look nerdier. I marveled at his confidence and admired his ability to project his intelligence into the room. When Robert pushed his hair away from his face, Uncle said, "You need a haircut."

"I don't want one."

"Fine, then." Uncle rubbed Robert's hair.

"You want to be an inventor?" I asked him.

Robert twisted his nose. "Yeah, make stuff." His hair fell back into his eyes. With my questions answered, Uncle talked about their last camping trip. Whenever his sons contested the facts, the lunchtime volume shot up at least ten decibels. After a volatile bout of storytelling, I piped in.

"What kinds of things did you and my mother do for fun?"

Uncle poked his last potato, stuffed it into his mouth, chewed and swallowed before saying, "She's eight years older. So, as soon as I could walk, I followed her everywhere."

"So, you were close to her?"

"They were two peas in a pod."

Grammy collected the dinner plates.

"Yeah, we were real close." Uncle lowered his head. "Up until she left... well, until she came back."

Grammy jabbed Uncle. Gramps leaned across the table to make eye contact with him. Uncle's eyes widened. Their antics were comical. Based on their buffoonery, anyone could see they were trying to hide something from me.

"Where was she?" Robert asked before I could.

"Who wants pie and ice cream?"

Grammy's question started I do's going around the table like an echo. She went for pie. Uncle collected our used flatware. Gramps went for ice cream. I gathered the serving dishes. In the kitchen, Uncle scraped the dinner plates. I waited for Grammy to leave with the pies before speaking.

"Where did my mother go?" I asked him.

"Maybe we can talk later." Uncle turned his back to me.

I waited a few minutes. Then I pleaded with him, "Please tell me where she went?" I repeated myself four times.

He refused to respond. To reserve my option to discuss things later, I withstood the urge to walk out of the house, get into my car and drive back to Brackwood.

Back at the table, Grammy dished out pie and then passed each dessert plate to Gramps as if they worked on an assembly line. He topped those slices of pie with vanilla ice cream and then handed them out to everyone. During dessert time, they told more stories while my ice cream melted into the pie.

Being too obtuse to see how their actions had affected me, nobody bothered to make room for me in their stories, although I sat right at the table with them. I felt like an unwanted stepchild. Wasn't I a part of their family? My mother sure belonged to their family. If she had been dead, I believe they would have told stories about her. They might have told stories about her childhood, about how she lived and perhaps about how she died. What secret did they hide? I thought about how Uncle said, *until she came back.*

Although I should have noticed years ago, I had missed their odd behavior. My mother never discussed her past. Heck, she never shared anything personal about her life. Some event caused the Millers to disengage from her. They hadn't spoken about their reasons, but I knew people well enough to decipher whatever happened wasn't good.

Their avoidance sparked my mission to uncover the truth. They all played the same game, but Uncle disappointed me. No matter what, I intended to find out where my mom came back from.

After supper, Uncle invited me to the county fair. I pounced on the offer thinking he might open up to me. Uncle and the boys piled into my car for the drive over. Lillian shouted from the entrance when she saw us. We walked up to her. Her curly, burnt umber hair coupled with her curvaceous body made her look cherubic.

Once we reached her, she kissed Uncle. She clung to him before making room in her consciousness for the rest of us. Then she hugged her sons. When she turned to me, she smiled, making her eyes even friendlier. "Having a good visit?" she asked.

"I'm helping out on the farm."

"No farm work for me—ever," Lillian chuckled.

We crowded around the ticket booth evaluating the options until Lillian and I decided not to go on the rides. Based on our decision, I got three tickets for unlimited rides. When the attendant gave me the wristbands, I asked for forty raffle tickets. I separated them, giving twenty each to the boys.

Jack looked at his brother. "Told you she was rich."

"We can afford to pay you know." Uncle opened his wallet.

Lillian tugged his arm. "Let her do whatever she wants."

Robert creased the row of tickets, excited about winning a prize, he tore off the raffle side and separated each ticket before dropping them into the bucket.

"If you don't separate them, they won't pick your tickets."

Jack followed suit. He stuffed the stubs into his jeans.

Uncle almost put his wallet into his pants pocket, but he stopped. "Will you hold this?" he asked Lillian.

Robert held out his raffle tickets. "Can you take these too? I might lose them on the rides."

"You can't lose them in your pocket, stupid," Jack snickered.

Lillian put Uncle's wallet and Robert's raffle tickets in her purse. Then she took Jack's chin and lifted his face to make him look at her.

"That's enough with the name calling."

"Yes, Mama."

"Thanks for all those tickets. Can I call you Portia?" Robert asked.

"Works for me."

Jack tugged his dad's arm. "Um, can we go now?"

"Hold your horses." Uncle kissed Lillian. "We're off."

"Let's meet at the pavilion at eight," Lillian yelled.

Uncle waved his arm in the air, signaling his agreement.

After he disappeared into the crowd, we walked around the food vendors and then went into the pavilion. The bright room had rows of chairs facing the stage where a folk group played an old-timey tune. They reminded me of the *Steep Canyon Rangers*, except the fiddler wasn't half as good.

The music billowed. Some people danced, some ate, most milled around. My nose wrinkled against the smell of sweaty people. Going back out, we ran into my grandparents. I couldn't wait to get into the open air, but we stopped to speak with them.

"Good evening, Portia—Lillian. I see you're child free tonight," Grammy greeted us.

"I am, a night off." Lillian wiggled and then she chuckled.

Grammy touched my shoulder as she spoke to her friends; with a big smile on her face she said, "This is my granddaughter from Brackwood. She's an attorney."

Somehow, Grammy never remembered.

"Accountant," I corrected.

"That's what I said."

"No ma'am you said attorney." Lillian defended me. Her face had gone serious matching the edge of confrontation in her voice.

"Did I? Well, you know… they're all the same to me." Grammy giggled. Afterwards, she branched off into another conversation with her friends giving us an opportunity to leave the pavilion.

"I've been spying a corn dog. Want one?" Lillian offered.

"Sure, why not."

I accepted, although I'd never tasted a corn dog. Lillian paid for two of them. I bit through the sticky sweet fried cornmeal batter surrounding the hot dog. Yuck. I cringed. The off-putting sweetness combined with the rubbery-red-dye taste had me wondering what to do with that corn dog. Lillian gobbled hers down. Gingerly moving forward, staring right at it, I carried mine like a poisonous stick.

"You eating that?" Lillian asked.

"I don't think so."

"Give it here." She reached across my body.

My nervousness caused me to laugh. More than anything, I hoped not to offend her. "I'm sorry—"

"No worries, they're not for everyone."

"I'm happy to say, it's all yours."

We walked on. Rides were spinning round and round, lights flickered, smoke from meat stuffed grills puffed into the air, children ran about and gravel crunched under my feet as we meandered. I struggled to free myself from my sunken spirit. Unsavory thoughts hindered my ability to meld into the micro-environment created by the fair. We drifted to the strip where they had rows of carnival games.

The bright lights shone down on all the pay-per-play booths where they displayed throw away prizes of stuffed animals, trinkets, or posters. Carnival barkers shouted to entice us to play. They had the squeaky water gun game, the basketball tossing game and the pound of mallet swingers displaying their strength as they tried to win a prize with the ring of the bell.

At the bucket toss game, a man called out. "Have fun, win a prize. Three throws for a dollar." He held out the balls as we passed by him.

"Let's play." Lillian gave the man four dollars.

We threw our balls at the tilted buckets hoping they wouldn't bounce out. Every ball I threw landed on the stuffed animals surrounding the buckets. Lillian held her last ball. She studied the bucket's angle. "I'm going to make this one."

She tossed the ball underhanded using minimal force. The ball hit the back rim, bounced off and then fell in. The strangers who were watching cheered with us. Lillian asked for one of the black and brown bears. She cuddled the stuffed animal after the man handed it to her.

"So soft, feel it."

She practically shoved it into my face. I rubbed the bear. Then we walked along the strip. The bings, bangs and bongs competed with the carnival barkers.

Breaking the silence between us I said, "At lunch, Uncle talked about my mother coming back home."

"He told you about the reform school?"

I felt hot, lightheaded and dizzy. The crowd blended into a kaleidoscope of changing patterns. I thought about my words before speaking to make myself sound casual.

"Not much, what do you know?"

"Nothing. Your mother was already gone when I met Jack."

The hot sticky smell of cotton candy wafted past me. People shuffled from place to place. I concentrated on the bright lights until I found my voice. "Anything you can add will help. I don't even know the name of the place."

Lillian stopped, forcing a group of teens to navigate around us. "She went to Eucharist reform school."

"Where is it?"

"At the end of Old Mill Road. It's closed down."

"Do you know how she ended up there?"

"Nope, no one ever says anything about her. I heard something about a court case."

"A trial, do you know when?"

"Honestly, I don't. I'm sorry."

From that point onward, the spirit of the fair flirted with evil intent. Plus, I realized Lillian had shared everything she knew about the reform school. Besides, the fair was no place for serious conversation, so I stopped pressing her for information, tuned in to the festive vibrations around me and wrestled with the notion of having a murderer for a mother.

"Let's play this one." I walked up to the coin pusher machine digging in my purse for a ten-dollar bill.

The attendant gave me a roll of quarters. Breaking it in half, I shared the coins with Lillian. We took turns dropping quarters into the slots. A keychain teetered on the left edge. With the right push from the coins behind it, we surmised it would fall.

Lillian plunked four quarters into one of the slots. "I'm getting that keychain," she said sounding unreasonably serious.

I dropped three quarters into the middle slot, they rolled down the bar as the tray slid back exiting the chute just as the tray moved forward. Several quarters dropped off without pushing the keychain closer to the edge.

Lillian nearly pressed her head against the glass to study the arrangement of quarters. After she backed away, I suggested we concentrate on the middle slot to increase the odds of forcing more coins to fall off. "It's going to drop." Lillian bumped me with her hip. "Take this." She pushed the stuffed animal into my hand and then positioned herself in front of the machine, blocking access to the slots. She widened her stance and then strapped her purse across her chest.

I backed away. Her intensity made me laugh until my belly ached. She wanted that cheap keychain. I gave her the remaining quarters because watching her play amused me. Lillian inserted all the quarters I'd given her, plus the ones that had dropped down. Before hailing the attendant, she fished a five-dollar bill out of her purse.

Waving it above her head she shouted, "Five dollars."

"You know that keychain is worth less than a dollar—don't you?"

"I don't care."

She plunked most of those quarters into the machine before a group of coins fell off bringing the keychain down too.

"You won."

I laughed so hard; I almost couldn't get the words out.

Lillian jumped up and down before she collected the keychain. "See, I got it," she said when she turned around.

"But it cost you eleven dollars."

"Eleven dollars of good times. Didn't you have a lot of fun?"

"Watching you play? You bet I did."

As we walked along, Lillian attached the keychain to her keys, and I laughed even harder. We moved on to the amateur talent contest where we heard some okay comedy, listened to some bad singing and watched some fantastic dancing. By my urging, we wandered over to the fine arts exhibit.

They had a diverse collection of paintings, a few mixed media and sculpture pieces, along with artists giving mini-classes and demonstrations. We spent a considerable amount of time viewing the artwork before leaving.

Back at the pavilion, a new band had taken the stage. They had moved the tables to the sides of the room. People crowded onto the dance floor. The lead singer belted out, *I like that old time rock and roll*. The pavilion had become claustrophobic. Fortunately, minutes later Uncle showed up.

"Can we eat?" Robert said, speaking louder than necessary.

"Sure, let's get something." Lillian turned the bear to face him. She made it dance. Robert danced too.

"Where'd you get that?" Uncle asked.

"I won it."

Lillian passed it to Uncle. He tucked the bear under his arm. Once outside, we gathered near the food vendors. Robert wanted roasted corn on the cob and Jack wanted pizza. "Over here." Jack pulled his mother to the pizza stand. Up at the window, Jack turned to Robert.

"I'm getting pepperoni. What do you want?"

"Same."

Jack ordered two slices of pepperoni pizza.

"Make it three," I spoke from behind him.

"I guess four," Lillian added.

"Five," Uncle shouted over my shoulder. He tried to pay but I didn't let him.

"You told them I'm rich, so… tonight is my treat."

Uncle stepped aside. "All right, go ahead."

While Lillian and I went for corn, they picked out a table in front of the pavilion. "Let's decide how many before we order," Lillian said.

I figured the pizza would be filling. "Count me out," I told her. Then smoke billowed into my face. The smoky corn teased me when the vendor passed hot buttery cobs to his customers. "I meant count me in," I corrected.

Lillian ordered four corn on the cobs. After I paid, we settled in on the bench with the others.

Jack spoke with a mouth full of pizza, "Do you have a boyfriend?" he nearly shouted.

"Cut it out, Jack. Don't ask people such private questions." Uncle scolded with a hint of playfulness in his voice.

"Okay. Sorry."

My cheeks had gotten warm, perhaps rosy too. The misty sky was short on light, so no one saw me blushing. Feeling thankful for Uncle's intermediation, I escaped into the mesmerizing lights of the Ferris wheel as they shone blue, yellow, red and green while it rotated round and round to nowhere.

"Yuck!" Jack pulled his head back and stuck out his tongue. "This corn sucks."

I thought the corn had the right amount of crunch, salty sweetness and butter. "Trade you for my pizza," I offered.

He dragged my plate across the table. "That wasn't a fair trade."

"It's fair. The pizza is too greasy for me. This corn is delicious." Jack took a bite of the pizza. "Okay, if you say so."

We lost ourselves in a lively conversation until fair workers interrupted our unity. Their singsong voices broadcasted the coming event when they called out, *Raffle time. Raffle time. Get your tickets.* We'd reached the end of our festive outing, stars shone through clear patches in the cloudy sky and Robert shot up like a firecracker before running towards the pavilion.

"Let's go in," he shouted.

The beeps, bangs and clangs of the fair faded when we stepped inside the pavilion. We found a spot at one of the tables. Robert spread his tickets out, reviewing each number before putting the tickets down on the table. "They use the last three numbers." Robert told his brother.

"What if some people have the same number?"

"See the letter in front?"

Jack nodded.

"They use that too. It would take at least twenty-five thousand people to repeat."

"You're making that up."

"No, I'm not."

Jack took his tickets out, not making a fuss as Robert had done, he spread them out on the table.

"Can we talk tomorrow?" I whispered to Uncle.

"Sure, why not. Come by the house."

During the raffle, Robert traded two of his tickets for prizes. On his first trip to the stage, he picked out a toolkit. The second time, although no one prompted his generosity, he chose a paint set for his brother. When the raffle ended the crowd filed out of the pavilion. We stayed behind, kidding around until the crowd thinned to a trickle. I drove off having made a plan to get more information about the reform school.

I readied myself early Monday morning. At breakfast, I told Grammy I had business in town. Around ten o'clock, I drove half a mile down the dirt road connecting Grammy's house to Uncle's. On the other side of the farm, I rang the doorbell. When Lillian saw me, her face brightened.

I stepped into her updated kitchen, with Grammy's old tree table still in the center of it. Otherwise, the kitchen looked new and modern. They had uncovered the wood beams in the ceiling to add character, painted it a ducky yellow and replaced the wood floors with ash-colored planked tiles. A smart choice for the rugged nature of farm life.

"I love the changes you made in here," I said.

"Thanks." Lillian smiled.

"Why does it look so much bigger?"

"We took out the industrial stuff," Lillian said.

We sat at Grammy's old tree table.

"With this kitchen… all the new appliances and that stove, I feel ashamed of my absent cooking skills."

"Good luck. Cooking is not for me," I offered.

"I traded being a working psychologist for full-time mothering. Cooking hasn't caught on yet."

"I didn't know that."

"Yeah, cooking isn't for me either."

"I didn't know you were a psychologist."

"I am. Want tea or something?"

"I'd love a cup of coffee. Where are the boys?"

"They're out farming. It's the first day of summer break but Jack woke them up anyway."

Ending the small talk, I hurried to say why I'd come to see her. "I've been thinking about this reform school business but I'm afraid to ask Uncle about it."

"Honestly, it wouldn't help. Everyone clams up when it comes to your mother."

"I wonder what happened."

"Me too. Why not ask your mother?"

"She'll never tell me."

"You sure?"

"Very. It's why I want to unearth the truth."

"What's your plan?"

"Don't know yet. How did you find out about the reform school?"

"We drove to the place one day. Jack said Frances had been in there for a while. He wouldn't say more."

It was difficult to believe Mom committed a violent crime; yet only thoughts about murder filled my head. I knew the issue would nag at me until I had closure.

"What if she killed someone?" I whispered.

"Why are you thinking that way?"

"She committed a crime, got sent to reform school. It could have been murder. There's no way to know."

"I doubt she did anything violent. Let's find out." Lillian filled my coffee cup, put a bowl of strawberries on the table and then raised my hopes when she dialed the police department. Her voice became more subdued the longer she spoke on the phone. A frown flashed across her face when she hung up. Without her saying so, I knew we were out of luck.

"Sorry, you need more information," Lillian said.

The police told her we needed either an incident date or report number to obtain any information from them. As it stood, I remained ignorant of all the particulars. I didn't know the crime; I didn't know the year the crime occurred, and I didn't even know who or if there had been a victim. I had zero facts.

Reality tamped out my hope. Although bursting with the desire to know the truth, I understood wishful thinking wouldn't yield any answers and I also knew, asking my mother, Gramps, Uncle or Grammy would have been as effective as asking a rock.

Intrigued by—or at that point, obsessed with the whole reform school secret, blood rushed to my brain and my defeated attitude faded. A surge of energy ran through me as I considered another idea. Denten is a small town, so I figured all those years ago, the papers likely reported everything.

"I'm going to search old newspapers," I told Lillian seconds later.

"For what?"

"Certainly, I'll find news about the crime and the trial."

"Excellent idea. Go this afternoon."

"I will. No reason not to."

"Where will you start?"

"At the library. Is there another place?"

"What year will you search first?"

"Let's see, Mom went to college in 1971. Maybe I'll start in 1968."

Lillian grinned. "Keep me posted. I want to know everything."

The library is in the center of downtown Denten. Although any number of crimes could lead to reform school, during the short drive over, I concocted all kinds of murder scenarios. I entertained myself with thoughts about—who Mom might have killed, why she might have killed them and what weapon she used to kill them.

I parked a block away from the library giving myself a chance to ease my nerves. Vacillating between apprehension and eagerness made my jaunt feel much longer. When I stepped into the coolness of the library, I trembled with the excitement of discovery. At the information desk, I approached the attendant for help.

"Which papers were in circulation in 1968?" I asked.

The woman deepened the wrinkles around her mouth when she tightened her lips. "Let me see, the Denten Post and... what is it you're researching?"

Shame threatened to freeze my vocal cords. I swallowed hard. Somehow, I felt guilty. I read the woman's name tag. Her name was Barbara Salisbury. I kept my voice strong and smooth. "Barbara, would you mind directing me to the papers?"

Her smile helped me to relax myself. When Barbara turned around, I glanced at her weathered neck. Following her arm, looking from her shoulder down past the tip of her pointing finger, my eyes landed on the sign on the back wall.

"See the sign hanging there?"

"Yes, I see it."

"That's our Microform Reading Room. All the older papers are in there. Good luck with your research."

I slogged to the back of the library. Learning how my mother became persona non grata would require a commitment to poke around in the past. I questioned my readiness. Filled with doubt, I retrieved six 1968 Denten Post microfiche cards.

Focused on the headlines, the scanning moved at a clip. Headlines like *Assassin kills Merriweather, Martin Luther King Slain* and *U.S. GIs Accused of Village Massacre* were easy to screen out. Yet, several hours later, I hadn't found anything about my mother. I scanned every 1968 archive sheet before moving on to 1969.

With my goal set to finish the 1969 stack, I picked up another sheet. Holding the plastic card up to the light, I inspected the illegible ink stains before placing it under the glass to start the tedious task of scanning for news related to my mother, Eucharist or murder. There were headlines about business development, crimes, the government, elections and other diverse subjects. None of them involved Frances Miller or Eucharist.

At two o'clock, I phoned Grammy to let her know I would miss dinner. I started in on the 1970 archives. To complete the stack, I restricted myself to one single depressing break, a break long enough to stir up my pessimism. I finished my search. Turned out, there were no articles in any paper that pulled back the curtains on all those secrets.

For fear of the anxiety alone, I had avoided the subject of my mother after Sunday supper. Would circumstances force me to ask Grammy, Gramps or Uncle about the reform school, I wondered?

The following morning, I chose to work the farm while I figured out a new plan. At breakfast, Grammy put a bowl of oatmeal in front of me right when I sat down. "You have a good day yesterday?" she asked.

"I spent the day working in the library."

"What business you got down here?"

Gramps stared at me, expecting an answer. Heat rushed to my face. I sipped my coffee. It wasn't as though I had spied on them, but I had been sneaky and deceptive.

"None. Things come up," I told him to hide my dishonesty.

"I guess people with money can work while sitting on their butts," Gramps said.

"Jack, be nice."

I clinched my jaw, shutting down my desire to pour out my feelings. Gramps finished his breakfast and then he stood behind his chair glaring at me. With a loud sigh, he pushed the chair under the table.

"Plan another day on your butt?" he asked.

"Don't mind him. He's bitter." Grammy picked up his bowl.

"You coming—or not?"

"I am, Gramps."

He went outside. When his red shirt disappeared, I touched Grammy's arm. "Why don't you talk about my mother?"

"She's been away for forty years now."

"Yeah, I know, but she's not dead. Did something happen?"

"I'm sorry to say so, but you won't be finding out from me."

"Don't you think we should talk things over?"

"Nope, I don't. Regaining the peace took a mighty long while."

"What does that have to do with me?"

"Best not to stir the pot."

"Do you love her?"

Grammy bent forward. Her copper eyes were soft yet penetrating. "I love your mama. Always will." She carried the dirty breakfast dishes to the sink, leaving me dumbfounded as she walked away.

Grammy, like my mother, never articulated her feelings about anything. Emotions swarmed over me. My tears flowed down my cheeks. I lifted myself out of the chair, but before I reached the door, Grammy confronted me. "What's come over you?" she asked.

"My mother is…" I began to sob. "Why did my mom go away to reform school?"

Grammy stepped away from me. "Did Junior tell you that?"

"I figured it out myself. I went to the library—"

"To the library?"

"Yes. Please tell me what happened?"

"It's been ages. No good will come from bringing it up."

"Something is psychologically wrong with Mom."

Grammy's usually delightful face became sorrowful. Tears filled her eyes. She sat in Uncle's chair.

"You sadden me. My heart always imagines her well."

When I touched Grammy's hand she didn't flinch, tighten or move away. What she did was—overwhelm me with her embrace.

"Nobody cares or remembers her." I cried on her shoulder.

She pushed me back to arm's length. "Fran is a part of me. I'll always remember her."

"What happened to her pictures? It's like she never lived here."

"We said goodbye to Fran same day she married your father."

"What do you mean?"

"Her wedding day was one of the saddest days of my life."

"You went to her wedding?"

"We all did. Right here at our church."

"She married in Denten?"

"Where else would she go?"

I heard the door slam. Grammy baulked. Her eyebrows shot up, deepening the wrinkles between them. Then her eyes widened. She focused on my face.

"What are you two doing?" Gramps said.

"I'm upset, that's all," I said.

"What you got to be upset about?"

"Things. I'm afraid I've managed to upset Grammy too." Acting like a farm girl might have, I wiped my eyes on my shirt-sleeve. Gramps shook his head as though my distress irritated him.

"It figures. You coming or not?"

"I'm coming."

"Women." Gramps headed for the door. "You on the rag?"

"Jack, enough. Don't be crude."

"Let's get moving, Portia."

Grammy hugged me. I heard Gramps exhale. I squeezed Grammy's hand, loosening my grip as I turned to leave.

Outside, the sun hinted its inevitable appearance. The cloudy ground radiated a gray film into the air. The morning fog hovered over everything causing me to think of graveyards and bad news.

"We got a lot of work today. First, we gone clean out the chicken coops. Let you get a real look at farming."

Gramps worked alongside me all morning while we cleaned the chicken coops. Although I spent the morning around chicken poop, I got butterflies in my stomach whenever I thought about my discussion with Grammy. She bowled me over. If my mother married forty-years ago as Grammy said, I didn't know the truth about anything.

Throughout the morning, I combated my emotional stress over the secret my father kept from me. Knowing he hid the truth tainted my memory of him. That little lie caused me to question the accuracy of everything I knew about my parents.

After the chicken coops, we hopped into the haul truck to drive over to an isolated section of the farm where three rows of heaping compost stretched down the land. The manure bombarded my nose in the same way air freshener might saturate a closed room. Gramps dumped out a load of straw next to the first pile before we exited the truck.

"What a foul smell." I covered my nose and mouth.

"It is. We need to put this straw on top and you can't do it with one hand." Gramps took out the pitch forks.

"I need a mask. This must be the worst job on the planet."

Gramps chuckled. "Now you see how lucky you are to have such a soft life?"

"If this is the alternative... then yes."

"It's not the worst job. Your nose gone adjust. See the third mound over there?"

"I see it."

"It's ready. Almost got no smell. This one just starting."

"Let's work over there," I chuckled.

"You'd smell this one no matter what. Come soon we gone bag that row to sell."

"You sell compost?"

"Don't, I sell soil. We use Junior's cow manure to make it."

"Does it bring in much money?"

"Pays for itself with no waste. We better get this straw on top."

Using pitchforks, we threw straw on top of the manure. Gramps hurled straw from one side, leaving me to the other side. It's the crappiest job. Tending the dark mounds of stench became my late morning work. I had to push my misgivings to the back of my mind, to let go of my dreary outlook. More than an hour later, Gramps put down his pitchfork. He knew what he was talking about—I stopped smelling the manure. I dropped my pitchfork and then patted my jeans with my gloves.

Gramps removed his gloves. "You hungry?"

His voice startled me. Acclimating to the silence caused me to lose track of time, but his question prompted me to check in with my stomach. "I'm starving."

"My stomach's a timekeeper. Tells me right on the money when to stop working," Gramps laughed.

The work had been tiring. I felt exercised. Going back to the house, I nodded off in the truck. When we walked inside, Uncle stopped talking. Gramps didn't appear to notice. I pretended to do the same and headed to my room to shower off the morning's dirt.

With washed hair, brushed teeth, dressed in clean clothes and having an empty belly, I hurried to the table. Gramps and Uncle talked about cows. Their conversation ended abruptly, and I filled up the space. "I know why you stayed on Uncle."

"Yeah, why?"

"It's the food. Grammy's a wizard in the kitchen."

"You might be right. I love Mama's cooking."

Grammy put a bowl of her canned peaches on the table. "We're mighty lucky you love farming too. I take comfort knowing you're right up the road."

"I'm a farmer to the core Mama."

Gramps chimed in. "He got his inheritance early. That's why he came back. Free house—free farm."

Uncle grimaced as if Gramps had punched him in the belly. "Now that's pure lies. You know what I've done here," he shouted.

"When we built this house, you were off working for that industrial farm. You didn't care then."

"How else was I to care for Lillian and the boys? Besides, I work here now, don't I?"

"All you got from us. I'd a come on back too."

"Dammit Papa, what's your problem?"

"Me? You got the problem. I'm speaking truth."

"I earned my degree in agriculture. Got some experience, now I'm here. What more could you want from me?" Uncle ranted.

Grammy asked Uncle to settle down, but he was still steaming. "Don't let him rattle you. He knows you deserve everything you got. Where would we be if you hadn't come on back?"

"Retired," Gramps drawled.

"Retired? Well, if I'm stopping you, go ahead. Retire."

Uncle pushed back his chair. The squeal on the polished cement floor caused me to jump. Grammy caught hold of Uncle's arm before he passed her. He stopped but kept his back to her while she spoke.

"You worked all morning. Don't let him ruin your meal."

Uncle took his seat again.

Grammy passed the gravy to Gramps. She glared at him before letting go. They had some kind of silent communication going on and I think she got her way because Gramps took the gravy without saying anything.

Uncle fumbled with his fork. "Mama, I'll speak to you for the rest of the day. I'm not talking to him."

Gramps sneered. "All right by me."

Uncle poked the air with his fork synchronizing his words to each jab. "You've never paid me one penny," he said.

"Thought you was done talking to me?"

Grammy focused on Gramps. "We should all stop talking. Now everybody hush," she said making me feel shamefaced for stirring up trouble. Instead of apologizing, I closed my mouth. We ate the rest of the meal in silence until Grammy brought out a pie.

During the summer months, lunch lasted about three hours. We farmed from five thirty until noonish. When possible, we stayed inside during the hottest part of the day. Midday breaks benefited me. I used the time to check e-mails, read, or make phone calls while digesting my food.

No matter how long the break, overeating was a poor choice. Ignoring my own good judgment, I ate a slice of apple pie. Everyone had a slice. With pie in my belly, I planned to rest in my room but then Uncle said, "Do you want to retire Papa?"

Gramps' face went blank. "Sometimes... sometimes, I do. No use dreaming about it. I don't want to sit around waiting to die. What would I do if I retired?"

"Travel." Grammy sounded optimistic.

As she picked dishes off the table, I wondered if Grammy had a list of places she wanted to see.

"Where would you go?" I asked.

"Anywhere, I haven't had a vacation since I don't know when."

"Mama, I don't think you've ever had a vacation. We all need one."

"If you want, I could look at your books." I made eye contact with each of them.

"Huh, we don't need your fancy city help."

"No Papa, I think we do. The finances are the hardest part of managing the farm."

"I could help clarify your financial options."

Uncle sliced another piece of pie. "Mama, you got ice cream?"

When Grammy left us, I pressed for a decision. "Well, what will it be?" I asked them.

"Come by the house after supper," Uncle said, and that settled it.

Gramps had us back at the manure pile after our break. Somehow, I didn't mind being out there because Uncle's decision had carved out an opportunity for me to ask him about Mom.

Together, we piled on the load of straw and then Gramps used a turning machine to combine the straw with the manure. His competence alone got the job done. I was useless. The whole time, I dreamt up ways to goad Uncle for information about my mother.

After we finished that job, I had another shower and then rested before going to Uncle's house for some answers.

At eight o'clock, I knocked at Uncle's door. The boys were already in bed and Lillian cleaned the kitchen. Uncle led me to his office at the back of the house. Toys were on the floor along with dirty boots, shoes and boxes. The desk had piles of paper, ledgers, mail, electronics and stray cups on the surface. The disorder made me the tiniest bit uncomfortable.

"How do you work in here?"

Uncle shrugged. "It's the marvels of farm life, I guess."

"If you say so," I laughed.

Uncle settled himself in his chair and then he moved a pile of papers to another spot on the desk.

"Is that enough room for you?"

"If I have a corner, I can work."

"What do you need from me now?"

"Let's talk about your bottom line first."

"What do you mean?"

"Give me a rough estimate of the farm's gross income."

"About two hundred thousand, so far this year. That includes the food market. We sell our produce, Mama's pies and jams and the various goods we stock throughout the year," Uncle said and then moved a stack of papers to the floor.

"Where's the payroll?" I scanned the ledger Uncle gave me. There were no payments to him or my grandparents. "I don't see your names here," I said.

"We don't get paid. We buy what we need. It saves money."

"Not exactly, you end up paying more taxes. Plus, you lose some benefits. Each of you should have been paid employees long ago. Do you know why it's setup like this?"

"Like I told you, I don't have a clue. Papa always did things this way."

Lillian appeared in the doorway. "Would you like anything?"

"Maybe. What are my options?"

"Wine, milk, coffee and tea."

"Decaf?"

"I don't have decaf coffee."

"I'm asking about tea."

"Sorry, I don't have the decaffeinated kind."

I signaled for Lillian to hang on by putting up my pointing finger. I turned to Uncle. I patted the stack of ledgers in front of me.

"How about you let me take these for a while?"

"Sure, if that's what you need to do."

"Sorry Lillian. Water will be fine."

"If you're done, why not hang around with us. You mind?"

My heart pounded. I filled my lungs with oxygen hoping to clear my head. I didn't want to miss my chance to talk to Uncle. "Not at all—" I forced myself to lie because I feared hurting Lillian's feelings. Uncle steered us into the living area, and I sheepishly followed him.

A smoky gray, U-shaped sectional filled the room. I sat on the middle couch thinking it was the friendliest seat to occupy. From the kitchen side of the sectional, Lillian offered wine.

"Yes, please," I said. Alone, in the room, I acquainted myself with the numbers in one of the farm ledgers.

When Lillian returned, she gave me a glass of water and put a bowl of strawberries in front of me. Uncle brought two wine glasses and a bottle of wine.

"I'm having beer," Uncle said before plopping down on the perpendicular sofa to my left and then Lillian stirred up trouble when she sat next to me.

"Dig up anything interesting?" she asked with a big grin and sparkly eyes.

I widened my eyes hoping she'd keep quiet.

"Dig up?" Uncle guzzled his beer.

"Portia has questions for you."

Bobbing her head towards Uncle, Lillian egged me on. I signaled for her to cut it out. Lillian shrugged. Her giggling should have frustrated me, but I laughed too.

"What's the secret? Spill the beans."

"Go ahead. Ask him."

Uncle had a lopsided smile. He looked sideways at us. I avoided quizzing him. I said, "I've been thinking about my mother's wedding."

"Why, what about it?"

"Whatever you can share. I don't know anything."

"Want to see the pictures?"

"You have pictures?" Lillian and I said in unison.

Uncle leaped off the couch.

"You're the worst Lillian. A real villain."

"I am. You can't beat the results." Lillian chuckled and then poured wine into my glass and then we both laughed really hard. Uncle came back with a faded green photo album. He extended his arm across Lillian's body and put the worn-out binder in my lap.

I stared at it.

"What you waiting for?"

Uncle reached across Lillian's body again, in one swift motion, he recaptured the album and positioned himself on my other side. Being sandwiched between them made me feel like a child. With the album resting on his legs, he flipped the cover open.

"Want to start at the wedding?"

Lillian touched his leg. "Start at the beginning."

Right then, Uncle pointed to a five-by-seven black and white baby picture. "That's your mama." He tapped the photo on the odd page. "And that's me."

Tape stains had darkened the corners of the photos. I wanted a closer look but restrained myself. Pages later, after much anticipation, we viewed the wedding photos. The first picture showed my parents standing in front of the church where they married.

Although I thought myself prepared to uncover my mother's past, I got more than I had bargained for. "I can't believe…" I felt tears behind my eyes. My voice cracked.

"What's wrong?" Uncle asked putting his warm hand on my shoulder, making me feel calmer but I was still unsettled.

"Can't believe what—are you upset?" Lillian asked while studying my face with an intensity that made me nervous.

"Not really… I've never seen Mom's childhood pictures."

"Tell you what; I'll split them with you."

"Are you sure? I don't want to take your pictures."

Uncle flipped the page.

"Yep. Wish I had more, I found these in the closet after my folks moved out. They probably didn't even remember having this album."

Lillian turned her whole body to look at me. "You are upset."

"I guess, a little. It's not the pictures though."

"Then what is it?" Uncle asked.

"I always thought my parents married in 1976. We have tons of their wedding photos at home."

"They got married in '68. See?" He pointed to a picture of himself standing in front of the church.

"You remember the wedding date?" I asked.

"I wasn't even nine… it happened some weeks after she came back home from… no, I don't remember."

"You don't have any idea of the date?"

"Can't say I do. Look, we have on coats. Winter of '68, as close as we can get."

My whole being shuddered with despair. Whatever happened to cause a sixteen-year-old girl to marry a thirty-eight-year-old man couldn't be seen in a photo, but I wanted to know what happened.

After my talk with Grammy, I suspected my mother had gone to one of those reform schools where unwed girls had babies without embarrassing their families.

I turned to Uncle. "Was she pregnant?"

"Was who pregnant?"

"My mother."

Uncle threw his head back when he laughed.

He mocked me, although I'd asked a sensible question. My skin reddened and I wanted to leave the room.

Lillian frowned. "What's so funny?"

"She wasn't pregnant, okay. I don't remember everything, but I know that much."

Regaining my wits, I quieted my anger over Uncle's maniacal laugh. "Well, you obliterated my theory."

"What theory?"

"About my mother being pregnant."

"I'm telling you… she wasn't," was all he said, ending our conversation. A somber mood soaked into the room.

Lillian stopped being playful.

I kept quiet.

Uncle flipped to the first photo in the album, removed my mother's baby picture and then page by page he selected photos until a pile formed on the couch next to him.

With the photos divided up, Uncle excused himself. Lillian and I went outside to talk. Under the night sky, we examined the facts I'd collected. The details were insufficient to extrapolate the missing pieces about my mother's flight from Denten.

We had both come to believe she'd been pregnant. At the end of the night, I was no closer to the truth. If anything, my ignorance had grown bringing my curiosity right along with it.

Lillian poked out her bottom lip. "What are you going to do now?"

"Go back to the library. Look at earlier papers."

Over the next few days, I worked the farm with Gramps and then spent the evenings searching the archives. Accepting Uncle's boyhood memories as confirmation, I recast my net to include Denten publications from 1964 through 1968. The time frame more than covered the period my mother would have spent away from home.

To speed up my search, I used the same tactic. I read the headlines. Most were easy to ignore. Two headlines caught my attention, both occurred in 1966. The first alleged a local teen had burned down a grocery store and the second discussed how a young boy polluted the river by dumping trash over the bridge. When the weekend came, I hadn't found a single piece of information to bring me closer to finding out what happened in Denten.

On Saturday morning, Gramps showed me how to weed and spot pests. At the spinach crop, he listed everything to look for, he spread his arms to illustrate the magnitude of the job. Taking in the lushness, I turned my body one-hundred-eighty degrees to look at the densely planted rows of green.

I'm not going to like this work, I thought. Gramps squatted, dropped to his knees, pulled at, turned over and plucked spinach leaves while I watched. It was slow work. A few minutes later, he yanked out a wad of pigweed by the root. Blocking the sun with his bucket he looked up at me. "Look here," he said.

I studied his thinning hair and red skin, forgetting about the weeds he'd pulled. "You should wear a hat," I told him.

"Now you sounding like my wife." He held out the spindly bundle. "Pigweed can be a big problem."

"What should I do if I spot any?"

"Pull it on out the ground."

I had no problem differentiating pigweed from spinach. Pigweed has veiny diamond shaped leaves like basil, but it also has reddish roots and if you rub them, they feel a bit furry compared to spinach. When Gramps pulled out a bunch of lambsquarter weed, I couldn't distinguish it from spinach even though it had an earthy green scent.

"Those smell good. Can you eat them?"

"Sure can. We gone eat these. You already been eating some."

Gramps dropped the bundle into a bucket before swiping through the spinach. I followed him up the row. Together we inspected patches of spinach for cutworms, slugs, snails, aphids, beetles and leaf miners.

"What about this?" I thought I'd spotted a lambsquarter weed.

"That ain't none. Remember, they're paler green."

"It looks the same to me."

"They different all right."

Gramps removed a bunch of lambsquarter from his bucket. He went over the characteristics again. They were almost the same shape of spinach. Ending the second lesson, he held the lambsquarter right up against the spinach and I noted the subtle difference in color.

"We won't find too many, they grow best when it's hotter."

The neat rows of spinach stretched out, seeming to spread the green cover for miles. "One row at a time," Gramps had said earlier. "That's how you get it done." Farm workers scattered about; they inspected the crop with us. Scanning my area, I looked at the work ahead, realizing the tedious job would keep me occupied all day, causing me to lose a chance to scan through the newspaper archives. I thought there had to be a better way.

"Why don't you spray the weeds?" I asked Gramps.

"Could… if I wanted to poison the food. Best to prevent weeds settling in. That's the natural way."

"Do you use pesticides anywhere on the farm?"

"In a pinch, we might use neem oil or Bt. They the more natural products. We got to avoid those too… if we can."

"Wouldn't pesticides make this less tiresome?"

"Sure might, never rush things that need time. Nothing worse than going against nature."

We went back to inspecting. A few rows over, I saw some pale green leaves shooting up. "What about that?" I pointed.

"Those are carrots. Leave that one right there." Gramps yanked another bunch out of the ground. Dirt dropped off. The freshness reminded me of cutting cucumbers. He inspected them and then pushed the dirty carrots close to my face. "If we had a worm problem they'd be attached to these carrots."

He picked off a ladybug releasing it into the air, it fluttered around us. When the red speck landed atop the spinach, I said, "I'm always amazed at all the ladybugs around here."

"Wouldn't be, if you was a farm girl."

"Why are there so many?"

"We release them to keep aphids in check."

I followed Gramps up the row. He waved me over to him. I stood by his side. He pointed to a leaf. I stooped to get a closer look. "See that?"

I nodded.

"Those are leaf miners. The tan bumpy trail is a dead giveaway."

Gramps used a fine-tip scissor tool to remove the infected leaf. He put the clipped leaf into a bin he carried on his waist. I turned over several leaves looking for pests. Remembering to search for leaf miners, I checked each leaf for the tan bumpy trail. I moved along rifling through the spinach.

"Found some," I called out surprised by my own excitement.

Gramps inspected the leaf. "Indeed, you did."

He handed me the snipping tool. I clipped the leaf while he watched and then put it in his bin. He nodded his approval. "You spoke truth earlier; I should wear a hat." He squatted to inspect the crop. Then he turned to me. "You're on your own pumpkin. If you need me, I'll be right here beside you."

My love for Gramps blossomed. The farm suited him, I doubted he wanted to retire. I decided to buy him a hat. Somehow, working with him made me feel proud of the tiniest things. Plus, he acted kinder. I focused on the job, hoping my help lessened Gramps' workload. Emptying my mind while inspecting the spinach put me in the zone just like running always did. I let myself enjoy it.

Several hours later, Gramps stood over me. "You head on back, I'll finish up," he said.

I set off towards the house, finding leaf miners and a few slugs rounded out my day. Since the library closed early on Saturday, farming caused me to miss an opportunity to search more newspapers. No matter, I had worked out a new strategy for my next visit to the library.

On Sunday, I walked into the library seconds after it opened. My strategy was to skip the 1967 archives in order to search 1968 again. That day, I bypassed everything except the marriage announcements section hoping to yield results. Unexpectedly, none of the papers had announced my parents' wedding. I was baffled. In the sixties, most people published marriage announcements, plus my father's parents were very formal.

My oversight occurred to me after exiting the library. Almost to my car, I remembered my parents married in winter. Back inside, I worked my way through the 1967 October and November archives.

Next, I lifted the glass to insert the December sheet. I pushed the microfiche up, down, left, right until I spotted it. They published on December 20 in the section headed *These Couples Will Wed in January.*

The announcement read:

Foster – Miller – A January 20 wedding in First Council Church is planned by Frances Dianne Miller and Howard Conrad Foster III. The bride-elect is the daughter of Jack and Margaret Miller of Miller Farm. Mr. and Mrs. Howard Foster are parents of the prospective bridegroom.

Sadness filled my heart, but I hurried to leave the library as I had promised to show for Sunday dinner. I drove back thinking about my mother. She married two weeks after her sixteenth birthday. Why did my grandparents let her marry an old man?

At the house, I tiptoed into my room from the porch to avoid everyone. Lillian knocked a few minutes later. She sat on the edge of the bed facing me.

"I saw you sneak in. Are you hiding in here?"

I shook my head and hunched my shoulders. Leaning against the headboard with the announcement in my hand, I read it to her. "My mom was a child when she got married," I let all of my angst come out.

"Sixteen is young but—"

"Barely sixteen is different."

"You're saying there's something—"

Grammy opened the door before Lillian finished her thought. She stood in the doorway looking upset. I knew she had waited for me to get back. Scowling, she stepped into the room.

"Come now, time to eat. No more dilly dallying."

Lillian had her back to the door. She mouthed, "Sorry." She had a big grin on her face. I didn't harbor any ill will, but I felt remorseful over delaying everyone's meal. Certainly, if Grammy had known how wretched I felt, she might have insisted I skip dinner.

Suppertime passed by in a foggy haze. Not because I found it impossible to engage with everyone. The truth is… I didn't speak or socialize and everything tasted bland because lost in my own thoughts, I wasn't fully there.

After supper, Gramps slept in his chair, Uncle helped clean the kitchen, Lillian, Robert and Jack played Skip-Bo. I sat on the porch thinking of home. The boys' laughter mixed with my sadness. I considered going inside to surround myself with their cheerful voices but then Grammy came out too. Her rocking chair squeaked as she pushed back and forth.

"You feeling ill?" she asked.

"No, I'm thinking about Mom."

"Is she ill?"

"I don't think so."

"Then, what's gotten into you?"

"I'm upset about the circumstances surrounding my mother's marriage. Everything about it is all wrong."

"Is that what you're moping about?"

"My parents claimed they got married in 1976. They lied."

"So, what, they lied. Are you hurt?"

"In a way. Mom went to reform school. She married a man old enough to be her father. Everyone is keeping secrets from me."

"We're just living. I can't see how you're hurt."

"I told you. Something is wrong with her." I had raised my voice, but then felt awful for being disrespectful.

"Let's have a walk," Grammy whispered.

We left the merriment behind us. All the farm noises had stopped for the weekly day of rest. The somber quietness fitted the emptiness that had fallen over me. Grammy led us into her orchard where she settled herself on one of the harvest stools scattered around the farm. I sat in the grass, shadowed by an apple tree.

"Did you know your father was my friend?" she began.

"No, you never told me."

"Well, he was. He wanted a wife. Fran needed a place to be."

"A young wife?"

"Your mama wanted—"

"She was a child."

Grammy clenched her jaw. "You don't have the whole picture. Everything is not always simple."

"She married your friend." I shouted out friend like a curse word, although I knew my father to be a kind, loving person.

"You're missing the point."

"Maybe if you were forthcoming, I wouldn't."

"Your grandpa wouldn't look at her or talk to her."

"Just tell me what happened. I know she didn't get pregnant. What could she have done that's so terrible?"

"She did what she did."

I waited.

When Grammy didn't bother to explain, I slowed down my thoughts, crossed my legs like Buddha, relaxed my body and then said, "Why can't you be honest?"

"Portia, you're pushing me. Why you so fixed on this?"

"I want the truth."

She sighed. "I'm speaking truth."

Grammy stood up. The green leaves of a low branch hid her eyes from me. I needed to see her face. I stood up too. Looking up at the trees, she pulled a handkerchief from her apron and then patted the tears dripping from her eyes.

"Sorry, go on Grammy."

"Well, he refused to let her leave the house. She deserved better, and I trusted Howie to take her."

Grammy used a nickname that neither my mother nor my father liked but she called him that anyway. I wondered if she knew how much he hated that nickname.

"You forced her to marry him?"

"Nobody forced her to do anything. I told Fran she could go live with him if she wanted to," her voice quivered.

Grammy sat down again.

I positioned myself in front of her and then sat cross-legged under the same tree. I rubbed my hands through the prickly blades of grass. "What made them get married?" I asked.

After a lengthy pause, she said, "Fran was strong minded. Her defiance always got her into trouble." While she told me, Grammy waved her hands in the air and her face had an interestingly devious *who knows* expression on it.

I wanted her to share how or what type of trouble my mother got into all those years ago. I waited until I felt levelheaded before speaking again.

"You didn't say how they ended up getting married?"

"Your clever Mama asked Howie to marry her."

"She asked him?"

Grammy nodded. "I lost her forever."

"Why did you lose her?"

Tears dropped from her eyes.

I went over to her. Limiting my contact with her, I extended my arm, getting just close enough to touch her shoulder. Saying something like, "don't cry or there, there now," would have sounded trite, so I just stood there waiting amongst the apple trees.

Clusters of tiny bright green apples hanging from the branches attracted various birds. From somewhere in the trees above, a Baltimore Oriole tweeted its unique flute-like song. I searched for its bright orange belly but couldn't spot it.

After a respite, Grammy stood up. "You should be more grateful. Grandpa thinks so too," she said.

There were no positive words to speak in reply. She was wrong. Moreover, she deflected her own shortcomings on to me. She often did. I had seen her use the same sneaky method to manipulate others, especially Uncle.

Although, I saw right through her craftiness, I didn't force my will. My refusal to bully Grammy meant the reform school secret remained intact but grew in my mind. While walking back, Grammy hooked her arm around my elbow. Then we strode arm in arm until we reached the house. I kept thinking about her remark, *she did what she did.*

At breakfast the next morning, I looked away when Grammy put a plate in front of me. It hadn't mattered. She turned away too. A barrier had formed between us after our talk, and I wasn't interested in knocking it down. I had to leave the farm.

Before leaving, I debated the merits of asking Gramps about my mother. I'm glad I chose not to ask because it would have been a sizable mistake. Except for farming or religion, he didn't have much to say to me anyway. I refused to give up; yet, sticking around, hoping for a miracle would have wasted my time.

Neither Grammy nor Gramps protested when I announced my plan to leave. My grandmother packed a lunch for me. She seemed glad to see me go. Without me around, she safeguarded her secrets. On the other hand, it seemed Gramps would unwillingly miss me after I left them. He hugged me with sad eyes. "You being around made the days go faster," he said.

I hugged him tight.

Before I got into my car, Gramps prayed. He prayed for my safety, he prayed for my happiness and although he didn't think it necessary, he prayed for me to find love. I found his positive prayers beguiling. I wondered why he couldn't be as positive when he wasn't praying. If he were, being around him would have been more pleasant.

As it stood, I left them, suspecting I'd stayed my last stay at the Miller farm. Gaining insight into how my mother ended up in reform school became my chief goal. My investigation wasn't over. I intended to gnaw at it until I burst over with facts.

Ready to move forward, I checked into the Denten Beach Resort. Later on, I drove to the courthouse. As I climbed the stairs of the oldest building in Denten, my hands got cold. My fears were unfounded, but bizarre ideas about Mom's criminal past filled my mind. I had to know the truth.

To quiet all those fears, I imagined the two-story brick building as a vault. I needed to unlock it. With the right combination, I expected to find answers. In the lobby, I used the directory board to locate the records office on the second floor. It was only a tiny room with three terminals and a solitary woman sitting behind a desk reading a book.

I interrupted her saying, "Excuse me, I need court records from the sixties."

Horizontal lines appeared in the woman's forehead when she looked over her glasses. She put her pen down.

"Do you have a case file number?"

"No. I don't."

"Do you have a judgment date?"

"I have a name."

"Do you know the type of case; is it civil or criminal?"

I lowered my voice, ensuring the pace of my words reflected my irritation with her silly questions.

"Is there a way—to perform—a name search?"

The woman rolled her eyes. "It ain't free honey."

"How do I get started?"

"It's going to cost fifteen dollars."

"I don't mind paying," I smiled working to appear friendlier.

"If you're sure you want to pay. We might not find nothing— but the clerk can run a search for you."

Across the hall, my heart went into overdrive when the man scribbled on his notepad. After completing the transaction, the clerk gave me a receipt and then walked away. I could hear him typing on his keyboard. My foreboding thoughts resurfaced. Although I had difficulty admitting it, the likelihood of finding the truth terrified me.

Pacing the room, I waited for the results and then hurried to the window when I saw the man coming back.

"Sorry ma'am, there were no cases matching your criteria."

"Are you sure?"

"I am. Checked for both plaintiff and defendant."

"Criminal and civil cases too?"

"Yes Ma'am."

The clerk had the details right. He had searched for Frances Miller as plaintiff or defendant from 1960 to 1970. Feeling crushed, I walked back to the lobby. When I spotted the information counter, another possibility occurred to me.

The attendant had the job of giving out information, figuring he might have answers, I went over to him. He was a tiny man. While speaking to him, I made sure to look at his face instead of at the top of his head.

"Do you have any information about Eucharist reform school?"

"No. I don't. The city didn't run it."

"Who did?"

"Some church."

"Do you know which church?"

"I'm not a church man myself, so don't know."

He leaned right, then left looking behind me. I looked back. A young girl waited behind me.

"Certainly, you've heard something."

"Haven't. Do you have a government related question?"

"No sir." I thanked him and then exited the building.

Saddled with failure, I navigated up Old Mill Road toward Eucharist. I drove up the dead-end street until I came right up to the dilapidated building with its boarded windows.

The 1900s L-shaped gambrel roofed building had two stories. The lower floor had expansive windows; they were as tall as the entry doors. A series of upper windows marked the rooms where the girls might have slept—possibly where my mother once slept. Up near those windows, some of the burnt earth-colored bricks had crumbled where the mortar loosened.

I imagined a heavy windstorm collapsing the building to the ground. The spiked barbed wire fence with its, *Danger, Keep Out*, signs quarantined the relic. Rusted junk concealed what used to be grassy areas out front. A large field spotted with wildflowers stretched out behind it. I imagined children running around back there. I walked about wondering how to surrender to my failure.

The mystery of Eucharist rested somewhere in a forgotten grave. I wanted to dig it up. Going as far as I could go, I had explored the path I discovered. With all avenues leading to dead ends, Eucharist became my only untapped link to the truth but traipsing around Denten seeking answers wasn't a possibility for me. Back in Brackwood, I intended to execute a criminal background check on Frances Miller, find out more about Eucharist and then plan how to get answers.

With unyielding determination, I would capture the golden nugget of truth as a personal treasure.

Lillian and I met for lunch Tuesday afternoon just before I headed home. I shared my failure at the courthouse and my visit to Eucharist.

"Why not call it a beginning," Lillian smiled.

"What makes you say that?"

"We're building a relationship and my kids love you."

"I came to Denten to get away. Now I'm leaving wondering what grisly thing happened here."

"I honestly don't think your mama committed a serious crime."

"You don't?"

"No. If she did, don't you think you would have found something in the papers or at the courthouse?"

"I guess. But I'm not giving up. Something made them give her away."

Lillian had a thoughtful smile on her face. "Listen Portia, if you decide to pursue this, do it for yourself. Not your mother."

It had been years since I connected to someone, and I perceived Lillian welcomed my friendship. I vacillated between dumping my anguish and keeping it to myself. Predicting I'd shatter our budding friendship, I chose not to divulge my personal troubles or discuss my mother's issues.

Someone at the next table laughed too loud. We looked over at her. When I turned back, Lillian fished around in her paper bag sized purse. She set her keys on the table, then a book, her wallet, cell phone and then at last she held a small, gift-wrapped box over the table.

I took it. "What's this?"

"Robert made it. He says you told him to."

"It's true, I asked him." I shook my head in disbelief.

At the time, my motives weren't very noble. I wanted to stop him asking for gifts and doubted he would make anything for me. I tore away the comic paper he used as gift wrap. Lillian drank her tea while she watched me. I sensed her searching my face for signs of approval.

Robert had made a Rubik's cube trinket box with perfect dimensions. Each side had yellow, blue, green, red or orange squares with the classic black gridlines. He'd also painted the center square on each side its opposite color. The green top had a blue center square.

Opening into two halves, protrusions on the bottom half fit into the top half like a jigsaw puzzle. He left a note inside. *Remember my birthday*, he had written on a piece of notebook paper.

"You should know… Robert worked out the math by himself. His brother helped paint the squares."

"I'll find a fitting place in my home. Please pass on my message and say thank you too."

Robert's gift pleased me. I rubbed my thumb across the top while signaling for the server to bring another cup of coffee to keep me perky during my drive back to Brackwood.

My time in Denten was ending whereas my friendship with Lillian had blossomed. I worried we'd lose touch after I went home. Then I remembered Uncle saying he needed a vacation.

Following my intuition, I said, "If you want, come visit this summer." I fiddled with the box.

"The boys and I would love to come. Will the Fourth of July week work for you?"

"Yes. Now is better than later, while I'm taking time off."

"I think I can convince my husband to come too."

"If you do… you can stay in the guesthouse my father built for his parents. It's a beautiful cottage house."

"A private getaway might seal the deal."

"There's a pool and spa."

Lillian's eyes brightened. "We love swimming."

"We can go to the lake if you want—"

"We're coming. You don't need to sell me."

"I know. I'm excited about your visit."

"Me too. I'm looking forward to it."

Leaving Denten wasn't all sadness, visiting the farm actually set some positive things in motion. I nurtured my friendship with Lillian, tracked down loose details about my mother's life in Denten, plus learned the truth about my parents' marriage. Lillian had it right. My time in Denten had indeed been a beginning because it springboarded my drive to untether myself from my mother.

Though it wasn't a total gain, my vow to unearth the secrets of Denten started the process of seeking answers. Something unsavory transpired in Denten and whatever occurred formed a chasm between my mother and everyone who had loved her. That's why I headed for Brackwood with an aspiration to mend my family.

PART THREE

The Visit

Farming had given me new insights, but I had to reengage my Brackwood life. During my first week back, I kept busy with my to-do list. At its completion, I had hired a personal chef. After several interviews, I settled on Simon Hunter, a rugged, carefree man. I instantly liked him. Yet, it was the sample meals he prepared that pushed him to the top of the list. He moved into the two-bedroom house where Mr. Wooten, our previous cook, had lived years earlier. The house is three acres away and has a separate road leading to the property and a trail connecting it to my house.

Next, I prepared the guesthouse for Uncle's visit. My father built the four-bedroom cottage for his parents, but no one had stayed there after Grandmother Foster died in 2003. Like the main house, the guesthouse had a maintenance schedule. Even so, for my own peace of mind, I ordered an inspection of the plumbing, gas line and structure. Once I had the-all-clear, I stocked the pantry with the items Lillian requested.

With the house business completed, I had a solid week to myself. My alone time proved more rejuvenating than my trip to Denten. Feeling rested, I let my mother know I had returned to Brackwood, and I invited her over for dinner.

Mom and I were somehow close but always awkward. Her aversion to my affection, taught me to substitute closeness with long conversations, travel, trips to museums, hiking, elaborate meals and other things she agreed to do with me. Hoping to make our visit pleasant, I planned a special meal for us.

Her arrival on Friday at 6 p.m., marked the end of my isolated existence. I met Mom at the car to prevent her using the side entrance. We walked around to the front of the house where we entered through the seldom-used front door. I steered Mom into the dining room.

Simon had set the table, putting us in the middle chairs as I had asked him to do, thus we sat across from one another as if it were a typical weekly meeting.

"This is formal. What's the occasion?" Mom asked.

"Nothing—just dinner."

"Shall I bring in the food?" Mom offered.

I sprung up, not giving her a chance. Simon brought the soup to the table. After the introductions, he ladled red pepper fennel soup into our bowls and then retreated to the kitchen.

"This is scrumptious," Mom said with her eyes closed. "What made you do it?"

"I know you like soup."

"Why did you hire a cook?"

"He's a chef, not a cook. Unlike you, I can't cook, and I prefer not to clean the kitchen."

"This soup is creative. Not a dish I'd prepare."

"If you wanted, you could hire your own personal chef."

"I don't like strangers about the house more than necessary. I value my privacy."

"I know. He's staying in the cabin where Mr. Wooten lived."

"I'm glad you're doing what fits you best."

Seconds later, our conversation switched to work, moving us right into familiar territory. Our meal became a working dinner and I connected with her, although we remained emotionally alienated. I didn't mind. I loved how my mother brightened as she updated me on the changes at work. During my absence, Mom had renewed her love for going into the office. She also landed two new accounts. First, as I had forecasted, ACC Foods hired our firm because Mom's analysis prevented massive penalties and fees.

In addition to signing with Foster & Co., they recommended another large firm, Betea Juice. Mom exclaimed, "I've been thinking maybe I'm too young to retire." Those words made me feel as though she'd let me out of a pressure cooker. "You were right about Jarod," Mom continued after Simon served the entree. She tasted her food. "Very delicious."

"That's marvelous. How?"

"It's well balanced. I never would have thought to pair chicken with apricots and the arugula is—"

"How was I right about Jarod?"

"He's extremely knowledgeable. Promoting him to COO allowed me to eliminate all operational duties from my position."

"What does that change for you?"

"I'm back to organizational issues and big clients. I don't miss doing the everyday accounting things."

"Brilliant Mom. Maybe you should stay another twenty years or so," I offered somewhat seriously.

Mom pressed her napkin to the edges of her mouth. "Will you be back to work soon?"

"Sorry, not yet."

"You'll inherit the firm no matter what."

"I know. Right now, I'm not ready to be CEO. Maybe not CFO."

"I thought we had an agreement."

"We do. And it hasn't been six months."

Mom stroked her chin.

I shrugged my shoulders.

Promptly changing the subject to end my discomfort, I jump-started my commitment to avoid needless lies. In Denten, my family weaved and nurtured a host of secrets. Disclosing where I'd been prevented me from doing the same.

"I don't want to keep secrets. So, I'm telling you now... I've been in Denten at the farm."

Mom crossed her knife and fork on her plate before removing the napkin from her lap. Her delayed response sent my head spinning. I felt like a house-bound dog, waiting to be let outside. After some thought Mom questioned me. "What did you do for two months?"

"Mostly farm work."

"You did farm work?"

"Yes, me. Unbelievably, I liked it."

"What made you start farming?"

"Gramps did. He insisted farming was great for thinking."

"Did it work?"

"I figured a few things out." To stop feeling anxious, I added, "I have pie from Grammy."

"You do? What kind?"

"Peach—your favorite."

We finished eating and then Mom strolled down the hall. She had a few quirks, her disinclination to eat dessert at the table was one of them. When I asked where she'd picked up the habit, Mom said, "Can't remember, but sometime before my college years." On occasion, my father teased her about it.

Nevertheless, when we had dessert, she insisted we go into the den. Most of the time she watched the news. After Mom left the table, I found Simon in the kitchen. As I stepped in, he unplugged the percolator before pouring the hot coffee into a porcelain coffee pot and then he added the coffee to the tray with the cream, sugar and slices of pie.

In the den, I placed the serving tray on the ottoman in front of the sofa. I filled our coffee cups, adding a cube of sugar and a splash of cream for Mom. On my way home from Denten, I purchased a rustic photo album in a gift shop where I stopped to stretch my legs. Seeing it, sparked the idea to give Mom a piece of her life back. To fill out the album, I mixed in the Denten photos with photos of her life in Brackwood. Where possible, I added notes.

During a commercial break, I pressed the mute button on the remote. When Mom turned to me, I held out my gift as if it were a rare jewel. I had wrapped the album with glossy purple paper and tied on a velvety purple bow.

Mom untied the bow. She rested the gift in her lap, worked her fingers through the paper to unwrap the ornate wooden box and then looked at me. "Keep going." I smiled.

When she removed the photo album she said, "Pictures?" She flipped to the first photo, "The Miller Kiddos," she read the tagline aloud. I had used Gramps' words. Whenever his grandsons were around, he'd say, *there go the Miller Kiddos*. I neglected to share where I picked up the expression.

Mom loosened her baby picture, held it up and then stared at it. After a long look, she put it on the couch next to her before turning the page. "The beginning," Mom read the next label. She lingered on a photo of herself holding Uncle Jack when she was around nine or ten years old. He looked huge sitting in her lap. In the photo, Mom smiled while looking down at him.

"Where did you get these?"

"Uncle Jack."

"This is a very thoughtful gift. Thank you." Mom pointed to my pie. "Take that away before I eat it." She had already eaten hers. I laughed but I didn't dare move. I sat there watching Mom flip through the pages. Midway through, she turned to a four by six photo of her parents standing on the church steps.

Mom slammed the album shut. The thump startled me; it seemed to rattle my brain. Things were going wrong again. My mother gawked at the album, and I readied myself for her backlash.

"Did the pictures upset you?"

Mom didn't respond.

I waited there, giving Mom time to gather her thoughts because I believed the photos might inspire her to share something new about her life. After a respectable pause, I removed the album from her lap. I placed it between us on the sofa.

"Would you like me to get rid of it?"

"I never thought I'd see his face again."

Mom's voice had been reflective. She picked up the album and then searched for the photo. My dad stood next to his mom in the background. I had unsympathetically placed those wedding pictures in the album to invoke a confession. I thought—or hoped seeing them would force Mom to correct the lie about when and how she married my father.

"You thought you wouldn't see Dad again?" I asked hoping to make good on my hidden agenda.

"I'm talking about my father. What did he say?"

"Nothing, I got the photos from Uncle."

"What did he say?"

"Not much… he did say, you married when he was eight and he hasn't seen you since."

"I'm not responsible for not seeing him."

"Why haven't you seen him?"

"Not important." Mom stood up, pressed the album to her bosom and then said, "Thank you for this."

Feeling surprised by Mom's gratitude and lack of anger, I squeaked out, "You're welcome." When I looked up, Mom kissed my forehead and then rubbed the kiss with her thumb.

"Tell me more about your farming experience."

Mom sat down again. Her upset over Gramps' photo left me feeling out of sorts. To my dismay, we hadn't reviewed or discussed those photos as I'd hoped.

Instead, we discussed the farm. I told Mom about greenhouse farming, the seedlings Gramps grew in them and how we planted the crop.

Mom laughed when I said, "I'll never be a real farm girl."

"I wouldn't have minded," Mom admitted.

"You're a lot like Gramps you know."

"Farming suits him. I suppose it might have suited me too."

"Did you want to farm?"

"Not really, but maybe I'll buy a farm when I retire."

"You would move to a farm?"

"No. But I could buy a farm, somewhere warm, where I could escape to on occasion."

"Where would you go?"

"Maybe some Island… far away from everything."

"I could see you packing up and taking off."

"First, I'd need to retire."

Our chat ended with me telling Mom about leaf miners. She went straight to bed without asking about her family; not her parents, not her nephews, or her brother. I probably should have told her about Uncle coming to visit.

Our conversation was so pleasant. It was a welcomed change from how things had been before I left for Denten. Talking about Uncle might have spoiled things and selfishly, I just wanted to enjoy my time with her.

Lillian and I chatted almost every day after I left Denten. Her solution to telling Mom about their visit was to wait, which meant not telling her at all. Lillian figured it would be best to just invite Mom over after they arrived.

"Let her see for herself," she told me.

Although I cast my vote with Lillian, I suspected she'd given me bad advice. In a way, I had listened to Jarod too. When Mom and Uncle met again, whatever was going to happen, was just going to happen.

My uncle arrived the following Thursday evening. The next morning, I invited Mom for the holiday weekend. Had Mom scrutinized our conversation, she might have sensed my nervousness. To keep my uneasiness at bay, I spent the morning studying the Miller Farm books Uncle brought down with him. I was glad for the distraction because work always prevented me from thinking about anything not related to accounting.

About an hour before my mother arrived, I stopped working but busied myself doing minor things around the house, like propping up pillows and repositioning vases. While I fussed around, everyone else lounged by the pool or swam. At one-thirty, the security notification system announced, "Front gate opened; code 4-2-4-9."

During Mom's drive up to the house, I collected Uncle. We stood in the entryway waiting for her. My mother stepped inside, put her bags down and then looked up.

"What's this? You have a beau?"

"Maybe you should look again Sis."

Grinning like a lottery winner, Uncle stepped forward. I saw recognition come across Mom's face. She stepped back.

"Wait, what's going on? Jacky?"

"Yes, it's me."

Uncle opened his arms. He expected an embrace, but my mother pulled her head back, twisted her face and then backed away from him.

"No, no, no… this is not going to—"

"Aren't you glad to see me?"

"After forty years… no, no, I'm not."

Uncle lowered his arms. "I see Frank still fits."

I looked from Mom to Uncle. "Frank? Who's Frank?"

"It's what I call your mother."

Feeling a bit cautious, I gathered my mother's bags and then headed into the house. They followed me into the living room. Absent of goodwill, Mom scowled, sat in Dad's chair and then folded her arms across her chest.

"Did you have a good day?" I said cheerfully.

"You should have told me he would be here."

"If I had, you wouldn't have come."

Mom turned her whole body to me. "Portia, you robbed me of my choice."

"I, for one, think she made the right decision."

Mom rotated, rested her hands on the arms of the chair, leaned forward and stared at Uncle. "You for one… what did you think when you never wrote or called or came to see me?"

"I would have… I never had your address or phone number."

"What are you talking about Jack?"

"You put us out of your life. You didn't call or anything."

"I put you out? I put you out… a real humdinger huh? Or anything?"

"I missed my big Sis. You didn't care how I felt."

"Stop telling lies."

"Frank, you left us."

"Really… did I?"

Those snake veins popped out on Mom's neck. They were going in circles. She straightened her blouse. Uncle sat on the sofa across from us. He clenched his hands and then pushed his fist into the sofa leaving dents in the cushions when he scooted forward.

"Mama brought me to Hanover, we stayed three whole days. You never came to our hotel."

"What did you expect after seven years?"

"If you cared, you would have met us there."

"Did you write, did you, Jack?"

"No but…"

"I was getting my MBA. I didn't have time to waste on people who didn't matter."

"What do you mean didn't matter? I begged to visit you."

"I wrote for three years. I called too. They changed to an unlisted number to stop me calling."

"I never got any letters, and I didn't know about the phone number. Sorry Frank."

"As I said… people who didn't matter."

"So that's it?"

"What do you want… paragraphs?"

Mom turned away. They were both stuck in their version of the truth. I wanted to stop things from getting worse. Children gravitated to my mother, and she loved it. I gambled meeting Uncle's children would alleviate her angst.

"Want to meet your nephews?"

I motioned for Uncle to go get them, hoping those boys would make things peaceful again. When he left the room, I took his place on the sofa. A headache formed above my eyes. Deceiving myself, I expected Mom to become excited when she saw her brother.

At the same time, I hadn't given Uncle any warning. What could I have said? Perhaps, I should have suggested he give Mom space. Perhaps, I should have discussed her issue with affection. Perhaps, I should have thought things through and called everything off. Even now, I'm not sure. I just know I should have done things differently.

I heard the quick pops of flip-flops before the boys entered the room. They had wrapped themselves in pool towels, yet they dripped water on to the wood floors. Lillian wore a sundress over her bathing suit. I appreciated her modesty. After Uncle introduced his wife and children, Mom smiled but she didn't say hello or speak to any of us. We all looked at her sitting there with her hands in her lap. She looked right back at us.

"Can she talk?" Robert asked.

"Yeah, stupid." Jack slapped the back of Robert's head.

"Mama, he hit me. Tell him—"

Lillian stepped between the boys. "It was nice to meet you. Who's hungry?" she asked.

The boys shouted, "I am."

Lillian led them out of the room. I thought she had reacted too fast. A few minutes longer would have given Mom time to warm up to them.

After they walked out, we just sat there until Uncle said, "Frank, I swear to you, nobody showed me any letters."

"I believe you. Your father could be harsh."

"He can be. I'm sorry about all of this."

For an instant, I thought they would reconcile. It wasn't fated. Mom narrowed her eyes. "How shall I account for the thirty years since you grew up?"

Uncle pivoted. "How would I have known where to find you?" He exited the room.

Interfering with family relationships was bad business. Who was I to pick the scab of unhealed wounds?

We left her in Dad's chair. An hour passed before she toted all those bags to her room. In spite of my allegiance to Mom, I had no idea how to help her work things out. All I wanted was a joyful visit with everyone.

To help us settle in together, I planned a lighthearted evening hoping to get things on the right track. Around dinnertime, I knocked on Mom's door. She didn't respond to my meek, tap, tap, tap, so I knocked harder. She called for me to come in. Not seeing her in the reading room, where she usually stayed during the day, wasn't a good start, but I went on with my task anyway.

Mom had stretched out on the chaise lounge in front of her picture window. Taking a deep breath, allowing my body to relax, I stood in front of her. "Are you angry?"

"Yes and no," she answered without facing me.

I smiled. "Come eat with us. We're in the outdoor room."

"Give me a minute," she said, staring into the woods.

Mom wore teal sailor pants and her walking shoes were next to the pecan chair. She hadn't planned to leave, but she did plan on taking a walk. I left her there. Not having to argue about how I had tricked her felt like Christmas day. I wanted to jump for joy like a child.

"Is she coming?" Uncle asked when I returned.

"Surprisingly, yes."

When my mother entered the room, she smiled, headed over to the bright yellow sofa where she planted herself at the edge of the round ottoman, right in front of the boys.

"Tell me your name?" Mom pointed.

"It's Robert."

"Are you, my auntie?" Jack asked.

"Guess I am, Jacky boy."

"That's not his name," Robert said.

"It's what I called your father. Have you two been to the creek?"

"You got a creek?" Robert asked.

Mom nodded. "Want to go?"

The boys got excited. The outdoors made my mother more open to people. Like Gramps, nature tranquilized her brashness. Being in the woods with her was fun. I encouraged Lillian to let them go. With the okay, the three of them trudged across the Sahara granite patio, past the pool and then disappeared into the woods. The creek was a quarter mile away. Supper would be ready before they reached it.

With Mom out of our sights, Uncle leaned into Lillian. "I don't get her," he said with a hint of angst.

"I bet she's glad you're here." Lillian rubbed Uncle's back.

He sighed, "That's just wishful thinking."

"She's still here, isn't she?" Lillian made a good point. Nothing stopped Mom from leaving.

The three of us went outside to the patio, where we waited for Simon to finish preparing dinner. Sitting out in the open, with the serenity of the woods around us, Lillian unexpectedly probed Uncle for information.

"Why did Fran go to reform school?" she asked.

I latched on to Lillian's boldness. I nodded my head. "Yeah, what did she do to get sent there?"

"They never told me."

"Was she there long?" I asked.

"A couple of years, I think."

We had a minuscule break from our musing because Simon brought dinner out. We filled our plates. Before eating, Uncle mouthed a blessing. Lillian tasted her food without waiting for him to end his silent prayer.

"What do you remember about my mother coming back home?" I asked when Uncle opened his eyes.

"She was skittish. Cried all the time like a big 'ole baby."

"Let's not be insensitive. Babe, you know something must have happened at that place."

"What did Grammy do when she got back?"

"Not much. Mama tried. Papa was pathetic."

Lillian caught my eye and then widened hers before asking, "What about the court case?"

"I don't know anything about it."

Lillian leaned closer to him. "Wasn't it a religious reform school?"

"Yeah, the church ran it."

"What church?"

"Ours, the First Council Church. Well, my parents' church."

"The same church from when you were a boy?"

"That's the one." Uncle looked around. "Pass the bread?"

"Didn't you say you were afraid of their pastor?"

"Yeah, when I was a boy. Pastor Joseph is a mean one. I never liked him. He ran the reform school."

They had an extended conversation, perhaps even forgetting I was there. During those minutes, I tucked away the information Uncle unintentionally gave me. I even collected the clue that helped solve the mystery of Mom.

They were still talking when Robert raced up to us saying, "Look Papa, I can whistle." He positioned an acorn cap between his thumbs, widened his stance, fluttered his lips over the acorn top and sounded out a spitty bluup, bluup. I couldn't see his technique, but I knew why his slobbery blow made no sound.

After his failed attempt, Robert pulled another acorn top out of his pants pocket and gave it to his dad. Uncle blew between his thumbs to bounce air inside and then out of the acorn top.

It sounded out… fweet—fweet. Once he'd expelled his breath, he looked up. With soft, hopeful eyes he focused on Mom.

"My big sister taught me how."

Mom smiled.

"She's awesome huh?" Robert shouted. He seemed overexcited and Uncle patted his back to calm him. Working with his boys, giving multiple examples, positioning their hands and laughing, Uncle taught them how to send their own fweets into the air.

Jacky finished his supper and then stood in front of us until he had our attention.

"Can everybody call me Jacky now?" he asked.

From that moment on, we called him Jacky. After a brief chat at the table, Mom hauled the boys away. They played games. First, she taught them Clue and then Sorry. At some point, they switched to Skip-Bo—Robert's favorite game.

While Mom preoccupied herself with the boys, Uncle, Lillian and I swam. That night, one of my favorite activities became highly unenjoyable because being in the pool made me feel like an intruder. They flirted around in the water without swimming at all. To end my discomfort, I hurried my laps and then retreated to the spa.

After a while, I excused myself for the evening. Before I could leave, Uncle asked if Mom would speak to him again. With me sitting at the edge of the pool, flicking the water with my feet, Lillian explained why he needed to be patient.

Somehow, she ignored my mother's negativity towards him. Instead, she pointed out how my mom doted on their sons, shared her knowledge of nature with them, had endless patience and kept their behavior in check when they became rowdy. I don't know how she managed to do it, but Lillian brought the phantom mother inside my head back to life. I aspired to her benevolence. Even so, my admiration didn't stop me from sympathizing with Uncle.

My mother's rigidness stirred him up. At the same time, sympathizing didn't stop me from noting that Uncle had acted like a pigheaded brat. He hadn't given Mom a chance to come around and he kept escalating things. Of one thing I was sure, it was his job to cope with his disillusionment not Mom's or mine.

Meeting again after forty years, must have been challenging for them, but things should have been easier for Uncle. After all, they hadn't sent him away, married him off and then stopped speaking to him. Logic aside, I feared Uncle's fortitude would wear thin if my mother continued to ignore him.

Saturday morning, Mom trotted into the kitchen, her perkiness clashing with my grogginess, the excitement spilling out of her as she readied herself for a brush with nature. She wore her typical apparel, ash Patagonia quandary pants, a long sleeve t-shirt and hiking boots with a backpack slung across her shoulders. I assumed she planned one of her all-day treks out into the woods.

"Are you leaving now?" I asked.

"No, I promised Robert and Jacky a hike."

I turned the page in the book I read. "Today?"

"Yes, to the lake."

Mom poured herself a cup of coffee. She had pumped herself up with the idea of hiking to our lake house with the boys. Her tactics were all wrong. I wanted to go too.

"Maybe we can all go?" I offered.

Mom frowned. "Is that my only option?"

I knew Lillian would enjoy a day away from her kids. I wasn't going to tell Mom though. I sipped my coffee.

"Probably." I focused on my book.

"Will you please ask your uncle about a hike?"

It was only seven o'clock. I hadn't had breakfast or finished my first cup of coffee. "Let me eat breakfast and get dressed first," I said.

While we waited for breakfast, Mom conversed with Simon. As they talked, I read my book, making a big effort to ignore them because their excitement annoyed me. I felt childish. Simon seemed happy for Mom. I should have been happy for her too. Yet somehow, my bitterness took over. The more she connected with those boys, the angrier I became over her ability to show her affection for them.

At eight-thirty, I knocked on the guesthouse door. The boys were sleeping, Uncle drank coffee and Lillian ate breakfast. They had allowed themselves to sleep in. Once again, I felt like an intruder. With haste, I invited them for a hike to the lake house with my mother.

Uncle put his cup down and then he hugged me.

"Gee whiz—fantastic. I'll have a chance to talk to my sister."

Instead of squelching his enthusiasm, I suggested they prepare themselves for a full day away from the house. Uncle went off to wake the boys. When he left us, Lillian agreed to meet up at the house in an hour.

As promised, they gathered in the outdoor room at nine o'clock. Pointing to Robert's shorts, Mom shook her head.

"That won't do."

"He's fine," Lillian countered.

"He needs long pants and long sleeves."

Lillian didn't budge. She lifted her yellow print sundress. "See, I'm wearing shorts too."

Mom marched into the house. Moments later, she handed out lightweight, waterproof backpacks. Everyone set off to fill their packs. Although I had clothes at the lake house, I added a couple of one-piece bathing suits, shorts, a t-shirt, protein bars, water, jeans and a summer dress to my pack.

Before setting out, Mom touched Robert's shoulder, "You be extra careful," she told him.

"I will."

We headed out past the pool into the woods. The five-mile hike skirted past the creek until it bordered the lake front. From there, we'd head down to the house. Our voices interrupted the birds as we walked along the uneven trail. About half a mile in, we scampered to the base of what we called, the sledding hill.

As a child, I had a blast sledding down the hill with my parents every winter after the first snowfall. By the time I turned fifteen, we had stopped going because my father could no longer hike to the top with us. As we climbed, I invited everyone to come sledding that winter.

"I'm coming," Jacky called out.

He thumped his brother and with uninhibited excitement, ran up the hill. Robert ran after him. Their laughter filled the woods until seconds later, a cry echoed around us. I heard the scream prior to seeing Robert tumbling down the hill.

"My leg," he cried out.

Robert hobbled over to his mother, abandoning his brave face, obviously in pain. He sat on the ground grabbing his bloody leg.

"Nothing's broken," Lillian said after she franticly inspected his entire body.

Fishing around in her pack, Mom squatted next to Robert. She found her first aid kit and then squirted water on his leg. After clearing the dirt, she inspected the wound.

"It's only a scrape," she told him. Turning to Lillian Mom said, "Long pants," as though Lillian were a child.

What could she say? Mom had it right. It must have been something about boys. I had walked in those woods for years without injury. Mom opened a disinfectant wipe.

"This might sting. But you're a champion—right?"

Robert closed his eyes when he nodded.

"He ain't no champion," Jacky laughed.

Uncle pulled him away.

Mom put her head closer to Robert's leg, dabbing it until she removed all the blood. Afterwards, she held up an assortment of colorful Band-Aids.

"Pick a color," she told him.

"I like red." Robert chose the pink one.

The woods filled with laughter. "He's color blind like you Jack."
"He sure is." Uncle laughed too.

Robert favored his left leg until he forgot he'd hurt himself.
Mom didn't take any chances though. For the rest of the hike, she
guided us through the woods, giving special attention to Robert
but also allowing time to explore various paths at her discretion.

We stopped twice to let the boys climb trees. Along the path,
my mother pointed out various flora and fauna, the same way
she had with me as a child. By the end of our hike, Robert and
Jacky had a collection of miscellaneous objects stuffed into
their pockets.

When we arrived at the lake house, Uncle tossed his pack on
the ground before running towards the water. His family did
the same and then took off after him. Mom and I went inside to
get ready for lunch. Once the table had been set, we transferred
the food into serving dishes.

A bouquet of wildflowers with sprigs of fresh wheat springing
up through the purple-blue veronica, apricot stock and natural
thistle filled the center of the table. I moved the arrangement
and then placed a salad of field greens in its place.

While Mom freshened up, I went out to get everyone. Uncle
and his family cavorted at the edge of the lake. Instead of disturbing them, I stood under the eaves listening to Lillian giggle as
Uncle chased her along the shore. When he caught her, he lifted
her off her feet. She shrieked until her sons came over to tug
at their father's arms, then she laughed. "Thank you," Lillian
howled. "You're my heroes."

They plopped onto the grass and then I left the shelter of the
porch. "You're all wet," I said when I stood over them.

Lillian got to her feet. "Your mother is a genius."

"She is?" Robert asked.

"Yes, she is. We have dry clothes."

Mom might be a genius, but she also despises dirt. I got towels for them and asked them to leave their wet shoes and socks on the porch. After somewhat drying themselves off, I showed them inside.

Upstairs, I pointed out which rooms they could use to clean up. Lillian, marched up to each door, peeked inside until she stood in the doorway of the room with the picture window and queen-sized bed. She disappeared for a minute.

"We'll change in here," she said when she came back out. Pointing to the next room, the one with bunk beds, she said, "The boys can clean up in there."

"You can see everything from up here."

Robert leaned over the mezzanine railing. I pulled him back. We looked down into the great room. In the center of it, a large Persian rug covered the area where the furniture sat. Two charcoal sofas faced one another making a passageway to the fireplace. A pair of dusty rose armchairs capped off the opening. I looked through the panel of windows at the front of the house, recalling Uncle's lighthearted play with his family. I thought of my father, wishing he were with us.

"Ready?" Mom called up to me. She stood in the middle of the great room with her head tilted up.

"They're cleaning up." I turned to Robert, "You need to clean up too."

When he scooted off, I showered in my room. Making myself presentable, I pulled an icy blue patterned boho sundress over my one-piece bathing suit and went downstairs. I somewhat read a book and somewhat stared at the lake as I waited on the sofa.

Lillian came down first. She looked aimless but smiled, making her face as bright as the cobalt blue, red and yellow tie-dyed sun dress she wore. She looked like a beloved painter's palette.

"Can I help?" she asked Mom.

"Everything's under control," Mom said.

A few minutes later, the boys came down. Mom commandeered them. She put her hands on their shoulders, walking them over to the table. "Sit here and here," she told them. Mom placed herself in the chair between them. They sat on the side of the table facing the lake.

Uncle stepped behind the chair across from Robert. Frowning, he shook his head and then ever so slowly, sat at the head of the table. "Thanks so much for doing this, Frank."

"It's a pleasure. Let's eat."

"What about the blessing?" Jacky asked.

"We don't say blessing because—"

"Why don't you say it?" Mom suggested.

Jacky opened his palms to hold hands with Mom and Uncle. First, he bowed his head. Next, he said, "Thank you, God, for this food. Bless the…" He opened his eyes. "Who prepared it?" he asked.

Uncle chided him. "Go on, say the blessing."

"Bless the hands that prepared it. Amen."

"Thank you for today. I really enjoyed the hike," Lillian said.

"Why didn't we know you before Auntie?" Jacky asked.

"Sometimes families drift apart," Uncle answered.

"I didn't drift nowhere," Robert responded.

"Anywhere," Mom corrected.

"Anywhere, where?"

"It's anywhere, not nowhere," Mom chuckled.

"Then where did you drift to?"

"You know, I heard about you before you were born."

Jacky perked up. "What about me?"

"You too," Mom said.

Robert had a thoughtful expression on his face. "But why didn't we know about you before?"

Mom turned to her right, holding his attention, she said, "I can't change the past. What is—is. Let's move on from here. Maybe make up for lost time?"

"Okay, are you getting me a birthday present?"

"Robert!" Lillian shouted. "Why do you do that?"

"What do you want?" Mom ignored Lillian's anger.

Robert looked from his mom to his dad. "I want a telescope and a microscope, not the toy ones. Real ones."

A red hue spread over Uncle's face. He slapped his own leg. "I told you to wait until Christmas. Now stop asking."

Robert looked down into his plate.

After some silence, Mom said, "Why shouldn't he have them?" Her voice had been inquisitive and non-confrontational.

Lillian shook her head. "He's only eight."

"And he's about to be nine. Most of all, he's smart. Why not let him explore whatever intellectual thing he wants?"

"He needs to pick one." Uncle stirred in his chair.

"You're in trouble." Jacky poked Robert's arm.

Mom tapped Jacky's hand. "Why should he pick? Let him have both. I'd give him both."

"Damn you Frank. You practically ignored me, now you're spoiling my child and turning him against me."

"I'm not turning him against you. You think giving children tools to explore the world is spoiling them?"

"If they're expensive things."

"I'm simply suggesting you give him those things. Nothing more."

Everyone just sat there without saying anything, but I knew Mom had been sincere. During my formative years, she had given me whatever educational thing I asked for. I had a telescope, science kits, electronics sets, plus various things I tired of without remembering I wanted them. She wasn't trying to harm anyone.

A good minute passed and then Uncle let out a heavy sigh. "You know, since you left Denten and got rich, you think you can just do whatever you want."

"What do you mean?"

"I'm saying you're the one who got sent away and came back half-baked. Not me."

Mom narrowed her eyes. She turned to Uncle. "I'll thank you to never mention that again."

Uncle raised his voice. "Sorry, you left—not me."

Mom walked over to him. She stood over him and Uncle sat in his chair looking up at her as if he were shocked. Mom swore at him. "You selfish... you're acting like an—"

Lillian steered the boys away and rushed outside.

I could feel my heart pounding. I excused myself to go out with them. As the fresh air washed over me, I eased the door shut to trap their voices inside, but still their brawl diluted the tranquility of the lakefront view.

Jacky marched off the porch. Lillian went after him. Robert apologized when I sat down next to him.

"Are you upset?" I asked him.

"I didn't mean to make Papa mad."

"Trust me. It's not your fault, even though you feel like it is."

Robert slumped with his chin touching his chest, unhappiness all over his face as he pouted. Assuming my seated meditation pose, I interlaced my fingers, relaxed my shoulders and put my hands in my lap. In between periods of staring at the lake, glancing at Robert and longing for solace amongst the trees on the distant shore, I wished for Mom and Uncle to end their dispute.

Jacky stayed at the shore throwing rocks into the lake, but Lillian came back to us. She stretched out her arm, opening her hand to Robert, she said, "Let's take a walk."

Hand in hand, they went off to collect Jacky. I left the porch too. We all escaped the heated voices. Jacky, Robert and Lillian walked along the shore. I slipped out of my sandals, pulled my dress over my head and then waded waist deep into the cool water before stretching out to immerse my body.

Under the water my mind cleared. The fighting rendered me powerless over keeping the peace, but I clung to the possibility their quarrel might make things better between them.

Having cooled myself, I swam to the dock. I lifted myself out of the water and sat facing the lake. Appreciating the summer breeze, I swung my feet while I mulled over the disastrous afternoon.

Lillian startled me when she touched my shoulder. She stood over me with Robert and Jacky by her side. She put my shoes next to me and then held out my dress. I pulled it over my bathing suit.

"Are you okay?" Lillian asked.

"I'm sorry. I'm so sorry." Robert had tears in his eyes.

After I gently tugged Robert's hand, he sat next to me—or more like slumped against me. I put my arm around him. Lillian sat next to me and placed her right arm around my shoulder and her left arm around Jacky's back. There we were, sitting at the edge of the pier, feet dangling over the water, staring out at the lake.

Our commune ended when Uncle yelled out to us. He said, "Lillian, come quick."

Terror shot through me. I ran, leaving the others to catch up. Uncle filled the doorway. The alarmed look on his face matched his voice.

"What's wrong?" I demanded.

"I don't know."

Tears filled my eyes when I saw my mother curled up on the sofa. My legs felt weak—I stood there helpless, not knowing what to do. After a moment, I put a blanket over her.

"What happened in here?" Lillian asked Uncle.

"She wouldn't talk to me. I grabbed her shoulders."

"And then this happened?" I asked.

"No. When I shook her, she freaked out."

"You shook her?" No one could miss the anger in my voice.

"Not now, Portia," Lillian commanded.

The boys stared at Mom. Uncle and I did too.

"Portia, get a small paper bag. Jack, please take the boys outside."

Uncle steered them right out the front door. I found a paper bag.

Lillian knelt in front of Mom with the bag in her hand and then she placed it over Mom's nose and mouth.

"Breathe in through your nose," she repeated several times.

"I don't think she can hear you."

"She hears me. Get another blanket."

Feeling bewildered, I stood there with the blanket in my hands, not knowing the right things to do. Lillian met my eyes. Her face softened. "She's having a panic attack. It can't last forever. Cover her feet and then hold her hand."

I hesitated. My mother would not have wanted me to touch her.

"Can you rub her arms?" Lillian asked.

I rubbed Mom's arms while Lillian encouraged her to take a deep breath. Uncle walked up to us. Lillian spoke like a drill sergeant ordering troops when she commanded Uncle to stay outside until she came for him. Uncle obeyed.

Lillian coached Mom until she sucked in air through her nose. Her breathing slowed, becoming steadier with each breath. "Now, keep taking regular breaths," Lillian said as she removed the bag.

The moment the bag left Mom's face, I instantaneously stopped rubbing her arms.

"What should we do now?" I asked.

"Let her rest."

Lillian removed my mother's shoes and then sat on the sofa with Mom's feet in her lap. "Relax your legs. Feel your legs relax," she said. I watched from the other sofa, rubbing the fabric until I resorted to counting with my eyes closed. I wanted to help. At the same time, knowing there was nothing I could do allowed me to stand-by without interfering. By the time I reached three thousand, it seemed Mom had fallen asleep.

"Please, ask Jack to see if the boys are still hungry."

Moving deliberately, I went to do as Lillian had asked. Outside, the air hinted of rain. The earthy freshness cleansed my thoughts. When I reached Uncle at the shoreline, I avoided his eyes.

"Lillian wants you to feed the boys," I told him.

"I'm sorry, I need a minute." Uncle walked away.

I went over to Robert hoping he didn't feel too heavyhearted.

"How about we get a drink? You want one Jacky?"

"Do you have soda?" Jacky asked.

"Yes. Let's go see what kind."

During the exchange between my mother and Uncle, Mom cleared the table. I foraged for leftovers. Finding everything neatly tucked away, I imagined Mom putting food into those containers while Uncle followed her around. She probably went back and forth to the refrigerator or cabinets as if he were invisible.

Everyone besides Jacky had lost their appetites. He ate leftovers but Robert stuck with soda. When Uncle showed up, I went for a shower. Later, when I came back down, the sofas were full of sleepers. Uncle had already gone out to sit on the porch. He just stared at the lake. I decided to join him. Lillian came out too.

The sky had turned gray. Calm waters lapped at the shoreline. From the porch, everything gave a false impression of peacefulness. Thinking to resolve our immediate issue of getting back home, I sat next to Uncle. Without intending to, I grilled him.

"What were you thinking?" I asked.

"She wouldn't answer me."

I didn't say anything.

Sometimes, misery followed misery when my mother got into one of her defiant moods. My emotions exploded. My feelings confused me. I was livid but had empathy for Uncle too, but condoning his actions wasn't possible. How could anyone ignore the physical assault? He had grabbed Mom; shook her and then amplified his offense by yelling at her. My fury pushed me into silence for fear I might fling irrevocable words.

At the peak of my confusion, Uncle stood up. "We need to get back. The boys are tired," he said.

Lillian reached for his hand. "We can't leave now."

She looked through the window behind us. I looked too. Jacky and Robert were sound asleep. My mother could have been awake. Regardless, I felt we shouldn't disturb any of them.

"Let's stay here tonight," I offered.

Uncle faced the lake. "We'll need our things."

"I'll get a car to take you to the house."

"Jack, you go." Lillian said.

"Sure, I'll pack up everything. Then drive our truck back."

We both went to my house. I figured going along with him would be easier than talking him through the security.

That evening, we were all gloomy. When everyone went upstairs, I sat on the sofa across from Mom prepared to stay with her all night. An hour later, Lillian came back down, showered and in her pajamas.

"Today has been super weird. How are you doing?" I asked.

Lillian nodded. "The shower helped."

"I'm sorry this hasn't been a stellar vacation."

"No worries. I would like to speak with your mother in the morning."

"Do you think she'll talk to you?"

"I know she will. Maybe you can find something for everyone to do for a few hours."

I kept my thoughts to myself. The idea of spending time with Uncle didn't please me one bit. Yet, I would do what Lillian asked. If she believed it was the best way—then I did too. Although I respected her optimism, I also held on to my doubts about her ability to get through to my mother.

Right after we agreed to make space in the morning, Mom curled herself into a ball. When Mom sat up, she had a blank, not-really-there look on her face. Suddenly, Lillian sprang up. With a back-and-forth lullaby movement, gentle stroking of

Mom's hair and a soothing voice, Lillian consoled my mother as someone might a child.

"You're safe," she reassured her.

Those actions seemed to tap into an ancient rhythm and Mom slowed her breathing. I think she sighed. As a witness to whatever pain and agony Mom suffered, I still managed to begrudge her acceptance of Lillian's altruism.

Going off to bed, I entrusted my mother to Lillian. Before falling into a deep sleep, I thought about the best way to deal with Uncle's sour attitude without diving into my own funk over what happened. The whole ordeal made it difficult to be around him. On top of that, he refused to own his part in spoiling the day. How would I avoid a confrontation with him? We were bound to bang heads.

The following morning, I went for a run. The dew had softened the ground and the cool morning air had the freshness of rain after a drought. I sucked in the pine fresh air. My heart pounded faster, my arms swung freely and my face relaxed as I ran forward. I was free. All the while, the alternating rise and fall of my feet, made me feel as though I glided through the air.

Outside of my movement, a stillness had settled into the woods. A rare twig snapping, the rustling of small animals and birds tweeting contributed to the peacefulness. After running a few miles, sweat formed on my back and my mind cleared. I ran in the shadow of trees, interrupted by flickers of light, until I reached the creek.

Bustling water brought me to an abrupt halt. Mossy rocks spotted the muddy earth with patches of vivid green. A yellow-headed bird pecked at shrubbery on the other side of the creek.

The serenity of the woods should have eased my mind, but it set me thinking instead.

A sunbeam emblazed my body. While absorbing the cosmic energy, I tried to collar my thoughts but failed. Instead, I let everything playback in my head. Uncle's aggressiveness contrasted his otherwise gentle manner. His behavior puzzled me. I pondered whether or not to confront him.

He hadn't exercised any level of kindness or common sense when he grabbed and then shook my mother. Yet, for strange reasons, I unwillingly empathized with Uncle. I felt like a traitor because I understood his actions, perhaps envied them. What could be done? It had happened; no one could take it back. I reasoned spilling my wrath on to him wouldn't improve anything. Having made my choice not to confront him meant only that moment mattered.

For several minutes, I meditated in that haven where trees had replaced people. As I ran towards the boat house, the idea of an adventure on the lake filled my head. Lillian wanted space. She would get her space. The rest of us would have some fun. In the boat house, there were kayaks, an old wooden canoe, a large fiberglass rowboat, jet skis, a once-used pedal boat and my dad's twenty-foot Luger.

I stroked the Luger, letting my fingers run across each letter. My father named the boat, *Merchant of Venice,* after his favorite play. I loved his boat. In the summer of 1990, my father launched it into the lake, then navigated to the Merrimack River and finally into the North Atlantic Ocean, where we spent two of the happiest weeks of my life. Dad's Luger wasn't an option.

Kayaking required skill. I scratched it off the list, but the rowboat made good sense for a trip down the lake—it was also the best choice because the boys were too young for jet skis. I hoped Uncle would cheerfully come along without upsetting anyone.

When I returned to the house, Uncle and Lillian were at the table. Mom had disappeared from the sofa. I searched the refrigerator and cabinets for suitable breakfast foods. We didn't have anything except leftovers. I called Simon. He made no fuss about preparing breakfast for us at the lake house. Forty minutes later, he arrived with a big smile on his face, a cheerful greeting and boxes of foodstuff.

Simon looked lumberjack rugged but had a calm and gentle nature. In the kitchen, he prepared breakfast for each of us. I had eggs, toast and fruit. Uncle had oatmeal. Lillian decided on fruit and coffee until the boys came down. Simon suggested pancakes to them. Lillian looked impressed.

"You're making pancakes without the mix?" she asked.

"Yes, it's not a problem." Simon laughed. His robust laugh made the rest of us laugh too; thus he triggered the first light-hearted moment of the morning.

"I'm going to try those pancakes," Lillian told him and then when they were ready, she ate three of them.

After everyone had filled their bellies, I shared my plan to take a trip down the lake. Right away, Uncle expressed his excitement, but when he looked at Lillian, she reached out for him with a sad expression.

"I'm sorry; I'm staying here," she said.

"Why?"

"You know why, Jack."

"I'm not too crazy about leaving you. We can all stay."

"Please, go with the boys. It will help them enjoy the day."

Uncle carried his bowl to the sink. He began to wash it. Simon eased the bowl away from him. Uncle released the bowl and then he spun around to face us.

"This is supposed to be our vacation."

Lillian went to him. She slipped her arm around his waist while kissing him on the lips. Jacky played on his device. Robert buried his face behind a book. They appeared oblivious to their parent's parley over the day's plans.

"You're right babe." Lillian said.

"You think I'm being selfish—"

"I love you and you love your sister… don't you?"

"She doesn't even notice you."

"You don't know that."

Uncle stepped back causing Lillian's arm to fall away. "I wanted her to treat me like a brother—not a stranger. Everything went haywire."

"I know. Remember, you were a child when she last saw you."

"Shouldn't matter, I'm her brother."

"Honey, can't you see, you are a strange man to her."

"All she had to do was talk to me. But she wouldn't—"

"And you tried to force her—"

"I never forced her to do anything."

Everyone looked at them after Uncle hollered. Lillian clasped Uncle's hand urging him towards the kitchen door.

"Let's go look at the boat," I said, when they stepped out.

Uncle showed up as I taught the boys about water safety. "What's cracking?" he said when he came into the boat hangar. His friendliness seemed forced. I smiled and then gave him a life vest. Not taking time to hear my safety instructions, he wandered off. "How about this here one?"

Uncle climbed into the pedal boat. Jacky climbed in with him. Mom had innocently gotten the boat for my college graduation party, thinking it would be fun for everyone. It wasn't and I loathed it. No one had used it after the event. We should have gotten rid of it. I intended to make known my contempt, but the three of them were already inside bouncing around looking happy.

Their excitement made me happy for them, but still, I wanted to say the boat needed maintenance. I couldn't lie to them. They were overjoyed. I figured if a peaceful day required using that thing, then I should accommodate them.

"Pedal boat it is… you still need to wear the vests," I told them. So, there we were, the four of us unhousing the ten-foot, banana yellow pedal boat. We rolled the boat to the shore using its dolly. After pushing it into the water, we tied it to the dock and dropped the anchor. With the boat secured, my lack of knowledge about how to use it needed correcting.

I searched for the user manual. Half in and half out of the boat, I rifled through the compartments. I felt as silly as I must have looked leaning over to poke my head into all the hidden cubbyholes. My search ended when I spotted a waterproof pouch in the storage under the back seat.

"Found it." I held up the manual.

When I faced everyone, Uncle insisted we bring food and water with us. Once we rolled the dolly to the boat hangar, we went back inside. Mom had restored her pristine look. Jacky and Robert hugged her. I wanted to hug her too. Instead, I addressed our current problem.

"We need to pack a lunch," I said to her.

Mom leapt off her chair. She fished out a cooler from underneath the island cabinet.

"Let me." Simon gripped the cooler.

Mom released it and then went back to her breakfast.

"Can you come with us?" Robert asked Mom.

"I'm tired today. You go have fun."

"I'm sorry I ruined everything. I don't want a telescope—" Robert stepped up to her chair.

Mom knelt bringing herself to his level. "I know you do, and you didn't ruin anything."

She had him sit next to her at the kitchen island. They carved out their own private space. Whatever the subject, it excited them.

"Bet you're still asking for stuff," Jacky teased Robert.

Neither Robert nor Mom gave credence to his comment. When I looked over at him, I noticed Uncle had walked away. I tapped the back of Jacky's head and then pulled him into my side.

"Be nice," I said.

Jacky leaned against me. "Can we go now?"

"Hang on. We're almost ready."

Lillian touched Mom's shoulder when she came into the kitchen. Mom didn't recoil. I wondered how she'd react if I touched her. Unfortunately, I lacked the courage to try; the risk of humiliation was too high.

"Feeling better?" Lillian asked when she sat next to her.

"Much better, thank you," I heard Mom say.

Reading the boat manual, I learned the rudders for the joystick navigation were under the boat. They worked in reverse. Left was right and right was left. I laughed to myself. The navigation mocked me. Like my relationship with my mother, everything about the boat seemed upside down and backwards.

While we waited, Simon wrapped leftover sandwiches in butcher paper. Then he added them to the cooler along with some fruit, nuts and drinks.

"Are we ready?" Uncle asked as he gripped the cooler.

"Yes," we answered.

Lillian walked out with us. Before stepping off the porch Uncle kissed her. She whispered something to him while they hugged and then she let go of him.

Once we lifted the boat's canopy, Jacky and his father steered us into the lake. I guided us southwards to a tiny island where locals swam. We'd gone down the lake a ways when I asked, "Want to see a fairy pool?"

Jacky laughed. "No such thing as fairies."

"I swear—it's a real—no kidding fairy pool."

"Even I don't believe in no fairies," Robert snickered.

After we finished laughing, Uncle decided to let the boys have a look. We traveled straight until we cleared the jetty. Subsequently, they turned the boat left to round the peninsula and there dipped between the forested rock formations, beckoning to us, was one of my favorite spots. A pool of calm waters with a sandy beach. Some local folk were already swimming.

"There it is," I pointed.

Uncle's eyes widened with wonderment. "It does look like a fairy pool," he said.

Robert leaned forward, poking his head into the front of the boat. "Can we swim?"

"I don't know?" Uncle looked back.

"The water is perfect right now. I think—"

"She says it's perfect. Can we Papa?" Robert stood up.

"Remember no standing in the boat," I reminded him.

"If you want? It's up to Portia."

"Let's go," I said.

They navigated around to the other side of the peninsula where we anchored our boat. Exiting, we walked the wharf until we reached the sandy beach. Those boys dropped their life jackets, peeled off their shirts and then jumped into the water faster than I could step down. Uncle collected their things.

On the beach, I put out a towel and then gave Uncle the towel bag. He took one out too. I laid out, letting the sun extinguish my dark thoughts while the boys frolicked in the water. Their gleeful voices rose into the air. The fortress of evergreen trees lining the unreachable distant shore held out promise of an escape into another world. The lushness beckoned to me. I stripped down to my bathing suit, moved to the edge of the sandy beach until the cool water covered my feet.

"Do you plan to swim?" I asked Uncle.

"I'm going to keep an eye on my sons."

"Watch from the water. It's perfect for a swim. I promise."

Uncle shook his head, his attitude threatened to block the gaiety of our outing. The murky space around him seemed contagious and I had no desire to slather around in it. Escaping into the water, I stroked my arms, left, then right and kicked my legs to propel my body away from the beach. When I perceived the strong current of the open waters, I turned around. With the current as my guide, I swam laps until I felt exercised.

Back on the shore, Uncle and I watched the young swimmers take turns diving off a high boulder we all called the jumping rock. I had done the same as a child. A local boy stood on the rock, with a holler, he splashed into the water. Robert mounted the rock next. I looked on feeling afraid he'd hurt himself. I couldn't liberate myself from my uneasiness. My anxiety rested in my fear of Uncle's boundless anger. If one of the boys injured himself, I knew he'd blame me. I'd never live it down.

"Does that frighten you?" I asked staring out at Robert.

"Sure does. Got to let them live you know."

Uncle didn't break his gaze. We watched Robert ready himself. He squatted, squeezed his feet against the rock, standing up he balanced himself, grabbed his nose and then jumped. I held my breath until his head popped up.

"I never felt scared when I jumped off that rock."

"You didn't know any better. I bet your parents were terrified."

"I never knew. But I get it now."

When the boys exited the water, they flopped in the sand. Robert put his head on his father's leg. "We're hungry," he said.

"That man says we can eat with them."

Jacky pointed to the children standing with their parents. I turned to look. Jacky's new friends waved their arms in the air. I waved back. Uncle shook his head without bothering to look where Jacky pointed.

"We have our own food," he said.

"Papa, please, please, please, let us eat with them."

"Cut it out, Jacky. We don't know them."

Jacky pouted, displaying his dissatisfaction.

"I'm hungry," Robert said.

"They do need to eat," I offered.

"Can't we at least eat—over there?" Jacky asked.

Uncle evaluated the picnic area behind us. "Tell you what, we'll go over, but we'll eat the food we got. Agreed?"

"But Papa—"

Uncle sat on a boulder bringing himself face to face with Jacky. His voice sounded calm but firm. "No buts. Those are the terms. Now, you choose."

"Fine." Jacky's negotiating ended.

Uncle stood up. "Let's get the food."

He carried the boys' things back to the boat. Robert ran ahead, Jacky followed. I put our towels back into the bag, slipped my shorts on over my bathing suit and then I followed too.

Jacky took his food to the other picnic table where he sat next to the couple's daughter. He offered his soda to her and then smiled big when the girl took it. Jacky must have gobbled down his food without breathing because in less than ten minutes he and the other boys tossed around a football on the beach. Between throws, he glanced over at the girl.

A curly haired woman with golden brown skin came to our table. She glistened in the sun as water dripped from her hair into her face. Before speaking to us, she beckoned to her husband.

"I'm glad you came over." She sat with us.

"We don't want to impose." Uncle said.

"I'm Alex Hansen," her husband said when he reached us. He sounded like one of those people who always included their last name whenever they introduced themselves.

"Sorry, manners. I'm Kathy. How about you?"

"Jack." Uncle extended his muscled arm across the table.

The curly haired woman turned to me.

"I'm Portia. Nice to meet you," I said.

Jacky called out to Robert. He hurled the football capturing Uncle's interest. He and Paul ran off with Robert to play on the beach. "I'm a lawyer. What do you do?" Kathy asked after we sat quiet for a while.

"I'm an accountant."

"So why did you become one?"

Kathy slipped into her t-shirt; her curls had stopped dripping. The air felt chilly, and I put on my t-shirt to delay my answer.

"Although nobody forced me into it, some might think so. At least a little."

"Why would they?"

"All the men on my father's side, except for my dad's father, became accountants. My dad started teaching me the principles of accounting when I was a kid. I might be brainwashed." I smiled.

"Both my parents are lawyers. I felt forced into it. What did your grandfather do?"

"He invested in real estate and steel."

Kathy laughed. "That's a long way from accounting."

"Sure is," I agreed.

There were times when I wished to have inherited my grandfather's independence or sense of industry, but that was another matter. Kathy and I talked about our careers until everyone came back to the table. Another hour of eating and playing around passed before we left the tiny island.

At the boat, I climbed in front to ensure a smoother, quicker ride back. Late into the afternoon, we pushed the pedal boat back into the hanger. Before going inside, we removed the rowboat and then tied it to the dock because Uncle wanted to have some private time out on the lake with his family. When we stepped onto the porch, Lillian hugged her boys and then kissed Uncle. The boys excitedly told her about the rowboat.

Inside, Robert ran over to his Aunt Frances. Jacky joined Robert on the sofa closest to her. Mom spoke softly. Her relaxed face matched the easiness in her manner when she asked the boys if they had had a fun time. Robert relayed how he swam in a fairy pool. Jacky added details about the jumping rock.

Mom listened to them from the armchair. Snuggled on the other sofa with Uncle, Lillian joined the conversation. The boys, with full animation, Mom's encouragement, lots of laughter and a host of questions from both Mom and Lillian, recalled their adventure. I quietly left the room. After a shower, I called Jarod to share my day with him.

An hour passed before I came back down to an empty house. Everyone had gone off to enjoy the outdoors. At four o'clock, there was plenty of sunlight left to take a stroll along the lakefront.

Walking northward, away from the house, I headed straight toward Mom coming the other way. I stopped when I saw her. I stood there watching how the wind blew her turquoise palazzo pants to one side. She had looped her sandal straps over her fingers, dangling them by her side, letting them swing back and forth as she walked. I expected her to turn away when she saw me, instead, her face lit up and she quickened her pace. I started walking too.

"You can't always get what you want," Mom said, when we met up.

I jumbled my words but managed to give the expected reply. "I'm glad we're here together. It's been a while." Mom smiled. "Since my graduation party."

My mother reached out to me and then stopped. She almost touched my arm. Our exchange was awkward; yet my joy overshadowed my musings about her odd behavior. I wanted us to spend time together. Sensing she did too, I requested she join me for the rest of my walk. Mom turned around. She looped her arm around mine as Grammy had done a few weeks earlier.

Our mother-daughter moment catapulted me to my girlhood days of unhurried relaxed living. We walked farther down before stopping to enjoy the evening sun. I waded into the water until it rose to my ankles and then pressed my toes into the rocky sand. Mom rolled her pants up to her shins. She waded in too.

We stood in the evening sun which made everything golden. The warm air had a steady interruption of cool breezes, and I relished the moment. Mom flicked her foot. The water splashed and then rippled away from us.

"I've been talking to Lillian," she confessed.

I picked a rock out of the cool water.

"She's a psychotherapist you know," Mom added.

"Yep, I do." I flung the rock into the lake.

"Well, I'm going to think about getting help with my life issues."

A thousand questions raced through my head. More than anything, I marveled at her changed attitude. "Sounds good," I managed to say.

Mom wrapped her arms around her body as if she tried to warm or hug herself.

"I might. I don't know if I can. But I want to."

"It's a start Mom."

We lingered until the golden rays stopped shining on us. As we walked back, Mom decided to take everyone out for dinner. She wanted to go to "a lovely restaurant."

The weekend had been difficult for everyone. Feeling the need for space, Lillian wanted to stay at the lake for the rest of their visit. It was a perfect idea. As I explained how to arm and disarm the security system, Uncle put his face close to the panel.

"Press this at night?" he asked.

I nodded.

"She's mental, you know."

"What? Who are you talking about?" I stepped back.

He laughed. "Who else? Your mother—my sister. She's crazy, off her rocker, bonkers."

Undeniably, my mother targeted her kindness, but she always nurtured and catered to children. She had been especially welcoming to her nephews. Those unkind words tumbled out of Uncle's mouth, dirtying up every good thing, causing me to brew an unstoppable hatred of his arrogance.

Mom's conduct might have made him feel bad. Sometimes, she caused me to feel bad too, but hurt feelings didn't give him or me cause to call her crazy. At the restaurant, Mom alienated Uncle in every way she could manage.

We all noticed. She maximized the distance between them by sitting at the opposite end of the table. He could have been on the moon because Mom ignored him with unwavering completeness. When he spoke, Mom turned her head away from him. She reserved her words for Jacky, Robert, Lillian or me. I had never seen Mom treat anyone that way. Her deportment may have been childish, but she didn't merit his disrespect.

My irritation mounted until I said, "Do you need more attention... are you a child?"

My words catapulted out before I could call them back. I always work hard to prevent my words from cutting into people. Yet, it seemed Uncle deserved the sting of the truth.

"I'm not the one who's nuts." Uncle shrugged.

Why did he always need to say such hurtful things? No matter his opinions, I couldn't ignore his callousness. I shoved the security booklet into his hand. "What's your problem?" I shouted.

Lillian came down from putting the boys to bed. "What's going on?" she asked as she approached us.

"Ask your husband. I'm leaving."

"She's pissy because I told her Frank is cuckoo."

"What an ugly thing to say."

"Didn't you see how Frank acted? I'm not blind. Are you?" Uncle shouted at us.

"You assaulted her yesterday." I fumbled with my key fob trying to reduce my anxiety.

"Wait a minute, I'm a criminal now?"

"She means you touched her in a demanding way," Lillian inserted. Uncle waved his hands in front of his chest.

"Wait a minute, I've never harmed a woman in all my life."

"But you're the one who upset everything, not my mother."

"How is this my fault? Someone should figure Frank out. She should—"

"Be what you want her to be?" Lillian frowned.

She looked exhausted. I wondered how long she had attended my mother the night before. She probably needed sleep. I had to put an end to the bickering for my own sanity and to show respect for Lillian. I grabbed the door handle.

"I can't do this. I'm going home." Not allowing time for their protest, I walked out.

On the Fourth of July, an inescapable funk fell upon me. Lillian and I had planned a cookout for the kids. The boys had been so excited, talking about all the hotdogs they wanted to eat. Lillian was even going to try her hand at making some potato salad. Mom was going to bring corn to roast and an apple pie. Still, we canceled because an opportunity for merriment had turned sour, leaving behind the fetid odor of discontent. I was so bummed. To vaporize my anxiety, I spent the morning painting by the creek.

Later, I hoped to remedy my loneliness by spending the evening with friends. Jarod came along to keep me company. Sitting right next to him, I thought about my broken family. The possibility of Mom and Uncle adopting an amiable relationship seemed hopeless. Although I couldn't say why, Uncle's attitude towards Mom tarnished everything. It seemed, he sought to miraculously vanish forty years of estrangement, but no matter how angry I felt, I always managed to see Uncle's side of things too. That's because I thought, although to a lesser degree, Mom shared the blame. To push Uncle away, she rained down her anger as though she were a gray cloud of doom.

Jarod brought my attention back into the room when he gave me a glass of wine.

"You were lost in thought," he said.

"Sure was. I'm thinking about family feuds."

"What happened?"

"My whole family is broken to pieces."

"Weren't you supposed to be with them tonight?"

"Yes, that's why I'm bummed. We had to cancel."

"I'm truly sorry. Want to talk about it?"

"Not right now. I'm trying not to play gatekeeper."

"Gatekeeper?"

"Yeah, I'm trying to do what you always advise. You know, to let whatever happens, happen."

"It's always a good idea."

"Yes, especially with my mother and her brother."

Jarod cocked his head, giving me one of his contemplative smiles. "What would you be able to do anyway?"

"That's the problem. There's nothing I can do except keep them away from each other, but it's the opposite of what I wish to do."

"It's a no-win situation." Someone called Jarod. "Be right back."

When he walked away, I feasted on dark thoughts as if they were potato chips. I valued Lillian's friendship. Together, we'd found ourselves stuck in the middle of someone else's controversy. If our relationship suffocated under the weight, I would blame Uncle. Jarod had spoken the unsweetened truth. It was a no-win situation.

The sky exploded with pops of red, blue and green. Jarod came for me after the first burst finished. I set aside my musings to enjoy the fireworks.

The following morning, I called Lillian to talk things over. First, I apologized for walking out on her. Next, I told her how awful I felt about the fighting. That's when she proposed a birthday party for Robert. She thought it would be a good way to mend things. It sounded like a brilliant idea to me. We both noticed how my mother had attached herself to Robert. The two of them had some kind of bonding experience.

Their connection gave us reason to suspect Mom would come to his party. The next morning, I went out to get a few gifts for Robert. Simon met me at the door when I got back. "I signed for some boxes." He extended his arm holding out an envelope. "Thanks," I said sniffing the air. "What's that yummy smell?" "Garlic butter mushrooms. I'll put on the fish in a minute."

The envelope had a note from my mother. She had written, "Please take these packages to Robert's birthday party."

If not for the party, she would have shipped the boxes. Mom had listed Uncle's house on the farm as the ship-to address, using my address as the sender. I put the boxes in my car, had a tasty lunch and then diddled away the afternoon painting in the woods near the guesthouse. I looked forward to a fun, low-drama evening celebrating Robert's birthday.

While we unloaded her packages, Mom drove up. After she cut the engine, I opened her door. "I wasn't sure about coming," she said, still sounding apprehensive.

I sighed. "I'm sorry about the other day, but I'm glad you came."

Once inside, the boys sat the boxes in the middle of the floor next to the one I'd carried in earlier. I added my gifts to the pile. Mom hugged the boys and Lillian. Robert shook the smaller gifts until Uncle planted his hands on Robert's shoulders. "We should eat now, so that Robert can open his birthday presents," he said.

"Alright then." Lillian kissed Robert's forehead.

"I'm too old for kisses," he mumbled.

"Not for mine." Lillian skipped into the kitchen.

We laughed at her silliness. Mom and I followed her.

Earlier, Lillian had informed me of her plan to make Grammy's biscuits. My curiosity about how things turned out exceeded my patience. A plate of golden-brown biscuits sat on the counter. "Those biscuits look perfect. What else did you make?" I grinned.

Lillian laughed, "What are you implying?"

"Nothing. I'm curious," I joked.

"I baked a chicken, steamed green beans and there's salad."

Lillian opened the oven to show off her baked chicken. Steam went into my face when she lifted the lid from the pot with the green beans in it. When she replaced the lid, I hadn't seen anything except steam. "You changing your ways?" I bumped Lillian's shoulder with mine.

"Everything looks yummy." Mom ignored or missed the banter between us.

When it came time to eat, the boys sat next to my mother. Uncle jerked out his chair. Then he mumbled, "I guess, that's that."

Lillian grimaced. "Remember not to fill up on biscuits," she told us.

"We love biscuits." Jacky chomped off a chunk of his biscuit. When he patted his stomach, Uncle laughed like a kid. I couldn't help myself, I laughed too. Then I tasted my biscuit. Lillian had done a good job.

"Just like Grammy's," I told her.

"Liar," Lillian smiled.

While we filled our bellies, Robert reported on his fishing expedition. He had never gone fishing before but caught a fish off the dock using worms he dug up himself. Although he flung my father's old rod into the water, he didn't know what to do when the fish tugged the line.

"He fell right on-off the dock," Uncle slapped his own leg.

"He made a big ole splash," Jacky laughed.

Uncle waved his arms over his head. "You should have seen his face when he came up."

Mom looked worried. "I'm glad you know how to swim."

"He's fine. We ate that trout for lunch." Lillian picked up the dishes. When she took Robert's plate, she teased him. "My little provider," she giggled. They laughed at their inside joke.

"Are we ready for cake?" Lillian asked us.

We were all too full for cake. Lillian decided we should sing happy birthday, let Robert blow out his candles and then open his presents. Everyone helped clear the table. Then we sang happy birthday in front of the glowing cake. While the last words of the *happy birthday* song vibrated around us, Robert closed his eyes, mouthed something and then blew out all nine candles with one breath.

Afterwards, he jumped up, ran into the living room and then sat in front of the pile of boxes stacked between the sofas. Like cattle, the rest of us, herded into the great room behind him. Mom sat across from him giving herself the best view of his face. Jacky and I occupied the chairs facing the fireplace.

"Happy birthday from Mama and me," Uncle said.

Robert ripped the paper off the gift. He frowned when he saw it was a portable gaming device. A moment later, he grinned. "Maybe I can program it or take it apart." He hugged his parents.

"Sure, whatever you like," Uncle said to him.

During my childhood, my parents always gave me the most perfect gifts. Sliding two boxes down the coffee table until they were in front of Robert, I hoped to have done the same for him. First, he opened the hefty hard-backed book: Electronics Projects for Beginners. His eyes filled with excitement and then he flipped through the pages.

"Every word... I'm going to read every word." Next, he opened my last gift to him, a Robotics set. "Boy, wow!" He examined the box but didn't open it.

When he quieted himself, Mom pushed one of her boxes over to him. She used a pocketknife to cut the tape. Robert knelt on the floor, removed the packing paper and dug into the box. Crumpled paper covered the floor all around him before he pulled out his present. Lillian sucked in her breath the moment she saw it. Jacky did too.

Robert jumped up and down. He ran around the sofa with the box held over his head. "Aww man! I got a telescope." His voice shrieked making him sound like a girl.

"It's programmable," Mom pointed to the box.

"Can we open it?" Jacky asked.

Robert joined in, "Yeah, yeah, yeah. Please?"

"Let's wait until we get home."

Uncle shook his head, took loud angry breaths, with his fist tight he folded his arms across his chest. Lillian rubbed Uncle's arm and then reached for one of the boxes. She raised her eyebrows and then slid the largest box in front of Jacky. "This one's for you."

Jacky put his hand over his heart. "I didn't ask for nothing— promise, not me."

Mom smiled. "These gifts are for all the birthdays and Christmases I've missed. I've missed a lot more of yours Jacky boy."

He grinned. "Oh boy... thanks Auntie." With the top layer of packing paper removed, Jacky pulled out a digital drawing pad. "What's this?" he frowned.

"Empty the box," Mom reassured him.

He took out an unlabeled cardboard box and then placed it on the floor. Next, he removed a box with a picture of a wooden art case. "Aww man," Jacky ripped off the plastic. "It's a real art kit." He opened the box, slid out the wood case and then opened every drawer to reveal an array of coloring pencils, soft pastels, charcoals, paints and brushes. The top of the case converted to an easel when lifted. He opened, then closed it, then opened it again.

Mom interrupted. "There's more," she said, pointing to the box.

Sensing Mom packed the boxes herself, I looked inside and then lifted out a large sketchpad. With the cardboard side facing up, it had made the box look empty. Underneath, Mom had placed sketchpads of varying sizes.

"You scored," I handed Jacky the sketchpad.

He peeked into the box. "Aww man." Jacky sounded astonished. "How did you know... how did you know?"

"What is there to know?" Uncle asked.

Mom faced Uncle. "He loves drawing." She scrutinized him in a way I had seen a thousand times. Her voice made clear she thought him clueless or an idiot.

"Well, I knew. We knew," Uncle looked at Lillian.

Lillian sighed. "I know he doodles a lot."

"What about that one?"

Mom pointed to the cardboard box Jacky had placed on the floor. He loosened the flaps, opened the box and with a gasp, flopped back on to the floor with his feet tucked under his buttocks.

"Oh my God—Oh my God," he repeated while staring at the ceiling. His excitement filled the room.

"Let me see." Robert reached for the box.

Jacky bounced up, grabbing the box, he said, "It's a laptop."

"Let me see it," Robert said.

"Let's open yours buddy," Uncle suggested.

Mom gave him the pocketknife. Uncle sliced through the tape and then returned the knife after pulling back the flaps. We watched Robert lift out a microscope accessory kit. When he saw it, he fished through the packing paper until he picked out the microscope. His excitement burst out of him. Mom gave him a semi-professional, binocular compound microscope. It was indeed, a real one.

Robert tore away the plastic and then fiddled with the microscope. He busied himself with the premade slides. When he finished going through the kit, he hugged Mom.

"Thank you, Auntie," he said.

"You're welcome." Mom rubbed his hair.

Robert cheerfully went over to his father, but Uncle had a menacing look on his beet red face and refused to look at the microscope.

"What will you inspect first?" Mom asked.

"I'm going to look at cow poo." Robert held his head high.

We laughed.

He looked from person to person; he cocked his head.

"What?"

We laughed harder and then he laughed with us.

"Thanks for your generosity." Lillian hugged us.

The boys thanked us again.

"It's too much." Uncle looked deplorable.

He walked away from us to go stare out the front windows. Lillian touched his back when she went up to him.

"I'm grateful. So are the boys."

Although Uncle had become sullen, he helped stack the empty boxes next to the kitchen door and he put the gifts the boys weren't using next to the fireplace. Robert busied himself studying the items in his microscope accessory kit. Mom explained the digital drawing pad to Jacky. Lillian sat on the floor looking over Jacky's laptop.

About an hour passed before Lillian served cake. Soft music played in the background. We had branched off into separate conversations. Mom and I were discussing an art exhibit we wanted to see at the museum until Jacky blurted out, "I'm going to make cartoons for a living."

His announcement caused Uncle to leap out of his chair. Uncle kicked the boxes we'd stacked by the fireplace. "All this stuff… all this stuff. It's too much."

Jacky ran over to him. "Papa, please stop it." He tugged his father's arm. Uncle stopped and then he glared at Mom.

"You happy now? Proud of breaking up families? Want him to be deviant too?"

The words came out of his mouth like bullets. Tragically, Uncle came to his senses the instant my mother left hers. She bolted from her chair, marched over to him and pounded his chest. Uncle put his arms up and then stepped back.

"You're just like him. Just like him," Mom screamed.

Her bun unpinned. Her hair whipped into her face. Her elegance vanished right before our eyes. For an instant, I sat stunned. Willing myself to move, I hustled the boys away from them.

"Did he break my computer?" Jacky asked.

"I'm sure everything is fine. Don't worry."

"What's wrong with them?"

Robert's confusion reflected my feelings. I guided the boys to the table. Mom's sweaty face reddened. She looked wild. Seeming to tire, my mother bent over, placed her hands on her thighs and within seconds, explosive sobs cut through the room.

I went to her. I strained to decipher her words when she said, "Take me home."

I gathered her things. While I supported her, Mom and I walked to my car. She melted into the seat. Not a single word passed between us on the drive to her house. Just making it to her bedroom, she collapsed onto the bed.

Unable to console her, I covered her with a blanket and armed the security system. When I drove off, I found myself ready to confront Uncle.

Back at the lake house, I entered without knocking. The door opened to the sound of Uncle screaming. Robert ran to me. The force of him charging into me almost toppled me over. He clutched my arm. Seeing the boys all frightened like that made me want to cry. They didn't need to mope around feeling bad. I guided them upstairs and told them to shower before going to bed.

"Don't leave," Robert said at the top of the stairs. He clung to me, wrapping his arms around my waist, seeming afraid to let go.

"Everything will settle down. Go shower. I'll wait right here."

Uncle's voice sporadically invaded my consciousness while I waited in the mezzanine. A few words or sentences drifted my way when his volume increased. For my own sake, I tuned him out. Jacky joined me on the Shinto bench after he showered. When Robert came over to us, he smelled of cucumber melon body wash and water dripped on to his pajamas. I rubbed a towel over his head to remove the excess water from his hair. Once we sat on the bench with Jacky, I looked at each of them.

"What should we do now?" I asked them.

"Can I sleep with you?" Robert asked Jacky.

"If you want—what do I care?"

"Will you tell us a story?"

"I'm not a baby. I don't need a stupid story."

Robert didn't need a story either. Jacky's brave face hadn't fooled me. He was afraid too. He walked into the room and then plopped on the lower bunk.

I thought about how my parents might handle the situation. My father would have cheered them up, somehow getting them to laugh so that they would feel better. But my mother, she would have calmed them and put them to bed.

Entering the bedroom, I said, "I'll tell Robert a story. Jacky, don't listen, if you don't want to."

"Fine." Jacky's spitefulness contrasted his naturally playful tone.

Once they settled in bed, I began the story. I used the most soothing voice I could muster. Remembering how my guided meditations often induced a hypnotic effect on me, I tried it on the boys. I adopted the same tone as the woman who led my meditation sessions. In a matter of minutes, they had both fallen asleep.

When I stopped reading, I noticed Lillian listening from the doorway. Uncle stood behind her. Seeing them inflamed me. All the things Uncle had said hit me hard. My angry thoughts welted up to the surface; same as they would have had he beaten me with a hammer. I closed the bedroom door, preparing to unleash a firestorm, intending to blow it his way.

I pushed past them.

At the bottom of the stairs, Lillian tried to apologize. "Please forgive us. We—"

"What happened is unforgivable."

"It's not my fault." Uncle slid his hands into his pockets. "Frank didn't need to flaunt her money in my face."

"Why do you hate her so much?"

I felt a pain in my throat from reaching a volume I never used, screaming to be heard by someone who didn't care—to make sense of what was happening.

"She hates me. Hates our whole family."

"That's ridiculous."

"Come on Portia, you're not stupid. I see how she treats you."

"She treats me fine. She makes your children feel special. But I agree, she didn't fawn all over you."

Uncle smirked. "What did I ever do to her? Nothing, that's what."

"Maybe all the nothing, is the problem," I said.

Lillian walked away. We followed like ants. In the great room she flumped down on the sofa. Uncle dropped down next to her.

"Portia, you're not making any sense." He crossed his arms.

"Are you serious? It's been over four decades since everyone stopped caring about her."

"I care about your mama." Lillian countered, allowing her misplaced defensiveness to escape her.

Those words stuck to me like tape folding in on itself. A measure of animosity brewed between Uncle and me when I shouted, "I don't mean you or your boys. I'd think you'd know that." I deplored my words, the moment they gushed out of my mouth.

Lillian looked morose. She put her hand to her mouth. Her chin trembled and then tears rolled down her face. I knew I had skated on the emotions of a friend. Worst of all, I had affronted the one person who had remained clear-headed throughout the visit.

I wanted to apologize. To tell her how sorry I felt for my unkindness. Instead, I questioned Uncle about his tirade. Sounding as angry as I felt, I said, "I'm listening... what, did she do, to you?"

"She left me. That's what."

He leaned forward placing his hands on his thighs. I pitied him. Standing over them, I wanted to scream, get out. I controlled my tongue to prevent making an abysmal mistake. On rare occasions, my parents squabbled. When they did, they never walked away from one another. On the other hand, I had made a habit of storming out. It was exactly what I wanted to do right then.

Countering my impulse, I sat on the sofa, primed for a reconciliation. I imagined my buttocks glued to the cushion.

"Do you think everything is about you?" I asked Uncle.

"No... but what she did broke everything."

"How exactly did she do that?"

"I'm not going to talk about it—ever."

"And why won't you talk about it?"

"Because... I don't have to. She broke things good with her filth."

His words felt foreign to me. Lillian had gone quiet. But that statement pushed her right back into our dispute.

"You lied to me?" she asked.

"I'm not the filthy one. I planned to forgive her. Except she—"

"You were going to forgive her?"

My volume made Lillian jump. How could Uncle have called Mom filthy? Those despicable words described many things. My mother was not one of them. How had he come to see her that way, I wondered.

When Lillian came over, she reached out to touch me.

I stood up. "I'm done," I said.

"Let's get everything out in the open."

Lillian tried to mediate for us. It was obvious Uncle had a character deficit, and it wasn't going to become my problem. His rancorous outburst had depleted my patience.

"There's nothing to say. Your husband is a child."

"We should—"

"Done." I raised my arm into the air, walked out the door and then slammed it shut behind me.

They went back to Denten the following morning. Before their visit, I ordered a criminal history report on my mother. Turned out, she didn't have felonies, misdemeanors or violations of any kind.

At the time, the news relieved my anxiety. Then, Uncle attacked his sister and had a violent reaction to everything about her. He all but accused her of having committed a heinous crime.

If my mother had a criminal history, I speculated it was sealed or expunged. For the rest of the week, I deliberated about what to do next. Those brutal episodes of intense anger between Mom and Uncle pushed me towards Denten. Some unknown thing had caused Grammy, Gramps and Uncle to have a low opinion of my mother and I needed to know how it came to be that way.

On the night when Uncle spoke openly with Lillian, I scribbled the name of his childhood pastor in my journal. That man, Pastor Joseph, became my only lead to understanding what happened way back in the sixties.

Whatever the thing was that broke my family had to come out in the open. It was time. Somehow, Uncle's visit made the Denten secret an elephant. I proposed to hunt it down and kill it.

PART FOUR

Standout

Armed with information about Eucharist, I prepared to dive into our family secrets. I didn't waste time getting started. By 10:00 a.m. the following Sunday, I had checked into the Denten Beach Resort.

The next morning, I ran, ate breakfast and then phoned the Denten First Council Church. When the secretary answered, my mouth went dry. I hadn't thought things out. Not having any legitimate church business, I claimed to research the history of the Denten First Council Church. "Everyone says Pastor Joseph is the man to see," I said to her after explaining my fake project. "Is it possible to put me in touch with him?"

"He's here right now, in an elders meeting."

"Do you think he'd be willing to talk to me?"

"I imagine he would. Can you get here before noon?"

"Sure can."

Feeling lucky, I waved my arms in the air, picked up my keys and then headed over to the church. When I arrived, it was only eleven-thirty, so I drove around to the back of the old stone building, passing the maple, birch and hemlock trees that dotted the grassy boulevard in front of it and then I waited in the parking lot.

At eleven fifty, I exited my car. My nervousness combined with the coolness of the shaded path and an eerie chill passed over me as I walked under a cluster of maple trees. Beads of sweat dotted my forehead when I gripped the forged iron handle on the large oaken doors. Envisioning every single barrier crumble to the ground, I opened it.

Entering the church where my parents married, I recalled all those photos Uncle showed me. One of them had a long shot with the church's clock tower rising into the sky. Individual faces were difficult to pick out from the dots of people standing on the stairs. I wondered if the whole town had attended Mom's wedding. Inside, I crossed the foyer to speak with a petite woman in the office to the left of the church doors.

"Good afternoon, I'm Portia. I called earlier."

The woman smiled. "Yes, I'm the church secretary, I remember your call. My name is Phoebe. Nice to meet you."

"Should I just wait here?"

"Yes, the elders will be done soon."

During the short wait, I paced the lobby thinking about how to introduce myself to pastor Joseph. Seeming to magically appear, a group of men burst into the hall from one of the meeting rooms. Their voices filled the space as they headed to the exit doors. I saw Gramps in the middle of them and turned my back. He came down the corridor, talking with the elders, giving me a fright but exited the church without noticing me.

Soon after, a doddery old man, wearing a yellowing white shirt, so thin I could see his undershirt, painstakingly pushed his feet forward but made steady progress down the hall. When he neared the foyer, the secretary called out in her cheerful voice.

The younger man who walked next to him said goodbye. The pastor shuffled over to us.

"This young woman wants to know about the history of our church," Phoebe said, sounding proud or honored to announce my phony project to him.

"She does?" Pastor Joseph extended his arm. During our handshake, he clasped both his hands around mine, shaking too hard and gripping too tight.

"I know you're a busy man. May I take you to lunch or something?" I offered.

"Or something? What exactly do you suppose that something might be?"

"Sorry sir, I'm imposing."

"You not imposing. I'm eighty-seven. I'm retired from just about everything. There's not many somethings for me to do. This here council meeting, about the only something I do do." He stood there in his shabby brown pants, held up by his faded red suspenders, waiting for me to say something.

"My name is Portia Foster. I hoped you might have time to talk with me this afternoon."

"To you? Whatever for?"

"Church history... remember?"

Phoebe saved me from lying to him. His aged skin hung out of his short-sleeve shirt when he rested his heavy hand on my shoulder. He focused on my face as if we were intimate friends. "Tell you what, the church secretary here—Miss Phoebe, she usually takes me on home." He looked at her. "Want a break today?" he asked.

"I got lots to do here. I don't mind at all."

The church secretary held up a stack of papers as proof of her workload. The pastor dabbed his cloudy eyes with a thin handkerchief he pulled out of his saggy pants. Amid all of his unsightliness, somehow, he exuded authority.

"Alright then," he turned to me. "I'm supposing, you can drive me on home now."

Everything happened fast. Too fast. I exited the church feeling a fraud. At the church entrance, I jumped out to open the passenger door. The pastor tucked in his shirt before getting into the car. After he buckled up, I walked around to the driver side.

"How does a young lady, such as yourself, afford a car such as this?" he asked when I closed my door.

"Where to?" I responded.

"Is this one of those beamers?"

"It is."

"Well, anyone with such a car as this, can certainly take me to lunch." He checked his watch. "How about Tiny's?"

"Works for me."

I didn't need to think about it. I drove away ready to get answers.

Tiny's happened to be the oldest and busiest diner in Denten. Although there were a number of people waiting in the reception area, the host showed us to a table when she saw the pastor. She put us right in front ensuring the old man didn't need to walk too far. Several people greeted him as we walked to our table.

The host put a menu in front of me. Then she stood next to the pastor while she told him the specials. "I bet you'll be wanting the meat loaf," she offered with a smile.

"That's right, I do." When the host left us, he said, "Now, how is it, that I might help you today?"

Leveraging his eagerness, I expected to coax him into a conversation about my mother. Four decades had passed; yet I hoped he remembered her. The lunch crowd made the diner noisy. Raising my voice, I leaned forward so he could hear me better.

"Is it true… your church ran the Eucharist reform school?"

"Sure did, I left my home in Virginia to see to it."

"When was that?"

"Around 1951, '52. I was a young thirty-something, with a head full of ideas on helping young folks."

"Did you achieve what you set out to do?"

"Think we did. Closed down in '82. Were you even born then?"

I laughed. "Barely."

He laughed too, causing his top dentures to drop down. He pushed them up using his middle finger.

"Why did you close?"

"Everything ran its course."

"What kind of reform school did you run?"

"The same kind, any decent Christian would run. The kind putting young folks on the road to Christ."

"Was the school for boys or girls?"

He paused. "What's this got to do with church history?"

"Isn't the reform school a part of the history?"

"That it is."

"I imagine the reform school was important to you." I flattered him hoping to put him at ease and to counter his defenses.

He leaned back. "I set out to win young girls over to Christ. We made proper women out of those errant girls."

"How'd you do that?"

"Daily regimen."

"What was the regimen?"

"We had strict rules, a dress code, most important worship and daily prayer."

"What type of dress code?"

"Girls had low cropped hair. They wore long sleeve shirts, white socks, skirts to the ankle and closed shoes."

"You chopped off their hair?"

"That we did."

When the food arrived, we took a small break from our conversation. Every fork of food challenged the pastor because his hand shook when he lifted his arm. Concentrating on the arduous journey to his mouth, he managed to avoid dropping his meatloaf.

His messy chewing disturbed me. He was loud, opened his mouth too wide giving me glimpses of his masticated food. Exercising an odd counter measure, I oscillated between looking past him, focusing on his eyes and looking at my plate to avoid his unsightly mouth.

"What was the purpose of the dress code?" I asked, picking up where we left off.

"Modesty kept those unruly girls on the road to Christ."

I wondered what he meant by modesty—I wondered what he meant by unruly too. Leaving my curiosity for another time, I avoided digressing into other matters like clothing choices. "If you don't mind, please describe a typical day at Eucharist?"

"Wake time, prayer time, scrubbing up time, work duties, worship followed by reeducation."

"What is reeducation?"

"Well now, we had ourselves a caseload of offenders whose actions went against the word of God. These folks, especially the deviant ones, needed special programming."

My food curdled in my mouth. Putting my fork down, I swallowed hard and then looked straight into his eyes.

"Do you remember Frances Miller?"

His knife clanked on his plate. With a look of disgust on his face he asked, "Is this another stunt by that Bowman woman?"

"I'm sorry sir; I don't know who you're referring to."

"Madeline Bowman, bane of my existence."

"I don't know anything about her," I reassured him.

He looked past me. "Hers was a challenging case... back in sixty-six or sixty-seven when folks respected the word of God."

I stared at him. "Whose case?"

"Some girls, like corrupt Madeline, committed offenses against God. We rectified their sinful ways."

"What offenses?"

"Sins against nature."

"I'm not sure I understand."

"I'll let you research for yourself. You obviously not a woman of God." He stared without blinking, seeming to sum me up.

"How did you know your treatment worked?"

"I'm no psychiatrist." His boldness faded, he lowered his eyes and avoided mine.

"You're saying you helped the girls to—"

He squinted his leaky eyes. "Look now…" He raised his voice. "Tell that woman not to send fancy lawyers around pretending on me."

"Sir, I'm not a lawyer. I don't know who Madeline Bowman is."

"I'd like to end this attack so I can enjoy my supper."

"What can you tell me about Frances Miller?"

He ignored me.

For the rest of his meal, he refused to look at me or acknowledge my question. I ushered him home when he finished eating. At his house, I helped him onto the sidewalk.

Before he walked off, he muttered, "Thank you for the lunch. Good day now."

By the time he went inside, I had already driven away. During our meeting, I had written two words. '*Madeline Bowman.*'

Hidden in the pastor's catty remarks was an implied connection between my mother and Madeline Bowman. Suspecting I'd guessed right, I went back to try my luck at the courthouse, hoping to find a court case related to the Bowman woman.

At the clerk's office, a man in his fifties or sixties attended the counter. When I asked for cases involving Madeline Bowman from 1966 through 1969, he tightened his mouth and glared at me.

"You don't want to get tangled up with her. She's bad news."

"I'll go where the research takes me."

"What kind of research you doing?"

I focused on him and then leaned forward. I kept my mouth shut, letting my defiant stance do the talking.

"Suit yourself." He went away.

The click, click, click of his keyboard pushed me closer to finding answers. The man slid a piece of paper across the counter when he reappeared. I reached for it and then he slapped his hand down, right over the paper. I dropped my arm to my side. I stood tall matching his gaze until he removed his hand.

At the records terminal, I tapped the first option to select criminal cases. Using the on-screen keyboard, I entered the case number 69-C1-00134. A case popped up from the summer of 1969. I clicked *print record* and then took the ticket the machine spit out to the clerk. After paying, an hour passed before they called my ticket number. I rushed to get the document.

Hurrying to get outside, I shoved those papers into the exterior slip pocket of my tote bag. Holding the document awakened my phobia that my life would crumble around me. My heart pounded. The thumping in my chest became intense. Inside my car, fearing I'd have a heart attack right in the parking lot, I phoned Lillian.

Hearing the distress in my voice, she asked if something was wrong, I couldn't stop my tears.

"I'm fine… I'm—"

"You're what?"

"At the Denten courthouse." My sobs became uncontrollable.

"In Denten? Stay there. Jack will bring me right over."

"Please don't…" I wiped my nose.

"Take deep breaths. Promise you'll wait."

I promised but felt stupid for calling. I stayed because I couldn't drive anyway. I felt as if a heavy blanket prevented me from moving. I reclined my seat and then waited. Lillian slipped into the passenger seat when she arrived.

"What's going on?" she asked.

I turned to her. "Where's Uncle?"

"Farming. I didn't get him."

Relief washed over me. I put my seat in the upright position. Lillian looked into my eyes and then she patted my tears with a tissue. Reaching into the back seat, I removed the document from my bag. Lillian flipped through the pages. Before she could read it, Grammy tapped the window, startling both of us. She opened the back door and then sat behind Lillian.

"Did you get here today?"

"Yes, this morning," I lied to avoid confrontation.

"You ill or something?"

"I'm fine. Sorry for bothering you."

"Lillian was saying, we had to come get you."

"Hope I wasn't a bother."

"She told me you broke down. Everything seems good here."

"The car is fine."

"You coming to the house?"

"She's staying with us," Lillian lied. While I appreciated her desire to protect me, nothing could entice me to stay at her house.

"You still cross with me?" Grammy leaned forward, putting her hands on the headrest.

My throat tightened. I focused on the steering wheel. "I'm not angry with you," I said.

"You just can't be bothered to come by?"

Grammy bombarded me in a way that electrified my anxiety. Feeling the weight of the situation, I shut down. I just stared straight ahead. Lillian sprang into action. She got out of the car, opened Grammy's door and somehow persuaded her to leave the parking lot. After Grammy drove away, Lillian opened the driver side door.

"Let me drive." She grinned. "Where are you staying?"

Her words induced an unexpected sensation of relief.

In my suite, Lillian sat at the table reading the document. I opened the patio doors before sitting down next to her. The sea air freshened the room. The waves crashing on the beach distracted me, giving me a second to disassociate from my troubles. I imagined myself swimming in the ocean.

"There's nothing in here about your mother."

"Nothing?"

"Not a thing. This case is Madeline Bowman against Eucharist Reform School."

"You sure?"

Lillian nodded. "What were you expecting?"

"You remember the pastor your husband talked about?"

"I sure do."

"Well, I met him today. He seemed repulsed when he spoke her name."

"Whose name?"

"Madeline Bowman's. I'm wondering if she's the missing link to figuring out what happened with my family."

"I get that. But why were you upset?"

I considered Lillian's question. My family lived down the road; yet it wasn't possible to depend on them. They were angry, dishonest and full of spiteful venom towards my mother. Plus, the thought of my mother being a criminal caused me to develop a fearsome mistrust of her.

Everything seemed bleak. If my speculations turned out to be true, I wouldn't have anyone to rely on. "I suddenly felt alone in the world," I said, opening up to her.

"You're not alone. You'll always have me… the boys and Jack too. We all love you."

"After the fiasco at Robert's birthday party?"

"Yes, it wasn't your fault."

Realizing, I'd extricated myself from everyone I loved caused me to feel horrible and I wanted to fix everything. But how could I? Uncle, along with my grandparents, made feeling a part of their family a bleak prospect.

Although I wished things had been different with my mother, they weren't. She alienated me too. Thus, a healthy relationship with any of them seemed impossible. I avoided a disagreement with Lillian by changing the subject.

Pointing to the papers on the table, I said, "What does it say?"

"She claimed Eucharist abused her."

"What kind of abuse?"

Lillian lifted her eyebrows, inhaled and then exhaled through her mouth. "Shall I summarize for you?"

I studied her face. "Yes, please."

"The lawsuit claimed they sexually assaulted and physically abused her. It also alleges unlawful captivity."

"They held her captive?"

"That's what it says here."

"What did they do?"

"There are no details. They dismissed the case without a trial."

"Do you think they were prostitutes?"

"I doubt it."

"Uncle called her filthy."

"Yes, I remember." Lillian became agitated.

"And he talked about deviants. He said she sinned against nature."

"Who did?"

"The pastor did."

"Who did he say sinned against nature?"

"I'm not sure. I couldn't figure out if he meant my mother or Madeline Bowman. I don't have a clue what he meant anyway."

Lillian sighed, rested her palms on her thighs, looking right at me she said, "I think he's saying either the Bowman woman or your mama is gay."

The room closed in on me. Lillian confused me. That pastor had a nasty attitude, an exacting honesty and a hatred for Madeline Bowman. He hadn't said anything about my mother. My mother, who never dated anyone after my father died, had neither men nor women on her radar. I stood behind the chair next to Lillian.

"He didn't mean my mother," I said.

"I'm sorry to say this, her own brother called her deviant."

A twinge of disbelief prevented me from listening to Lillian. Her words eluded me. I walked away, undaunted by the evidence. Standing in front of the patio doors, I focused on the waves crashing onto the beach. The roar of the ocean swooping in and then out again seemed to beat against my morbid reality but didn't wash away my despair.

"Portia, everything is going to be just fine."

Lillian tried to coax me out of my funk. Her gentle voice sounded reassuring, yet somehow ineffective at the same time. When I turned to her, she ripped the top page off the document. She pushed the ragged piece of paper across the table.

"There's an address. Go check it out."

"You're saying to track down this Madeline person?"

"You have another idea?"

I shook my head like a child. "No."

"Well, there's your answer. Go tomorrow."

Lillian picked up the paper. I took it. Checking out the address was a good next step.

During the drive back to the farm, Lillian accused me of being insensitive. She tried to shame me because I hadn't checked on my mother before leaving Brackwood. It didn't work. One thing I knew for sure, to the point where I wouldn't even argue about it was… going to my mother's house would have wasted my time. Even so, before heading out, I phoned her. She hadn't answered. From years of struggling to connect with my mother, I easily deciphered when to push and when to walk away.

"She would have ignored me," I said redoubling my resolve.

"Maybe she would have welcomed your concern."

I laughed. "She wouldn't have."

"Does she know you're here?"

"She might guess where I am."

"What would make her think you're here?"

"I left her a voice mail."

"What did you say?"

"I said, it was time to continue my journey." I chuckled to hide my nervousness. Since Mom had been yo-yoing through life for decades, it seemed fitting to let her recover without beseeching her to be well again. Lillian mentioned how all the feuding saddened her, causing a bit of anxiety to seep into me, but I kept myself from mentioning the source of all the friction. I didn't need to tell her.

With my eyes fixed on the road, I said, "I'm eager for everything to settle down."

Fortunately, the day hadn't been a total loss. The pastor led me to Madeline Bowman. I believed tracking her down could unvault the truth about Eucharist. It was time to open an old wound to let the pus drain.

To get into the right frame of mind—to increase my chance of finding someone at the address, or to work up the nerve, I spent the morning in the hotel spa. Stalling accented my flawed logic and strange ideas spun around in my head making a mist of my courage. Unfortunately, nothing was going to change the dread I harbored about going to that address. I needed a game plan.

As a cover, I drafted a story, rehearsed until I felt confident and at three o'clock found my way to the address. My courage faded away right in front of the house listed on the court document. I thought... what if dangerous people live in there? Circling the block for a third time, I considered the risks of knocking on that door.

Boosting my mood with a host of affirmations I'd heard countless times at various team building meetings, I parked on the other side of the road alongside the public green space, making sure people saw me there. When I rolled down the window, the fresh scent of cut grass came through with the ocean breeze. I listened to the girls skipping rope. *Down by the river, down by the sea,* they sang. Their innocent voices lured my thoughts to simpler times.

A young boy sped by on his bike. He hiked onto the curb to cycle down the sidewalk. Several people busied themselves on the block. Some people sat in the blue-green grass under the trees, while others sat on their porches. I let my consciousness mingle with the sounds of children playing. Their happy voices propelled me to the door of 8032 Orleda Drive. A strange house with a connection to my mother's childhood. I knocked.

A gray-haired woman answered. I focused on her blue eyes instead of her broken yellow teeth. I stood tall, making use of my height.

"Is Madeline Bowman available?" I asked her.

The woman clutched the doorknob and then turned into the house to ask if Madeline planned to come around later that day. Someone yelled back. The woman widened the door. "She's not coming today."

"Thank you," I turned to go.

"Did she invite you to have dinner with us?"

I stood confident, thinking I'd look more official. "She didn't. I'm doing some research on Eucharist." I used one of my rehearsed lines.

"Did you check at the Woman's Center?"

"What women's center?"

She pushed the door forward, leaving a small opening. I could see her teeth. "The Standout Women's Center."

"The what?"

"Do you even know Maddie?"

"No, I don't know her, I'm—"

"I wish you Jesus folks would stop hounding us."

She slammed the door. Standing on the steps, I debated whether to knock again or not. I wanted to explain, but I had already lied. Certainly, the stained-tooth woman wouldn't have answered again. Knowing I had flubbed it, I listened to the rope jumpers chant, *Banana, banana split, what you get in arithmetic?*

Before driving away, I made good use of the information the woman gave me by calling the Standout Women's Center. Madeline wasn't there, but I left a voicemail. Not risking it, I left my name, phone number and then went a step further. I said, "You might remember my mother, Frances Miller."

Grammy had invited or somewhat summoned me to dinner after our encounter at the courthouse. Although I would be early, I pulled away from the curb and pointed my car towards the farm.

Barrels of harvested peaches sat on the porch. They looked perfectly ripe. I liberated a big one and sunk my teeth into the bright yellow-orange fruit at the reddest spot. The sweet creamy peach flesh filled my mouth and juice ran down my arm. Inside, Grammy came over to me carrying a kitchen towel. First, she dried her hands and then she patted the juice on my arm. I felt like a child, but I liked it.

Grammy had spent the whole day cooped up in the kitchen, canning peaches, making preserves and baking pies for the market. There were stacks of boxed pies on the table. According to her, the pies flew off the shelf the same day she delivered them to the store. However many she had planned for the store didn't matter to me. I just wanted a slice of the one she'd serve after supper.

"Seems you got a lot done today, Grammy."

"I did. What you get up to today? Helping Jack?"

"I have my own project."

"What you working on?"

Visualizing the pastor's face and recalling the sound of his voice, kept me from responding. I sat at the table.

"Anything I can do to help?"

Grammy carried over a bowl of boiled potatoes. She sat the bowl in front of me.

"You can help peel these."

"How did you meet my father?" I asked.

"When we were little, your father came running through the field flying his toy airplane. He waved his arm in the air like this." Grammy stretched her arm straight over her head. She said, *neow-neow-neow* as her hand rose and dipped in the air. I laughed at her mimicking an airplane flying overhead.

"What were you doing out there?"

"I was having tea with my dolls."

"Did he speak to you?"

"He didn't see me. I ran after him—I told him I was gone tell my papa he was trespassing."

"You said that to him?"

"Yeah, sure did." Grammy laughed.

She went back to the stove to put chicken into the hot oil. Once the skin started crackling, she coated more chicken with flour. Before coming back to the table, she turned the cast iron skillet until the handle pointed at the wall behind the cooktop. Grammy used Gramps' chair making it easier for me to enjoy her animated face when she resumed her story.

"He told me to go ahead if I wanted my papa to lose his job."

"Your father worked for Gramps Foster."

"He did. This whole side belonged to him. My papa was the tenant farmer until he died."

"You grew up here?"

"Yes, right next to your grandpa. He grew up in Junior's house."

"How did you get the Foster farm?"

"After my papa died, your grandpa worked the land. Later we got it from your papa."

"Did my father scare you out there?"

"He didn't scare me. I was seven or eight at the time. I said...
let me see your airplane."

I laughed. "What did he do?"

"He let me see it. Then we ran through the field. We were
friends from then on."

"What was he doing here?"

"Nothing, sometimes he came with his papa."

"Did you ever go to his house?"

"No. When he turned ten, they sent him off to boarding
school. We wrote back and forth sharing our secrets. During our
teen years, we were inseparable when he came home."

Grammy looked solemn. After a meditative pause, she
returned to the cooking chicken. The whole chicken-frying
process seemed messy and dangerous. I liked the results though.
By suppertime, I'd already eaten a crispy golden wing.

Once the potatoes were ready, Grammy called Gramps. He
washed and then came to sit with us. He hurried through the
blessing, loaded his plate and then ate for a few minutes before
saying, "Want to know what Portia been up to?" He didn't wait
for her response. "She's running around town pestering folks,"
Gramps continued.

I supposed the pastor had spoken to him about our meeting. I didn't care. Neither he nor the pastor had any good will
towards Mom. I wanted to know why, and I aimed to exercise
my freedom to enlighten myself.

"He's right," I said, denying him control over me. "I'm asking
questions about Eucharist."

Grammy frowned. Although I touched a nerve, she didn't
say anything. Gramps stared at me. I stared back. He pointed
and then jabbed his finger in the air. His cadence heightened
the anger in his voice.

"You need to stop nosing about. Ain't nothing to find out."

"I'm going to do what I want to do. Not want you want me
to do." I said, hoping to deflate his ego.

"Let it alone, Portia. We straightened your filthy mama out."

"Filthy?"

"That's right. You ain't deaf."

"You're referring to my mother—your daughter. You don't act like you love her at all."

"She shattered my love to pieces."

"How?"

"The things been done, and we saved her soul. She should be grateful. Now, she's a decent woman, as God intended."

"What are you saying?"

"She sinned in the eyes of the Lord is what she done."

"What kind of sin?" I tempted him to give away what irked him.

"Nothing worth mentioning. We turned our backs on her in accordance with the Lord's will."

Grammy hung her head, patted her eyes and then left the table. Gramps angrily pushed his chair back before going after her. I knew she cried out there. Like my mother, stress caused me to lose weight. During the silence, I ate out of necessity, plus the food tasted delicious and I didn't want to lose my appetite before I could finish eating. Most of all, I knew, whatever upset Grammy wouldn't be shared with me anyway. A fact, I'd come to accept.

Right before Grammy appeared, Gramps called out, "Peggy, you wanted the same thing I did."

"I didn't and you know it."

"Sorry for the upset Grammy," I said, when she entered the kitchen.

"Portia, please don't stir things up."

Grammy placed herself across from me, same as when we peeled potatoes and then she dragged her plate until it sat in front of her, but she didn't eat. Her mournful stare caused the energy to drain from my body. I psyched myself up—or dare I say, built an emotional wall to ready myself for a battle.

Even my compassion for Grammy wasn't going to change my course. Terrible things happened. I had the court document as proof, and it seemed my grandparents had condoned it. Maybe Grammy had regrets, but I had no desire to let her off the hook. "I'm going to pursue this to the end," I said.

"You only gone find a deviant girl got straightened out by the word of God," Gramps said with a lot of venom and then he stood behind my chair. I turned to look at him. He puffed up. It seemed he wanted to pounce on me. Gramps wasn't youthful, but he had powerful hands with strong forearms and biceps. For a minute, he intimidated me. I kept my eyes on him until he moved away.

"Do you care what might have happened to her?"

"Know what happened."

"Tell me and then I won't go around town looking for answers."

Gramps banged the table, dropping his fist from above his head to hammer on the wood. Grammy jumped. I closed my eyes but didn't move. For a second, I felt defenseless sitting there. I considered standing. Worrying I'd escalate things, I stayed seated.

"For goodness sake, let's just eat."

Grammy's request didn't deter Gramps. "She got married," bang. "Moved away," bang. "Now she lives a clean life. End of story."

"A clean life? She—"

"Portia please. Stop this."

How Grammy projected all the messiness on to me escaped my understanding. Gramps had raised his voice, pounded the table and called names, but she pushed his rage and her fear onto me. I wasn't the bully. Her habit of asking me to let things go, grated on me that night. We were polar opposites. I would scratch at an issue until it pained me. Grammy on the other hand, never analyzed anything unless forced. There was no way to do what she wanted.

Her effort to boss me around infuriated me, but after a moment, I dropped it. There wouldn't have been any benefit to discussing the issue anyway. Gramps was adamant about his right to kick my mother out of his life. He had dug into his position, acting as if he had a monopoly on how everyone should think. I didn't agree with him. Neither my protest nor my reasoning would have restored his sanity.

At some point, I thanked Grammy for dinner and walked to the door with her trailing behind me. When Grammy hugged me, she brought her lips to my ear. *Please tell your mama I love her*, she said. Grammy may have been earnest; no matter, I wasn't a proxy for obtaining my mother's forgiveness. I never relayed the message.

Although Gramps' rage was short lived, I presumed he would have preferred to pound me instead of the table. While he managed to restrain himself, his explosive hostility angered me. I've yelled, cried, shouted but never hit anyone; yet, without contemplation, I braced myself to defend against him.

Unfortunately, we had all failed to communicate. Gramps harped about what I should or shouldn't do, Grammy shut down and I stood defiant. Worst of all, no one listened. Forty years of antipathy, heartbreak and rebuke had solidified a habit of clamming up.

After that night, it no longer mattered. While I battled with them, Madeline Bowman left a voice message. She wanted to meet with me Thursday morning. Only my death would stop me going.

Madeline oozed confidence. On her way over to me, she spoke to different people, stopped for mini conversations with some and directed others to do this or that, all the while spilling her energy into the room as she moved forward.

Her pixie haircut matched her youthful manner, but she needed a haircut. Although her blonde highlighted hair was cropped on the sides, every few minutes, it fell into her face.

Before she reached out to take my hand, she brushed her hair away from her eyes.

"Everyone calls me Maddie," she said while shaking my hand.

"Thanks for meeting me."

"I'm running fifteen minutes late. Can you wait?"

"I'd be happy to wait."

"Good. I've cleared my calendar for the rest of the morning."

Madeline disappeared down the hall. A brief encounter with her led me to a series of comparisons. I judged Mom and Madeline were both confident women. In most ways, my mother is reserved, traditional and closed off. On the other hand, Madeline seemed stylish, modern and cordial. My comparisons were irrational. Still, there I sat, making assumptions. For example, with a high measure of irrational thinking, it came to me that Madeline was more thoughtful than my mother.

Quieting my mind, I halted my appraisals to concentrate on what I wanted to say. Soon after, Madeline strutted back into the lobby. Her head came to my shoulders and her feet turned out like a ballerina with her heels touching to make a V shape. Excellent posture I thought, surmising she might have aspired to become a dancer. Madeline asked the receptionist to hold her calls and then she turned her radiant face to me. I couldn't help smiling to match her exuberance.

In her office, she closed the door and then crossed the room to sit behind her desk. I sat on the soft leather sofa to her left. Before she said anything, I'd begun to feel self-conscious and slightly nervous. Fortunately, Madeline took charge, giving me time to settle in.

"Do you know anything about the Center?" she asked.

I shook my head. She labeled Standout as "a happy place," she founded to cater to Eucharist survivors. Those who needed help could get legal services, short and long-term therapy, temporary shelter and substance abuse rehabilitation. Standout offered these services for free to Eucharist survivors and their families too.

"Little Portia is all grown up."

Madeline changed lanes faster than I could accommodate. Her statement shattered my sense of obscurity about my purpose. I had come face to face with my mother's past but lost my footing.

"Do you know me?"

"I saw you a few times when you were a child."

"You did?"

"Yep, I held you once."

"Sorry Madeline, I don't remember meeting you."

"You were a baby. How can I help?"

Madeline smiled. She leaned forward putting her elbows on her desk. Unable to entrust my feelings to her, I dodged the question. "I met Pastor Joseph. He sure hates you."

Madeline threw her head back, her eyes closed. It took her far longer than normal to stop laughing. "I know. Winning my lawsuit still eats at him."

"Didn't they dismiss your case without a trial?"

"In 1969, when I was sixteen, they ignored me. Their dismissal inspired me to become a lawyer."

"You filed another lawsuit?"

"Sure did. The case lasted two years. We won in April of eighty-two."

"I'm going to take time to read the transcripts."

"It's a lot to take in."

"Your lawsuit claimed they abused you. What happened?"

"You're full of questions with no answers."

Madeline straightened papers on her desk. I felt dauntless; even though my fierceness belied my uneasiness, I questioned her again. "Will you tell me how my mother ended up at Eucharist?"

"Ah, I see." Leaving her desk, she sat in one of the guest chairs, swiveled to face me and then fixing her sea blue eyes on me, she said, "How is Fran?"

Her seriousness made me uncomfortable but captured my interest too. I felt small.

I thought about lying; but decided being genuine served me best. I relayed the circumstances of my mother's marriage, shared how everyone had rejected her and then talked about how she didn't have any friends. Madeline leaned forward, looked into my eyes, nodded, frowned or bit her lip as I vented my frustrations. Becoming emotional, I lowered my head to hide my eyes from her. I didn't want to cry during our first meeting.

I ended by saying, "In March, she freaked out."

"What do you mean freaked out?"

I recounted Mom's breakdown at the doctor's office and the fiasco at the lake house. My desperation became clear to me for the first time.

"I think she's losing her mind," I admitted.

Madeline sighed. "Eucharist was harsh."

I suspected Madeline might be gay. But certainly my mother wasn't that way. She was married and had me. I stood up, putting my hands on my hips, looking right at her face, I said, "Did you get my mother into some kind of trouble?"

When Madeline stopped laughing, she sat next to me on the sofa. "I loved her," she said.

I leaned away but gave her a sideways glance. The room felt hotter—seemed smaller. I wanted to open a window or go outside.

"You loved her?"

"Yes, and if I were a gambler… I'd bet she loved me right back."

"Are you saying she's gay?"

"I can't speak for her."

"How did you end up in Eucharist?"

"I told you. We loved each other."

"They sent her to reform school for that?"

"We got caught kissing."

Knowing my mother kissed Madeline mystified me. My mother wasn't affectionate in public or private. On the night before my father died, he sat on his hospital bed listing all the things he intended to do when he returned home. Tears spilled from my mother's eyes like a swollen river. She knew he wouldn't come home again. I knew too.

Mom hugged him and then kissed him on the mouth. I'd seen my parents hold hands when they walked together, hug, bump shoulders, peck on the lips or even cuddle, but before that day, they had never kissed openly or passionately in front of me.

Feeling timid, I pushed myself to say, "My mom kissed you?"

"Yes, many times."

"Where?"

"On the mouth."

"I want to know where you were when you did all this kissing."

"Everywhere. We kissed in her room, my room, inside, outside…" Madeline used a funny voice.

"All right, I get what you mean." Although I hadn't intended to laugh, I did. "They took you to jail for kissing?"

Madeline twisted her face. "Jail? We were never in jail. The church had our parents sign us into their reform school. We kissed there too. At night we clung to each other."

"There were no charges—was it legal?"

"Kissing?"

"Being sent to reform school."

"We were minors. Our parents decided and it depends."

"What depends on what?"

"Reform schools aren't illegal, but what Eucharist did is."

"Pastor Joseph claimed they corrected you."

Madeline's eyes grew softer. I thought she might cry. For an instant, the strong woman faded. Her shoulders slumped and she straightened her blouse. "If I had to guess, I'd say he's a psychopath—a very cruel man," she said.

"Why did they ignore your first lawsuit?"

"It was a case of small mindedness."

"What do you mean?"

"Denten was… and still is, a small town. Back then, they got away with their injustices."

"What did they do to you guys in there?"

Madeline went back to her desk where she scribbled something on a notepad. "I have a proposition for you to consider," she said a moment later.

"What is it?"

"You want to read the court case, right?"

"Yes, I think I should. Don't you?"

"It's up to you. If you do, the information might trouble you. But Standout can help."

"I'll go to the courthouse tomorrow."

"No need. You can read everything right here. We have the transcript, depositions, testimonies, pictures and letters from past residents."

"Sure, I'd love to read them here."

"Good. I'm going to assign a therapist to work with you."

"I don't think that's necessary."

"Please trust me on this. In exchange for access to our resources, you must see the therapist at least twice a week."

"Twice a week?"

"More if you want. I'm going to assign Janice Moore. She's one of our best therapists. She's here Monday through Friday from 8:00 a.m. to 5:00 p.m., later, if you need her. During your time here, Janice will be assigned to you and only you."

"Don't let me trouble you."

"Trouble? It's what we do at Standout, especially for people like you."

"I don't think—"

"Those are the conditions. It's up to you."

"Do you think I'm mentally ill?"

"No, I don't."

"Let me think about your terms."

"We have everything you need. You'll never gain access to certain artifacts otherwise."

"If I agree, may I start tomorrow?"

"Either way. Please let me know before five."

Madeline walked me to my car. When she hugged me, I clung to her, letting my tears land on her blouse. She kept her arms around me until I let her go. During our embrace, the needy feeling inside of me shrunk a tiny bit.

"Thanks for everything, Madeline."

She smiled, softening her eyes. "Call me Maddie," she said, turning away from me. In seconds, she disappeared behind the Standout doors.

After Standout, I went to see Lillian. By going to the farm, I risked a brush with Uncle and his sour countenance. I didn't care. Madeline had punctured my reality causing my emotions to leak out into the universe unresolved. I needed help.

The boys ran out when I drove through the farm gate. Jacky opened my door after I cut the engine. He was so cute and such a gentleman. His excitement delightfully extinguished my apprehension about coming around to the farm.

"Hello Cousin Portia."

"Good afternoon, Jacky."

Robert gripped my arm. "Will you look at the night sky with me?"

I didn't respond.

"Please, no one wants to," Robert added.

The honest answer was no, but I just nodded my head. Regardless, he would have to wait anyway. As we walked onto the porch, I sensed my mistake. My insides itched with rage and confronting Uncle would have been the only way to scratch that itch. Something I wasn't ready to do.

"I don't want to cause trouble," I said to Lillian.

"You're no trouble."

Lillian sent the boys to clean up for lunch. Realizing I needed to eat too, I said, "May I take you to lunch?"

"Let's see, Jack is with his folks—so of course."

"How about Tiny's?"

When the boys found out we were going to Tiny's they acted as if I'd invited them to Disney Land for roller coaster rides. They danced around pretending to be girls. Lillian laughed harder and harder until she begged them to stop being silly.

When they finally stopped, Jacky said, "Can I drive your car?"

"I don't think so." I laughed, but he was serious.

"I drive the tractor all the time."

"Maybe I'll give you a lesson sometime soon."

Jacky started dancing again. Lillian pulled him close to her and then kissed him on both cheeks.

"Okay, okay," he screamed and wiped his face.

Those kisses calmed both of those boys down and then we left the house. At the diner, before we ordered our food, Robert pulled out his electronics book and Jacky drew in his sketchbook. Lillian ordered for them and then we chatted about Standout.

Although the diner chatter had peaked, leaning closer and speaking in a low tone, I said, "I met Madeline today."

"How did it go?"

"I liked her. She's a lawyer. There was a trial."

"Did you go back to the courthouse?"

"I didn't need to. Standout has all the files. But there's a catch."

"What's the catch?"

I listened in as Robert described the robotic bug he wanted to build. Then I watched Jacky draw it. "Maddie, that's what everyone calls her, she thinks I should talk to a Standout therapist twice a week."

"That's a wonderful idea."

My heart sank. Knowing Lillian spoke not only as a friend but as a psychologist too, I avoided asking for her justification. Sidestepping didn't prevent her asking me questions.

"What if you get overwhelmed again?"

"I'm not sure I want to invest so much energy—"

"Be honest with yourself Portia. Haven't you already?"

I studied Jacky's drawing. His bug had a red body with sprinkles of black dots like a ladybug.

"What kind of ladybug is that?" I asked him.

"It's my robotic bug spy machine. I'm gonna—"

Robert spoke over him. "He stole it from me."

"You collaborated. Seems like a win-win to me." I supplied another viewpoint for him to consider while Lillian waited for my answer. Although I wished to deny the implications, I returned my attention to our conversation.

"Feeling coerced is no fun," I said.

"You'll find out what happened and have someone to advise you." After she said that, I turned my attention to the boys, promptly dropping the subject. Jacky flipped through the pages of his sketchbook, and we ended right where we started—Robert's robot bug.

"All the ladybug dots have weapons in them." Robert pointed to one of the black dots.

"Why do they have weapons?"

"It's an incognito crime-fighting robot."

"So cute."

"Told you... should've made it a mean bug," Jacky insisted.

The boys spent the rest of the meal arguing about it, until Lillian had Jacky put the sketchbook away when their dessert showed up. She had turned over the dessert menu, pointed to a dessert until the boys settled on chocolate cake with ice cream. They gobbled down every single bite.

"I'm so full." Robert said when we got to the car.

"Just right." Jacky patted his belly, to mimic his father, making us laugh at his silliness.

When we drove up to the house, I saw Uncle on the porch with his face behind a sheet of paper. He peeked over the top. Right away, he stood up, folded the paper and tucked it into his shirt pocket. Perhaps, he wanted to avoid me too. "Maybe we'll get together again in a few days," I said as Lillian exited the car.

"Aren't you going to look through my telescope with me?" Robert came to my window.

"What about drawing on my computer?" Jacky opened my door. "Please, please, please Cousin Portia."

"Come on, he's harmless," Lillian cajoled.

The three of them stood on my side of the car looking down at me until I gave in to them. As we neared the house, Uncle walked down the steps. He marched down the path looking irritated.

"Portia," Uncle grunted.

He turned his head to avoid my eyes. If my mind wasn't playing tricks on me and I don't think it was, I'd say he picked up his pace right as I started to greet him. His petty behavior spurred my decision to stop playing games. Right then, ending my doubtfulness, I decided to go back to Standout.

When I arrived at Standout the next day, a stout woman greeted me at the door. She focused her gray eyes on me. Her pale skin complemented her auburn hair. Smiling a perfect smile, showing her perfectly straight and perfectly white teeth, she greeted me.

"Good morning, I'm Janice Moore," she said. "Are you Portia?"

"Sure am."

We shook hands.

Her painted nails matched her hair. Janice had a peaceful demeanor, making her seem comfortable with herself, the world and even me. Right away, she put me at ease. Undoubtedly, in just a few seconds, I deemed her one of the most pleasant people I'd ever met.

"Are you going to be with me all day?" I asked her.

"No. But I'm going to show you around... get you settled in."

"Thank you. I appreciate it."

The woman assigned as my therapist moved her shapely frame to the right, then we strolled down the corridor side by side. During the tour, Janice harped about their benefactor. Someone who had donated five hundred acres to Standout.

After touring all the key areas, we exited the two-story V-shaped building. Out in the courtyard Janice said, "You're special to us, you know."

"I am? Why?"

"Well, your parents were a big part of Standout."

"My parents? Please explain."

"Let's take things moment by moment."

Janice led me past the patio area. Red astilbes, big blue lily-turf, scruffy lemon verbena and lavender lined the walkway, yet the calming fragrance of lavender filled the courtyard. I noted the fountain at the center. The trickling water soothed me. A brick wall, camouflaged by sage bushes, stretched out past the building, ornamental railings on top brought its height to over six feet. From the street side, no one would guess the wall hid a tiny fairyland. Janice continued past a section with manicured grass, rustic flowers and herbs. We stopped under a sycamore tree, right in front of a bronzed plaque.

My heart quivered. There was an image of my father on it.

"Take a moment." Janice pointed to a bench off to the side. "I'll be over there."

Her green dress clashed with the orange butterfly weeds when she sat on the bench. Butterflies landed on the flowers under the tree and in my stomach. I married my consciousness to the trickling water until my dizzying thoughts drizzled out in itsy-bitsy spurts.

The plaque had a dedication inscribed underneath my father's bust. It began, *Howard C. Foster*. The next line read, *Our Standout Man*, followed by:

> *We dedicate this courtyard as a symbol of thanks to our bene-factor who donated these five hundred acres to Standout Women's Center.*

It was dated 1986. My father never mentioned Standout or the nature of his business in Denten. When my grandfather died, I inherited over seven hundred acres from him. The estate, with its grand house, where we had vacationed often, once included the Standout property. Without knowing anything about Standout, I had a connection to it.

I went over to sit with Janice. Chirping all around us, hummingbirds darted in and out of the bright red flowers on the pineapple sage bushes.

"My parents never spoke about Standout."

"Now you know. Change anything?"

"A little."

"I remember you running around the day we broke ground."

"I don't remember being here."

"You were only five or six years old."

"Why was I here?"

"Your father was more than a benefactor. He served as a board member and his Firm handled our accounts."

"Did you know my mother?"

"Yes. We were friends at Eucharist."

Not expecting an answer, I asked, "What was she like?"

"Very feisty. She raised hell. Never let them run her."

"My mother?"

"Yes... your mother. She stayed strong and she sure helped me. Let me take you to the files."

Just like that, she headed back inside, ending the tour and our conversation. Even so, I had already decided I liked Janice because she was frank with a gentle tone.

"We thought this a fitting place," Janice said.

They had put all the case files in the Frances Miller-Foster conference room. Reading the dedication made me apprehensive about snooping into Mom's past.

Thinking my actions would invade her privacy, I couldn't walk through the door.

I turned to Janice. "Can we talk now?"

"Sure can."

Janice swayed down the hall, her green dress flowed around her legs. The plaque next to her door said *Janice Moore, A Standout Founder.* I stood in the doorway. Her cozy office had a courtyard view, with a long peach couch sitting right in the center of the room. Janice crossed her legs when she sat in the brown and white paisley chair across from the couch. Entering her office, I walked over to the chair to her right and then settled into it.

"That's a zero-gravity chair. Leaning back might help you relax."

I had too many questions. Relaxing sounded like a copout. I sat straight and crossed my legs.

"How did you become a Standout founder?" I asked.

"Many of the women named in the lawsuit helped establish the Standout Women's Center."

"What did everyone do?"

"Those who could… gave money. Others donated time."

"Which did you do?"

"Both."

"I'm glad you're a founder."

"I remain grateful for my part in Maddie's project."

"What did you donate, in terms of time?"

"I developed the Standout process."

As both a Eucharist survivor and a psychiatrist, only Janice could do it. She closed her psychiatric practice, donated two years to building the program, became the first client, then the first Standout therapist. She spoke at length about their process. They had tons of support programs there. Their emphasis on therapeutic partnerships was what I liked most of all.

At Standout, they aimed to heal survivors without stigmatizing them. Before making the program official, Janice herself went through the process guided by Dr. Huslinger an expert on anxiety disorders. She made everything sound so friendly.

"I may have gotten more out of the deal than Standout," Janice admitted to me.

"How's that?"

"Cognitive behavioral therapy alleviates PTSD and other anxiety problems. I, myself... benefitted from those therapies."

"You had to get psychoanalyzed?"

"No. I had to break away from psychoanalysis."

"It must have worked out, you're still here."

"So it did. You ready to review the files?"

I focused on her. After a lengthy but strangely comfortable pause, I said, "Not yet. How did my mother help Standout?"

"First, she recommended her firm donate accounting services to us. Second, she managed the building fund."

"How did my father get involved?"

"He was our accountant. When he learned about the trouble we had finding a place in Denten, he donated this land to us."

"So, she knows about this place?"

"Your mother?"

"Yes, my mother."

"Indeed. You know she does."

"How often does she come here?"

"I don't think she's ever been here."

"She should come here for help. Don't you agree?"

"What kind of help do you think or sense she needs?"

"I'm not sure."

"Why do you think she needs Standout?"

I rehashed everything again but added the craziness of those breakdowns Mom had had all my life.

"How do you feel about what you've told me?" Janice asked.

I resisted her attempt to turn things around. "As I explained, she needs help. Do you know what happened to her?"

"Your mother can tell you about her experience."

"She won't. Do you think whatever happened to you at Eucharist, also happened to her?"

"Perhaps. Some. More. Less. We had vastly different experiences."

"What happened to you at Eucharist?"

"Why is it important to you?"

"It's not."

"Well, if it's not, you'll find out everything you want to know from the case files."

"I want to know because my mother needs help."

"Maybe you're in need of help?"

"If she gets better, I can live my life."

"Interesting… here's what I'm willing to do. I'll give you an overview of Eucharist. Then you may determine for yourself why Maddie filed the lawsuit."

"Sounds fair." I pushed back into the chair before closing my eyes.

Janice explained how Eucharist had used aversion therapy on the girls housed in its facility. She quickly jumped to electroshock therapy, after breezing by some of the allegations of abuse.

"Did the shocks hurt?" I asked somewhat knowing the answer.

"They hurt like hell. Nowadays they anesthetize people prior to administering shock."

"Why did they shock you?"

"To induce electrically stimulated seizures."

"They made you have seizures?" I turned my head to look at her.

Janice nodded.

"Did it cause brain damage?"

"Probably not."

"I'm not understanding why they did it?"

"To brainwash us… to make us more compliant."

"Did they brainwash you?"

Janice stood. "I've given the overview. Are you ready to read the case files now?"

I sat up. From her overview, I conjured an idea of what to expect, but I wasn't in the right frame of mind to begin reading those files.

"Maybe starting on Monday would be better."

"I agree. I'll be here at seven o'clock."

Later that evening, the silvery sand stretched out like a country road. The moonlight cast a blue hue over the water as the waves crashed on the shore. I ran into the blue night.

During my run, I pondered whether it was judicious to stir things up, reveled in the hope of stopping the emotional servitude that had over-run my life and after running several miles, squashed my qualms about digging into Mom's past.

On Monday morning, I began my review of the Eucharist case files. Madeline claimed Eucharist failed to act in the best interest of the girls placed in its care. She alleged the residents suffered sexual abuse, physical violence and sadistic mind games. In her opening, she stated her intent to show how Eucharist, First Council Church and the State breached its duty of care to Eucharist residents.

She told the jury, "This is not a lawsuit against religion or religious freedom. But about the human rights violations and abuses committed at Eucharist."

For almost a week, I reviewed the evidence, looked at photos, listened to recordings and read letters. Two of those days went to studying the medical records Madeline subpoenaed from Eucharist. Four days into it, I began my review of the State's witnesses. Madeline's cross-examination of Dr. Henry D. Parkinson stood out.

Madeline Bowman: From your testimony, we learned you give all Eucharist residents electroshock therapy. Can you explain why?

Dr. Parkinson: Electro convulsive therapy is an effective psychiatric treatment for correcting maladapted girls. Proper use creates a gateway to help them succumb to the teachings of the reform school.

My mother received electroshock therapy three times a week for three months. In subsequent years, she had maintenance shock therapy once a month, for over two years.

Mʙ: They give up. They stop struggling—right? Do you agree with those teachings?

The State's lawyer objected. "She's badgering the witness. If you want an answer, then let him answer."

The Judge sustained.

Mʙ: Do you agree with those teachings?

Dʀ.: My beliefs don't govern my treatment. Both homosexuality and hysteria are mental disorders. I treat mentally ill patients.

Mʙ: Do you classify all Eucharist residents as patients?

Dʀ.: Yes, I do.

Mʙ: As Eucharist is not a medical or psychiatric facility. Can you tell us why you consider the residents mentally ill?

Dʀ.: We're dealing with maladapted girls.

Mʙ: Would you classify Eucharist as a psychiatric institution?

Dʀ.: I suppose not.

Mʙ: You diagnosed every Eucharist resident, past and present as mentally ill. Is that correct?

Dʀ.: Yes.

Mʙ: Is it also correct to say your methods helped push the doctrine of First Council Church? Does your... to make it simpler, treatment facilitate brainwashing?

The Eucharist attorney objected, saying Madeline had asked a compound question.

The judge overruled him.

Dʀ.: Mine is an effective medical treatment.

Mʙ: What diseases do you treat?

Dʀ.: We treat maladapted girls.

MB: What are the medical diagnoses for these, as you say, maladapted girls?

DR.: For some homosexuality. Others may have acute mania and varying diagnoses.

MB: Could you list other diagnoses?

DR.: I don't recall. Several others.

MB: For thirty years, you've treated girls from all over the state and girls sent by First Council Churches from all over the country. The diagnosis is homosexuality or hysteria for every resident. Nothing more. Would you like to modify your testimony?

I searched through several medical records. There were no other diagnoses given. They listed Frances Miller as *homosexual deviant*.

DR.: It looks like you have your answer.

MB: Perhaps. Would you say, Eucharist incarcerates girls whose offenses, if committed by an adult, wouldn't be considered a crime at all… anywhere?

DR.: Yes.

MB: With the state as a partner, First Council Church criminalized girls. Afterwards, Eucharist labeled them mentally ill, deviant or hypersexual. Would you agree, Eucharist misused its power by operating as a mental institution?

The State's attorney objected. He accused Madeline of misstating testimony. That time, the judge sustained and instructed Madeline to hold all conclusions for her closing argument.

MB: Would you call Eucharist a mental institution?

DR.: In many ways… yes, I suppose some might say so. You must remember, Eucharist girls have a high degree of mania. Once we stabilize the mood, these girls go on to live productive lives. They recover from their atypical or antisocial tendencies.

At some point, with my head already spinning, the examination shifted focus to shock therapy, moved on to allegations of rape and torture, but ultimately ended with the details of *The Way Treatment Plan*.

The tiny kernel of truth about Eucharist sparked in my mind before igniting into a blazing flame in my heart. They had done those things to my mother.

Approaching Janice's office, I worried she'd cut off my senses by putting a paper bag over my face to slow my rapid breathing. That didn't happen. Instead, she walked outside, setting a fast pace which forced me to suck in the fresh air. We walked right through the courtyard, and I peeped at my father's bronzed bust as we passed the sycamore tree. Several steps later, the brick path petered out into a dirt trail dotted with bluish-purple sage bushes.

We trudged along as heavy air fell down on us leaving behind a hint of sage. Soon after, the trees became dense, and the woods encased us.

"It might rain," I said mostly to myself.

"Sure might. Did you eat this afternoon?"

I shook my head. "I'm not hungry."

"For now, we walk." Janice slowed the pace.

"Sweet birch, hemlock, beech," I pointed to the trees as we passed them. Birds tweeted all around us. If my mother had been with us, she would have identified the bird calls.

Ten minutes later, the woods thinned. The path had led us to a log cabin surrounded by clusters of red maple trees. Floral scents from the pink, lavender and blue foliage lining the pathway to the stairs blended with the moist smoky air.

All manner of women gathered on the wrap-around porch. Some clustered together, others kept their own company, some talked, and a few stared out into the woods.

"Welcome to the House of Refuge," Janice said as we approached the steps. Somebody waved when we walked onto the porch. She waved back.

Women swarmed her like groupies, cackling voices grew louder, the peacefulness vanished and through all of it, Janice smiled showing her teeth.

"This is Portia Foster," Janice finally told them.

A few women hugged me. I shrank away, allowing Janice to engage with them by herself.

"Let's talk later," Janice said to someone. After she stepped back, she nudged me forward, motioning for the women to let us pass.

"You hungry now?" Janice asked.

"I need to eat."

We made our way to the left side of the porch where a woman, with salt and pepper pigtails, checked the temperature gauge on the barbecue grill.

Janice hugged her. "Good evening, Macy. Any good stuff left?"

"Not much. You don't need much no how." Macy bumped me with her hip. "You're not a big girl." She winked her right eye before lifting the grill lid.

Smoke billowed into my face and the smell of roasting meat awakened my appetite. Macy laughed, livening up her whole face, testifying to how those crow's feet etched around her eyes.

"This is ready." She swiped to the right with the tongs. Rows of ribs and chicken with perfect grill marks lined the racks. "This is not." She swiped to the left.

Janice's eyes widened as she gawked at the meat. "Oh boy, Macy, you outdid yourself."

Macy, a little stooped with age, held out two plates in her knotty hands. I took one and waited.

Janice pointed into the grill. "I'd like… that one and that one."

Macy put those ribs on Janice's plate.

I gaped at the rows of meat.

"What you waiting on… you vegetarian or something?" she teased.

"No. I'm not—"

Before I could choose, Macy plunked a rib on my plate. "That's beef honey. You'll love it." Then she added chicken. "Here's a chicken leg, you're going to love that too." Macy jabbed the air with her tongs. "Other non-meaty stuff over there."

We stopped at the other table before Janice led me around to the back of the cabin where an old beech tree stood in the middle of a grassy area about fifty feet away from where we sat on the porch. A wide-spreading crown of dark green leaves branched out from its sturdy trunk and gave cover to a cluster of sea blue Adirondack chairs. The majestic tree tempted me to leave the porch.

"How old do you think that tree is?" I asked Janice.

"I'd say… maybe two hundred years or more. I love that tree."

"Yeah, why?"

"It's old, been through a lot but it's still standing. I am that tree," Janice chuckled.

I looked at the women gathering on the porch. They were all older. I guessed the youngest to be in her forties.

"Are all the women here from Eucharist?" I asked.

"Perhaps, now is the right time to impart the Standout Rule."

Janice lifted herself out of the chair, balanced her plate in one hand, held her drink with the other, walking mindfully she stepped off the porch. I followed her. Putting distance between ourselves and the cabin, the voices faded to a whisper.

Under the tree, Janice seated herself in one of the blue chairs. I preferred the grass. Once settled, Janice leaned forward, looked down at me, stroked her chin and waited for me to look into her eyes.

"Our rule is… we don't ask anyone about their past."

"I'm sorry for—"

Janice put up her finger.

I closed my mouth.

"If someone wants to chronicle their experience they will do so, without prompting."

She locked her eyes on me until I nodded.

Chagrin over having asked Maddie and Janice about their experiences consumed me. I hadn't realized my selfishness. Growing callous wasn't my idea of goodness, but somehow, I had neglected to consider that my probing might cause harm to others. Working to escape my guilt, I imagined myself on a nature retreat and stared out into the dense forest of trees on the other side of the pond.

"I'm guessing something disturbed you today," Janice asked, bringing me back to reality.

I sat my plate on the grass. "I read about the way treatment."

"Then you felt anxious?"

"I also read testimony given by Dr. Parkinson."

"Can you be more specific about what upset you?"

"What they did to those girls."

"Learning what happened made you feel…?"

"Angry. Furious. They bound my mother to—."

"You were angry… what else did you feel?"

"I felt anxious. My heart thumped. I wanted to run and never stop. I panicked because…" I looked away for a moment. More women had arrived. "I don't know." There was a lump in my throat and Janice saw right through my pretense.

"I'm sensing you may have felt helpless," she said.

"They were cruel. Why did they do those things?"

"I nearly went mad trying to figure that one out. There's no way to know. Moving past what happened; living in the moment is the best way for me. Everyone here strives to do the same."

Janice pointed to the cabin. I looked around. Smoke lifted into the air. Lots of women were on the porch.

"Do you know what this is?" she asked.

"What, what is?"

"This gathering?"

"What is it?" I asked.

"Refuge night. Once a month, during the full moon, Standout hosts a gathering here at the cabin. Women come from all over. The Connecticut and Denten women come most often."

"Are men welcomed?"

"Yes. All Eucharist survivors and their families can come. I used to bring my husband and children."

"You were married?"

"I am married. My husband … they sent me to Eucharist because I loved him."

"How old were you?"

"I was fourteen. He was sixteen."

"Did he come back to Denten?"

"No, his parents sent me to him. We're from Appleton."

"Where was he?"

"In college. He went to Yale. I went to live with him there. Never went back home after Eucharist."

"Then you married him?"

"I finished high school first…" She smiled. "Then we became Mr. & Mrs. Lyndon J. Moore." Janice looked angelic. Her husband obviously contributed to her happiness. I wished for someone to make me smile the same way.

"Where is your husband now?" I asked her.

"Home or at work. He's an engineer. He stopped coming years ago," Janice nodded as if agreeing with herself.

"What about your children?"

"They're all grown up. Long ago, when you were a child, we had lots of children here. Nowadays, with everyone getting older, our children don't come."

"Do you want them to come?"

"I leave it up to them. But it's more fun now. We do things we couldn't do before."

"What types of things?"

"Well, sometimes we have a full-fledged bohemian camp out," Janice giggled looking somewhat devious.

After our discussion, until a little past sunset, wallowing in my sorrows, I loitered on the porch hiding in plain sight. No one approached me. Several women, like me, enjoyed their solitude in the midst of others.

At night fall I socialized with the Eucharist survivors. Without quizzing anyone, I extrapolated that they were a diverse bunch. Some were wealthy, some poor, some educated, others not so educated, some were well reared and others were not. Regardless, Eucharist had tortured them all.

Around nine o'clock, I spotted Janice on the porch near the cabin door. Before I could say goodbye, she grabbed my hand pulling me inside where women danced to bluegrass music. I guess Janice wanted to be in the middle of the hilarity because she used her large hips to bump her way to the core, dragging me in with her.

My arm rose with Janice's arm when she danced to the music. Her exaggerated movements made me giggle. Grinning and bobbing her head to the music, Janice bounced around doing a hop step. I capitulated. I lifted my other arm to mimic Janice, letting the fiddle move me, I danced with her. When Janice released my hand, she danced in a circle with her eyes closed, shook her head wildly and then disappeared into the crowd. I never saw her again that night.

Surrendering to the music, I coalesced my individuality with the hoard of nameless women. Sweat formed under my arms, along my temples and then down my back. I had danced for at least an hour when the music stopped.

Maddie yelled, "Moon bath."

Everyone filed out, moving into the woods. I followed. They migrated to a pond where the women stripped. Maddie was butt naked on the grass.

"Are you a standout woman?" she shouted.

"Yeah!" they called back.

Their roar resonated in the midnight air. Maddie jumped in. The others jumped in after her. In the moonlight, lingering at the edge fully clothed, moved by the strength of their affirmation, I stripped and then jumped into the pond. The cool water cloaked my body. I glided to the other side reveling in the sound of frolicking women.

On the other side, I lingered in the darkness until I felt rested. I swam back in the silky waters, guided by their rowdy voices. Once dressed, I situated myself under a tree. Lying in the grass, gazing into the heavens, I fell asleep. At dawn, I parted ways with the Eucharist survivors, but refuge night had rekindled my spirit. Janice had corrected my course. Taking her advice, I strived to stop driving myself nuts.

Flooded with energy, I walked out of the forest and then drove straight to Brackwood. I happily capitalized on the rejuvenating effects of Refuge night.

At home, I cleaned up, napped and then met Jarod for a late lunch at Fu da Garden, his favorite restaurant. We sat in a private booth with the curtains open. Yet, the low lights created a romantic atmosphere contradicting our rapport. While we waited for our meal, I somewhat told Jarod about my undertakings in Denten.

"I intend to reunite my mother with her parents," I finally admitted to him, but his response unbalanced me.

"Why are you responsible for their relationships?" he asked.

Although I seldom felt nervous around Jarod, I began to feel restless. He made a good point, but he didn't know the whole story. Things were complicated and I couldn't say why.

"These are more delicious than you promised," I said after tasting an edamame dumpling.

Jarod smiled. "You're skirting the issue."

"I guess I'm not responsible." I put down my chopsticks.

The server placed our Applewood smoked sea bass on the table. The whole fish sat atop a bed of chopped fennel. The sweet woody aroma stimulated my appetite.

Jarod served himself a portion of sea bass. "The head is my favorite. The cheek is tender."

"We're perfect together. I like the tail best."

Jarod had several bites of his food then he said, "If you want, you can tell me anything."

Filling him in on Standout or the court case would have been awkward. Everything I did in Denten involved my mother.

"I don't want things to get weird," I told him.

"Weird? Why would things be weird?"

"You work with my mom, so I'm limited in what I can say."

"Why do you need to control everything?"

"I'm not trying to control anything."

"You're trying to control me. You're deciding what I'll say or do."

"Don't you think things could get weird?"

"Why would it? This is our relationship. Not Fran's."

"I want to be extra careful. Wouldn't you?"

"No. I'm capable of setting boundaries. Why not let whatever happens, happen?"

"Honestly, I just can't…"

Jarod crossed his chopsticks on his plate. He searched my face then lowered his eyes.

"It took a plane crash, but now I know… I'm not in control. I have each day to live as best I can."

His words touched me. I didn't know what to say. I reached across the table placing my hand on his. Deep down, I knew my ability to set boundaries was questionable.

He looked into my eyes. "I miss our hikes."

I removed my hand. "I'm sorry about canceling last week. I can't say when I'll be home again but first on my list is our hike."

"What if we did something really fun tonight? Maybe we could go dancing."

"I've already made plans. Afterwards, I'm going back to Denten."

"No problem, when you get back then."

We finished our meal without much conversation. That was my fault. Unfortunately, I'd managed to push him away. Controlling or hurting people wasn't what I set out to do, but there was no turning back. Things were already in motion. Besides, who would instigate broadening Mom's circle if not me?

❖

On Monday morning, I had the most unpleasant day tackling the testimonies from Eucharist employees. Each testimony highlighted some aspect of the abuse that happened to many of the Eucharist survivors. The ghastliest amongst them came from an orderly named Larry Walsh. Madeline called him as her witness.

Madeline Bowman: How many years did you work as an orderly?

Larry Walsh: Just under fifteen years.

MB: Did your duties include raping girls?

Lw: No, I didn't never rape nobody.

MB: Oh? How would you characterize what you did?

Lw: Well, they got a device for doing male intercourse.

MB: Are you referring to the machine Mr. Joseph calls the Way?

Lw: Yes, Ma'am.

I studied the pictures of the Way machine for a second time. The monstrous contraption was a sinister device used to torture the girls identified as homosexual deviants.

MB: How did you use this machine?

Lw: First, I prepared the girl.

MB: Please explain how you prepared the girl.

Lw: The girl removed the underwear. On the table, we spread the legs, leaving the skirt over the hips. We strapped the legs to the table. Right leg—then left leg. Did the same to the arms, then we strapped down the hips.

MB: Were the girls compliant—did they submit willingly?

Lw: No… not at first. But in time, they didn't fight.

MB: After binding the girl to the table, what did you do?

Lw: We would push the machine in position—step back, turn it on for five minutes and wait.

MB: Did you watch?

Lw: Had to, case something went wrong.

MB: Did you enjoy watching?

Lw: Can't say I did. I was doing my job.

MB: What happened when the machine failed?

Lw: If it broke—Doc made me do it.

MB: Please discuss what you had to do.

Lw: Pastor kept telling me, the treatment helped those girls recover from their deviant ways. Then Doc told me, if I don't get it done, I'd be needing a new job.

MB: Are you admitting to raping girls… to keep your job?

Lw: Stop saying rape. Wasn't no rape. Doc and Pastor says, I had to administer the monthly treatment to those girls in a consistent manner. So that's what I done.

MB: I know, from experience, what you did. Again, I ask, what did you do when the machine broke?

Lw: Doc had me take the place of the machine if it was broke. To do the same to the girls.

MB: How often would you say the machine failed?

Lw: Don't know. Maybe three times a year or less.

MB: Did other orderlies perform the functions of the machine?

Lw: I'm sure they did—if it broke.

MB: To your knowledge, did Dr. Parkinson or other officials such as Calvin Joseph, perform the duties of the machine?

Lw: I never seen them.

MB: Do you recall if any officials were in the room when you forced yourself on those girls?

Lw: Yeah, Doc was. At least once or twice.

MB: Do you think you had a right to brutalize girls—like you did me—and other innocent girls?

Lw: You was gone get it one way or another. Me, machine or somebody else. I didn't want to. I needed my job. I prayed on it. Pastor kept saying I was doing the Lord's work. Says, I had to follow the will of God to turn back the Devil. He said I was saving souls.

Mʙ: When you impregnated three girls, were you… doing what you labeled, *the Lord's work*?

"Objection! Asked and answered," the Eucharist attorney challenged. "Is she a witness?" he added.

The judge overruled him.

Lᴡ: It weren't easy to not spill my seed.

Mʙ: Would it have been prudent to use a condom and thus avoid pregnancies all together?

Both the State and Eucharist attorneys objected, saying Madeline had asked a compound question.

The judge overruled again.

Lᴡ: Pastor told me they needed a true experience. Getting pregnant was a true experience, he said. I didn't want to be the Daddy of those deviant girls' babies.

I dropped the binder to halt my review of Larry Walsh's testimony. Studying the artifacts proved as problematic as Madeline had warned.

Discovering how the First Council Church supported the egregious undertakings committed at Eucharist caused me great anguish. "I'm going to make sure everyone knows what happened here. Right the wrongs they did," I told Janice when I marched into her office. In that moment, I wanted to broadcast the facts all over the town of Denten.

"The past can't be fixed," Janice countered.

As we discussed Larry Walsh's testimony, my grief became unbearable to me. "That church has no right to operate," I said, wanting to provoke some kind of action, although I didn't know how, what kind or for what purpose.

"Standout is a testimony to what happened."

Certainly, Janice was wrong. Their work hadn't made a dent in the minds of Gramps, Pastor Joseph or the clerk in the records office. Worst of all, they couldn't counsel or reach isolated women like my mother who desperately needed help.

"I want the church shut down. That's all," I insisted.

"First Council has thousands of churches all over the world. How would you shut them down?"

"I'm talking about the one here in Denten."

"How could shutting that one down help you?"

"Give me peace. Right a wrong."

"I sense you're feeling helpless again."

Her words agitated me. Although she had it right, I wasn't willing to say so. Hoping to hide my eyes, I lowered my head and then defended my position like a linebacker protecting a football.

"That's not it. Those church people should be punished."

"All of them—the innocent ones too?"

"Every one of them," I heard myself saying and then with a smirk, I added, "Worldwide."

"The burden of your pain belongs to you. Hurting others won't change anything."

"I'd feel better."

"For a while, revenge will trick us into thinking we feel better. In the end, it doesn't work."

"I'll take my chances."

"I'm guessing you want to avoid your feelings?"

Sitting up in the chair, I crossed my arms over my chest and then rejected her irritatingly accurate declaration.

"Nope, I want my feelings fixed."

Janice put her elbow on the arm of the chair. Then she held her chin. "You know that can't happen."

"I've been twisted up for years. Turns out, my mother had every right to neglect me."

"Being neglected made you feel…?"

"Worthless."

"Feeling worthless meant what to—"

"It's that Church."

"Taking vengeance won't make you feel better. All you'll likely do is… bring unwanted attention to the victims of Eucharist."

"Someone has to destroy the whole organization," I said, gripping tighter to my position.

"Do you hope to avenge your mother?"

Her question shattered my defenses. I moved away. I plopped down on the couch. "You're right. I do," I admitted.

Janice prevented me from creating distance by sitting in the chair next to the couch.

"Who specifically, do you want punished?"

Janice sounded compassionate, yet her demand for my veracity unnerved me. She was trying to atomize my fury and somehow, she had peeped into my brain.

"Nobody. Everybody. Whoever," I almost shouted.

"Who?" Janice tilted her head, working to maintain eye contact with me. I stretched out on the couch and then turned my head into the cushions, but she peeked around my façade anyway. "I'm guessing you want to punish your grandparents."

My eyes ached. My nose became stuffy. I wished she'd shut up. Sitting up, I screamed, "Yes, I want to punish them."

Janice sat back. "Good. Now you've admitted it. Let's explore those feelings."

We spent an hour talking about it. By the time I wrestled my revengeful thoughts to the ground, I had also bottled my rage. Although absent of the determination to destroy the town of Denten and the First Council Church, my anger hadn't completely vanished. I recalled Madeline's cross-examination of the President of the First Council Church, Pastor Ned T. C. Winston.

Madeline Bowman: How many member churches belong to the General Conference of the First Council Church?

Ned Winston: We have over eight thousand churches.

Mᴮ: In addition to your churches, you have more than seven hundred schools. Three of them are reform schools. How many of those schools received approval from your General Conference?

Nᵂ: All of them.

Mᴮ: What is needed for approval?

Nᵂ: We require a curriculum and operating budget. For reform schools, we also require a detailed program with specified outcomes.

Mᴮ: Did Eucharist submit the required documentation?

Nᵂ: Yes.

Mᴮ: Earlier, you testified that your organization couldn't be held liable for the actions of one of its member churches. You remember saying that?

Nᵂ: Yes.

Mᴮ: Good. Last year, your General Conference expelled an entire congregation. Will you please tell us why?

Nᵂ: They weren't in any way in harmony with our teachings on human sexuality.

Mᴮ: Did that Church support its homosexual members?

Nᵂ: That's right. They did.

Mᴮ: In 1980, your executive committee kicked out one of your member churches. What happened there?

Nᵂ: The pastor and his congregation advocated for gay rights.

Mᴮ: Was that church in harmony with your teachings?

Nᵂ: No, they were not.

Mᴮ: Now, I'm going to ask my final question Mr. Winston. Are the Denten First Council Church and its reform school, in harmony with your teachings on human sexuality?

Nᵂ: Yes, they are.

The First Council Church unapologetically vilified innocent girls by supporting Eucharist. The cross-examination proved it. There was nothing I could do about what happened long ago. Even so, accepting the facts didn't diminish my mother's pain. My heart ached for her. If I could have, I would have let her know how angry and sad I felt about all of it.

At the end of the day, hoping to quiet my brain, I ran along the beach. In minutes, the glow of the moon, coupled with the whoosh, whoosh of the waves crashing on the shore, put me in the zone. During my run, I vowed to embrace my mother along with all of her idiosyncrasies. I conjured a new image of her transformed into a Standout woman.

On Friday, I read the depositions Madeline's team took from Eucharist survivors. Most testimonies concentrated on the way machine, other awful aspects of Eucharist or Pastor Joseph's counseling sessions. Like in all things, there was an exception.

They deposed a woman who had no complaints. In her deposition, she swore Eucharist improved her life. Just having food every day, clean clothes and attending school contributed to her adoration of Eucharist. According to the woman's testimony, her promise not to fornicate made living in the reform school a breeze.

The testimony of Helen Kimbrel, on the other hand, flabbergasted me. "How did you come to see Jesus or angels?" Madeline asked her during the deposition.

Helen responded, "My first Way treatment made me feel crazy."

"It made you see angels?"

"I pretended to see angels."

"How did you pretend?"

"Whenever I thought Pastor could see me. I'd start praying or read my Bible. I even asked him to help me know Jesus."

"Did Eucharist make your life better?"

"It taught me how to lie."

"Can you say more?"

"I never seen Jesus or no angels. Reading the Bible helped Pastor believe me."

"What do you think he wanted you to say?" Madeline asked.

"In my meeting, Pastor asked me if… *a woman lying with another woman* was a sin. I told him it was. He asked if I wanted to turn away from lustfulness. I said I did. I told him Jesus revealed the truth to me. He liked that word, revealed. He used it all the time."

"How did saying you saw Jesus help you?"

"Soon as I confessed, I didn't have to have those disgusting treatments no more."

"What disgusting treatments do you mean?"

"The machine, those films, everything."

"How would you classify those experiences?"

"Painful—I was only thirteen. The pain down there made me scream but they didn't stop."

"Could you say what you mean by down there?"

"You know. My place."

"For the record, can you say what you mean, for the record?"

"They put something in my vagina."

"Sorry to cause discomfort. I must ask, did the machine or the electroshock make you claim to see Jesus?"

"Both, I think. Especially the machine. Being honest, I never saw nothing. Pastor smiled at me. Then he asked if homosexuality was a sin? I smiled back, said it was and told him Jesus revealed it to me with his angels."

"Do you believe that way now?"

"Yes, it was a terrible experience."

"Let me restate the question for you. Please say if you believe homosexuality is a sin?"

"I don't know. Don't know if I ever did. Back then, I heard some girls had easier stays if they agreed with Pastor. They were always talking about how to convert to right thinking. When he asked if homosexuality was a sin, I guessed saying yes was right thinking."

"What do you think now?"

"Still don't know. I was almost fifteen when they sent me home. I for sure liked girls. But I liked boys too. I protected

myself. Made things a lot easier. After Eucharist, I don't have
no sex with nobody. Never."

They listed the state prison as Helen's address. Years earlier,
they had convicted her for armed robbery associated with drug
addiction. Helen Kimbrel wasn't alone. Others had given depositions while in prison. Before Standout, many Eucharist survivors
had drug problems, spent time in jail or were homeless.

In the courtyard, I thought about the depositions. Mostly
thinking about how Helen Kimbrel chose to lie, it didn't take
long to own my timorous nature. Siding with Pastor Joseph was
the road to improved conditions. Like Helen, I probably would
have claimed to see angels, converted to his way of thinking or
do anything to avoid what they did to those girls.

After some time, Maddie joined me. I smiled when I saw her,
but I wasn't ready to be friendly.

"I hear you've been pushing through the material," she said.

"I'm waist deep in the awfulness."

"Pure hell," Madeline mumbled.

"Did all those things happen to you?"

"I pretty much suffered the same fate as those girls who were
considered deviant."

"Do the depositions cover everything they did?"

"Cover everything?" Maddie glanced around the courtyard.

"At least it wasn't every day."

Maddie nodded her agreement.

Sweat broke out on my forehead. I couldn't stop saying
stupid things. No matter how I felt, inconsiderate words escaped
my mouth. "It must have been awful there," I said hoping to
redeem myself.

"The thing is… shrouded in religious innocence, they set out to psychologically abuse us."

"How?"

"A few ways… mostly they pushed ideas of sexual normalcy. These notions, in my opinion, represent an oversimplification of the complexity of life."

"What do you mean oversimplification?"

"I mean…" Maddie shook her head and then sucked in fresh air. "who we are and how we become who we are is not constricted to narrow philosophical viewpoints."

"I don't want to offend you… how was that abusive?"

"Maybe forcing us to adopt their views seems harmless. Regardless, it was not—it's a type of rape. They bombarded us with their ideas until they corroded our natural love for life and ourselves, putting in its place mental illness and self-hatred. That's abuse."

"I'm sorry Maddie. I didn't mean to imply Eucharist wasn't cruel."

She didn't say a word. I shut my mouth—though it was too late. The weight of all the Eucharist information seemed to drop down on me. Feeling I had no right to cry, I held back my tears. I lifted my knees into my chest and then wrapped my arms around my legs, putting my chin on my knees.

The lavender bushes swayed when a strong current swept through the courtyard and the air filled with their sweet aroma. I vaguely remember saying, "I'm cold." At least I think I did because Maddie put her warm arm across my shoulders. From the corner of my eye, I looked at her. She seemed so wholesome and healthy. I wished my mother were well too.

"Do you hate my mother for leaving you?" I asked.

"I don't. I'm guessing you hate her."

"Yes, sometimes I do. More often than not, I love her."

Maddie pointed to a large silvery blue butterfly. We watched until it flew away.

"How do you think that happened?" she asked.

"It likes the butterfly weed."

Maddie chuckled. "How did you come to sometimes hate her?"

"Don't know. She makes everything harder."

"When she makes things harder, you hate her?"

Escaping for a moment, I considered how to mix my paint to obtain the bluish-purple color of the flowering shoots on the lavender bushes. Fixing the vibrant color in my mind, I returned to the conversation. I said, "No. Mostly it's when I feel she doesn't love me."

"I'm betting she loves you very much."

Maddie looked sympathetic. Although her sympathy moved me, in my mind, she had it all wrong. An orange-bellied robin sprinkled itself in the birdbath. During that tranquil moment, I ruminated on my thirteenth birthday. When I woke that morning, I ran up to my mother and for the first time, she refused to embrace me.

"Did I do something wrong?" I had asked.

"No. Today you became a woman. It's your birthday."

I tried to hug her, but she kangarooed away from me. My confusion must have collided with my father's because he picked me up.

"How's my angel this morning?" he asked.

"I'm too big to be picked up Daddy."

"You mean too old, don't you? You're as light as a feather."

He poked me in the side to make me laugh. I threw my arms around his neck resting my head on his shoulder. When I stopped hugging him, he put me down.

"We have a magnificent day planned for you," he told me and then sweet-talked me into feeling excited about my party.

For the rest of the day, whenever my mom neared me, I'd walk away, find my father or leave the room. At my party, I continued avoiding her, setting a pattern that it seemed we couldn't recover from because we both made it impossible.

February 4, 1991, marked a momentous shift in my relationship with my mother. The warmth in her voice was gone. Instead of being attentive, she became dismissive. Instead of nurturing me, she distanced herself. Everything changed when she became my ultra-cold, sharp-tongued, scrupulous mother.

As I recall, for at least a month, I cried every night. Inexplicably, not even my father could lessen my grief. In time, the woman who teleported into my life on my thirteenth birthday became familiar to me and we settled into our unwonted strangeness.

Having recalled the experience, I said, "She just stopped loving me."

"What makes you think that?"

"It's true. The day I turned thirteen, my mother avoided physical contact with me, unless I was sick or injured. Even now, if I try to touch her, she stiffens and moves away."

"Makes sense to me."

"You think she should have hated me?" My voice silenced the birds in the nearby trees.

"Hold on now, please be patient. Each of us were told our mothers made us homosexuals."

"They told you that?"

Maddie sighed. "Yes. They did."

"Why would they say such an appalling thing?"

"Their theory is… attentive or overly affectionate mothers cause their children to become homosexuals."

"How do you know if it's true?"

Maddie became animated. "Their whole ideology is bogus."

"How do you know it's what my mother thinks?"

"First, I don't think she stopped loving you. Second, sometimes, for odd reasons, we embody ideas even if we detest them."

"She stopped liking me. Before I turned thirteen, it was different."

"Well, the myth contends affection towards pubescent girls by their mothers will turn them homosexual."

"My mother wouldn't adopt such an absurd viewpoint."

"Do you mean to be unsympathetic?"

"I'm not. She knows being loved doesn't turn you gay."

"And I'm certain she loves you."

"You can't know that."

"Her choice not to show affection was an act of love too."

"Not true. If it weren't for my father, I would have gone mad."

"Can't you imagine her anguish?"

"She didn't have any anguish."

"I'm guessing Fran wanted to spare you the burden she'd faced."

"She stopped liking me. That's all."

"Why do you believe her decision didn't cause her emotional pain?"

"Trust me, she wasn't troubled."

I concentrated on the Sycamore tree with my father's bust under it. Although I didn't look at Maddie, I felt her eyes on me.

She softened her voice, "I realize she hurt you. Are you unwilling to put yourself in her shoes for one minute?"

"You don't know her. She doesn't love me."

"You're seeing her through your pain. Fran went through an ordeal. She married a man although she's attracted to women."

"Yeah, I know—I guess—I don't think she's…"

"Don't think she's what?"

"I don't think she's gay. She loved my father."

"Sexual desire is not about love."

The idea of my mother longing after women was bogus. Her desire for intimate connections seemed permanently switched off. How she isolated herself was all the proof I needed and there was no reason to talk about it.

To end the conversation, I said, "Guess I'll go dig in again."

"Pick it up on Monday."

"I'm eager to get back to it."

"What's your plan for afterwards?"

"I haven't thought about it."

"Tell you what, if you break for the evening, I'll ask Janice to come in tomorrow. If she can't, I'll come myself."

"I could use a break."

Maddie stood up. "Will you have supper with me?"

"Sure. Where should we go?"

Maddie gave me the address of 8032 Orleda Drive. I would have dinner in the house where I first looked for her.

On the drive over, I considered my brashness. Had I listened when Janice warned me not to ask Eucharist survivors about their experience, I would never have questioned Maddie. Like a fool, I lost control of my mouth because I had allowed the testimonies to cloud my judgment.

Calvin Joseph's interrogations aimed to combat all sexual desires in those girls. I hated him. I suspected those defenseless young women also tantalized his depraved nature and having them as his captive audience undoubtedly thrilled him.

The looming threat of the Way machine caused many girls to confess. They confessed to committing sins against God and nature. They even declared themselves sinners, deviants, evildoers, transgressors and a host of other labels, intended to deflate their will. Pastor Joseph demanded compliance and those girls gave it to him.

Regardless of my upset, my rudeness was indefensible. Reading about all the vile things stuck me right in the middle of my mother's nightmare. I felt pitiful. I wanted to wake up to a reality where those things hadn't happened. It was easy to see how that misogynistic pastor plotted to damage the lives of every Eucharist girl. His program hadn't helped anyone.

Madeline had made it clear how Eucharist had abused innocent girls for three decades. Some turned into women who suffered from drug abuse, mental illness and other problems. The lasting emotional trauma spilled on to their whole families. Onto people like me.

We became their victims. In my mother's case, she lost her ability to function normally, love or trust. Talking with Maddie made it all so real for me. In so many ways, my mother's misery had landed on me, and I wanted to extract myself from the category of damaged woman.

When I parked in front of the house, Maddie waited on the steps. Seemingly, in the very spot where I had stood after the woman slammed the door in my face. She smiled when I reached her. After she nodded to the steps, we sat down.

"I stopped for a pie."

Maddie looked at the pie. "Welcome to our Standout house."

"Is this a group home?"

"No. Eucharist survivors or their family members stay here if they need support. I grew up here."

"How did this become a Standout house?"

"I inherited it from my mother."

She turned her childhood home into the main Standout house. It was the first of five. Many Eucharist women had used one of their houses while getting back on their feet. After filling me in, she stood up. Her heroic life made me feel small. In the house, the woman with discolored teeth greeted us.

"Aren't you that reporter?"

"She's not a reporter. Portia is family. She's the daughter of a Eucharist survivor."

"You sure Maddie? We don't need no trouble."

"I'm sure, Helen. Update me on what happened this week."

Maddie put her arm around the woman's back. They walked into the living room. I followed them. While Maddie reviewed the week, I waited in an oversized puffy blue chair. After Helen gave her update, they disappeared down the hall, leaving me in the puffy chair with the pie in my lap, wondering if that other woman was Helen Kimbrel.

Joining another Standout event didn't appeal to me. Psyching myself up wouldn't have been possible. A quiet evening with engaging conversation, followed by a good night's rest was what I craved. Although, voices drifted into the room, no one came around. Sensing my mistake, I decided to leave, but then Madeline walked into the room. She waved her hand saying, "Follow me."

The dining space had six folding tables laid out in two rows of three, with enough chairs to seat forty-eight. "There sure are a lot of chairs in here," I said feeling regretful.

"We have only three guests right now; two Standout employees and we make seven."

"Why all the tables?" I asked.

"Any Eucharist survivor or their family is welcomed for Friday dinner. We're always prepared."

"Do you generally have many people?"

"Not these days. Let me take that pie." Maddie placed the pie on a table in front of the windows at the back of the room. I stood next to her but chose to stare out the window.

"What was it like growing up here?"

"Okay, I guess. We're standing in my bedroom right now."

I looked around. I twisted my face. "You slept here?"

Maddie laughed. "I gutted the place… redesigned it to make it a Standout house."

"You had an apple tree right outside your window."

"Right now, there's an apple tree and two peach trees back there. My father loved peaches. He planted peach trees before I was born. Those trees were planted six years ago."

"Peach trees smell amazing when they bloom."

"They do. Your mother spent a lot of time out there with me. We ate peaches right off the tree. See that big oak tree in the back?"

"Yes," I nodded.

"That's the tree we sat under when we talked about little girl things."

The evening sun streamed through the window. The rays turned her blonde hair golden. I wanted to ask, what kinds of things. I'm glad I didn't. All the same, I treasured those unforgettable memories she shared with me. My heart gladdened to hear how, for a time, Mom had a happy childhood. Maddie turned away from the window.

Hesitating, I turned away too but retained an image of Mom playing out there in Maddie's backyard.

"Will you help prepare dinner?" Maddie asked.

"I'd love to."

The kitchen smelled oily and meaty. Somebody was frying hamburgers. A young man put tomatoes in my hand. Confused by his presence I looked at Maddie.

"This is Cole. He's been here for…" she turned to him.

"Three months, since my mama kicked me out."

Cole was pretty. His silky brown hair flowed down his back contrasting his smooth bleach white skin. He looked like a girl. In fact, only his protruding Adam's apple made me realize he wasn't.

"How do you want these?" I lifted the tomatoes.

Cole scrunched his face. "Beats me. I'm no cook. I'm chopping lettuce. Do you like tomatoes?"

"I love them. Maybe I should—"

"Not me… hate 'em," Cole said.

Everyone laughed when Cole pretended to gag. Someone gave me a knife. Squeezing into the gap between Cole and Maddie, I sliced the tomatoes. With everything ready to eat, we put the food on the serving table under the window. While I filled my plate with tomatoes and vegetables, Maddie came over.

"You getting along okay?" she asked.

"Yes, I think so."

During our meal, Cole piqued my interest when he talked about becoming an architect.

"What college will you attend?" I asked him.

"I don't know. I'm only going to tenth grade now."

"No reason to rush," Maddie reassured him.

Cole was a fifteen-year-old child, but his manner made him appear older. I thought about his mother's pitilessness. She had denied him a home for being his natural self.

"Why do you want to be an architect?" I asked after thinking about his situation.

He hugged himself. "I don't know. My father wanted to be one. Now he's dead."

"Did you know I went to school with your papa?" Maddie touched Cole's hand.

Cole shook his head. He rocked himself.

Maddie patted his hand and then she explained how his dad joined the army right after they graduated from high school. "Your papa had already retired when he came back to Denten."

"When did he come back?" Cole asked.

"Can't remember exactly, but shortly before he met your mama."

Cole's sadness swept over the room, but then Maddie told stories about his dad until she had everybody laughing.

Cole lapped up her words in the same way I had when we looked at the backyard. The young man had lost his place in the world but received the supportive attention necessary to keep him away from trouble. I loved the support system Standout created and exulted the minor role I had on Cole's support team that night.

Although my idea of a good evening went astray, I doused my opposition to sharing my time with the other folk. In the end, the evening proved nutritive. Cole commanded our attention, allowing me to immerse myself in his life story. Thankfully, doing that liberated me from my own woes for a few hours.

Dinner with Maddie redirected my thoughts. Unfortunately, my improved mood had limited longevity. On the drive back to the hotel, my thoughts flung around until they landed on my sessions with Janice. Our conversations had dug deep into my insecurities to stir up my hidden pain.

A long run or a chat with Jarod always made me feel better, but I was too full for a jog. When I shared my sadness with

Jarod, he said, "Do something fun." Right after talking to him, I signed myself up for a weekend wellness retreat at the hotel. It started early the next morning. The brochure promised the weekend would renew my spirit. Lillian agreed to join me and I signed her up too.

Before falling into a deep sleep, I had already begun to feel better. Taking a break from the court case delayed my reading of Calvin Joseph's testimony.

PART FIVE

Clarity

We selected a meditative hike as our first event. The catalog promised a moderate hike into the state park with a catered lunch in the woods. Before lunch, we would have an hour on the beach. I hoped to use the time to run or swim. Making sure to prepare, I slipped a pair of shorts over my bathing suit and instead of hiking boots, I put on my running shoes.

At seven-fifteen, I met Lillian in the lobby and together we found the cluster of people waiting for the hike to begin. Outside the hotel doors, we stepped onto a wooden path. It led us straight into the woods. With clear blue skies, the day seemed off to a good start until the guide bombarded us with non-stop mandates.

"Connect with nature," he had said when he began to grate my nerves. "De-stress, let the environment move you," he continued.

Gentle winds rippled through the trees although the sun grew warmer. The soothing whish, whish of the early morning waves muted when we stepped into the woods.

"Return to your roots. Feel the land, its history, your ancestors."

I stopped. The group trudged ahead. The guide's voice faded, allowing me to perceive the vividness of my surroundings. Taking a five-minute break alleviated my agitation, but it returned when I caught up to the group. Every step became heavier. Six miles began to sound like a thousand as the irked sensation grew bigger.

"Enhance your self-awareness as you listen to your inner-self," the guide said.

I found Lillian. "He's irritating."

"He is?"

"Yes, with all that talking."

"Really? The instructions take my mind off the walking. Makes me consider the nature stuff."

I padlocked my mouth. She was enjoying the hike. Leaving Lillian, I walked alongside the guide.

"Is the path well marked?"

"Are we going too fast for you?" He widened his fake smile.

"Too slow, I want to run. Do you think—"

"This is a guided hike."

"It's the guiding that's problematic."

I neglected to filter my words because I monumentally disliked his interpretation of guided hike.

"I'm responsible for this group. We all—"

"Thank you." I walked back to Lillian. "Do you mind if I leave you?" I asked her.

"You're going back to the hotel?"

"No. I'm going to run ahead."

"All right then, see you later. Enjoy."

I trotted to the front of the group.

The guide called out, "Wait a minute. We should—"

Breaking into a jog, I let every step quiet my brain as the distance pushed his voice out of range. Without the constant prattle, my mind emptied. The soft path under my feet reminded me of home and I had a surge of energy. The woods vibrated with birdsong; small creatures darted about. I ran faster. In an instant, I forgot my reasons for being in Denten. Sustaining a fast jog for twenty minutes and then slowing to a fast hike ensured the group wouldn't catch up with me. Wind rustled the trees causing cool breezes to flow over the sweat pouring down my back.

An hour of brisk hiking brought me to a clearing domed by a canopy of pine needles, cedar, birch leaves and oak boughs. Pockets of red oak created a crimson glow giving the forest a magical quality. The cedar trees reminded me of Dad's cologne and hiding in our panel closet where Mom stored her woolen clothes. The spot resembled a medieval gathering place. I imagined a hobbit popping out to say, "Hallo, hallo."

I followed the sound of undulating waves, steadily growing louder as I neared them. For a short time, I rambled along the shore. Missing the serenity of the woods, I trekked back to the peaceful glade where I sat atop a boulder under a canopy of trees that blocked the sun. I assumed the Buddha position, closed my eyes and used the opportunity to think about my life.

Days before, Janice had insisted my relationships would remain unsatisfactory until I unveiled my inner life to the people I loved. Her words stung. Like Jarod, she examined my desire to control my world, but she also encouraged me to embrace my vulnerability. It wasn't easy for me. Anyone could have a good look at the woman who raised me and know it couldn't be easy for me. From her, I learned, keeping my feelings private served me best. And that's all there was to it.

Sitting in the woods contemplating my life brought a deep-seated hazy funk down on me. It threatened to never clear up. I felt defeated. Right there, I pondered how I might allow people to know me, how to change my life, or how to step away from the dreariness filling my heart. I found no answers. Next thing I knew, the guide tapped my shoulder.

"You found the spot. The hike continues to the ocean. Want to join us?" he asked.

A ray of sun pierced through the canopy. The group gathered around the boulder where I sat. I shielded my eyes to focus on them. They gazed upon me as if I were a museum exhibit or ancient relic.

"I want to swim," I mumbled.

"Me too," I heard others say as I scrambled away from the giant boulder, leaving the group, taking long strides towards the ocean. Lillian ran to catch up. I slowed down. As we neared the ocean, I concentrated on the waves. It was high tide. Removing my clothes to expose my bathing suit, I peeled off my socks feeling the sand grow hotter under my feet as I waited there.

The horizon mesmerized me. I wanted to plunge into the water, but I stayed at the edge of the shore letting the water cool my feet because Lillian stopped to pick up my things. I felt bad. Her mothering wasn't what I wanted or needed. After she put everything into a neat pile, she came running over to me. "How's the water?" she said.

"Perfect." I made myself smile.

Lillian clutched my hand, pulling me into the ocean with her, releasing me as she dived into the water. I waited for the next wave. When the wave crested, I swam inside the tube as my father taught me. The collapsing wave disabled my senses and I imagined myself deep in the depths of the ocean.

Again, and again, I jumped into the ocean, surrendering myself to the experience as the energy drained from my body. After a long swim, I joined Lillian on the beach.

"We have thirty more minutes. Do you mind if I walk along the beach?" I asked.

"Sure don't. I'm happy here."

She gazed at the horizon. I headed down the beach, sand squishing between my toes, water lapping onto the shore tickling my feet, the crisp air sweeping over me, all without including anyone else. I ran back. "I'm sorry. I invited you."

"I'm enjoying myself. Go ahead, walk."

Lillian was easy going. Being alone wouldn't have bothered her, but I put my clothes on and then sat with her. "This is our retreat. What would you like to do?" I asked.

"I'll walk with you."

While we spent time on the beach, the hotel had transformed the woods into a rustic lunch spot. Three tables with natural centerpieces filled the clearing. Tree bark, leaves and branches poked out of the woodsy centerpieces on each table. Goblets would have made the setting more medieval.

Hikers chatted sending a buzz of noise through the woods. All the talking ruined the peacefulness. We passed through the buffet, selecting various foods. Carrying my plate, I bobbed my head towards the boulder where I had meditated. On the flat surface of the huge rock, we had a measure of privacy. After a period of silent eating, Lillian threw a walnut from her plate to a squirrel sitting between the trees. We watched it nibble the walnut while we talked.

Without warning, Lillian made the conversation serious. "What's going on with you?" She leaned back resting on her elbows.

"I'm just a bit unhappy right now."

"You don't say?"

Her tease made me laugh. "I'm an emotional wreck."

"Honestly, I'm worried about you."

"I wanted to know what happened to my mother. I never thought I'd find what I'm finding."

"Like what?"

"Eucharist tortured her."

"What do you mean tortured?"

"They abused those girls in unimaginable ways."

"So disheartening. Does your therapist help?"

"Yes. I'm thankful for Janice."

"What's troubling you today?"

"Apparently, I'm incapable of being vulnerable."

"You think so?"

"Probably. I don't let people get close to me."

"Why not?"

"I learned from my mother—I guess. We're like pets to each other."

"That's kind of deep."

I felt sick about failing my father. I tried to match his goodness, but always acted to protect myself instead. "My mother was friendlier when my father was alive. We both were," I said feeling overly honest.

"Why was that?"

"I don't know." Some of my teenage feelings resurfaced. "I feel like a loser right now," I admitted.

"Really, why?"

Right then, it was impossible to say. I just kept thinking about how Eucharist had violated Mom in unthinkable ways, annihilated her innocence and robbed her of her personhood. They had broken her. She probably would have been stellar if all that nastiness hadn't happened. How could I have said anything about—why?

Lillian looked at me, giving me one of her tell-the-truth grins. "What are you thinking about?" she asked.

"I feel cheated. Hurt. Stunted."

"How do you feel stunted?"

"My life could have been better—easier."

"What's wrong with your life?"

In my unqualified opinion, my life was rotten. Still, I wanted to crawl into a hole somewhere. My selfishness made me feel uneasy. People had far bigger problems than I did. I guessed at a good answer.

"I could be more adjusted."

"Adjusted to what?"

"I don't know. Something."

"Did you talk about this at Standout?"

"No, maybe I'm just being silly."

"Talk about it." Lillian stood up. "Before I forget, I'll tell you now… Jack's coming with the boys later today."

My disappointment seeped out of me. Adopting a nonchalant attitude, I stood up too and then stretched my arms into the air to release the tension in my back.

We rejoined the group for the quarter-mile hike out of the woods. Lillian and I talked until they loaded us onto the bus. On the ride back to the hotel, I kept silent but thought about ways to avoid Uncle for two days.

Back at the hotel, I cleaned up and then met Lillian in the spa for our shiatsu massages. Feeling both relaxed and tired afterwards, I opted out of the next event, leaving Lillian to enjoy it by herself. I took a nap. Later, scampering around for my robe, sleepy eyed and full of reluctance, I went to the door. When I opened it, Uncle stood there clutching two worn out boxes.

"Can we talk?" he asked.

I stepped aside to stop myself from closing the door on him and then stepped back, opening the door wide to let him cross the threshold. Although the hottest part of the day had passed and the room was cool, I began to sweat. Sitting in the middle of the sofa forced Uncle to use the chair across from me. He put those boxes on the side table next to the chair.

"I apologize for how I treated you," he said.

"It's what you did to my mother—not me."

"I know, I know. I was wrong. I'm sorry."

"Tell her. Not me."

Uncle raised his eyebrows. "Don't you think I would, if I could?" he asked me.

"How would I know?"

"Can't you just listen to me?"

"Fine, go on."

"The first Monday after we got back, Papa went to his church meeting. When he left, I told Mama about Brackwood. How I thought Frank had gone mad. She said, I'm sorry."

"Why did she say that?" Uncle continued as if he hadn't heard me. "She went into the storage pantry and came out with some boxes."

I pointed, "Those boxes?"

"Let me finish. Mama gave me a box. Not those."

"What about those?"

"Those are for you. Just read this." He unfolded a piece of paper and then held it out to me.

Jacky boy,

You're the only reason to stay in Denten. But you know I can't. I'm going to miss you so much. I love you. I'm going to write every week. Promise to write back. You're the best brother on the planet. Remember that.

My mother had written to him on her wedding day. "Grammy gave this to you?" I gave the note back to him.

"Yes, a whole box of them."

"That's awful."

"My wife always says err on the side of love. I didn't with Frank or you. I messed up. Last week, I should have apologized when I saw you. But… I felt horrid about everything."

Tears rolled down his face. Those tears put me on edge. My ability to handle any kind of meltdown was questionable. Besides, I didn't want to comfort him if he did breakdown.

"Are you okay?" I asked.

"I'm fine." Uncle straightened himself in the chair.

I opened the patio doors to let in the ocean air and then I gave him a glass of water. "What did Lillian think?" I asked when I sat down again, hoping to ward off a possible breakdown.

"She doesn't know about the letters."

"Why didn't you tell her?"

"I'm telling her next. I wanted privacy. I opened and read all of them alone... by myself."

Grammy's underhanded manipulative behavior perturbed me. Uncle's thoughtlessness was another matter. I wasn't going to let her evil doing be his excuse.

"Why should the letters make any difference to me?"

Uncle winced. He pointed to the boxes on the side table. "Mama asked me to give these to you."

"What's in them?"

"Didn't look. Here's the thing Portia, those letters made me realize how I failed. I was a sucky brother."

"They did, how?"

"Well, I never asked for Frank's number."

"Why didn't you?"

"Fact is... I assumed she preferred not knowing me."

His honesty was insightful. I hadn't considered how everything affected him. A little boy had been stuck in the middle of the madness. I started coming around to forgiving him when he said, "Also, to put everything out there... I lied."

"Lied about what?"

"I know why Frank left. I went to the trial."

To keep myself from yelling at him, I took a deep breath and then looked out past the balcony. People were enjoying themselves on the beach. Their laughter, the fresh air, the crashing waves, made me want to step away from him. I had worn myself out, but his confession infused me with energy.

"You were selfish not to tell me," I said to him.

"Yeah, I know. But I preferred not to think about those times. Before the trial, I didn't know why she left or anything about what happened at Eucharist. I only went for the first two days. I got too upset to go back."

"Why did you call her deviant and filthy?"

"I'm a blockhead. I grew up hearing Papa say those things all the time. I was fuming… that's what came out."

"You were cantankerous."

"I know… but living with Papa after Frank left was horrific. She was the lucky one. She got everything."

"What did she get?"

"Your papa sent updates. When my papa wasn't around Mama would tell me about Frank's life. Everything sounded fantastic to me."

"So, you were jealous?"

"For sure."

"What did you find out at the trial?"

"They talked about what happened in there."

I felt tears in my eyes. "Why did you shake my mom?"

"I kept shouting… did they do those revolting things to you? But—"

"Knowing about Eucharist made you shake her?"

"No. I wanted her to say they hadn't done those awful things to her. I wanted to stop feeling guilty for not helping her."

His words allowed me to identify with him. But I didn't want him thinking I overlooked his cruelty. Making eye contact with him, I said, "I'm not going to pretend I understand. I do, however, comprehend feeling guilty and helpless."

"She kept asking why I wouldn't write back. She thought I hated her."

No matter how much he might have wanted it, I refused to mollycoddle him. The whole Miller clan had contributed to the pain my mother endured. "You could not have done anything to help her. Besides, she had been abandoned by everyone." My unsympathetic tone reflected the facts as I had come to know them.

"Not me. I thought she abandoned me."

"Everyone abandoned her—including me."

"You're right, I guess. I never tried to contact her."

"I can't imagine how alone she felt after Eucharist."

"I swear… Mama gave me the letters a few weeks back. Afterwards, I understood everything."

"I believe you. What are you expecting me to do?"

"Nothing—okay. The whole thing hurt me too. I'm just trying to apologize to you." Uncle lifted the boxes, twisted his mouth, bent forward so I could reach them, making sure to let go only when they were safely in my hands.

"Guess, I should leave you be." Uncle stood.

"You plan to tell Lillian soon?" I stood up too.

"I'm going to tell her now."

Uncle hung his head. He looked devastated. I put the boxes back on the table next to the chair and then surprising myself, I hugged him. I felt his muscled arms squeeze me.

"Sorry you felt so lonely growing up," I said before he walked out.

I reflected on what Uncle said about how my grandparents acted all those years ago—their inability to accept their own daughter, a child who loved and needed them. All that new information forced me to look inside myself. Fearing my own anger would lead to endless bitterness, I happily released my grudge against Uncle. Afterall, the ordeal had hurt him too. I disagreed with how he had handled things with Mom; yet, imagining the depths of his childhood sorrow allowed me to move on.

I carried the boxes to the table and peeked inside the top box. Grammy had jammed letters inside like canceled checks. I flicked my index finger across the top of each letter. She had opened them. I plucked a letter from the middle, read the return address and then dropped the letter as if it were on fire. My father sent them to her.

The second box had a host of browning letters inside. I shimmied out the first letter to avoid damaging it. I read the address, falling back into the chair, holding the letter away from my body, gawking as if it were a nude man as I came to recognize my mother's handwriting on the envelope.

In January of 1968, a few days after her wedding, my mother had addressed her letter to Mrs. Margaret Miller. I forced out the last letter, it was post marked May 24, 1971, just a few years before Mom graduated college. I replaced the letters I'd pried out and then closed the box.

I opened the first of my father's letters, written in 1968, a few months after Mom left Denten. He began with a warm salutation: *My dearest Peg*, but the body of the letter read like a report. He housed my mother in a New York apartment, hired a woman to live with her—someone he described as a surrogate mother. He also contracted a tutor to home school my mother for an entire year.

My father reasoned ...remaining at home wo*uld afford Fran everything she needs to begin school on a good footing this fall.* At the end of the letter, he scribbled Mom's new address and phone number. I believed the letter reflected his goodness, but I couldn't understand why Grammy refused to contact her little girl.

The things I would do to see my child popped into my head; like run through traffic, sell everything, go broke, or eat cat food, anything—beginning with divorce. How Grammy managed to stay away confounded me. Nothing would have stopped me from going to New York. Next, I read a number of letters where my father gave those updates Uncle spoke about. For her junior and senior years, my mother attended Brearley. A private high school for girls. A letter dated April 8, 1970, noted Mom's admission to Cornell and her graduation from Brearley.

At Cornell, Mom had a modest apartment in Ithaca with her surrogate mother. Months later, my father wrote ...*without exerting influence, Fran has decided to venture into the accounting profession.* I suspect Mom's decision confirmed her love for my father.

He proclaimed his love when he wrote:

Due to distance, I'm limited to weekends with Fran. She is growing into a fiery woman. Our discourse is lively. My continued wish for her is family and new friendships.

In May of 1974, my father invited my grandparents to Mom's graduation. He wrote, *Fran graduates summa cum laude, an achievement not to be missed.* The tickets were still in the envelope.

Juggling depression, grief and anger stirred up those old comfortable fears of monsters under the bed, public embarrassment and falling off a cliff. I marveled at my mother's ability to remain sane. She had endured a steady stream of rejection. The Eucharist survivor, who had become my mother, had kept everything from me.

In letter, after letter, my father's words engrossed me. He had escorted my mother through the madness, laid a new foundation over her old one, giving her the tools to tamp down her Denten life as though she'd never lived it. I might have read those letters all night long if the phone hadn't rung. Lillian invited me to dinner. Cuddling a box of letters was nostalgic, but it wasn't fellowship.

When I came into the lobby, Lillian rushed over to me. "Did you look?" she asked.

Robert chimed in, "Look at what? I want to see."

"What if it's poop? You're such a nut job." Jacky poked him.

"I would look with my microscope."

"Good evening, what a strange greeting." I grinned.

"Hello cousin Portia." Jacky hugged me and then Robert and Lillian did too.

At the table, Uncle leaned close to me. "Well, did you look?"

"Letters, both boxes are full of letters."

"I want to read them." Jacky took out a sketchpad.

"They're not your letters." Uncle told him.

Lillian picked up the buffet menu. "I'm going to try the Korean glass noodles. Did you read any yet?"

"Not many," I lied.

"What you waiting for?" Uncle asked.

"Want to come read them with us? We can make a night of it."

Lillian tempted me and I feigned indecisiveness, although I didn't consider her offer. Uncle had the right idea. It was a private matter.

"I'd rather not." I said after some delay.

"Well, just come hang out."

I liked Lillian's alternative suggestion, so I postponed feasting on those letters in order to spend time with them. We played games until around nine. Afterwards, the boys camped out on the floor to watch the movie they selected. Getting comfortable, I snuggled with a blanket on the short end of the L-shaped sectional, leaving the other side to Lillian and Uncle.

Everyone fell asleep. When I awoke, I went back to my suite and crawled into bed without reading any letters.

Lillian knocked at five fifteen the following morning. "Let's go. A meditative sunrise walk awaits us."

Her zesty voice fought with my groggy head. "Why are you so chipper? It's not even six o'clock. Let's skip it." I got back into bed.

Lillian followed me. Laughing like a child, she yanked my covers off. "Oh, no you don't. You invited me—remember?"

"We can do the next thing." I pulled my knees up to my chest wishing to have my blanket back.

"Was that a joke?"

"It wasn't. Go without me." I teased.

Lillian reviewed the retreat schedule. "Look, yoga afterwards."

"You like yoga?"

"I do. Before popping out two babies I was quite good."

"Fine then, you convinced me. I'm coming."

The sun erupted from the ocean right when we joined our group. By the time we navigated to our yoga destination, the sun had shed its golden skin, causing the sky to explode into a crisp palette of orange, yellows and misty blues.

We claimed mats at the front of the yoga platform making it easy to see the changing ocean sky. First, we completed three rounds of sun salutations. They invigorated me. To my consternation, the yoga continued with a series of challenging poses. They didn't bring joy or peace to my being as the brochure promised.

Yoga had been torturous. My only accomplishment had been serving as Lillian's sidekick for the morning. As we walked back to the hotel, Lillian stopped abruptly. I bumped right into her.

"Sorry… but I have to ask… who wrote those letters?"

I felt the cool sand between my toes. "Did you enjoy the yoga?"

"Yes. Did you?"

"I loved the sun salutations and the relaxation pose. You on the other hand are a pro."

"Very funny. Flattering me won't work. My husband left me out, now you're doing the same."

"No, I'm not. I just want to read them alone, so I can think about each one."

"Un-huh, you're leaving me out."

"I know. I'm sorry."

"For now, I'll let you get away with it."

"Thank you," I sighed.

Lillian's face lit up and then she pointed. I saw Robert running to her. "You had better come clean later on," she said opening her arms to scoop Robert up. Her hair sprayed out, seeming to dance in the ocean breeze as she carried Robert on her back.

"Where'd you go?" he asked.

"Exercise. I did yoga with Portia."

"I'm hungry."

"You are? You sound unhappy."

"Yes, because I'm hungry."

"Well, let's see if we can fix that."

Robert had Miller genes. He was going to be forever skinny. Lillian carried him for a few minutes. "How about I put you down?" She squatted until Robert's feet hit the sand. He climbed off her back, ending his piggyback ride.

The three of us headed over to Uncle and Jacky. They were throwing a football back and forth on the beach. When we reached them, Lillian put her hand on Jacky's head nudging him towards her. He relaxed into her side. Then she slung her arm around his shoulders. He clung to his mother with one arm and tucked the football under the other one.

"Are you hungry?" Lillian asked him.

"I'm starving," Jacky said.

"You want breakfast, or shall I take them?" Lillian asked Uncle.

"If you don't mind, I want to go for a walk."

The four of us headed off to breakfast. When Uncle showed up, we were already eating. He helped himself to Jacky's pancakes.

"Papa, get your own." Jacky laughed.

"Why? These are perfect." Uncle forked more pancakes into his mouth. Jacky turned away with his plate. Then Uncle turned to me. "So, who sent them?"

They pestered me until I told them the boxes had old letters from both of my parents in them.

"Did you read Frank's letters?"

"Just some of my father's so far."

"I'm glad you have those letters," Uncle sounded earnest.

I wiped breadcrumbs off the tablecloth. "My mother's letters are unopened," I volunteered.

Uncle clasped his hands. "Mama is stubborn… just like Papa."

"I'm sorry Portia. We have tonight. You're invited to read them with me." Lillian mimed opening a letter.

Jacky laughed.

"Maybe. We'll see."

"Do what works for you," Uncle instructed.

His eyes widened when his food arrived. Lillian reminded me of the Nutritional Health session starting at eleven o'clock. We excused ourselves. Without yielding to my desire to read more letters, I showered and then went to the next wellness event. I whittled away the afternoon in workshops as Lillian pressed me to attend them. During a break, around four o'clock, we said goodbye to Uncle and the boys. They were going to have dinner with my grandparents.

For the next hour, we attended the last workshop. In it, we learned some new relaxation techniques. The most valuable tips focused on relaxing under stress. I practiced every one of them.

When the wellness retreat ended, Lillian went to her suite excited about spending the evening alone. I passed the night away reading my father's letters. In 1976, he sent a wedding announcement. My father had written:

Once again, Fran and I are to wed. This time I requested she marry me, thus making this marriage our choice. She correctly says a man given to my proclivities should not live alone. Both of you had foresight, a wife did guarantee my inheritance. While I care nothing for my father's money, it also ensures my grandfather will leave the Firm to me.

We shall remain platonic. As before, I receive her as my companion. For the first time, we reside under the same roof. We have grown fond of one another. I desire us to function as lifelong allies.

At eight-fifteen, Monday morning, I found Janice in her office. She sat in her cushioned chair reading a book. I paused at the door. After a knock, she waved me in. Her smile loosened the knots in my stomach, but I leaned back in the zero-gravity chair before saying anything to her.

"My father was gay."

"How did you find out?"

"He wrote…" I sat up. "You knew?"

"We worked together for years."

"I wish I didn't know. It's upsetting."

"What's upsetting about it?"

Not having a good sense of what bothered me, I focused on what I believed to be my parent's wayward decision.

"What made them have a baby?"

"Does it matter?"

"Yes. They were both pretending to be normal."

"Pretending? They made a life together."

"An abnormal life. A weird one."

"What does normal mean to you?"

"I don't know. Not pretending."

"Did you feel loved growing up?"

"Yes, very much… especially by my father."

"Sounds pretty good for not so normal people."

"Who knows," I countered.

"Love is a very broad thing."

"I wouldn't know because my whole life is a lie."

Janice narrowed her eyes, leaned forward and then put her hand under her chin. I readied myself for her insight.

"What about your life is a lie?" she asked.

Her words disappointed me. I hesitated. "Everything is a big lie."

"When you think your life is a lie, you feel?"

"I feel like a freak. Who am I? I'm a lie."

"What lie is that?"

Janice looked into my eyes, stoking my fury. From my point of view, life dealt me a lousy hand. Absent of insight about what made my life a lie, I stormed out.

❖

I went back to the case files and started reading the last of Madeline's examinations. She called the psychiatrist, Dr. Susan Huslinger as her expert witness. The doctor testified about how The Way Treatment caused Post Traumatic Stress Syndrome (PTSS). In a white paper, the doctor gave a concise overview of how Eucharist traumatized those girls. She proposed a five-part solution to treat PTSS. The solution, according to Dr. Huslinger, marked a paradigm shift for treating stress disorders. Janice integrated each recommendation into the Standout process.

Diving into the Eucharist testimonies, I worked my way through the transcript. The lawyer, J. E. Morgan, represented Eucharist and the First Council Church. He called Pastor Calvin Joseph as his first witness. Madeline cross-examined him.

Madeline Bowman: How did you develop the Eucharist regime?

Calvin Joseph: I prayed; consulted with the church elders.

My grandfather wasn't an elder back then. Being absent from the list slightly redeemed him; although, it hadn't stopped me hating him.

MB: Did you consult any doctors, psychiatrists, or women?

CJ: They didn't need to be. The Lord revealed the way. We hired a like-minded psychiatrist to oversee the program.

MB: Your school has been shown to abuse girls. Will you continue to sanction those methods?

CJ: We don't cause no harm. We right errant behavior.

MB: Please describe for the court, what the treatment entails?

CJ: We provide corrective experiences.

MB: Please list these corrective experiences.

CJ: You ought to know. Corrected you—didn't it?

Madeline asked the judge to order the pastor to answer. Several directives later, he responded, "We give spiritual counseling, daily chores, mental and social correction. These combine to form The Way Treatment Plan."

MB: Will you allow me to make substitutions?

CJ: It isn't my court.

His sinister face came to mind. I visualized his laugh blending with those of the townsfolk.

MB: Does spiritual counseling, which you provide, consist of forcing girls to brand themselves sinners, evil-doers or abominations?

CJ: Bible teachings point the way. As revealed by God.

MB: Does your spiritual counseling seek a pledge to turn away from the sin of homosexuality or lustfulness?

CJ: You made the pledge… didn't you? We are very successful.

MB: At torturing girls? Your treatment—

"Argumentative, she's testifying," the Eucharist lawyer objected.

The judge sustained and then Madeline pleaded with him saying, "Your honor, please instruct the witness to answer the question."

The judge instructed him to answer.

CJ: Yes, confession is prerequisite to embracing the Lord.

MB: Many Eucharist residents have testified that your program tortured them until they conformed to your wishes. How will this evidence change your program?

CJ: We correct in accordance with God's will. We don't use torture.

MB: Many say Eucharist tortured them. Do you say otherwise?

CJ: Our program saves souls.

MB: Let's move on to mental correction. Would you say your treatment uses electroshock effectively?

CJ: Yes, when combined with the word of God.

MB: For what purpose do you use shock therapy?

CJ: We feel electroshock puts young girls into the right state of mind to receive my counsel.

MB: Is it brainwashing?

CJ: The word of God lets us reach the minds of errant girls.

MB: Why do you rape Eucharist girls with your machine?

CJ: Rape? The Lord doesn't sanction rape.

MB: Has any Eucharist resident ever consented to having the Way machine used on them?

CJ: It's used for social correction. You don't need permission to teach the will of God.

MB: Did the machine forcibly penetrate these virgin girls?

CJ: That's right. Homosexuals are taught God's will for them.

MB: Let's see... do you contend rape is the will of God?

CJ: Social correction is not rape. Our methods work. You ought to know. You turned out fine as ever, didn't you?

MB: You're right. I certainly do know. At fourteen, both your machine and your orderlies raped me. I left Eucharist traumatized, broken and depressed. But, no, I wouldn't say I'm fine.

The Eucharist lawyer called out, "Objection!" He continued, "Argumentative and she's testifying again."

Calvin Joseph retorted, "The Lord works in mysterious ways."

The judge sustained. He added, "Counsel will refrain from giving testimony and Mr. Joseph, you remain silent unless answering a question directed to you."

MB: Eucharist, as you've been shown, causes severe emotional trauma. Yet you allege your program is beneficial to your residents. Can you explain?

CJ: What you wrongly call emotional trauma, is a scar. The scar reminds girls to avoid sinning against God.

MB: Who's idea was it to scar young girls with the Way machine?

CJ: Dr. Parkinson recommended we use the machine.

MB: Did you ever observe the process?

CJ: No, I never did.

MB: Are you aware of the persistent mental health, social and medical problems Eucharist survivors endure?

CJ: I pray on it.

MB: You know about the issues but choose to ignore them?

CJ: I pray for the soul of every Eucharist offender.

MB: These offenders, as you refer to them, are any guilty of murder?

CJ: No.

MB: Did they commit any crimes?

CJ: No, But—

Mʙ: Would you say, Eucharist with the support of First Council Church and the State incarcerates or institutionalizes young girls for non-criminal offenses?

Cᴊ: *Render to Caesar the things that are Caesar's; and to God the things that are God's,* Matthew 22:21.

Mʙ: Please answer the question.

Cᴊ: We follow the word of God. Romans 13:1. *For there is no authority except from God.*

Mʙ: You imply neither your church nor the State need obey the law.

Cᴊ: For there is no authority except from God and those which exist are established by God.

Mʙ: Are you God's authority on earth or something?

Cᴊ: Yes, I am, in matters governing those at Eucharist who have sinned against God.

Mʙ: The First Council Church has over two thousand ordained ministers. Are they all representatives of God's authority?

Cᴊ: Some, like myself, are given the authority directly from God.

Mʙ: Is it correct to say, you believe God sanctions your program and you serve as his administrator?

The Eucharist lawyer objected saying Madeline had asked a compound question.

The judge sustained.

Mʙ: Are you… and only you, God's administrator at Eucharist?

Cᴊ: Indeed, our way is the Lord's way. If you will discuss the process with me, you will come to understand how and why it works.

Mʙ: Sir, I assure you… nothing you do works.

Madeline ended her cross-examination. She had spoken for all the women imprisoned at Eucharist. She proved Calvin Joseph, with the Church's backing, used the Way machine, and sometimes orderlies, to rape girls. To him, it was a cure for homosexuality. He had no trouble admitting it. Even with Madeline in front of him, spewing the facts as she did, he denied hurting those girls.

Yet, I believed he knew—deep down—had to know, the harm he caused them. There was no doubt in my mind that every girl who had stepped through the Eucharist doors condemned for their sexuality knew it. He had been delusional. To justify his own wickedness, Calvin Joseph likened himself to a god. I was sure, and I'd bet all those girls abused by him, were sure too... he wasn't even a decent human being.

Any half decent person in the courtroom knew too. But according to First Council's twisted logic, homosexuality infringed upon a sacrosanct rule. They supported their pastor and approved his actions. Isn't kindness sacred too? They certainly overlooked that little fact. By refusing to step outside of their self-righteous arrogance, the church leaders were just as guilty, if not guiltier than Calvin Joseph.

That day, all the ugliness flooded in, making me cry for those innocent girls and their lasting mental anguish. An anguish many tried to extinguish with drugs that took them even further away from themselves and the people they were meant to be by nature. Without regret, Eucharist had crushed their spirit.

Reading Calvin Joseph's testimony drained me. The presentation by the State's defense was next in the lineup of artifacts. Wondering if I should press on, I read their witness list. I hung my head and covered my eyes with my hands. With haste, I gathered my things and headed right to the Standout doors. The Eucharist lawyer had subpoenaed some orderlies, an expert witness, a psychologist, that girl who liked Eucharist, their medical doctor and my mother.

To disentangle myself from the weight of those testimonies, I left Standout. In my suite, reading the last of my father's letters, a jarring fact sent me right back to the farm. When I arrived, Uncle and the boys were out farming. Lillian waited for me on the porch.

"What's in the box?" she said as I walked up.

"Ha-ha. You know what's in it."

"Changed your mind?" she opened the screen door.

"We'll see… I finished my father's letters—these are my mother's."

Lillian, seeming to move in slow motion, bagged up the vegetables she'd chopped before I arrived. With her kitchen tidied up, she poured iced tea for us. "What's going on?" she said after sitting with me. Her voice sounded carefree, but she had a worried look that always made me feel like a child instead of a friend.

I gulped down my tea. "My parents never had sex."

"That can't be true."

"Well, at least not with each other… I don't think."

"What makes you say so?"

"I'm a test-tube baby."

"You're a what?"

"You heard me right. My parents used in vitro fertilization to have a baby… to have me."

"What made them do that?"

"Well, it seems, my father was gay too."

Lillian opened her mouth. She dripped out her words, "No. Way."

"Both my parents, I think. I'm pretty sure."

"You're a little miracle. See, I said you were special."

"That's not the kind of special you meant." I laughed too hard, hoping to hide my gloominess. I'm sure there were many people who wouldn't have had an issue with a test tube conception. I wasn't one of them. The deliberateness of how I became a fertilized egg added to the list of things making my life feel abnormal. Even so, I couldn't change the truth. "The whole thing is kind of weird," I said, working to balance myself.

"I think it's wonderful."

"Well, I sure don't. It makes me wonder who I am."

"Really? I would go around saying, hey, I'm a test tube baby."

"I'm not doing that."

"Get a t-shirt." Lillian kept laughing.

"That's not funny."

"Did you have suspicions?"

"Who would think about being a test-tube baby?"

"I'm wondering if you suspected your parents were gay."

"No. Did they considered the ramifications of having a baby?"

"What ramifications?"

"Pretending, keeping secrets and telling lies. All kinds of things."

"Personally, I can't imagine their agony."

"I suppose. But I'm not getting a t-shirt."

"How about a green t-shirt with big white letters. Just put test tube across the back. Make people ask."

"I'm not getting one." I laughed.

We talked more about my parents' choice. I hadn't considered how they had given up a part of their identities. Thanks to Lillian, it became easier to see that they had paid an unquantifiable price to avoid the social stigmatization of homosexuality and how they had both lost the right to live and love as they preferred.

Over the weeks, I had handled my anxiety about Eucharist. My ability to discuss the issues with Janice without upset assured me, I could discuss the whole matter with Lillian too. I told her everything. For a time, sitting at her table, we talked about the atrocities perpetrated at Eucharist, the court case and Standout.

We talked until Uncle opened the door. He came in dirty and without the boys trailing behind him. "Where are the little ones?" Lillian asked and then walked up to him while he removed his boots.

"I let them go explore the woods."

Uncle pecked Lillian on the mouth. After washing up, he came over to the table. They kissed and hugged even longer.

"Did you know my mother came to Denten in 1982?"

"No. How would I have?" Uncle sat with me.

"She was a witness at the trial."

"I didn't see her."

"My father asked Grammy to meet up with them."

"Did she go?" Lillian gave Uncle a glass of tea.

"I don't think so. He didn't write again until 1991."

"What did he say then?" Uncle asked.

"He wrote to Gramps."

"What about?"

"They had some kind of agreement."

"What agreement?"

"Sorry Uncle. I have no idea." I tapped the box of letters.

My fear of violating my mother's privacy prevented me from opening them. They may not have belonged to her anymore, but I couldn't muster the resolve to read them. Earlier that day, I had explained my reservations about opening them to Lillian.

"You want us to help read them?" she grinned.

"I'm worried about—"

"These letters belong to you now," Lillian said.

"I don't want to—"

Lillian opened the box. "They stopped being Fran's when she mailed them."

"I'm done for the day, I'll help." Uncle offered.

I knew Lillian had it right and I knew they wanted to read those letters. So did I. Although I blissfully neglected to confess it, I preferred their help because all the disclosures in my father's letters had been difficult to accept.

"Sure, why not," I said.

While Lillian ordered pizza, Uncle pried out a small stack of letters to make room in the box and then he counted the letters. Grammy had crammed 146 letters in there. We agreed to separate the letters into three sections. Lillian collected two of Jacky's small sketches. Uncle mouthed the numbers as he counted to forty-five, stuck in a sketch with bright yellow patches on it and began again. With the sections marked, we decided to have Lillian read the first grouping, Uncle the second, saving the third for me.

To start, I picked up one of the browning envelopes from the table. Lillian counted—one, two, at three we opened the letters. The crunching made me feel as if we were doing something monumental. My heart raced. Lillian unfolded the letter she opened.

"Let's scan each one," she suggested.

"You want to back out?" Uncle asked.

I shook my head. There were too many letters. I needed their support to speed up the process. I read my first letter. Then I opened another one. When I finished my second letter, they were still reading their first ones. Lillian definitely read every word. So much for scanning, I thought. I opened a third one. "She wrote the same message every time," I said, after reading a fourth one.

Lillian stopped reading. "This one is about leaving Denten."

"I'm reading about her apartment." I read the letter Uncle opened. The letter parroted what my father had written. I picked up two of the letters I had opened, giving one to each of them.

Mama, please call or write. I miss you all. Lillian read aloud.

Uncle shook his head. "Refusing to read these letters is beyond belief. Mama—"

"Hated her. Gramps did too," I added.

"I wouldn't say—"

"Don't say it Lillian. Mama might not have hated Frank, but it seems to me, she may as well have."

"You have a point, Jack. But hate? She might—"

"Only care about herself." I said, stepping away from the table.

"What she did was mighty selfish. Doesn't mean she hated her," Lillian countered.

"Why wouldn't she read these letters?" I went back to the table.

Lillian poured tea into my glass. "I'm giving her the benefit of the doubt by assuming she loved her so much it hurt."

The blood drained from my face. Her assessment jumbled my thoughts. From my perspective, if Grammy loved my mother, she would have opened the letters.

Uncle set us back on track when he said, "I don't think we're ever going to agree." He was right. We decided to work backwards, having everyone open the letters in my section first. Our strategy, we reasoned, would allow us to pinpoint where Mom started her plea to have my Grandparents call or write to her.

We all grabbed one of the letters.

"Same," Lillian called out.

"Same," Uncle echoed her.

"Same," I reached for another one.

We continued this way until we silenced ourselves. Each of us knowing echoing 'same' would become depressing. Uncle opened the last letter from my section. I grabbed a letter from the next one. Same, I called out, increasing my pessimism. We opened letter, after letter thinking Mom would not have sent too many with the same message. We were wrong.

After a while, I conjectured my mother wrote that message in all except the first two letters. As my optimism faded, the boys bounced into the house carrying a pizza. We cleared the letters from the table while the boys cleaned up for dinner.

Lillian put a green salad and a stack of plates next to the pizza box. Jacky showed me his computerized drawings when he came to the table. He had created a little comic book. Together we reviewed his work and then discussed ways he might improve his technique.

"Jacky is a real artist." Uncle munched pizza. "I'm glad Frank recognized his talent."

"Aww thanks Papa," Jacky mocked his father's tone.

"I was a total butthead."

Robert laughed. "You said butthead."

Lillian held up Robert's electronics book. "He's done reading this."

"So what? Mister big brain can read."

"Exercise kindness Jacky. You know the rules."

"Sorry Mama." Jacky lowered his head.

"Did you see his latest?" Lillian leapt from her chair, motioning for me to follow her and then she walked into the living room. Something moved near the fireplace. I jumped back. Robert ran in laughing. Lillian laughed too. The electronic toy rolled forward, stopping in front of us. "See, I made a wireless remote for my bug." Robert showed me the screen on his gaming device.

"What kind of bug is it?" I asked him.

"No kind. It's Donnie."

"Donnie? What does it mean?"

"Nothing. I like the name. You see right there?" Robert pointed. "It's the solar panel and the skin too. That's the eye."

"It's brilliant," I said, loving how he'd used his electronics set.

"I helped."

Robert turned to Jacky. "No, you didn't."

"I drew it for you. I added it to my comic."

"Liar. That's not helping."

Uncle popped into the room. "All right, enough already."

He squeezed Jacky's shoulder. Jacky, chewing his pizza, laughing in amusement, turned to face his dad. "I showed him which colors to—"

Uncle lost his cheerful disposition. "Why are you carrying food through the house? Back to the table. Now."

"Yes, Papa." Jacky left us.

The rest of us clustered in the hallway where Robert explained his robot to me. He even let me try it out. I was awful, but Uncle was agile, and Lillian didn't even try. Jacky came back to have a turn with the Robot.

Once dinner finished, the three of us went right back to work. We ripped open eighteen months of Mom's letters before Lillian reached one with a different message. It had been addressed to Gramps. She read it to us.

Papa,

I love you. I wish you would talk to me again. At least let Mama come visit with Jacky. I'm married. You said get married. I got married. I did everything you asked of me. What more can I do? Please papa.

Your Scout

"Why did Gramps call her Scout?"

Uncle jumped up. He disappeared into the hallway where he rummaged through the closet causing the boys to run over to see what he did back there. I heard them teasing each other. Moments later, Uncle came back with Robert and Jacky trailing behind him like ducklings.

He smiled wide and proud when he sat the box he carried on the table. "Wait until you see it." Uncle opened the box. He fished around under the paper until he removed a greenish-brown ranger hat. "I found this hat in Frank's closet years ago. My papa gave it to your mama before… you know."

Using both hands, he passed the hat across the table. I took hold of it, noting my mother hadn't worn it much. The stiff leather band still looked new. Unfortunately, I also did a poor job of revving up excitement over the hat.

Robert touched it. "Can I wear it?" he asked his dad.

"Sorry son, you can't."

Robert leaned against Uncle. "I want one," he said in that begging tone children use to get what they want.

"Did you know your room used to be Auntie Frank's room?"

"You told us a thousand times Papa." Jacky rolled his eyes. "That's a stupid hat."

"I like it." Robert sat next to me, bringing himself closer to the hat. I held the hat over the table for Uncle to take it again.

"Frank loved that hat. Give it back to her."

"I don't want to take the hat from you."

Lillian reached across the table. She put the hat back in its box. We all kept quiet. Everyone appeared dejected as if we'd lost a baseball game or received bad news.

"I think your papa cried when he found that hat." Lillian sniffed to extinguish the seriousness of her words. Her tease sparked a round of banter.

Uncle balled up his hand, pretended to clear his eyes, his fist moving back and forth like windshield wipers.

"Did you do this?" Robert looking at his father, poking out his bottom lip, made a weepy face.

"I bet he cried like this." Jacky jumped in. He hung his head, shook his shoulders to mimic sobbing, all the while struggling to hold in his laughter. Lillian held her belly.

I sniffed, hung my head, put my head down on the table and then hid my face in my arms like a child.

Everyone kept laughing.

We were still laughing when Robert leaned into his father. "I'm sorry you cried Papa. I don't want to wear it." He cried for real.

Uncle hugged Robert until he stopped crying and then Lillian sent him to wash his face. His sadness had affected all of us. To cheer everyone up, Lillian decided we should go out for ice cream.

The boys shouted, "Yee-haw."

The tenderness their parents expressed moved me. My muddled emotions included sadness and excitement. Ice cream sounded good to me. I stood up to prevent my tears.

"Yee-haw," I shouted, making everyone laugh again.

After ice cream, we read the remaining letters. The boys were already in bed when we finished. While reading the letters, Uncle reminisced about the happiest parts of his childhood. By the end, Uncle had gone through a range of emotions.

One letter caused him to cry while another made him laugh. At one point, he vowed never to speak to his parents again. For the most part, my father's letters divulged everything I needed to know. I didn't learn anything new about my mother from her letters because she didn't express her ideas or feelings about anything.

She only talked about old stuff, farming, family and missing everyone. Seeing how Uncle valued those letters, I suggested he keep them. When he declined, I asked if he wanted to trade the letters for the ranger hat.

"Deal," Lillian said picking up the box of letters.

I couldn't help myself, I laughed. She was an angel and a villain all rolled together and I realized how much I loved her.

That Friday, I read my mother's testimony. The Eucharist attorney touted her as, "The epitome of how Eucharist transformed the lives of wayward girls."

At the start, Morgan asked, "Are you happy Mrs. Foster?"

"As happy as possible."

"Aren't we all?" Morgan retorted. "If only we could all be educated, successful accountants with millions of dollars."

"Irrelevant," Madeline objected.

The judge sustained.

Morgan claimed my mother had a magnificently normal life. He insisted the "redemptive lessons" Eucharist provided benefited her. He said, "Without them, her life would not have been so exceptional."

After asking a load of questions about her wealth, lifestyle, confirming her net worth and education level, he showed pictures of my grandfather's estate in Denten. The one connected to Standout. My father had converted it into a business retreat some years before he died.

Madeline objected. "The irrelevant questions continue," she said. That's when everything changed.

"Do you appreciate the corrective experience you had at Eucharist?" Morgan asked.

In typical Mom fashion, she replied, "I wouldn't say corrective."

"If not corrective then what?"

"Torture, abuse, rape. Possibly—"

Her response brightened my day. According to the transcript, Morgan stopped her from speaking.

"What's this... a change of heart," he said. "Mrs. Foster, are you aware, perjury could land you in jail?"

"Yes, I sure am."

"Is it true, when we deposed you, we asked if Eucharist had taught you what it meant to be a woman?"

"Yes, it's true. The lawyer sitting beside you did ask."

"As I recall, you said Eucharist taught you about being a woman. Isn't that also true?"

"It is."

"Then what's this change all about?"

"The lawyer simply asked if I had learned about being a woman. He never asked what I learned. I learned women had no rights... no power and—"

"Alright, enough of that, let's get back to the topic at hand. Would you have so much success if not for Eucharist?"

"How do you define success?" Mom deflected.

I covered my mouth when I heard myself giggle.

The attorney requested the judge instruct Mom to answer.

"Isn't she your witness?" the judge asked.

"A hostile witness it seems. Mrs. Foster personifies the corrective experience Eucharist provides. That's why we subpoenaed her."

"I'll instruct her to answer, but if she needs clarification, you had better provide clarification."

"I bow to you, your honor," Morgan said.

I couldn't stop my giggles, it seemed Mom had rattled him.

"Mrs. Foster, would you agree, achieving wealth, a career and high standing in society is testimony to your success?" he continued.

"No, I wouldn't."

"Would you like to define success for me?"

"No," Mom answered, and I giggled again.

"Let me attack this another way. Has your life been happy since leaving Eucharist?"

"No, it hasn't."

"You expect us to believe getting college educated and marrying your wealthy husband doesn't reflect how successful Eucharist is?"

"Are you asking about my success or Eucharist?"

"Didn't Eucharist teach you how to be a woman?" Morgan asked.

"No."

"Didn't Eucharist prepare you for a normal life in society?"

"No."

"Mrs. Foster, weren't you sent to Eucharist to correct your homosexual tendencies toward women?"

"You'll need to ask First Council Church or my parents."

"Do you deny being homosexual?"

"I'm suggesting you ask the people who sent me to Eucharist to explain to you why they sent me there. It wasn't my doing." Mom likely pointed while saying, "Ask my father. He's sitting right there."

"Are you a homosexual Mrs. Foster?"

I reminded myself to breathe. I read her answer.

"Possibly?"

"Yes or No are you a homosexual?"

"Possibly?"

"You have a child. Would a homosexual woman have a husband and a baby?"

"Yes. One might."

"Are you a homosexual?"

"Possibly?"

"Your honor, would you please instruct Mrs. Foster to answer yes, or no?" Morgan insisted. The judge told her to respond yes or no.

"No, your honor. I won't."

"What is the problem?" The judge interrogated her.

"I don't have a definitive yes or no answer. No one will force me to adopt one."

"Counselor, I suppose you have a truthful answer. Move along."

Mom wielded diversionary tactics like a magician. She must have maddened that lawyer. I loved how she stayed in control. At the end of his questioning, my mother hadn't championed his case in any way. She bested him. Even so, I wished she had responded yes or no about being gay.

On cross, Madeline asked, "Mrs. Foster, how many times did you meet with Calvin Joseph?"

"Zero."

"Why not?"

"I refused."

"Why did you refuse?"

"My father told Pastor to keep me. I didn't think it mattered whether or not we talked. Nothing was going to help my situation."

"What did you think would happen to you?"

"I thought they would keep me until I turned eighteen."

"The average time at Eucharist is twelve to eighteen months. How long were you held at Eucharist?"

"Over two and a half years."

"Did Eucharist declare your treatment a success?"

"No. Calvin Joseph just sent me home. He told us... my mother, my father and me, he said, I couldn't be helped. Eucharist decided to get rid of me too."

"One final question Mrs. Foster, how would you characterize your experience at Eucharist?" she added, "You may answer as you think best. Take whatever time you need."

The defense objected. "Calls for conclusion and narrative."

"I will allow it," the judge said. "She's your witness. If her response skirts the issue, you may object. Now, go on ahead Mrs. Foster, answer the question as asked."

"Eucharist tore me apart. They tortured, raped and shocked me all over my body; they acted to defeat my will and punished me because I refused to characterize myself as a sin… then they tormented me until they destroyed my peace of mind. It still haunts me."

In his closing argument, Morgan said Eucharist had reformed my mother along with "every woman who had ever crossed its doors." He beseeched the jury to review the list of women redeemed of homosexuality and lustfulness. He listed married women like Janice Moore, but only those who had children, wealth or professional careers. Absent from his list were the women who were single, in jail, on drugs or homeless. Madeline had submitted a complete list of survivors into evidence. Hundreds of Eucharist survivors were on it, stretching back to the fifties.

Morgan contended the jury needed to consider the ingratitude of the women who had benefited from the care Eucharist provided. Absent of evidence, he claimed Eucharist had turned lustful girls into decent, God-fearing women. He said, "Those who learned to control their sinful desires became wives and mothers instead of fornicators or hopeless deviants."

Morgan accused the mothers of Eucharist survivors of corrupting their daughters. He told the jury, mothers who had made homosexuals of their daughters had been "too sensual or showed their bare skin to these young impressionable girls."

He spoke again and again about sins. His main defense focused on bad mothering. He claimed, "Over-affectionate mothers push their children into homosexuality." He called them careless mothers.

When I read where he said, "such parenting caused girls to develop unnatural love," those words pressed upon me how my mother might have played the odds by adopting their philosophy to protect me from becoming homosexual. The truth is…

I would rather have been homosexual than hated. She had gotten it all wrong.

Morgan ended his closing saying, "Some mothers turn their daughters homosexual; others make them hypersexual. Eucharist successfully corrects that."

Madeline ended her closing saying:

> *Mrs. Foster, like all Eucharist alumnae, is an example of the lasting trauma, violation of freedom and assault to human rights Eucharist inflicted on young girls. Each of you on the jury, represent the only members of society who can provide justice to Eucharist survivors.*
>
> *As you have heard, the defendants are guilty of organizational negligence. They are also vicariously liable for the abuses committed by Eucharist staff.*
>
> *The survivors will never recover their lost childhoods. I want you to be their voices. Although no dollar amount is sufficient. This jury can help compensate them for all they endured at Eucharist.*
>
> *Thank you.*

The Christian, mostly homophobic, completely male jury awarded compensatory, general and punitive damages to the women of Eucharist. The State had to pay fifty-million dollars. Additionally, the judge mandated the State create a general fund for the survivors they sentenced to Eucharist. The jury awarded another seventy-five million from the First Council Church. There were no appeals.

My investigation ended. I returned the artifacts to the evidence boxes and then stacked them in the corner. Four weeks had passed since I'd read the first testimony. There were no more secrets to dredge up. Yet, I took no pleasure in the answers I'd found.

Standout offered a place where Eucharist survivors, their children and their extended families could find solace. It was a Center of healing. With all those factors in front of me, I still wished the pastor, the doctor and all those orderlies were in jail.

When I went to Madeline's office, she sat behind her desk with her head buried in a legal document. My knock distracted her. After she waved me in, I sat on her sofa with my legs crossed.

"I finished, the case files."

"Excellent. Your thoughts?"

"I'm wondering why no one went to prison?"

"I initially filed a criminal case, but—"

"Didn't they commit crimes?"

"Yes... but in law school, I realized the whole matter was bigger than what happened to me."

"I'm still confused, what made it impossible for you to charge them with a crime?"

"Nothing did. In civil cases, the loser pays in dollars, not jail time."

"I can't help feeling discontented. They deserved punishment."

"They were punished. Maybe not how you hoped."

Maddie recapped the key outcomes of the trial. She noted how the case exposed Eucharist and forced the court to shut it down. "They never harmed another girl and the state made stricter laws to govern reform schools," she said proudly.

She had a point, but the victory alone, wasn't enough to appease me. With my whole heart, I believed Calvin Joseph deserved punishment. The trial proved his actions were criminal; he belonged in prison.

"What about Calvin Joseph?" I asked.

"The trial sunk his spirit, hurt his pride and sent him off with his tail between his legs."

Contrary to her wishful thinking, I knew the pastor was still arrogant, inconsiderate and even worse, he had kept his status around town. As far as I could tell, the trial hadn't harmed him. Maybe it had initially, but he seemed to have recovered his pride.

"There's the doctor too."

Maddie scowled. "That so called doctor, Henry Parkinson, lost his license."

"Why aren't you angry?"

"What should I be angry about?"

"Because... no one went to prison."

"I came to terms with that prior to filing the case."

"I'll never make peace with it."

"Yes, you will. There's no other option."

I imagined Maddie was a superhero to the Eucharist survivors. If those things had happened to me, I wouldn't have been as forgiving. Heck, I might have been one of the women whose lives fell apart.

"Why did my mother testify for Eucharist?"

"I named over forty women in the class action lawsuit. None of them were my witnesses."

"I'm confused, why did they call her?"

"The defense did their own investigations. They had a right to subpoena whomever they desired. I'm guessing they figured she'd make a fitting witness for them."

I laughed. "They missed the mark with that decision."

"They sure did."

The distribution of the settlement allotted twenty million dollars to my mother. Yet, Maddie only received five point three million dollars, plus her fees and whatever percentage she collected as the trial lawyer.

"My mother received a rather large settlement."

"Did you know... she is the only Eucharist survivor who never admitted to sinning?"

"No, I didn't."

"Do you recall her release notes?"

I shook my head.

"Well, they pronounced her a non-redemptive deviant."

"I read where you told the jury."

Maddie came to sit with me on the couch. "Eucharist considered her their only failure. However, they tried to contradict themselves when they declared her an example of their success."

"Do you think the settlement distributions were fair?"

"Ultimately, the jury determined the amounts."

"Yes, I studied the personal injury metrics. But what do you think?"

Maddie had no issues with the settlement distributions. She explained how the jury used the metrics provided by the court to calculate the damages awarded to all the plaintiffs.

According to her, the metrics worked in Mom's favor. The main source of disparity resulted from Mom's testimony. By testifying, the jury saw my mother's mental anguish up close and couldn't deny it. As a witness, my mother's medical records, the extent of the torture she endured, and her incarceration time got more scrutiny than any other woman listed as plaintiff.

"Guess I'll get going," I said after Maddie broke things down for me.

"What's next for you, Portia?"

"I'm heading home Monday afternoon."

"I hope you'll consider a few months at Standout with Janice."

"More therapy?"

"When we last talked, I sensed you had a lot to work out."

"You're right. I'm lost right now."

"Why not stay awhile… work things out?"

"I don't know Maddie, I'm ready to head home."

"I sure wish you'd reconsider my offer."

"We'll see. Have you had dinner?" I asked.

"No and I'm hungry too."

"Will you join me?"

"Sure. Love to."

During that dinner with Maddie, we discussed my desire to help Mom get better. I wondered if there might be a safe way for her to deal with her past.

"Help yourself first," Maddie advised.

Like Janice, she pushed me to focus on my own problems. Not having committed to more therapy, I planned to go home, but I had one final obligation. I'd sworn to have at least one Sunday dinner with Grammy before leaving Denten.

Problem was... emptying my mind of how Eucharist abused my mom. I just couldn't do it. Although the church had to pay money, in real terms it amounted to less than ten thousand dollars per church. Money didn't fix Mom and Gramps had a role in harming her. There was no way to spend an evening with him without feeling repulsed, but I wanted to keep my promise to Grammy.

Heat rose from my toes to the tip of my head when I saw Gramps sitting on the back porch Sunday afternoon. I recalled the lawyer's words; *she should be grateful.* Gramps had made the same statement a few weeks earlier. I wondered what part of himself he had turned off. He knew the truth about Eucharist, yet he never reconciled with my mother or disconnected from his church. At the very least, he should have redeemed himself by asking—no, begging for forgiveness.

As I approached the house, my gut knotted up, my jaw clenched and prior to stepping on the porch, I embodied my mother's strength. "Good afternoon," I greeted Gramps without stopping for his reply. Inside, Lillian hugged me which caused my anger to topple out into the room. "I hate him," I said.

Lillian took my hand. "Going for a walk," she called over her shoulder. We walked twelve paces past the front door then Lillian stopped. "Hate who?"

"Gramps."

"Why... What happened?"

"He went to the trial. He heard my mother's testimony. He sent her there. I can't stomach what they did to her."

"Maybe let's slow down," Lillian said.

She grabbed my other hand. We were facing one another like little girls. She squeezed my hands, closed her eyes and then took a deep breath. I took one too. I breathed deep, letting the air fill my lungs and send the scent of ripening apples up my nose. Lillian started walking again. Our stroll gave me time to calm myself.

Hidden by the apple trees in Grammy's orchard, we walked ever so slowly until I stopped to pluck a cherry red apple from one of the trees. The apple crunched as I savored the sweetness. I gave it to Lillian. She bit off a hunk and we passed the apple between us until only the core remained.

We started walking again. "Tell me what happened?" Lillian said.

"I read my mother's testimony."

"What did she say?"

Unable to contain myself, I grinned. "She made Eucharist look bad. She told the truth."

"That's why you hate Papa Miller?"

"No but… everything goes back to him."

"What did he do?"

"It's obvious. He calls her deviant. Says she's filthy. Plus, he didn't allow Grammy or Uncle to contact her."

"Surely Mama Miller had something to do with it too."

"I wouldn't know. I'm coming unhinged right now."

Lillian didn't try to console me. It wouldn't have helped anyway because surely, I had already stopped listening to her. We reached the end of the apple orchard and then turned around. As we walked back, I glanced around the farm; everything had depreciated, the buildings, the land, the crop, nothing looked as peaceful as it once did to me.

Going inside for supper wasn't easy. Yet, I endeavored to preserve my relationship with Grammy—to at least keep that from going sour. Finding no elixir to quiet my anger, I struggled to hide my rotten mood. I remained pensive, on high alert and ready for a confrontation.

Working to balance myself, I took the Sunday dishes out of the china cabinet. Although Grammy seldom wanted me meddling around in the kitchen, I stayed with her after setting the table. Fortunately, preparing dinner kept her from noticing my distress. At supper, flashes passed before me as I struggled to attach myself to anyone or anything. Time just moved along.

Robert laughed with Grammy. The smell of oniony pot roast drifted up my nose. Lillian whispered in Uncle's ear. In the middle of it all, Jacky showed his drawings to Gramps. Holding up the pages, grinning proudly, pointing here and there, he explained his work. Gramps nodded while he looked on.

When Jacky finished his little show and tell, Gramps said, "Good work. You'll make a fine cartoonist someday."

"I'm thinking animator now," Jacky corrected.

"You know Papa, I think we should get him into a class."

Uncle's toothy smile peeved me. He hadn't bothered to mention how he came to discover Jacky's talent.

Gramps looked right at me. "Good idea. Maybe he'll be a real artist."

"At least I'm not a failure or an evil liar," I shouted. The words just hurled out of me. My sulk had morphed into rage.

Even with my good intentions intact, I had insufficient power to stop myself from losing control of my mouth. Stillness beamed into the room. No one spoke, clanked dishes, laughed, or whispered.

Grammy ogled me. "Have you gone mad?"

"Like my mother? Maybe you should stop talking to me too."

"Yeah, she mad. We know you been with all those deviants at their devilish place."

"You're the devil Gramps. You… you hate everybody. You don't have a right to say anything to anyone. You should—"

"Let the past be," Grammy pleaded.

"No, not today. You should have read my mother's letters."

"I did my best."

"We all need to face the truth, Mama."

The boys swung their heads from person to person until Lillian told them to go outside.

"Close the door," Uncle shouted after them.

"Junior, what's done is done." Grammy pushed her plate forward.

"It's not done. You let my mother suffer… caused her abuse."

"I did no such thing."

My anger had shifted into spitefulness. Being catty bothered me, although I spoke the truth. I expected Grammy to start crying. Refusing to back down, I readied myself to ignore her high emotions. Tears wouldn't have affected me that day because getting to the truth surpassed my need to protect anyone's feelings.

Uncle didn't let her get off that easy. "Why couldn't you be brave enough to open Frank's letters?"

"What letters? Wasn't supposed to be no letters."

We ignored Gramps.

Uncle continued, "She begged to see us."

Gramps spoke louder, "How'd you get those letters Peggy? I had the mail put in my hand. Never let Martin do otherwise."

"Maddie's mama sorted the mail. She saved them for me."

"She committed a federal offense. I'd report her myself if she weren't dead already."

"Papa, what do you think you did, taking mail not addressed to you?"

"Everything sent to this house is mine. She got Howard's mail."

"Because he let you farm his land for free. The terms for letting Fran marry him." Grammy eyed Gramps.

"Papa did that?"

"He did." Grammy continued, "Worse still, he got this land from Howie for free too."

"How?" Lillian asked.

Uncle looked at Gramps. "I would like to know too."

"When Howard asked to have Portia visit us, your papa wouldn't let her come."

"Why would my father give away his farm?"

"He signed the property over to us."

"But why did he do it," I said louder than before.

"Howard was sick."

"Mama why aren't you answering Portia's question." Uncle stood over Grammy.

"Sit down Junior," Gramps demanded.

Uncle actually sat down. Then Grammy said, "Your papa promised he'd let Portia visit if Howard gave him the farm."

"Then he agreed?" Lillian asked.

"He wanted Portia to have more family."

"Papa swindled him?"

"I wouldn't call it that Junior. Things—"

"You should fix this… Please apologize to my mother," I said, locking my eyes on Gramps.

His face twisted and then he stood up, curling his top lip. "Since we in some kind of tell all. Your mama's dead to me. Want to know what done it?" Gramps shouted.

"Being gay?" I held his gaze.

"Marrying your homo daddy is what done it."

When Gramps rained down his lack of remorse, love or kindness right in front of us, my stomach did that thing that happens on roller coaster rides. I wanted to punch him in the mouth.

Right then, Grammy screamed. "Jack, you're unimaginably awful."

"Knew all along. You thought I didn't. Everybody knew your precious Howie was a homo," Gramps hollered.

"You finally done it Jack. You finally did."

Grammy pushed her chair back. The scraping echoed in my ears. When she exited the kitchen, chairs pushed back and shoes clapped the floor. We followed her like frightened cattle. Outside, she headed for her orchard.

Grammy stopped. "I'm sorry about the letters. I'm a coward. Didn't know what else to do."

"Forget what I said Mama. I'm sorry."

"No, you got it right son. I opened one of her letters after she quit sending them. She asked me to visit her."

"Why didn't you go Grammy?"

"Years later, I worked up the courage. Remember how we snuck off?"

Uncle nodded.

"It was too late. She didn't want nothing to do with me."

The freedom of Grammy's words surprised me. Then I realized Gramps hadn't left the house.

"What will you do now?" I asked.

"I can't leave my husband; he needs me."

"What do you want to do, Mama?"

"This is where I belong. Besides, I got nowhere to go and no way to support myself. Working the farm is all I ever done."

"You have us," Lillian countered and then held Grammy's hand.

Grammy stepped back but held on to Lillian's hand. "I love my son. But a woman needs a way out. I don't have a thing. Nothing at all."

"You're going to be fine," Lillian reassured her.

"I grew up right here. My father worked this farm until he died. Then my husband took over. Where is my life?"

I suspected Uncle renewed his love for Grammy in that moment. He went over to her shaking his head, put his arm around her back and then pulled her into his side.

"Let's go to my house," he suggested.

"Junior, I'm hankering on staying with you for a spell?"

"Okay by me Mama. The house belongs to you anyhow."

"No, it don't. The deeds are in your name. I made sure of that."

"I know Mama. I know."

"Hang on a minute. Come with me you two."

Grammy put herself between the boys. She stretched her arms to encompass them, together they disappeared into the house through the back door. When they returned, the boys carried pies and Grammy gave the tub of ice cream she carried to Uncle.

"We might have spoiled dinner. No reason to ruin dessert."

"What about Grandpa?" Robert asked.

"He's fine. He needs to think on himself."

"I'll drive you over Grammy."

We stayed in the car to talk after pulling up to Uncle's house. While out there, I asked Grammy when she found out about my father. She rested her hands in her lap and then focused on them. "I was in love with your father," she confessed.

"You were?"

"Yes, for a time."

I restated my question. "How did you find out about him?"

"Everybody thought a rich boy like him wouldn't want nothing to do with a farm girl like me."

"What did you think?"

"I didn't believe them. Back then, boys respected girls. I thought he would marry me."

"Did he say he loved you?"

"No and later, he told me he never had no feelings for girls."

"What did you do?"

"He broke my heart. But we pretended we were dating until he started college."

"He pretended too?"

Grammy's forehead wrinkled. "When he came home from boarding school, he courted me."

"Why are you angry with Gramps now?"

"Because… he knew all along about Howie."

"Why does his knowing upset you?"

"For a time, I loved your father more than I did my own husband."

I covered my mouth. "Wow Grammy."

"Your grandpa knew how I loved him."

"I'm sorry."

"It was as it was."

"My father is the best person I've ever known."

"Hope you can now see why I done what I done."

"He sure loved my mom and me."

"I'm still grateful to Howie."

"Did my mom know about him?"

"I told Fran he was like her. I said he wouldn't care who she loved."

"Thanks for what you did for Mom."

"You're a part of my heart Portia. You mightn't think so, but I'm overjoyed to have you in my life. When I saw your little self, standing at the door, all those years ago… it was like getting Fran back."

After our chat, Grammy tearfully served up dessert. Watching her bemoan her life, set me thinking about my own. Right there at the table, eating ice cream, I decided to go back to Standout.

My first session with Janice began the next day. For the first few weeks, I sequestered myself, avoiding everyone except Janice and Maddie. From the start, Janice targeted my errant desire to take responsibility for my mother's life. She surmised the root of my suffering had gotten tangled up with my goal to help my mom. I disagreed.

Whenever she pressed me, I denied every insight she made, even when she had it right. Silence became my tool to protect my inner thoughts, but Janice had intimate knowledge of all things Eucharist and she knew exactly how to whittle away my defenses.

One afternoon, responding to her gentle probes, she got me to share my secret.

"I'm unlovable," I confessed avoiding her eyes.

Putting my chin on my chest and then without anticipating it, I sobbed. My shoulders shook. Loud noises from deep inside gave themselves voice. My nose ran. I couldn't breathe, and I couldn't stop crying. I stretched out on the couch with my back to Janice. She put a blanket over me.

I turned to face the windows and then stared out into the courtyard. After Janice wiped my nose with a tissue, she said, "Let me hold your hand."

I stuck my hand out, leaving it on the couch close to my face. Janice sat on the floor next to the couch, making it so that she could see my eyes. She put her soft, manicured hand around mine. With Janice holding my hand, I cried until I fell asleep.

When I awakened, I peeked from behind the blanket to scrutinize her. Moments later, I sat up.

"Welcome back," Janice said putting her book down.

"I'm so embarrassed."

"For being human—for feeling—for crying?" she smiled.

"You sat there the whole time?"

"Not all of it." Janice leaned forward, smiled her friendly smile again as she held out a glass of water. I smiled back.

At our next session, Janice jumped right in, not giving me any time to retreat from my disclosure. "What caused you to believe yourself unlovable?" she asked as soon as I sat down.

"Well, I told you what happened on my thirteenth birthday." Janice nodded. "Then you felt different?"

"My mother's repugnance made trusting people difficult."

"In what way?"

"I couldn't get close to anyone. I thought… if I did, then they would reject me too."

"How did your mother's rejection make you feel?"

"Like a big pimple. Something she wanted to get rid of." I cried as my words tumbled out.

"I'm wondering what else you felt?"

"I may as well have died."

"You should have died because…"

"My mom stopped loving me."

"Not feeling loved—what was that like?"

"It meant, I wasn't good enough for her or anyone else."

"And there's the tragedy. Let's work on changing your perception."

Admitting my inability to feel loved launched me into a whole new realm of sharing my deepest thoughts with Janice. My sessions began to change my outlook. Although reluctant, I relinquished my habit of blaming myself for my mother's deficiencies and began to reconsider who I wanted to be in the world.

Weeks later Janice asked, "Who are you right now?"

"I'm an accountant," I told her.

"Tell me about who you are. Not your occupation."

"I'm not sure. Can you give me an example?"

"Let's see, I'm a mother, my husband's soul mate and friend. I am a compassionate nurturer." Janice smiled.

Looking away, I glanced into the courtyard. I didn't have a clue what she meant anyhow.

"I'm sensing you're not connecting with this exercise. Is that the case?" she asked looking into my eyes.

"Not quite."

"Can you tell me what it is?"

"You're right, I'm not getting it."

"How do you feel about homework?"

"Sure, I'll do it."

"I want you to make three lists. First, list the things you enjoy or want to do. Second, list the things you value. For the last list, put down what matters most to you."

"What do you mean what matters to me? Aren't those the same?"

"What's the same?"

"What I value and what matters?"

"They could be. You distinguish. Do you value honesty or kindness more than being an accountant?"

"I'm not sure about either."

"You will be. Do your best."

"When should I complete this assignment?"

"The weekend is coming, so how about Monday? Remember to be honest with yourself. There are no right answers. Be honest and you'll get there."

Having shucked off my insecurities about allowing others to know me, I spent many evenings at Uncle's house. That Friday, I elicited help with my assignment.

"Can you define who you are?" I asked Lillian.

"I'm me, Lillian."

"I know, but… what matters most to you?"

Lillian thought for a minute. "I treasure my family, especially my children," she said.

Uncle interjected, "For me it's farming."

"Isn't that your occupation," I asked him.

"I think it's both. I love farming. I don't think about much else."

Robert looked sad. "You don't think about us Papa?"

"Son, I think about you, Jacky, your mama and everybody in this family, but a lot of my time goes to being a farmer."

Robert came over to his father. "You mean the same way I'm always thinking about inventing things?"

"Yep, just like that," Uncle said.

"Then I guess I'm an animator. I see the pictures, the characters, what they do, what they say, where they live. Everything."

Uncle rubbed Jacky's head. "Whelp, then you got it right."

No one would have declared me an expert on the subject of values, but I thought Uncle had missed the point.

"There's more to it," I said.

"How could there be?"

"You didn't say what matters most to you?"

"I'm sure I did. Farming and my family."

Grammy sighed. "Keeping the peace matters to me. These days, I'm thinking I got my life all wrong."

"What do you mean Grammy?"

"Don't listen to me. I'm thinking too much."

"I'm glad you're saying how you feel," I said hoping she'd share more of her feelings with us.

"Best to keep my opinions to myself. I'm not one for telling the inner workings of my mind."

"I have news," Lillian said, changing the subject.

We quieted down. She stood before us as if she readied herself for a presentation. Although Lillian still had a cherubic face, she had lost a few pounds. Her clothes were getting looser, like the tan blouse hanging off her shoulder. She tugged her pants, covered her shoulder and then wiggled with excitement.

"I got a job." Lillian jumped up and down. "Bet you weren't expecting that," she said, dancing around the room.

Everyone rang out "Congratulations."

Robert went to her. "You're not going to be home anymore?"

"I start next week. I'll be here when you go off to school and when you get home. But on Saturdays, I work all day. Eventually, I plan to work full-time." She came back to the table.

Jacky hugged her, but Robert started sulking. Lillian put her arm around Robert's shoulders when she sat down.

Grammy patted Lillian's shoulder. "Congratulations. Wise decision," she said.

"Where is this job?" I asked.

Uncle squirmed in his chair. "She's going to be a psychologist at the Standout place."

"I thought about Mama Miller's situation. Then there's everything you shared about Standout."

"It's a magnificent program. But how did you get a job there?"

"I checked their job openings."

"Best thing I've heard all day," I said, feeling happy for her.

Grammy dealt the Skip-Bo cards and included me without asking if I wanted to play. After ordering my cards, I decided it was a good time to discuss the farm business.

"I want to let you know—" I began.

"You're moving to Denten forever." Jacky ran around to my side of the table.

I flattened the cards against my chest. He leaned into my shoulder. "No, I'm not. You're trying to look at my cards."

Jacky and I laughed.

"He's always cheating," Robert said. I put my arm around him.

"I finished setting up the business," I continued.

"Thank you, Portia," Uncle said.

"You'll need to do corporate and individual taxes."

"All of us?" Grammy asked.

"Yes, for the individual taxes—even Gramps."

"What does it all mean?" Grammy looked confused.

"You're all Miller Farms employees now. I set up an LLC organization like we discussed."

"Mama, you'll be getting your first paycheck."

"I will?" Grammy captured her tears with a napkin.

Robert went over to her. He stood behind her chair and then he draped his arms over her shoulders. Jacky leaned into her from his chair. She put her arm around his shoulders and with her other hand, she held Robert's hand as it hung down her chest.

"If you want, I'll be the Miller Farms accountant from here on out," I offered.

"Yes, Portia. We do," Uncle said.

"And there's one other thing. My father signed the property over to you, Grammy."

She held her hand over her heart. "To me—are you sure?"

"The agreement has your signature on it."

"That can't be right."

Grammy looked from me to Uncle. The news might have astounded her, but she owned the whole three-thousand acres. "It's true." I showed her the deed and a copy of the agreement with her signature on it. "Do you remember signing it?" I asked.

"A lawyer came by. He said, sign here—sign here, until he had all the signatures he needed. Jack signed too."

"He signed the rental agreement. You signed the quitclaim deed and the legal agreement specifying the terms."

"I never thought I'd own a thing. Never earned a nickel in all my life."

"You bring more money into this farm than you think. Your value-added products help support us. All the work you do… Mama, you should have been paid all along."

"Now, I can tell your papa what to do." Grammy chuckled.

Uncle leaned closer to me. "Why did you look those things up?"

"Because… I didn't believe what Grammy told us."

"I wasn't telling no lies."

"What do you mean?" Uncle asked.

"I didn't believe my dad would have signed the farm over to Gramps."

"It's just as I told you," Grammy said.

"Well, not exactly," I countered.

"How'd you get all this information anyway," Uncle asked.

"I called our lawyer. He sent the agreements. After Mom married in 1968, Gramps rented the land for one dollar per month. Their agreement would have expired in 1998. Then—"

"Why did he give it to Mama?" Uncle asked.

"I can't say. After Gramps allowed me to visit, my father extended the rental agreement, then on my eighteenth birthday, the lawyer filed a quitclaim deed giving the land to Grammy."

"Seems like, my papa swindled yours?"

"Morally, he did. Fiscally, not so much. I'd bet my father used the arrangement to reduce his taxes. He didn't need the farm."

"But Papa used Frank and you as leverage."

"Perhaps, he did."

"It's not fair. The farm should be yours."

"Not really, I'm glad he signed it over. When he did, he gave it to me too. You know, we may never have met otherwise."

"I guess. I'm still sore about all of it."

"Don't be. I'm not." I thought about another problem while we ate our ice cream. The kinks in the Miller Farms organization needed fixing. The issues weren't overly complicated. Uncle owned the house he lived in and the parcel it sat on. Grammy owned the land and the buildings on what had been the Foster Farm and Gramps owned the old Miller Farm and Market as sole proprietor. Everything needed to get integrated into the Miller Farms organization.

When they finished their ice cream, the boys left the table, then I said, "Uncle we also need to discuss a few issues related to the Miller Farms organization we setup."

"Why, what's wrong?"

"Nothing, I'll explain next week when we meet with Gramps."

"All right, good enough."

"Grammy, you'll need a will."

"Everything goes to Junior."

"Those are your wishes. Now you'll need to put them in writing to make everything official. It would be best to add him to the deed."

Lillian and I walked down the dirt road after everyone went to bed. We talked about how she had kept up her credentials and maintained her license. "I always knew I'd go back to work. This is sooner than I planned, but I'm happy," she said.

Her training would start the next week. When we got a good distance from the house, I confessed my troubles.

"Tonight, everyone knew who they were. I'm still figuring it out," I said feeling a bit childish.

"You're giving us too much credit. My boys are young. They don't have a clue. My husband and his Mama, well, they keep things simple."

"I wish I could too."

"You have a brilliantly complicated life."

Lillian grabbed my hand. Under the night sky, we walked hand-in-hand along the dirt road, the same way she often did with her sons. I felt childishly awkward, but I let her hold it. "I'm failing in every way."

"No, you're not." Lillian squeezed my hand.

My sadness resurfaced. "I still struggle with the little things. How would I know what matters?"

"Do the assignment. You'll figure it out."

"I hear you, but—"

"You've become a big part of us. We're healthier because of you."

Lillian's words warmed my heart and her positive framing helped. Had I gotten out of my own way; I would have trusted her discernments. Finding purpose or meaning outside of work didn't come easy to me. I was an accountant like my dad. It was the one fact about me, I never doubted.

In Denten, I put my life on hold. The three months pause gave me a fresh start. Unfortunately, my inquisitiveness stirred up a lot of pain, not just for me, but for my family. My good intentions had some unacceptably negative consequences.

When we got across the farm, the lights were on, and I suppressed my impulse to check on Gramps.

"I messed things up between Grammy and Gramps."

"Honestly, I don't think you did."

"Things are worse for Gramps."

"He's fine."

"But Grammy left him."

"Don't let your grandma fool you. She sends my boys over with his meals. In the mornings, she takes his breakfast herself."

"She does?"

"Every day; so, he's content."

"Meeting with Gramps next week will be difficult for me."

"Treat him the same way you would any client."

"Good advice, that's what I'll do."

Holding hands under the night sky, not thinking about anyone else, we turned around, continuing our conversation until we reached the house.

Another five weeks of intense therapy helped me to create boundaries. Boundaries which demanded self-reflection plus Janice's help. Help I resisted, until I had no choice but to accept it. Janice debunked my notions of normal, forcing me to find my authentic self.

My life had changed. Ending our last session, Janice asked, "When we first met, helping your mother seemed most important to you. How about now?"

"I'm my number one priority. Those I love are a close second."

Janice leaned forward; her smile made me feel warm all over. "You're getting there," she said.

I grinned. My progress made me proud, and I trusted Janice. She had helped me to become vulnerable, establish a support network and work out a healthy way of coping with life. Most of all, I began to see myself as a separate individual with my own wants, needs and preferences.

Knowing Janice was like having a fairy godmother, who had granted my deepest wish. I felt uniquely normal. After months of counseling, I was clearheaded about almost everything, but when it came to my mother, things were still a bit cloudy.

A difficult conversation loomed over me. I feared it. To reduce my anxiety and to increase my comfort level about the conversation, Janice role-played with me. Most often, she had me act as I suspected my mother would have acted. Nothing worked. It seemed I couldn't defeat my fear of getting vulnerable with Mom.

Right at the Standout doors, feeling like I'd already failed, I said, "I'm not sure about that conversation."

"You'll do fine, Portia. You have all the tools you need."

"Thanks for everything," I said, leaving Standout for the last time.

"I'm glad you searched here for answers."

"Me too." I hugged Janice. "I'll see you in Brackwood next month."

I went straight to Tiny's when I left Standout. Although Maddie had a busy life, we met for lunch every Friday. That day, I wanted to say something I'd been holding back for at least three weeks. Bombarded by my fears, I tapped the table using a technique Janice taught me to dispel my anxiety.

Twisting my mouth, I said, "Maddie, you've been like a mother to me for the past few months. I'd like us to continue our friendship. If that's okay with you." My body tensed as Maddie ruminated on my words.

"Getting to know you has been a pleasure," she said, after her thoughtful pause.

"Did my request weird you out?"

She hesitated again. "It didn't."

"Don't get me wrong. I'm honestly not looking to replace my mom or anything like that."

"Really Portia, it's nothing you said. The issue is… I don't feel deserving of the honor."

"You must be kidding. You are one of the most nurturing people I've ever known."

"To be honest, I do feel parental towards you."

Maddie frowned when she said parental, but when she laughed my body relaxed. I realized her discomfort wasn't about me.

"Please, don't feel pressured." I held my breath.

"I'm happy about our budding relationship."

"Thank you and I appreciate everything you've done for me these past few months."

"Standout works."

"I feel like I've won the life lottery."

Maddie grinned. "You did."

"I suppose, in many ways I have."

Maddie patted my shoulder in the same way Gramps liked to do. "Are we set to meet in a few weeks?"

"You bet. We have a solid plan."

Part Six

New Beginnings

Thinking about my father expanded my understanding of his actions. For a time, he had given up on Grammy. Between the years of 1982 and 1990, he hadn't written to her at all, but then in May 1991, my father addressed his letter to Mr. & Mrs. Jack Henry Miller Sr. He wrote, *Portia is coming for her first visit. I expect you to treat her with kindness per our agreement.* His prudent decision protected me.

By surrendering his land, my father gave me a place to be when things deteriorated between my mother and me. I surmise he knew it would happen. I had no way to connect those dots; yet I believed I'd drawn the right conclusion. Ten years after his death, my father's sacrifice yielded an unexpected dividend to me. Had I not gone to the farm, the summer of my thirteenth year on the planet might have corrupted my spirit. Instead, I had an amazing summer. The farm saved me. Without it, I would never have discovered Standout.

Digging into the past made clear how well my mother had held things together. Many women had fallen apart. With my father as her champion and her own ingenuity, my mother mapped out a coping style. She survived. Even so, I knew her nightmare hadn't ended.

Although my motives were somewhat selfish, I wanted Mom to feel better, to start living her life... to experience joy again. Besides, her mental wellbeing would allow me to move forward with my own life. Nothing I wanted to say to Mom could have gotten any easier. In fact, stalling might have made it harder, so a few days after returning to Brackwood, I invited Mom for dinner.

After we ate, I gave Mom the ranger hat. She sucked in her breath when she opened the box. Mom seemed transfixed until I spoke to her. "What are you thinking about?" I asked, feeling somewhat excited for her.

"Where'd you get this?"

"Uncle Jack found it in your old closet."

Mom extracted a piece of aged paper she'd hidden behind the leather band. She unfolded the note.

"To my little Scout. Love Papa," she read aloud.

"Why did he call you Scout?"

"We explored the woods together."

"Did he love the woods like you?"

"Perhaps. At the time, I wanted to be a forest ranger."

"When did he give it to you?"

"I think... I was maybe eleven or twelve. I wore this ranger hat all summer long. If they'd allowed it, I might have slept in this hat."

"Wear it on your next hike."

Mom looked girlish when she grinned. "I would look silly."

She tucked the note behind the band and then put the hat back into the box. I smiled realizing I'd missed her. The hat made her happy and she certainly needed some of the harmony she had back when she loved Maddie. The time before the whole reform school business dropped a load of misery on her.

"I don't think you would look silly."

It was a real, adult sized ranger hat. Mom took the hat out again, loosened the inside band to make it bigger and then put it on her head. She romped around the kitchen like a little girl until I said, "Why didn't you become a forest ranger?"

"I was young. Everyone grows up."

I disappointed myself when I blurted out, "Did Maddie ever see you wearing it?"

Mom froze. Realization swept over her face. She tugged her sleeve. Her worry lines became prominent. Everything I practiced evaporated. Wishing to recall my words, I tried to repair the damage.

"I saw where you played in Maddie's backyard."

Mom grimaced. "What are you saying?"

She took off the ranger hat. While I may not have picked an ideal moment to confront Mom about her lovingly reckless effort to influence my sexual preference, I let myself go with it.

"I met Maddie in Denten—gotten to know her."

"What do you mean?"

"Mom, I'm saying I met Madeline Bowman at Standout."

"Why were you at Standout?"

"I had some issues to work on and just so you know… Mom, it's fine by me if you're gay."

"Stop this silly talk."

"I'm not gay. And you can't make me gay, Mom."

"What's gotten into you?"

"Nothing, you matter to me." I waited.

Remembering the importance of accounting for my actions allowed me to remain silent. Mom sat down, she smoothed her pants and then scooted her chair under the table.

"These types of things disturb me."

"Mom, there's nothing wrong with being gay."

"That's not what I mean. It's what you're doing… bringing these things up like this."

"For the past four plus months, I've been in Denten. Maddie allowed me to read the case files at Standout."

Mom's eyes teared up. "I worried you might be out there trying to find things out."

"Do you wish I hadn't read them?"

"I never wanted you to know those things about me."

"None of that is about you. Inexcusable things happened to you. It was cruel."

"Well, it did happen. I've done everything to leave it behind."

"You've suffered... even married a gay man to escape your father."

Mom's eyes widened. She covered her mouth before turning away. After dabbing her eyes, she said, "He would never have wanted you to know that."

"I'm sorry Dad had to live a lie."

"You don't know what you're talking about." Mom put her hands in her lap.

"Grammy gave me his letters," I admitted.

"Then you know he was my best friend."

"I know, Mom."

"No... I don't think you do. I loved your father."

"He loved you too."

Mom smiled. "He certainly did."

"But you still had to live a lie."

"Your father would have been appalled by what you've said. We were life partners. We didn't live any lie."

"Mom... are you gay?"

"I don't know."

My heart filled with sadness. At fifty-six, my mother hadn't explored her sexuality. Despite her resistance, I believed Eucharist had ideologically colonized her brain. They won. Mom turned against herself. She revered heterosexuality.

Worst of all, she willingly harmed me to uphold those ideals. There was still time for her to erase those hate filled beliefs and I suspected she wanted to do it.

Trusting my insight, I said, "You have the right to know. I hope you'll let yourself know."

Mom considered my face. "You're not a homosexual?"

"No, I'm not. But, so what, if I was?"

"You could be. You've never brought anyone home."

"I'm not. I'm sorry to say this... but I've never been able to have a lasting relationship."

"I've been an awful mother—haven't I?"

"Given what you went through, everything makes sense."

"Maybe, I should have sent you to Boarding School."

"I'm thankful you didn't."

Mom tightened her jaw. "Your father wouldn't let me send you."

"I'm thankful to him for that."

"What made you do this—prying into my life?"

"You did. Your appointment...how you shut me out...my thirteenth birthday."

"Your thirteenth birthday?"

"You stopped loving me. I felt like a big pimple back then."

"A pimple? I am an awful mother." She put her head into the palm of her hand. I kept my eyes on her.

"What did you think would happen?"

"I thought you would be independent—strong—normal." Mom focused on me.

"By not loving me?"

"I love you. You, are, the best part of me."

"Then why did you do it?"

"Your father disliked my decision. I assured him, I had to do it."

"He was right... not you. I felt unlovable. What you did is not the reason I'm not gay."

"You don't know." Mom left the table.

"Yes, I do." My menacing tone startled her, but I continued anyway. "Those people psychologically abused you. Then you did it to me."

"Did what to you?"

I took a deep breath. My childhood pain, though not comparable to hers, was valid too. Our confrontation started to push us into our old habit of escalating beyond the ability to communicate. I needed her to hear me. Recalling my sessions with Janice changed our course. I tapped the table.

"You withheld all physical contact from me, you became firm—without a hint of gentleness. That's what I'm talking about."

"I thought you said you love me. It sounds like you hate me."

"For fourteen years, you've hated me. I've been vying for your love."

"I don't hate you. I never intended for you to feel hated."

"Good to know. I've struggled to let go."

"Let go?" Mom pressed her hands to her chest. "I'm not your mother anymore?"

"Of course, you are. But I can't live for you or in your shadow."

Mom hung her head. After a long pause, she said, "I wanted you to be independent. I can see how I might have been wrong to do what I did to you." She minimized her offense. I reminded myself of how harsh her protective efforts had been. She hadn't meant to hurt me, but her unjustifiable decision had remodeled our relationship into an unwinnable tug-of-war. We needed to change. Neither of us would get what we wanted if the battle continued.

Refusing to pretend otherwise and controlling my anxiety, I relayed the message I worked on with Janice. I clapped my hands.

"Well, if you want to improve our relationship, I'd like to help."

Mom raised her left eyebrow. "Are you a psychotherapist now?"

Ignoring her sarcasm, but keeping my voice even, I said, "Will you trust me... say as you would have... trusted Dad?"

"I don't know. What is this help?"

"Please come to the lake house next Saturday at 10:00 a.m. That way, you'll see for yourself."

"And if I don't?"

"What can I say? Then you don't. May I ask a question?"

Mom tugged her sleeve. "Ask."

"There's a gigantic barrier between us. Want to keep it there?"

"No. No, I do not. I protected—"

"I've forgiven you. If you want to improve—"

"I'll meet you."

Sharing my pain with Mom made me feel strong, in control and ready to move on. It was another step towards healing. Before Standout, I projected my pain, shortcomings and fears on to my mother. Releasing my fantasies, allowed my mother to just be a mom and not a perfect one. It freed me.

Absent of the emotional baggage, I began to know myself. I saw Mom too and ever so slowly, I let myself become her champion. First of all, my mother deserved peace of mind. Tapping into the nexus of support provided by the Standout community could help her find it. Second, she needed permission to define herself, a chance to become whatever or whomever she chose. Until Standout, I hadn't known I had the right to define myself. I doubted my mom knew she had that right.

Finally, I hoped my mother could open herself to the love around her. If she did, she would have Robert, Jacky, Uncle, Lillian, Janice, Maddie, Grammy, someday perhaps even Gramps and definitely me loving her right back. Doing so, would help her escape the hollow place where she hid herself.

We both knew the people who could guide her. To her, they were old friends, lost connections and estranged family. To me, they were new friends, my support and saviors. I hoped Mom would show up to the lake house.

I hiked Franconia Notch State Park with Jarod on my first Sunday back from Denten. The forest had refashioned itself from deep green into an autumn palette. Sprinkles of yellow, bright orange with dots of red and rust foreshadowed the winter. We hiked up Mount Flume for about an hour. Jarod seemed invigorated but I got colder by the moment. My sweater wasn't warm enough for the elevation. My teeth chattered.

Jarod evaluated my attire. "You're cold. I'm sorry, should have told you to wear something warm today." He gave me his jacket. With his jacket on, I started to get warm, but I rubbed my arms letting the body heat he'd left behind soak into me. "Let's head into the basin. It's warmer down there."

"I've never hiked here, or I would have known about the elevation."

"No apology needed. I love sharing my jacket with you."

We headed down past the rocky stream until the roar of cascading water dampened all other sounds along the path. Jarod pointed down to the clear water in the granite hole below us. He raised his voice over the gushing water as we walked down. "That's the basin," he said.

In the basin, we rested at the edge of a rock formation carved eons ago by moving waters. Jarod dangled his legs over the pool. Trees swooped down on us; the sun grew warmer. I reluctantly removed Jarod's jacket but kept it in my lap. Although I had stood him up twice, Jarod made our hike special. I felt ashamed of how neglectful I'd been.

"I'm glad you showed me this place," I said.

"My pleasure. I considered where to bring you based on our past hikes. I was sure you'd like it here."

"You're a good friend."

"Portia, I care about you."

"I'm working on being a better friend to you."

"You are a good friend. I think you've become my best friend."

Jarod leaned away when he looked at me. I admired him. I considered him my best friend too. I wished to say the same but chose not to lessen his disclosure.

"Thank you. You're special to me Jarod."

"You seem different."

"You think so?"

He looked me over. "Yep. I like the change."

His voice had been tender, contrasting his intense eyes. My body quivered. A year of cordial relations had passed because I hadn't found a way to express my romantic interest.

"In Denten, I thought about you often," I admitted.

"I like that you did."

"I'm sorry for being cagey for the past few months."

"You were busy. But I must admit... every day, I wished to hear from you." Jarod bumped my shoulder with his. Then he rubbed my back. His hand on my back felt good. My heart quickened. I wanted to kiss him. I stood up. "Sorry. Maybe... I shouldn't touch you."

I wanted to jump into the pool. "Too bad they don't allow swimming," I said as I moved away from him.

"This water is too cold anyway."

I stuck my fingers into the tiny waterfall then jerked my hand back.

"Bad idea—that's freezing."

Jarod laughed. "Told you it was cold."

"I know... but I would jump in for a minute. Wouldn't you?"

"Nope, I wouldn't. When it's freezing water, I'm not the guy. I'd watch you do it though."

"Ha, ha, watch me freeze."

"There's a natural pool like this one in Costa Rica. Perfect for swimming." Jarod reached for his jacket.

"Yeah, I know. My father took me to a few of those swimming spots. I loved them."

"Maybe we'll go together someday."

"Wouldn't be as nice without my father."

We hiked down the path, leaving the pool. As we explored the basin, Jarod made another suggestion. "We could swim in the Great Blue Hole. Ever been there?"

"I've never heard of it."

"It's a marine sink hole off the coast of Belize."

"You're teasing me?"

"It's real. I'll take you."

"I'll look it up first. I'm not going to let you throw me into a strange hole." I laughed.

We rounded the bend going away from the basin but stayed at the same elevation. Jarod stopped when the path became rocky. He extended his hand for me to hold. "I'm a skilled hiker—remember?"

Jarod looked embarrassed. I hiked past him. I regretted not taking his hand. Part of me feared touching him and the other part feared hurting him.

"What about Crater Lake in Oregon?" he suggested.

"I'd be happy to go with you," I told him.

"Let's go this summer."

I considered the possibility of taking a trip with him. In the same moment he asked, I started planning but hid my excitement from him. We hiked deep into the park discussing all manner of things. On the jaunt back, Jarod said he planned to reboot his life. For five years, he'd been recovering from a personal tragedy.

As we exited the park, he alluded to his plan to begin a new relationship. Don't do it—wait for me, I thought. I wanted to discourage him… to ask him to take his time moving on. Jarod is twelve years older than I am. He married during my junior year of high school. Then a year before I graduated with my MPA, his wife and children, along with his mother-in-law died in a plane crash. His boys were two and four years old.

When I graduated, Mom assigned Jarod as my mentor. Within the first few months, we became friends. Mom's decision to stop coming to the office, drew us closer, shifting our friendship into something special. To safeguard our professional relationship, I concealed my feelings for him. With Jarod, I could be carefree, talkative and freakishly content. If anyone had asked, I would have told them, I'd been falling in love with him for two years. I adored him.

Competing with his dead wife, dead children and his pining for those he loved became my unyielding fear whenever I considered the possibility of having a relationship with him. How could I fill the void?

I thought about how Janice would have advised me. I supposed she might say, take a chance or something like, get vulnerable or something more philosophical like, love requires an emotional connection. No matter, Jarod perplexed me. When I thought back to earlier interactions, I wondered if he had developed feelings for me months before I left Brackwood. While he intrigued me that day, I pocketed my yearning for him as I had to focus on my family.

For the next six days, I prepared for Mom's retreat. An idea I brewed after I found out about her friendship with Maddie, the Eucharist ordeal and the life changing work they do at Standout. When I first discussed my plan, I hadn't yet seasoned it into the fine idea it became later. At the time, both Maddie and Janice had reservations, but during my therapy with Janice, I worked on my own problems. When I brought my revised idea back to them, they agreed to help.

The weekend of Mom's retreat, I had a house full of people. Before leaving Denten, I invited Grammy for a visit, expecting she'd never accept. Without letting me know, that Friday, Grammy came to Brackwood. She walked through my door excited about getting away. Uncle came through right behind her with Lillian and the boys following him.

Uncle had defied Grammy's wishes. She asked him to drive her to my house and to pick her up the following week, but he prepared to stay with her. Although I assured him Grammy would have everything she needed, he said, "My mama ain't never been nowhere. I'm staying with her."

That same night I made a huge blunder. I had spoken with Lillian about the retreat, expressing my fears and reservations about what might happen out at the lake house. Grammy, having overheard everything, pressed me to let her come along. I couldn't discourage her. After multiple attempts, Uncle pleaded with her, Lillian suggested this and that and then we all gave up.

Ending our pleas, we agreed to let her come to the lake house to see Mom. Uncle insisted on coming too. He expected Mom to lash out at Grammy. So did I, but that didn't mean he should come with her. What it meant was… they both needed to stay away.

Maddie assured me things would work out. She and Janice agreed to have Grammy visit with Mom before they got started with their retreat. They figured, an hour, with Grammy would do. Despite my opposition, everyone ended up at the lake house. Uncle came for Grammy; Lillian came for Uncle and the boys had nowhere else to be without their parents. Those Millers had overrun me.

We arrived around eight o'clock Saturday morning to let Maddie explain the rules. The firmness in Maddie's voice surprised me. She didn't ask or demand, yet it was clear, Maddie was in charge. Grammy graciously accepted the terms.

Mom drove up at ten o'clock. Lillian and the boys waved from the shore when Mom stepped out of the car. Although she waved back, her face remained serious.

"I don't think I'm going to like this," she said when I walked up to her.

"You can thank me in the future."

"Is your uncle in there?"

"He is," I said, nudging her forward with my arm around her back.

Mom halted when Maddie greeted us at the door. She turned to leave. Maddie touched Mom's arm.

"Stay," she requested in her tender voice.

"This isn't right Maddie."

"Please come in, Fran." I supposed, seeing Maddie lured Mom into the house. Without hesitating, she allowed Maddie to direct her to one of the armchairs facing the fireplace. The mood was grim, but Robert and Jacky's jubilant voices coasted in, peppering the tension with their cheerfulness.

Mom kept her hands in her lap when she sat down. Maddie stood behind Mom's chair. I sat in the chair next to her forcing myself not to rub the fabric. I tapped my finger instead.

Uncle, keeping a watchful eye on Grammy most of the time, but shifting between Mom and me too, had a stern look on his face. He'd taken up a defensive position on the sofa across from Grammy and watched her with the same intensity he had the day his boys plunged into the water from the jumping rock.

"Grammy is here," I sounded as cheerful as possible.

"Hi Mama." Mom sounded like a child.

We waited several minutes expecting fireworks. Nothing. Just silence. Mom sat in the chair with her eyes closed. Acting against the standoff, I nodded to Grammy. She forced a smile. I pointed to Mom with my open hand beckoning Grammy to do something. She seemed years older as she made her way over to Mom's chair. She stood there looking at Mom for a few minutes.

"I've missed you," Grammy finally said.

An apology would have been a better start. But her behavior wasn't mine to control. Grammy knelt beside the chair. She pulled Mom close and then wrapped her arms around Mom. Although Mom kept her eyes closed and her hands remained in her lap, she rested her chin on Grammy's shoulder. After an extended hug, Grammy released her.

Mom kept staring into her lap as if someone had pressed her mute button. I wasn't sure if her response was good or bad. After a minute or two, I realized she wasn't going to have any sort of conversation with Grammy. I stepped forward.

"Is there anything you want to say to Grammy?" I asked Mom.

"I'm ready to go." Mom stood up.

She gathered her things paying attention to each item as if she were making a crucial decision whenever she lifted one of them. I felt remorseful about taking charge of her life. After all, I had closed off her options. In a way, I'd threatened to ostracize Mom like the rest of her family had done years ago. That's probably the only reason she agreed to meet me.

Mom seemed miserable. I wondered if I should call things off until Grammy said, "I'll stay with Fran."

My mother grimaced. She sat down again, letting her things drop into the chair next to her.

"No Grammy—you can't." I urged her forward.

We moved closer to the door. Before we stepped out, Uncle turned around. He said, "Frank, I was a really sucky brother. I'm sorry and I love you."

Mom's shoulders started shaking. Maddie went over to her. Grammy started to go over too, but I stopped her. At the same time, I put my hand on Uncle's back, turning him around and almost pushing him forward until we were outside.

Lillian was sitting on the porch. "How did it go?" she asked.

"Fine, I guess. I apologized," Uncle said.

Grammy wrinkled her forehead and then frowned. "She didn't hug me back. Or have anything to say to me." She started crying.

"Everything will fall into place," I said, feeling as if her tears were unfair or unnecessary—at the very least unhelpful. I walked off the porch, removed my shoes, stepped into the soft grass and crossed over to the rocky shore. I touched Robert's head when I stopped next to him. "Is the water cold?"

"Not to me. Can I go say hello to Auntie now?"

"I'm sorry Robert, not today."

I picked up a rock and threw it across the water.

Jacky counted, "One, two, three, four... ha, five times. How'd you do that?"

"I've lived near this lake all my life."

"You have to teach me."

"First off, pick your rock wisely."

"Yeah, how?"

"Look for the flattest rock you can find. Here, try this one."

Jacky threw the rock. It skipped once and then plunked into the lake. "Aww man."

"Now, let's talk about angles."

Both boys started throwing rocks into the lake. I stayed with them. It seemed to me, being outside for a bit would give Mom space to pull herself together. I used the time to teach them. I picked up the best skipping rocks and talked about angles. We threw rocks into the lake for at least thirty minutes. It had been long enough. That's why when Lillian yelled for the boys to come over to the car, I went back inside.

After fetching Janice from her room, the two of us stood in front of my mother. "Janice Moore is here to see you," I said, as if Mom had won a prize.

"Hello Fran. Do you remember me?"

"Funny. Of course, I do. You still cry a lot?"

Maddie laughed. "You did cry all the time." She sat in the chair next to Mom.

Janice laughed too. "Not as much now. Maybe because... you helped me stay brave, Fran."

"I remember. Whatever happened to that boy, Lenny?"

Janice sat on the end of the sofa bringing herself as close to my mother as possible. "I married him. He goes by Lyndon now."

Mom smiled, one of the most serene smiles, I'd ever seen come across her face. "Good for you," she said.

"Fran, Portia arranged this retreat so we could all spend some time together in this relaxed environment."

"I'm not ready for this." Mom faced Maddie.

"We're here to visit with you. Do you mind?" Maddie smiled. They kept their eyes on one another.

"No. But I'm not prepared for this—whatever it is." Mom scooted to the edge of her chair.

"Do you remember how we used to laugh so much until we had to pee?" Janice asked.

Mom nodded her head. "But Portia should have told me about—"

"When I requested you meet me today, I asked you to trust me."

"I'm trusting you. But—"

"This seemed the best way. Your friends wanted to see you."

Mom sat back. "You should have given me all the details."

"You do want to repair our relationship—don't you?"

"Yes. You know I do."

Maddie interrupted. "Maybe we can stir up trouble and laugh like the little girls we used to be long ago. What could it hurt?"

"What do I need to do?"

"Nothing. We thought you might like to have a retreat with some old friends," Janice said.

Maddie put her arm around Mom's shoulder. When my mother relaxed the same way she used to when my father touched her, I knew we were heading in the right direction.

"Are you expecting me to do therapy?" Mom asked.

"Goodness no," Janice laughed. "We are your friends, and we want to visit with you, have a reunion of sorts."

"Don't ask me any more silly questions, like I'm senile." Mom smiled. "How could I forget you?"

"Things happen." Janice smiled at Mom.

"Well, I remember you being the smartest one, but I'm not nuts."

"Fran, we both know you're not any more nuts than you used to be." Maddie said. They all laughed.

"But seriously, this week… if you're comfortable, I'd like us to talk about Standout. Is that okay?"

Mom nodded, her skin turning as red as the dusty rose chair she sat in. Janice caught my eyes. I knew she wanted me to leave.

I stood there anyway.

"I'm going now. Simon will prepare your meals. I'll see you in eight days," I relayed my information.

"Let me walk you to the door."

Maddie stood next to me. I didn't budge. I had things to say to my mother. I continued, "I let the office know you'll be out. You don't need to worry though. I'll be there."

Mom looked at me. "You're back?" she smiled.

"I think so." I smiled too.

"If there's nothing more Portia... we'll get started," Janice persisted.

"I'm ten minutes away if you need me," I said leaving Mom there looking strangely at ease and confused at the same time. I hoped she could endure the influx of emotions she must have been feeling. When I stepped outside, Lillian came over to me and I sobbed while she hugged me.

Lillian and I went straight to the guesthouse where Grammy prepared lunch. All of us took a short walk after supper. Later we played various games until everyone became sleepy.

Although we bonded, no one mentioned my mother. I suspected everyone had their own notions of what they wished to happen. As for me, I predicted Mom would give herself permission to explore every aspect of her person. In time, I hoped she'd disembody herself from her own fear of homosexuality. As the night progressed, I reminded myself that Maddie and Janice had recovered from their Eucharist experience. My mother could too. The Standout process worked.

The next morning, Grammy announced her intention to stay at my house until Mom finished her retreat. I recommended she go back to Denten as she couldn't help my mother in any way, but she refused to leave. It was irrational. Being at my house didn't bring her any closer to Mom than going back to Denten would have done. Besides, she had no way to know if my mother would associate with her again. Personally, I believed Grammy begged for disappointment.

In terms of Mom's well-being, I had faith in the love, professionalism and kindness Janice and Maddie would show her. If Mom allowed it, her friends would lead her away from the void where she sometimes dwelled.

On Sunday evening, while Simon stocked the kitchen with the things Grammy requested, I asked him about my mother. He thought she looked fine. But what did he know? They weren't friends. Although I must admit it, I remember how Simon smiled when he spoke about her. He had a little secret. I didn't ask. If I had, it would have violated my agreement with Janice.

"Do you think they can help your mama?" Grammy asked when Simon left the house.

"I would say yes. They helped me."

"You? What was wrong with you?"

"I felt unlovable—worthless."

"I can't believe you thought that. Look at everything you have."

There was no way I was going to have a tiff with Grammy over my own feelings. Even though her superficial analysis puzzled me, I reminded myself, she liked to keep things simple. Regardless, I wanted to tell her my material possessions didn't dictate my emotional health or self-worth. Putting her attitude aside, I relented to her inability to appreciate my self-esteem issues.

"You're right Grammy. I'm fine."

"I know. Look at this place."

My nose wrinkled. Grammy's words were exceptionally foul. She spoke from ignorance, oblivious to her offense. "Standout can help you too," I offered.

"What are you saying? You think I'm mental?"

"No, I don't. Wouldn't you like to have better relationships with the people you love?"

"You have a problem with me?"

"No, but… what about Gramps?"

"Marriage isn't perfect. Mine sure got a few snags right now."

"I'm confused. After everything he did?"

"All he done was lie about what he knew."

"He did more than that."

"You're talking about past transgressions. I'm talking about what happened a few weeks back."

"What do you mean?"

"From the beginning, your grandpa believed Howie was a homosexual. That's why he took advantage of him."

"Either way, I will never forgive him," I said, hoping she might see things from my point of view.

"You're not going to forgive your grandpa for what happened to your mama?"

"That's right."

"He loves you and he'd never hurt you."

"Maybe," I consented, but I wanted to tell her just how she had fooled herself.

"What do you mean? Maybe."

"Why would I forgive Gramps? He hates my mother."

"We all got faults."

"He has huge faults." I laughed.

Grammy frowned. "I'll grant you that too. So do I—so do you. You don't have to, but I love your grandpa. He lost some of my trust the other day. In time, I'll forgive him."

"Why?"

"Because he's my husband—a good one. Before you say so, I'll say it. He failed Fran. We both did."

"At Standout, you could work on all those failings."

"How's that? I'm not homosexual."

"Neither am I. They helped me."

"Well, glad for you."

"It's free. Certainly you qualify. They serve Eucharist survivors and their families too."

Grammy pulled her head back. She twisted her nose. "Hold on a minute now, I'm glad for the chance to have Fran back. Doesn't mean I need help from those homosexual women."

"There were heterosexuals at Eucharist too."

"Doesn't matter, prostitutes or homosexuals." Her bitterness filled the room.

"Grammy—why would you say that?" I shouted.

"That's what they were." Grammy looked through the pantry.

"They were innocent children."

"Please let it go. I'm not looking for no help."

"There's a lot you could work on. It's never too late."

Grammy bobbed her head from side-to-side. "Only thing I need to do is settle my feelings about what my husband did so long ago."

"Eucharist abused your only daughter."

"So you've said. I'm aware."

"You need to come to terms with what happened."

"What terms are those?"

Speaking in a tone that might have been somewhat harsh, I said, "About how Eucharist abused her."

"Pastor Joseph says they made her normal. I'm happy for her."

Her condescending tone incensed me; my insides seemed to burst. I had trouble keeping my volume down. Dealing with Grammy's ignorance ignited my contempt for her church. Beginning to see through her feigned innocence, her self-righteousness, the homophobic ideas governing her life and realizing she was bound to those ideas, infuriated me. I waited for her to leave the pantry. Then I studied her face.

"I believe you agree with Gramps," I said.

"He's a zealous man. He has his beliefs. I have mine."

"You know my father was gay."

"I like to think he straightened out when he married Fran?"

"We both know the truth. You gave me the letters—remember?"

"So I did."

"Mom is probably gay too."

"I don't think so. They never acted on it."

"What do you think about homosexuality?"

"I always say, love the sinner, hate the sin."

I loathed her statement, although I wasn't sure what she meant. "What do you mean?" I asked, delaying my judgment.

"Homosexuals are fine good people... if they don't commit the sin against nature."

"Do you agree with Gramps?"

"On some things, I do... others I don't."

"You wanted her to go to Eucharist too—didn't you?"

"I wanted them to help her. Not hurt her."

"You know they abused her—don't you?"

"What's done is done. Nothing I can do to change things."

Grammy wiped the table. I followed her around the kitchen like a puppy. I knew her bustle was an attempt to push away the painful truth about Eucharist and all the feelings that came with it. But I wasn't a therapist. I had no desire to assume the role for her. My simple wish was to benevolently hurtle her right into the truth.

"Gramps went to the trial. He knows everything and you should too," I told her.

"You may think me a bad person, but I never want to hear the horrors Fran went through."

"You sent her away."

"We talked about this. Your grandpa made her life miserable."

"I understand now. You—sent her to Eucharist."

"It sounded like a good idea. She ran around being with girls in the most awful ways."

"You mean kissing Maddie?"

"That's right. It's unnatural... an abomination."

"Does abandoning your daughter count as a sin against nature? Isn't that unnatural too?"

"Portia, don't start."

"Was her punishment natural? Did Eucharist have a right to hurt her?"

"She went. They were supposed to help and then send her home. Nothing made me madder than when Jack told them to keep her. They weren't supposed to do horrible things. I just wanted her home… I didn't care what she ended up as."

"What do you know about what happened at Eucharist?"

"Maddie's mother told me vulgar things happened there. She forgave Maddie her sins. I never let her tell me the details. I don't want you doing it. I forgave Fran." Grammy dabbed her eyes.

Her willful ignorance stupefied me. There was no way to let her words go unchallenged. "Why did my mom need forgiving?"

"She went against God. After a time, I didn't care. I forgave her."

"Did she go against God or you?"

"Both. That's all there is to it."

"What Eucharist and your church did was horrendous. Did you forgive them too?"

"Don't know what they did, so nothing to forgive."

"Grammy, don't you want to know the whole truth?"

"What for? The whole truth is just misery."

"Why are you afraid to know?"

"Maybe, I'm guilty too. There now, have I admitted what you want me to admit?" I kept silent. Grammy was guilty. No matter, I declined the invitation to spread out blame as if it were a warm cozy blanket. "Just know, I wanted her home," Grammy almost screamed.

"Why didn't you go get her?"

"Because, I wasn't a man. If I was, they'd done what I wanted." Grammy closed the pantry doors. "Just so you know… I accept that what happened to her was my fault too."

Grammy left me standing in the kitchen. She went down the hall to the guestroom as happily ignorant, homophobic and naive as ever. She had fooled me. Back in Denten, she acted as though she hated Eucharist. Turned out, she sought a magical cure for homosexuality.

Although she hadn't condemned my mother, Grammy couldn't step outside of her religious beliefs, even when it meant allowing her daughter to suffer rape and torture at the hands of a mad man.

She was the worst. Refusing to expose herself to the unpalatable abuses committed at Eucharist kept her feeling like an innocent victim. Unfortunately, Grammy's hankering to keep the peace let her bury her head in the sand. No matter how she saw things, from my point of view, she shared culpability with Gramps.

Once I realized Grammy's inability to contemplate the deeper meaning of things, I let go. Afterall, I couldn't force her to adopt a new coping style. She wasn't my problem. My life was enough to handle without adding her troubles to it, but I did feel sorry for Grammy. Nevertheless, I refused to use my energy to pity her.

Reluctantly, I harbored a measure of disdain for her choices because she had allowed fear to override her common sense. It must have been some kind of warped logic keeping her beholden to Gramps and her church. Worst of all, it seemed Grammy's sheltered life cost her more than she'd ever realize.

After our conversation, when it came to Grammy, I avoided talking about Standout, homosexuality or anything requiring self-reflection. Getting into my bed, I commended myself for keeping my promise not to check in with Janice or Maddie. I floated off to sleep envisioning Standout as a cocoon of wellness.

On Monday morning, I ate breakfast with Grammy, Uncle and Lillian. Somehow, we kept farm hours. Like me, Lillian looked unkempt in the morning; seeing her made me feel sane. Grammy, like Mom, seemed to wake up looking immaculate. Once I readied myself, I headed to my car toting some accounting books, feeling excited about returning to work. Lillian met me at the door.

"Jack is going home for a few days," she said.

"Is something wrong?"

"No, he has to work the farm." Grammy interrupted handing me a packed lunch.

"You shouldn't have done this, Grammy."

"Of course, I should have—you're sticks." Grammy kissed my cheek and then went back to the kitchen.

Lillian opened the door for me. "My sweet husband is afraid to leave his mama here alone."

"Alone? I'll be here."

"I know. But you have work. He wants me to stay with her. Do you mind?"

"Not at all, you're always welcome. But what about your job?"

"Don't worry, I finished my training before we came down. So far, I don't have any clients and we pushed back my start date."

"Oh, okay. See you tonight."

I stepped into my office before anyone arrived. It is the largest office in the building. My father and his grandfather claimed it before me. After my father died, Mom sealed it off. No one was allowed in it until she assigned it to me after I joined the firm.

A host of cherished memories came to mind that morning. I could almost see my father teaching me math or some accounting principle right at his desk. My desk. Then there were the times when I napped on his soft leather sofa while he worked late into the night.

The office had a bathroom, kitchenette and a rectangular conference table where we often had large lunch or dinner meetings. Being in there, steps you back in time. Everything remained as designed in the sixties, from the Danish rosewood desk to the paneling on the back wall. When I took over, I modernized the lighting to make it softer, changed out the artwork, leaving a few of my father's pieces and added some of my books to Dad's bookcases.

Coming back to work, I already had a goal to start a forensics department. It constituted my own, private, independent decision. That morning, I outlined my proposal. Just before noon, I unpacked my lunch. All the food Grammy prepared blindsided me. She'd sent enough for two or three people. There was soup, an assortment of raw vegetables and three half sandwiches. Picking up my phone, wishing he'd accept, I invited Jarod to join me. After he accepted, I put everything out on the conference table making a production of it, as we sometimes did for client lunches.

Purposefully, steering away from a business lunch vibe, I set the table with plates and napkins, played soft music, opened one of the bottles of wine we kept around for clients and finally satisfied, hoping for something which I couldn't name waited for Jarod.

"How is your first day back going?" Jarod asked, when he sat at the table with me.

"So far, so good. Are you hungry?" I poured wine for him.

Jarod nodded. "You know, I haven't had a homemade lunch since my wife died."

"Until my grandmother leaves, you're welcome to eat lunch with me every afternoon."

"What happens after she leaves?"

My skin tingled. "We can meet whenever you want Jarod."

"I feel lucky right now. Thanks for asking me today."

My eyes kept moving to Jarod's mouth when he spoke. My cravings for him were leaking into the room. Steering the conversation to business helped me ignore my longing.

"What do you think about forensic accounting?" I asked him.

"I don't know much about it."

"Really? I want to start a forensic department."

"How did you come to that decision?"

"I've always had a fascination with it."

"I didn't know that about you."

"Yep, I took all the forensic courses. Plus, I did an internship."

"You're really into it."

"Sure am. Do you think the Board will go for it?" I sought his insight.

"What do you think?" he countered.

"Forensics has the potential to increase our revenue stream with limited financial risk. So, yes, I think they will."

"How will you get things up and running?"

"Give me a few weeks. I'll have all the answers in my proposal."

"Sounds like a good plan. On another note, maybe we can eat in the park one day, while it's still warm or something."

Goosebumps popped up all over my arms. "Sure. Sounds fun. Wednesday?" I offered with a smile.

"That works. I'll put it on my calendar."

"What did you mean or something?"

Jarod looked into my eyes. "If you don't think it's weird… or inappropriate, can we have dinner this week? Not our usual hanging out… I want to have a date with you."

My heart pounded. "I would love to," I said, feeling nervous like a schoolgirl. Plus, I longed to kiss his wonderful lips.

"Portia, I've been wanting to say… I truly like you."

"I like you too—a lot." I felt stupid for adding a lot until Jarod kissed me. Kissing him back, I melted into him, feeling as though I loved him.

Jarod and I had our first date at Per Te Su restaurant that Thursday evening. He waited outside the restaurant and opened my car door when I pulled up. Inside, we checked our coats and Jarod gave the maître d' his name. He was so handsome. He wore a black turtleneck cashmere sweater with fitted gray tweed pants. I wore a navy-blue midi dress. It had a halter neck with intricate lace and my shoulders and back were out too.

"You look amazing," he told me.

"I think, maybe, I'm overdressed."

"I don't think so."

Jarod touched my arm and then took my hand as we followed the hostess to a small table overlooking the ocean. Right when we sat down, he ordered a bottle of wine for us.

"What did you actually do in Denten?" Jarod asked before we ordered our meals.

I felt cold. I inhaled. I preferred to tell him everything. Fearing his reaction, I watered things down. "I spent time with my family at the Miller Farm," I offered, hoping he'd change the subject.

"Is that the whole truth?"

"Maybe not. Why?"

"You're different; more relaxed."

Under the table, I tapped my leg one time, just like Janice taught me to do. To avoid having Jarod notice my nervousness, I took a deep breath too. I hesitated. Knowing that people have strong opinions about psychotherapy made me afraid to tell the truth. I did anyway.

"For a few months, I was in therapy with an amazingly brilliant and kind woman," I admitted to him.

"It sure seems to have helped your confidence."

"Honestly? The idea doesn't bother you?"

"Sometimes we need help."

"Would you go to therapy?"

"After my wife and children died, I saw someone—so yes."

During the rest of the meal, I told Jarod about Denten. I shared how I reconnected with my family, about Janice, about Maddie and Standout. Telling him allowed me to avoid secrets. I might have over done it though because Jarod didn't get a chance to say much. My elaborations lasted through dinner and dessert.

"May I pick you up next time?" Jarod asked as we prepared to leave.

Not having had a fancy date since leaving college, I awkwardly accepted by nodding my head. I smiled too. On the inside, I burst with excitement, feeling as if I couldn't wait for our next date. After the valet brought my car, Jarod rubbed his hand down my back as he kissed me. In that moment, I wanted to surrender myself to him right there.

Suppressing our thirst for sexual contact challenged both of us, but we controlled our lust. Jarod hadn't pressed me for sex. No matter, we were surely united in our desire for one another. Still, I managed to drive off feeling proud of my self-restraint.

Friday morning, Jarod found me in my office around 7:15 a.m., leaning over my desk, he kissed my forehead, he kissed my nose and then he kissed my lips before walking away. He stopped at the door.

"See you in five hours," he said.

The morning seemed to last forever. Throughout the day, I fantasized about the beautiful children Jarod and I would have together. When he showed for lunch, I had already placed everything on the conference table. Sitting close, we clowned around until I got serious.

"I must confess," I said with a rueful smile.

"Okay, I'm listening."

Jarod batted his eyes causing us both to laugh. From the chair next to me, I secretively clutched the cookbook I'd hidden earlier.

Smiling my devilish smile, I said, "I can't cook, so… if you want home cooking after my grandmother leaves, I'm giving you the instructions." I put the cookbook on the table in front of him and laughed again with my head thrown back.

Jarod poked my arm when I stopped laughing. I giggled like a little girl, which made me feel delectably embarrassed.

"I know you don't cook," Jarod said softly.

"You don't mind?"

"Sure don't. Why would I?"

"Cause I'm a woman." I batted my eyes.

Jarod pulled me to him. I rested my head on his shoulder. "I know a lot about you. I like who you are. Before you left, I had been thinking about how to date you for months."

"I'm glad you figured it out. What changed?"

"My job title. Being the COO puts us at the same level."

"I want to know why you started liking me."

Jarod took my hand. "Well, we spent hours and hours working on various projects after Fran stopped coming to the office. We ate dinner together; we hiked on weekends, we—"

"Are you saying it happened a while ago?"

"Yes, I wasn't ready. I am now."

"You never said anything?"

"Neither did you. When I saw you last week, my ache went away."

I sat up. "You had an ache for me?"

"Sure did. Talking on the phone wasn't the same. Being with you is much better. I missed you." Jarod leaned into me.

"How did you get so brave?"

"The last time we hiked, you were calmer—more grounded. I told myself not to miss my chance. Then you invited me to eat with you."

"I seemed grounded?"

"Yes. Happier, confident and more beautiful than ever."

I liked how Jarod described me and I felt contented around him. My excitement about the change in our relationship grew, making time speed by like a flash of awe. After work that Friday, Jarod walked me out of the building. Leaning on my car, with me leaning on him, he held me. After kissing me, he promised to cherish me as a lifelong friend. Those words reminded me of my parents, who had been life partners and friends. I wanted that too. Leaving Jarod had been difficult. I wanted to stay with him all night. Everything was going great between us.

On the drive home, I preoccupied myself by going over my first week back to work. Things could not have been better. That week, I renewed my love for accounting. Feeling more freedom in my life, I fine-tuned my forensic accounting proposal. Mom had made the firm more successful with electronic processing. I predicted I'd do the same with forensics.

Additionally, getting back to work proved exciting in ways I had never dreamt. My secret love for Jarod was out in the open. After our kiss, my life drifted into another lane. We had been cautious. In his mind, our positions put us on an equal footing. None of his fears about fraternizing would have mattered to me. I felt lucky to know Jarod.

It was his previous life with his wife, his lost sons and his dead mother in-law, that had me worried. His recovery had taken years. I didn't want to harm or disappoint him in any way. Months earlier, Lillian suggested I learn to accept love from others as easily as I gave it. I wanted Jarod's love. Yet, I surmised my fear over not being good enough for him would cause me to ruin my chance with him. Growing hopeful, I landed on something more positive. For the rest of the drive home, I only thought about Jarod's kisses.

When I got home, Lillian sat at the kitchen table. I poured myself a glass of tea and then sat with her. "Where is everyone?" I asked.

"Here and there. I'm kind of hiding out. How was the date?"

"I'm so confused right now."

"That's your response to a date?"

"No. I'm already thinking about marrying him. It scares me."

"Did he ask?"

"No. Yesterday was our first date."

"Oh. Why do you want to marry him?"

"I've known him for fifteen years. Aside from my father, he is the most phenomenal person I've ever known."

"You totally like him, huh?"

"I do. I know him, I trust him, I feel comfortable with him… am I getting ahead of myself?"

"What more do you need?" Lillian asked.

"I can't say. Reassurance maybe?"

"Why not help things along. Invite him over for dinner."

Even on short notice, Jarod showed up. He kissed me on the cheek after stepping through the door, confusing me with his restraint, until Robert spoke from behind me.

"You a soldier or something… are those army boots?" he asked.

Jarod didn't dress anything like a soldier. He wore a cream sweater, which made his caramel skin look delicious, navy pants and soft leather boots. Aside from being black, those boots didn't resemble army boots in any other way.

"I bet army boots are much stiffer than these," Jarod said.

"Yeah, but are you a soldier?"

"Nope. I'm just Jarod. What's your name?"

"Robert. Are you Portia's boyfriend?"

Jarod smiled, "I don't know. Maybe? I'll ask Portia. May I get back to you on that?"

Robert grinned. "I guess."

In the kitchen, I introduced Jarod to Grammy. "It's a pleasure to meet you. Portia shares those wonderful lunches you send. You're such an awesome cook," he said.

"Well, aren't you a sweetheart. I set my mind to fatten Portia up. Now I know why it's not working."

Jarod laughed really hard.

"Nothing will fatten me up. I'm like my mama and Gramps."

Grammy carried a large cooking spoon over to the stove. "Do you eat lamb?" she asked Jarod.

"I do. It's my favorite meat."

"Mine too." I leaned into Jarod. He put his arm around me.

"Aha, aha. He's Portia's boyfriend."

I had forgotten about Robert watching us. Grammy waved the spoon to shoo him away. But he stayed close, following us into the den, where I introduced Jarod to Lillian and Jacky.

"You're short," Jacky snickered.

"I don't think six-feet is short."

"You're shorter than Cousin Portia."

"Yeah, she has a couple of inches on me."

I eyed Lillian. She threw her hands up. I knew seeing how Jarod interacted with everyone was good for me. Lillian wouldn't have said anything to interrupt her boys unless they got out of hand. Jarod sat on the sofa next to Robert, placing himself in front of Jacky. On the other side of the ottoman, Jacky was on his knees, facing the sofa, using the ottoman to draw on as if it were a table.

A rainbow of pens, coloring and charcoal pencils laid out next to his sketchpad. Jarod leaned forward to see Jacky's drawing.

"What grade are you in?" he asked Jacky.

"I'm in the fifth grade because I skipped fourth," Robert answered.

"So what, he didn't ask you, did he? I'm in seventh grade."

"That's a cool character you're drawing."

"It's Beeveeton, the leader of Beevee Town."

"Yeah? Tell me about your town."

Jarod chatted with Jacky. Robert vied for his attention. Lillian and I escaped to the kitchen, leaving Jarod in the Den with the boys.

"What do you think?" I asked her.

"Oh my, how handsome he is." Grammy came up to us.

"He is handsome. Did you see how he gravitated to my boys?"

"He seems more comfortable with them than you or Grammy."

As we huddled in the kitchen, Uncle came through the kitchen door carrying a barrel of red apples. "There's more in the truck," he said.

"You're back." Lillian kissed him.

"Right on time for dinner." Grammy patted his shoulder.

"Mama wants to make pies tonight. I'd like some help bringing in all those supplies."

Lillian brought the boys into the kitchen. Jarod trailed behind them. When they entered the kitchen, Uncle looked Jarod over. "Who's this fellow?"

"It's Portia's boyfriend. I saw them kissing," Robert laughed.

Lillian held Robert by his shoulders. "Don't tease."

"Uncle Jack, this is my friend Jarod. Jarod, Uncle Jack."

They shook hands. Uncle eyed Jarod. "You look strong enough to help out," he said.

"Sure, I'd love to help."

Everyone except Grammy headed to the kitchen door. Uncle stopped us. "I think us men can handle it."

The boys vanished without protests. I stayed to help. Lillian pulled me aside. "Perhaps, you should let them unload the truck by themselves," she offered.

I followed them through the kitchen door and then crossed the courtyard to go into my studio. I sat spellbound on my stool in front of a blank canvas. I couldn't help myself, I watched Jarod carry in the supplies. Each time he crossed the courtyard, he captivated me. I loved how his chest and arms bulked up as he carried a barrel of apples.

Whenever he disappeared into the house, I held my breath waiting for him to reappear. At one point, he laughed hard, and I wondered what he found so funny. When they finished carrying in the supplies, I stayed in my studio to let Jarod visit with everyone.

While in there, I set aside a thirty-six by twenty-four-inch abstract painting depicting two lovers dancing in the forest. At least that had been my intent. Others might see a mess of blue, yellow and green with scatters of purple and red. The dancers as I called it, was one of my favorites. The solitude of the studio gave me time to reflect, and I thought about my mother.

Remembering how much I trusted Janice, plus reminding myself that Maddie loved Mom, helped me to stop worrying. With the two of them supporting Mom, she would experience the benefits of the Standout community.

For all I knew, those women had an extraordinary evening. With so many hours in a day, they had time to enjoy the lake, time to reminisce about old memories and a lifetime of experiences to share. They were fine, I told myself. Putting my mind at ease, I went inside.

"There you are... about to start without you," Grammy teased when I walked into the dining room.

She motioned for me to take the seat across from Jarod and then she sat at the head of the table. Lillian sat next to me with Jacky sitting to her left. Uncle sat between Robert and Jarod, and it seemed, Grammy had balanced the table to her satisfaction. When Grammy grabbed my hand, I bowed my head, readying myself for her blessing but none came.

Grammy said, "It seems Junior has taken a liking to your beau." She released my hand and then I looked at Jarod. He already had his eyes fixed on me. We locked eyes for an instant before we both looked away.

After her blessing, Grammy said, "I should just pass these sweet potatoes to Jarod, that way, he can just take Portia's serving from the get-go."

Everyone laughed at how Grammy poked fun at me.

Right then, Grammy started the food going from person to person with Jarod or me getting everything first. Throughout the meal, I gazed at Jarod. A few times, he had already been looking at me and other times, he didn't notice my ardent glances.

It had been years since so many people dined at my table. Having my family there eating, laughing and talking to one another made me feel whole. My life had developed texture and I experienced a richness I never thought possible after my father died. That night everything was perfect.

I woke early the next morning, taking my run before Grammy got started in the kitchen. Afterwards, I showered before going down to breakfast. Uncle and Lillian were already at the table eating biscuits, with eggs and breakfast meat. I limited myself to fruit and yogurt until Grammy shoved eggs in front of me saying, "I'm working on making you meatier for Jarod."

"Jarod likes me as I am."

"He sure does."

I smiled when Uncle confirmed my feelings about Jarod.

"It's too bad what happened to his family." Grammy sat down. "He told you about the plane crash?"

"No. Junior did."

Uncle grinned, looking as guilty as I believed him to be. "Sorry, but I just had to ask a guy like him, why he wasn't married. Didn't make any sense to me."

"What did you do last night?"

Lillian joshed, sounding as though she knew somebody's secret, but she didn't know mine. Her assumptions were all wrong. My sublime night would have disappointed her because nothing happened—not the things she hinted at.

"Jarod read in my studio while I painted him," I told them proudly.

"That's it?" Lillian grinned.

"I painted. Where are the boys?"

"Sleeping." Lillian took a bite of her biscuit. "Why can't I make them this fluffy?"

Grammy chuckled. "Likely because you're not a hundred. Over time you'll get better."

"Portia, I'm just going to ask. Are you dating Jarod?"

Uncle waited for my answer. "I think so… I hope so. Yes, we are… I guess?"

"Don't be so sure." Uncle laughed.

"We all liked him. My boys loved him." Lillian said.

"I think, I love him."

"You do?" Grammy put her hand over mine.

"Yes. We're taking it slow."

"Good plan." Grammy patted my hand.

I took her calloused hand into mine, holding it there for a few minutes while Grammy finished eating. Once she left the table, Grammy started heaving a twenty-five-pound bag of flour across the floor.

Uncle leapt from his chair. "Mama, I told you to let me know when you were ready."

"I'm not incapable..." She went on.

Lillian and I let Uncle deal with Grammy. We exited the kitchen.

In my studio, I gave Lillian the painting I had picked out for her. Without looking at it, she studied the incomplete portrait of Jarod. I had sketched his face, neck and shoulders, while he read his book. During that session, I also managed to block in the background, and add the shadow line

"This is splendid," she exclaimed. "You really did paint last night. I had no idea you were this good." She grinned.

"Thank you... it's just a sketch with a bit of shadowing," I said.

"Well, I can tell it's Jarod on there and I thought you painted landscapes. I've seen them all over the place."

"In high school, I went through a period of painting the farm. Those are the ones you've seen."

"They're good." She looked at the painting I gave her. "This one, however, is amazing. Dancers, I think."

"Yes, in the forest. The trees are all around them."

"Well, I can't make out trees. But I love it."

"Do you have a minute to talk?"

"Sure. The boys will sleep for at least two more hours. What's up?"

I had processed a host of changes, and everything moved faster than I could tolerate—being honest, it seemed I'd lost control. Life sprouted out, taking its own path. Loving how my

life felt at the time, worrying about losing my footing and fore-
seeing things cave in on me, kept me from being at ease.

"Everything is moving at lightning speed," I said.

"What do you mean?"

"I never thought—" I stopped talking.

"What's bothering you?"

"Nothing is wrong, but I'm afraid of the kaboom."

"What kaboom?"

"There's always a kaboom. Something devastating always happens."

"No, it doesn't. I'm sensing you're struggling with your control
issues right now. Is that the case?"

Standout had trained Lillian. Her adaptation was interesting
yet helpful. "I don't want anything to spoil how superb things
are right now. So yeah, I guess."

"When you become afraid, what happens?"

"I worry everything will spin out of control."

"What do you want to control?"

I looked at the incomplete painting of Jarod. "Nothing, I
don't want to stop feeling happy."

"Do you think controlling everything will help?"

"I wouldn't say so."

"What about going back to your old way of coping?"

"I don't know. I suppose not."

"Remember, you're going to feel somewhat offbeat. At least
until the changes you've made feel natural to you."

"You're telling me not to stress out?"

"That's exactly what I'm saying."

Lillian gazed at my paintings taking long pauses in front
of some. While she perused my studio, I thought things over.
Janice, Maddie and Lillian had it right. There was only one life
I could live. Just mine. I was already doing it, but I still worried
about Mom.

"What are you thinking about over there?" Lillian called out.

"Ordering a green t-shirt." I kidded.

"With big white letters?"

"Yep!"

"Honestly, what are you thinking about?"

She sat in the chair Jarod had posed in the night before. I felt as though she had squished his ghost. I focused on the unfinished portrait of him.

"What if my mother doesn't get better like you say?"

"You tell me. What if she doesn't?"

"I'm going to struggle. Already, I feel guilty about having an amazing week without her being around. Things are hard for her right now."

"The guilt is a part of the process. You'll be fine."

"My guilt is devouring me. I'm bracing myself for the worst."

"Trust me, I think Fran is going to be fine."

"I hope you're right."

"Of course, I am. I have a suggestion though."

"Let's hear it." I surrendered to Lillian's optimism.

"I looked up museums in Boston. Shall we go?"

"Yes, we should. Everyone will love it."

First, we visited the Fine Arts museum for Jacky. The next day, we went to the Science Museum. The exhibits astounded Robert and he tried to see everything. At closing time, Uncle had to promise to bring him back before we could leave the building.

Grammy had been as excited as Jacky and Robert because she had never been to museums like the ones we visited. Outside of her trip to see my mother, she hadn't left Denten since she was a small child. Her visit with me was also her first extended break from farm life. Everything fascinated Grammy. I marveled at her childlike ways. As I saw it, we were all adjusting to new things, while learning to accept one another. Grammy's life philosophy repulsed me. Even so, by the end of the weekend, I had no desire to challenge her. I simply held on to her love.

❖

Standout had fitted me with new glasses, allowing me to see the world from my own perspective. I no longer needed my parents' filters. After my exploration into the past, I esteemed my father's kindness in a new way. Both my parents loved me. Moreover, they had sacrificed for me, and I owed the richness in my life to them. They had given me, however offbeat their methods may have been, a full life with varied experiences.

On Monday afternoon, as I drove over to the lake house, I gave myself permission to live my life. I vowed to let it unfold with me acting in the star role. Each day, as I slid closer and closer to becoming a person my father would have admired, I wished the same for Mom.

The decision belonged to her alone. Standout, Maddie and Janice had set things in motion. If Mom wanted, she could expand her life. Going back to our old way of relating wasn't possible. My life had been forever changed. Moreover, I had untethered myself.

When I reached the lake house, my mother sat on the porch. As I walked up, she straightened herself. Mom had been leaning into Maddie. They were touching shoulders.

"Good afternoon, ladies." I smiled.

Mom's face turned red, yet I didn't give her a chance to say anything. I looked into her eyes, saying "You can't always get what you want."

Mom smiled. "But, if you try, sometimes you do."

When she reached for me, I sat down next to her. We held hands.

ABOUT THE AUTHOR

M. H. MUNDY writes about the things people do. Her stories spring from an obsession with human behavior. After a decade of studying and sampling the world's religions, Mundy settled into writing about what makes people tick. Her interest led to degrees in both psychology and sociology. Every day she embraces the complexities of being human.

Made in the USA
Columbia, SC
13 February 2023

11927903R00188